THE CONSCIENCE
OF ABE'S TURN

THE BIRTH OF THE CONSCIENCE
VOLUME 1

SEASON 1
EPISODES 1-4

J. TIMOTHY KING

The Conscience of Abe's Turn: The Birth of the Conscience, Volume 1 (Season 1, Episodes 1-4)

Copyright © 2007-2008 J. Timothy King. All rights reserved.

Published by J. Timothy King.

Read new episodes, stay up to date, and read special features at *The Conscience of Abe's Turn* website: `http://AbesTurn.com/`

First trade paperback edition, October 2008.

ISBN 978-0-9816925-0-0

Printed in the United States of America.

10 9 8 7 6 5 4 3 2 1

TABLE OF CONTENTS

"All power tends to corrupt and absolute power corrupts absolutely. Great men are almost always bad men, even when they exercise influence and not authority: still more when you superadd the tendency or the certainty of corruption by authority."

Lord Acton, in a letter to Bishop Mandell Creighton
April 5, 1887

With thanks to my parents,
     for teaching me always to be myself.

With thanks to my wife,
     for teaching me unconditional love.

With thanks to the late Harry Browne,
     for teaching me how precious is liberty.

PREFACE

I knew I was onto something when I started getting angry, disparaging emails. "Beyond improbable." "Pointless crap!" From someone I'd never met. This person actually read a few chapters—I checked—and was so incensed, went through the trouble to send me an email.

A scathing, negative review: *Abe's Turn* is beyond-improbable, pointless crap. That's my paraphrase, of course. As everybody knows (or so I'm told), cops and other government agents *never* trump up charges, *never* get the wrong end of the stick, *never* arrest the wrong guy, *never* take bribes, and *never* let their prejudices or personal feelings interfere with justice. And even if they did, they would *never* get away with it. And that is why (or so I'm told) law-abiding citizens like you and me *never* need to defend themselves. And by the way, drug laws are good for America.

Meanwhile, everything you see on TV actually could happen, especially the stuff in dramas like *Alias*, *Boston Legal*, and *Lost*. Not to mention everything you read in the daily newspaper.

Abe's Turn actually has a modest premise. The story's premise can't be the real reason for such vitriol. But this story *says* something. And throughout history, stories that say something have been those lambasted, denounced, and banned.

Stories that say things both in the themes they address and in their portrayal of those themes. *The Adventures of Huckleberry Finn* (still one of the most challenged books, in 2007, according to the American Library Association). *Uncle Tom's Cabin. The Color Purple. The Diary of a Young Girl* (Anne Frank). *Brave New World. Nineteen Eighty-Four. Slaughterhouse-Five. The Martian Chronicles. The Catcher in the Rye. Lord of the Flies. The Lorax* (by Dr. Seuss). *Heather Has Two Mommies. Death of a Salesman. Of Mice and Men. Ulysses. Harry Potter and the Sorcerer's Stone.* All of these have been banned somewhere in the United States. The *Harry Potter* books have been the most attacked of the 21'st century.

This first volume of *Abe's Turn* is the culmination of a decade of change. Its story brings together ideas from government politics, libertarian ideology, romance fiction, and Internet technology. I noted before that the story "says something." It says that if you give someone enough power, no matter how good a person that someone appears to be, he *will* abuse it. I talk more about the inspiration and motivation behind *Abe's Turn* in "Whatever Happened to Zorro?" a retrospective essay in the "Bonus Extras" section of this book. For now, the basic premise behind the story is summed up in two points: (1) Government officials have power. (2) Government officials are only human, just like the rest of us.

But *Abe's Turn* is more than just its story, because this story as I envisioned it could not be told within the confines of the traditional novel. Rather, it's an epic story made up of a series of smaller ones, because that reflects life. Just as none of us is converted by any single chapter, just as each of us is the culmination of all the stories he has lived, the story of the Conscience of Abe's Turn is a series of challenges, triumphs, and failures.

This story will, if all goes well, span 24 episodes over 3 years, 3 seasons, like the seasons of a television program, each season of *Abe's Turn* consisting of 8 novelette-length episodes. This volume contains only the first 4 of those episodes, the first half-season. The first of these seasons (the first 8 episodes) is entitled "The Birth of the Conscience," because it is the story of how the Conscience of Abe's Turn came into being.

By way of acknowledgment, I must thank my parents, my wife, and the rest of my family for their encouragement. More specifically: my father, who by writing his own book of memoirs unwittingly coaxed me to finish mine; my wife, who bore with me through months of reduced income, so that I could slog through innumerable hours of writing, editing, and marketing, instead of billing those hours to paying clients, the curse of the first-novelist; my mother, who joined my father and daughters in incessantly bugging me for news on "my novel," thereby forcing me to keep working on it, so that I would have some news to share.

Then there is Holly Lisle, a wonderful fantasy-romance author, who through her writing books, advice, and personal encouragement filled with been-there-done-that wisdom has done more for my writing than anyone else on Earth. And Perry Marshall, a shrewd and practical marketing consultant, who—unbeknown to him—with his newsletter and emails managed to convince me that this project is worth trying (even if it ultimately fails), that my passion is worth pursuing, and that I am worth every dollar I earn.

I also owe a debt of gratitude to the late Harry Browne, who at the age of 61 decided to run for president of the United States on the Libertarian Party ticket. Whatever the merits of this quixotic quest, without his authentic, straightforward, reasoned, honorable, peaceable case for liberty, during my own time of inner political turmoil, I perhaps still would not know where I stand or what I believe in.

Many others: The numerous writers who have read snippets of *Abe's Turn* and have reassured me that it does have its

good parts. All my friends who promised to "buy a copy" of
this book, even after I warned them what it's about. Tom
Metro, one of my oldest friends and colleagues, who patiently
listened while I droned on about writing and marketing and
the book industry, and who picked up the slack when I
couldn't put in the hours on our shared software-development
projects. Regular acquaintances from church and from syna-
gogue, who when I said I was "a writer," took me seriously,
even though I couldn't.

I must, however, emphasize that despite the support,
advice, and encouragement I have received, I am solely
responsible for everything in this book. The people I acknowl-
edge above had nothing to do with it. Yes, they provided me
love and inspiration. But if I am in the wrong, I—and only I—
chose to corrupt that love and inspiration. If I am a demented,
disturbed man, be assured that my parents raised me in a
upright, loving home. If my characters are unlovable, be
assured that my wife and children do love me. If my prose
falls flat, be assured that Holly Lisle wrote not even a syllable
of it. If this project turns out to be a business failure, be
assured that I did not actually follow all of Perry Marshall's
advice. And if my politics seem reprehensible, be assured that
I will never be able to explain them as well Harry Browne did.

PROLOGUE

He was born on Nine-Eleven. That is, on September 11, 1967. And his parents named him Theodore Webster Jackson. As a boy, he played football with his dad and his friends, watched the *A-Team*, and wanted to grow up to be a soldier of fortune, get married, and have an "old-style" family.

Instead, he graduated college in 1989, went to law school, and by 2001 was a partner at Hart, Zimmer, and Browne.

Somewhere in-between, he met Clydene Patrice Hobbes. Both young, both energetic, both enthusiastic, both idealistic and unashamed, both volunteers for the same political campaign, stuffing envelopes, and both lonely. They fell in love, but they needed to build their careers, or at least that's what they told each other. Years later, they finally got back together on Ted's birthday, the year he made partner. That was also the year Ted decided he was too young to play it safe and too old to be counting birthdays, but that's another story.

A year later, the two were husband and wife, not "old-style," but that didn't matter. Clyde kept him on his toes, and at the same time, he could open up to her—and she knew him —in a way no one else ever did.

They bought a house in the town of Abe's Turn and began a life together, became active in local politics, especially with controversial issues they both believed in. Each a busy profes-

sional, together they found time to stuff envelopes and deliver
signs for Suzie Smith in her successful campaign for town
selectman, or to collect signatures for a ballot question to elim-
inate the state income tax. Ted remembered introducing his
best and longest friend Michael to Harrison Scout, a PR man
who had previously worked for a noisy, minor-party senate
campaign that (much to the disgust of the incumbent candidate) successfully re-framed the election debate. Michael was
an expert PR and ad man himself. He was duly impressed.

But their most significant work as political activists
happened in their own living room, literally. It began over
coffee and cake on election day, November 7, 2006. Ted had
invited Michael, and Clyde had invited her friend and confidant, one Mira Jayson. After voting, as was their custom, they
would get together and opine on the certainty of politics. That
is, whether or not your candidate gets elected, you can be sure
that nothing will ever change, at least not for the better.

It was the first year, however, that Mira joined them, as she
and Clyde had only just met some months prior. Michael had
never formally met her, and his first order of business was to
make a pass at her.

Her response: "How do you know I'm not a lesbian?"

"Well, are you?" Michael asked, a twinkle in his eye.

"No, but you wouldn't know that as fast as you move."

"You want me to slow down? I can go slow," seductively.

"Maybe," Mira peered under her dark eyebrows at him, a
slight sneer on her lips, "I just want someone I can talk to."

That seemed to attract Michael even more than if she had
proposed finding a back room to get naked in. But it attracted
him in a way that he couldn't act on. And it was better that
they kept their relationship professional. One reason was that
Michael was Ted's friend, and Mira was Clyde's, and if something happened between them, it could make friendly social
gatherings very uncomfortable. Besides, it was no skin off of

Michael's nose. He went through women like he went through paper towels, avoiding long-term commitments with both. And it turned out that Mira was definitely the long-term kind of gal. They were clearly not made for each other. And if this weren't reason enough for them to keep their relationship professional, another reason revealed itself that night.

As the four sat recounting tales of their deals with the devil that is government, a new thread emerged that night. Surely, it had been there all the time, even if they had not noticed. Ted, as a criminal defense lawyer, frequently ran headlong into the two-faced nature of the criminal justice system. On the one hand, it releases the guilty in order to protect the rights of the innocent. On the other hand, it tramples over the rights of the innocent in order to get at the guilty, usually with the full blessing of the innocent it purports to protect. Clydene, too, had read enough horror stories online, ever since the Cyber-porn scare of 1995, stories of cops busting into the homes and businesses of average citizens, on circumstantial evidence, on anonymous tips, wrecking computers, stealing data. And usually, the enforcers had a personal bias to hate the accused, motivations that have nothing to do with the law. Sometimes, it all seemed too Orwellian to be true. But Ted confirmed that, yes, the law is at the beck and call of those who enforce it. If the cops really want to persecute someone, they can usually find a way to make it legal, even if they never prevail in court. Most people assume, incorrectly, that it actually works the other way around. And Michael backed up all these observations with his own file of personal accounts, collected from various people he had met, stories that hit just a bit too close to home, events that had transpired in Abe's Turn.

Mira was the one who pulled all these pieces together into a coherent thread. Something no one had considered before. Yes, it was bad all over the country. Yes, you could go online and find reason to fear the feds. But the feds have an entire country to patrol. What's the chance they'd end up in this town? When was the last time you heard of Mulder and Scully coming to Abe's Turn? Never? That's to be expected, because all the atrocities in Abe's Turn, they all happened at the hands of the local enforcers, and they were championed by the chief enforcer, Sam Baedes.

"Oh, Beady-eyes," Michael retorted. "Boy, have I got stories I could tell you about him!" And he would have gone on for several hours if Ted hadn't interrupted him.

And then there was Lando Benitez. He was Mira's own personal horror story. Lando had been visiting his sister and her family. He had come from Spain for an American vacation. His crime was being a Latino in the White section of town. He stopped his car to listen to music and enjoy the scenery, apparently suspiciously, because the cops "questioned" him.

Now, Mira, then as now a certified counselor, frequently volunteered for various organizations, to talk to victims of physical, mental, and sexual abuse. She did this for the same reason she became a counselor in the first place, because she cared. Through her training, she knew all the psychological symptoms of abuse, all the challenges the victim faces. She knew that victims tend to blame themselves, usually with the full blessing of their friends and family. Part of what she did was to help the victim hold the abuser accountable for his own actions, and to find the courage to take steps to stop the abuse. Through her experience, she had seen the physical marks, physically disfigured victims, but she also knew that the psychological disfigurement reaches much more deeply, is much harder to see. But she could see it, as clearly as anyone else could see the nose on a person's face. And she thought she had seen it all. But by the time she got to Lando Benitez, it was clear she hadn't.

She met him almost by accident. She was at the hospital talking to another patient when one of the nurses who knew her asked if she could take a few minutes to talk with him. Lando decidedly did not blame himself for his predicament. Far from being his fault, it was hers. Mira ended up spending hours talking with him. Most of his initial comments were sarcastic, passive-aggressive, intended to strike out at her for what had happened to him. Eventually, she convinced him that she had no association with the authorities, and in fact, if they found her talking to him, she would likely become a target of their ire.

But that wasn't the end of his travails, for he had apparently been identified as a target. Mira knew, because she kept in touch with him. Eventually, he cut his vacation short, because of official harassment and because he wanted to save his sister's family grief. That was Lando's official explanation. But Mira suspected that his brother-in-law may have all but thrown him out. By that time, he had amassed thousands of dollars in debt: fines, bail, hospital bills, repairs to the car after the cops "searched" it. Lando's brother-in-law picked up the tab, because he was family. But as far as Mira knew, he never forgave his sister's brother.

Mira told this story, still fresh in her mind, with such sentiment and passion that even Ted found himself being moved, and becoming angry at the villains of the story.

"The Chief even held a press conference," Mira concluded, "and talked about how 'our neighborhoods' were under attack and how he was fighting gang violence." Mira's voice started to waver.

Michael retorted, "We should just get rid of Beady-eyes and save at least one salary."

That was the beginning of the Committee for a Fairer Future, and the campaign against Chief Sam Baedes, and the events that led to the birth of the Conscience of Abe's Turn.

"Those who would give up ESSENTIAL LIBERTY to purchase a little TEMPORARY SAFETY, deserve neither LIBERTY nor SAFETY."

from the title page of *An Historical Review of the Constitution and Government of Pennsylvania*, 1759, excerpted from a letter from the Assembly to the Governor of Pennsylvania in 1755

EPISODE 1: HOW TO STAY OUT OF JAIL IN ONE EASY LESSON

Ted lumbered through the foyer of his home, following the sound of his wife's guitar back to her office. He waited for a few minutes outside the door, listening as she picked out a simple but beautiful tune on the instrument. The air smelled normal, plain, like nothing in particular. That meant that she had not had a chance to cook dinner, which meant she was overcome either with work or depression. And the fact that she was playing the guitar meant it was probably the latter, or maybe both. Ted pushed open the office door.

"Hi, Clyde," he said. "You had a day, too, I see."

She stopped playing. "Hey, you," she said kindly. "No, I was just thinking."

"Thinking. Sounds pretty scary. Or depressing," he said without cracking a smile.

She paused to gaze at the man towering over her in a suit coat and tie. Her eyes seemed to dwell on his graying rooftop.

I feel old, Ted thought. *Too old to be working twelve-hour days. Too old to dragging my butt home late, again.*

He bent down to kiss her. Their lips lingered over each other for a moment, and then they pressed gently but passionately together. Ted tenderly stroked her loose, fiery curls. Then he admired her creamy, slightly freckled skin, her arched eyebrows, her soft complexion.

She sighed.

She looks too young for me, he thought. *Too precious, too passionate.*

"What's for dinner?" he said.

"Well, I wanted to make chicken-curry soup, but I got distracted."

"So... Nothing for dinner?"

"Well, I was working on the QX project, and then the phone rang."

"So nothing for dinner."

"Well, I guess whatever you want. I had a late lunch, so I'm not really hungry. There's some bologna in the fridge."

Ted turned toward the kitchen.

Clydene set down her guitar and followed him.

"So I was working on the QX project. They're still screwed up. Another story." She took a breath. "And Mira called."

"Great," he said. "What does she need now?" He grabbed the bologna and a bottle of mustard, and headed for the kitchen table.

Clydene's curls bounced as she walked, like tight, little springs hanging from her head.

Really looks too young for me, Ted thought.

"She doesn't need anything. Well, nothing new, anyhow. She's been planning for that demonstration outside Town Hall."

"Yes." Ted snatched a loaf of bread from the shelf behind him.

"She thinks she's in trouble," Clydene said.

Ted paused. Then he breathed in. "She probably is."

Clydene regarded him. "Why? What do you know?"

"I know only what you do. Less, probably." He returned to his sandwich ingredients. "What do you know?"

"Remember I told you about that web form I coded up a

couple weeks ago?"

"Yes."

"I spent almost a whole day trying to get it working the way the analyst suggested. That was stupid. I should have stuck with my instincts."

"Okay."

"So I started over, and did what I should have done in the first place. And I had it done in an hour."

"That's a nice story. Is Mira designing software now?" He squirted a trail of mustard onto each of two slices of bread.

"No, but—" Clyde stammered. She started again. "When she gets a feeling that something is wrong, she's usually right."

"Okay. What's wrong?"

"Mira knows political activism."

"She hasn't been 'an activist' any longer than you or I," Ted retorted. He was beginning to get annoyed and wished that Clyde would stop beating around the bush.

"But she's better at it than we are," Clyde countered.

"She's also a perfectionist. And she sees problems that don't matter to the rest of us."

"So what? You think that means she's not in trouble?"

"I think that means we have to wait and see," Ted said.

"Wait and see if she gets hurt?" Clydene was clearly disturbed.

Ted stopped and looked at her. "No—"

"You believe in the Committee as much as I do. At least I thought you did."

"Ironic, isn't it? If she succeeds, I'm out of a job." That wasn't actually true, but a part of Ted liked arguing. And he was just too tired to be nice.

"You mean you'd have to get bona fide work, instead of defending victims? Is that your problem?"

Ted stared at her. "My problem is that I don't know how to

read the future."

"That's not funny, Ted."

"I'm not laughing, Clyde."

A pause. Clyde was staring at the ceiling. She seemed to be gathering her thoughts. Ted wished, if she wanted him to do something, she would just ask him, so that he could say "No," eat his sandwich, and go to bed. And if she didn't want anything, she would just say that, too, so he could just eat his sandwich and go to bed.

Clydene finally said, in that sad but firm voice that only Clyde knew, "I wish you could be a little more sympathetic."

Ted's heart softened. He really was old: old and tired. Too old to learn any new tricks, and too tired to try.

He replied as sweetly as he could, "Clyde, I'm glad Mira's your friend. And I'm fond of her, too. All I meant was that she's standing up to Sam Baedes. It stands to reason that she'll get into trouble. I don't know how or when. I've gone over the plan with her. She's not doing anything wrong. We both know that. But do you think that's going to stop him?"

"Exactly!" Clyde said.

"Indeed. And we'll both be there to stand up for her when the time comes. Right?"

Clyde was now staring at the pattern in the kitchen linoleum. Ted knew that pattern well. He had stared at it himself.

"Right?" he repeated, reaching out to caress her cheek.

"Right," Clyde agreed.

"Unfortunately, the next step is to wait and see what happens."

Clydene looked back up at him. "I just wish you could show a little more sympathy."

Ted touched her shoulder. He breathed in, then breathed out. Apologizing was the most difficult thing Ted had ever had to learn to do. But for numerous months, he had been making a concerted effort to be more understanding to those around him, and to apologize quickly, whenever he might have offended someone, even if he didn't really understand why they were offended. This was one of those cases. He knew he was arguing with Clyde, and she didn't feel like arguing, and the conversation was upsetting her, even if he didn't know why this particular conversation was different from any of the other friendly debates they had.

"I'm sorry," he said. He had learned the form of the apology from Mira herself. "I'm being insensitive. I'm tired, and I'm not thinking about how you feel. Please forgive me."

Clyde sighed and smiled a little. "I would really like a hug," she said.

So he held her for a while.

— ' c , —

Mira knew Chief Beady-eyes was out to get her. Of course, he was out to get her. Everyone knew he was out to get her. But Mira also knew he was on the verge of action.

She knew he was on the verge of action. But she didn't know *how* she knew. She just knew. She just had a feeling. It wasn't fear that gave her this feeling, because she didn't feel afraid. This surprised people when they first met her. This tiny, dark-eyed, raven-haired woman, not much bigger than a girl, stood up to tall, strong Sam Baedes, because there was only so much he could do to her. And because someone needed to stand up to him, and no one else would do it.

Maybe she had this feeling because none of his goons had harassed her in weeks, despite the fact that she had been planning for a big demonstration at the town hall, with protesters and victims telling their stories and hecklers and reporters drooling all over their notepads and everything. But that alone wasn't enough, because Baedes didn't make it a habit to get on her case indiscriminately. He always had a good excuse, no

matter how contrived it was, and he never did anything
overtly illegal. Besides, she had organized political protests
before with no fallout. Even so, this was the biggest yet. Her
demands for an independent council to investigate abuses in
Beades's department had started her troubles. That Baedes
would be called to account, this was the vision she held in her
mind. And Lando Benitez, he was the victim she held in her
memory.

There was something she had heard at the last envelope-
stuffing party, something that troubled her, though she
couldn't say why. It was an off-hand comment someone had
made. The words still rang in Mira's ears:

"He's all in on this one. You can be sure of it. Ol' Beady-
eyes is gonna stop us, even if it takes all of his men, even if
someone knocks over the Tangelo Street Diner."

The Tangelo Street Diner was a well known cop hang-out.
Clearly, this was supposed to be a joke, to build morale.
Because nothing pleases an activist more than to hear that he's
the top priority on his adversary's hit-list. An activist's biggest
fear is that he will be ignored. But the comment still gave Mira
pause. Not that she was concerned about herself. She wasn't.
She was, however, concerned that the protest go as planned. If
something went wrong, it would grieve and anger her to have
the press show up Monday morning to a non-event.

Of course, if he tried to shut it down, that could make for
an even bigger story for the press release:

Police-Abuse Protest Squelched by Chief

*Abe's Turn Chief of Police Sam Baedes today at the local
town hall oversaw the arrest of numerous demonstrators,
who were protesting abuses of power by the local police
force.*

*"This is a perfect example of the kind of abuse of process
we're talking about," protest organizer Mira Jayson said
from her jail cell. "We just want to have our say, to take
part in the democratic process. But he consistently shuts
down dissent on a technicality. Can't he take honest,
peaceful criticism?"*

And so forth.

That part about the technicality was just speculation on
Mira's part. And that was the problem. She knew something
had to go down. She just didn't know what, or when, or who,
or where, or how.

She had another concern, too, one that she tried to push to
the side every chance she got. While she was happy to be
arrested for the cause, she always grieved when others were
attacked along with her. Yes, she knew it was good for morale
and good for the cause. People who are willingly arrested for
what they believe in only believe in it more. But these were
people, human beings, and they were people she considered
her friends.

These thoughts filled Mira's mind as she drove quietly
down the road. She even forgot Ike sitting in the passenger's
seat next to her, until he broke the silence.

"Did you miss your turn?" he said.

Ike had been resting his eyes after a long, hot day on top of
a roof. He was sweaty and sticky and smelly and dirty.

Dirty. Mira loved the sound of that word, especially sitting
next to Ike. And sometimes she loved how he sweated and
how he stuck and how he smelled. And sometimes she loved
the rugged look of his five-o'clock shadow. Or the way his
short, straight hair clumped together after he woke up from a
nap. She blinked and forced herself to breathe, to get her heart
beating again. Thoughts of Ike often distracted her.

Being an apprentice roofer was hard, dangerous work. But

it was good work. Mira was glad he was making the job work, and that she had not misjudged him. Not many people would trust a parolee, and she called in some heavy favors just to get him the opportunity. She smiled at the thought.

He was right, though. She had missed the turn. Deep in thought, she had forgotten that she was going to drop Ike off at his place, on her way home from work.

"You're right. Sorry. I'll double-back," she said.

It was then that she noticed the flashing red and blue lights in her rear-view mirror.

"How long has he been behind us?" she asked, as she pulled the car over to the side of the road.

"Don't know," Ike replied.

Now that they had fully stopped, a uniformed man with a crew cut stepped out of the car with the flashing lights. He sauntered up to the driver's-side window of Mira's car and looked in. He was older than the two in the car, by at least ten years, but as fit as Jack La Lanne. Still, time had etched hard lines into his grim visage. His voice resonated with a deep basso quality.

"Do you know why I pulled you over?"

"No, Chief, I don't," Mira replied politely, "but I'm sure you have a good reason." There was a note of sarcasm in her tone that only she could detect.

Baedes pursed his lips. "Who's your friend?" he asked, motioning to Ike.

"Just a friend. Isn't it a little unusual for you to be making traffic stops?"

"In a small town like this, we all do our fair share." He looked in at Ike. "What have you been up to? Staying out of trouble?"

"Yes, Sir, I have."

"Think again."

By the look on his face, Ike could've been playing poker.

Mira eyed him carefully. But she believed him when he said he was keeping out of trouble.

The man at the window turned back to Mira. "Your registration expired last week."

A sudden tightness gripped Mira's chest.

"Driving with an expired registration is an arrestable offense," the chief added.

Silence. No one asked what he was going to do. No one even asked whether he had called in backup, though he surely knew whose car he was following and that Mira Jayson would offer no physical resistance.

Mira knew what was happening, though. This was it. This was his move. True, Abe's Turn wasn't all that tiny, and it was unusual for the chief to be making a traffic stop, no matter what he said. But Mira didn't have to deduct the true purpose of his stop. She could see it in his eyes.

He continued speaking to Mira. "You're also a convicted felon. It's a violation of his parole to be associating with you."

That sounded like bullshit. Neither Mira nor Ike challenged it, however.

The chief continued. "Mr. Morgan, slowly get out of the car, hands on your head, and come to the back of the car. Then you, Miss Jayson."

He followed Ike around to the back. Mira opened her door as instructed and was getting out, when suddenly a loud banging noise came from behind her. She swung around to see. The chief had Ike in a headlock. Ike was scraping wildly to get out of it. Suddenly, Ike was free and staggering backwards toward the side of the road. The chief came after him and knocked him to the ground.

Without thinking, Mira had run up to the back of the car, and now she tried to get to Ike, who was struggling to sit. Suddenly, the chief's billy club, propelled by great force, whacked Mira in the forehead, sending her body smashing sideways against the car. She might have seen Ike pinned and then handcuffed, were she not unconscious.

— 'c, —

"I need you to export the brochure to Flash and download it to their server before you leave."

Michael looked up from his desk at his boss's face. "Uhm... Why do you need that?" he said, grinning slightly. He decided to play a little cat-and-mouse with the pointy-haired one, since it was already half past six in the evening, a time when normal people had already gone home for the day.

"I told them we would do it today."

All at once, there were squeaking and shuffling noises from the adjoining cubicles.

"O-kay," Michael sang, as though considering carefully his next words. "We're happy to do whatever needs to be done," he said. "And I'll do my best. But I need you to check with me first before promising the client something that makes no grammatical sense."

The man smiled. "Riiiight," he said, playing along.

Michael continued, "I mean, if I have to promise to deliver gibberish, you at least have to get my sign-off on the gibberish I'll have promised to deliver."

The woman on the other side of the cubicle wall suddenly guffawed loudly.

"Michael Kelly, everyone!" said the man. "Let's all give him a big round of applause!"

The office erupted in applause and hoots and laughter.

Michael segued into his best Elvis impersonation. "Thank you. Thank you very much."

After the commotion died down, the man continued, "Seriously, though, can you do that?"

"Uh, seriously, it's gibberish." He found that the direct approach almost always worked the best. Besides, it gave him a chance to verbally poke at the man, and that was always good for a laugh.

The boss's eyes narrowed, his face turning into a scowl.

"I'd be happy to call him and see what he wants," Michael quickly added. "If it's easy enough, I can even bang it out before I leave. Probably it is. Otherwise, I'll get on it first thing tomorrow."

The man shook his head. "I'd rather that we arrange a conference call tomorrow." He meant he wanted to arrange a meeting, using the conference room's speaker-phone.

"Okay," Michael said. "We can do that. But he's probably waiting for something. That's why he called you. Let's try to set something up right now. Is there a conference room free?"

"No, the—"

Michael put up his hand. "I'm going to call him right now and clarify what he's expecting."

"I don't think that's such a good—"

"If we can't deliver it tonight, I'll hand the phone over to you, and you can schedule a meeting for tomorrow morning. Okay?"

The man frowned, sighed. "Go ahead."

But before Michael could make the call, the phone rang.

He lifted the receiver to his ear. "Hello. This is Michael."

"I'm glad I caught you," said the voice in slow, measured tones. "This is Ted Jackson. You'll never believe what happened."

"Um. The Abe's Turn Post Office now opens all mail for signs of inflammatory political truth?" Michael sneaked a peek at the expression on his boss's face.

"No, but close enough," the voice continued. "Mira's been arrested."

"Well, she should have been staying out of trouble," Michael said in the deepest voice he could muster, mimicking the big, burly police chief.

"Not so funny today, I'm afraid," Ted said.

"Hey, mocking Beady-eyes is always funny."

"Hilarious."

"You're making fun of me," Michael said.

"What tipped you off?"

"Sometimes, I don't get you, Ted. Are you joking, or are you pissed?"

"I'm pissed at the world, pissed at the system, pissed at God, and pissed at the man who thinks he ought to be telling God what to do."

"You know, for a minor character, he sure does use up a lot of our legitimate complaining time," Michael observed.

"You think he's a minor character?"

"He ought to be a minor character. Humble public servant and all that."

"I'm afraid you're not being realistic," Ted said. "The system doesn't actually work that way."

Michael sneaked another peek at his boss, who was waiting impatiently. Michael held up an index finger and mouthed, "Just one second."

"No witty rejoinder?" Ted said.

"What did he pick her up for?"

"Driving with an expired registration."

"Shit," Michael said. "I knew I forgot something."

"Doing the right thing is sometimes as hard as getting away with murder," Ted said.

"Murder might be preferable. Anyways, I have to get to a meeting. Thanks for telling me, though."

"Isn't it a little late for a meeting?"

"It's a late meeting."

"Speaking of which, can you stop by my place tonight? So we can have a late meeting, too."

"Or a prayer vigil," Michael said.

CHAPTER 2

Baedes was in the middle of filling out an arrest report in his office. He looked up from his desk to regard a tall, athletic woman dressed in a blue uniform, who had just entered. She was awe-inspiring, not just for her physical prowess and beauty, but even more for her accomplishments. Pale and soft from one angle, she stood as an amazon from another. Her academic achievements were significant, having earned a degree in Criminal Justice, having graduated from the police academy with flying colors, and now having made an outstanding young officer. She brought passion and dedication to the job.

All of Baedes's force was made up of fine officers. He stuck up for them, and they were loyal to him. But occasionally, Baedes met one that made his heart swoon. Not in a romantic way. Pamela Burns was much too young for him. She made his heart swoon in a proud, fatherly way. Just her being here was a credit to Abe's Turn and to him for hiring her and to the society he had worked so hard to build here. His chest swelled with pride, but he suppressed the feeling.

"I have those records you wanted," she said.

"Good," he said. "Has Miss Jayson been processed?"

"Yes, Sir," she said.

He took the folder full of papers.

"Ike Morgan is still waiting outside," she said.

"I know," Baedes said. But before she left, "Do you know why I haven't talked to him yet?"

"Not exactly."

"Because he's a bargaining chip."

The woman looked confused.

"Sit down, Burns."

She sat.

"Unfortunately, the law doesn't always do so well on its own. Sometimes the guilty need a little help to bring them to justice."

"Ike Morgan needs a push?" Pamela looked confused.

"No, Mira Jayson does."

"You aren't talking about..."

"I needed to make sure she was arrested in a way that would stick."

Officer Burns nodded. "That makes sense."

"So I made sure Ike Morgan and I got into a scuffle. That would guarantee not only driving an unregistered vehicle, but also resisting arrest, attempted assault, and anything else I can think of to throw at her."

"But what do you put in the report? Do you lie?"

"No!" Baedes said. "Never lie. Everything in my report is one hundred percent God's honest truth. Morgan and I were in a scuffle. That's the truth. Jayson charged at me. That's the truth. I made a split-second decision. That's the truth. All truth."

"Didn't you risk exposing yourself by getting into a scuffle?" she asked.

"Know your adversary," Baedes said. "These two probably wanted to be arrested. I was safe."

"Well, I guess she'll have some trouble getting on her high horse from the depths of a jail cell." She smirked.

"Indeed." Baedes grinned. "Don't worry, you'll pick it up quickly enough. You just need to get a little street-smarts under your belt."

"I appreciate your tutelage, Sir," she replied.

Baedes still grinned. "Send in Ike Morgan on your way out."

"Yes, Sir." Officer Burns nodded, rose, and was out the door.

Ike entered, his hands handcuffed in front of him.

Baedes had returned to his report. Without looking up, Baedes motioned Ike to a chair.

Ike sat.

"I'm just finishing up your arrest report," Baedes said, still writing. "But I haven't decided yet what to do with you."

— ' c , —

Clydene had never been to a prayer vigil. And this night, she really didn't feel like praying. Cursing, yes. Punching a bag, maybe. Ripping a pillow to shreds, definitely. But praying? No way. She was all prayed out. So instead of praying, the three friends sat in the Jackson's living room and chatted and nibbled stale cookies and sipped burnt coffee. Or rather, Michael and Ted chatted and nibbled stale cookies and sipped burnt coffee, while Clydene seethed.

"I must admit," Ted began, "I didn't let you in on the whole story over the phone."

"Didn't think I could handle it, eh?" Michael said. "Well, you were probably right."

Michael's spooky, sapphire eyes cut through the air between them. Actually, the spookiness came more from how his irises were set off by his black hair. The contrast made them stick out visually, like little glowing blue orbs.

Who can? Clydene thought.

"I do think you can handle it. But I thought I should tell

you in person," Ted said.

Michael took a notebook and pen from his pocket. "Okay. What's the situation?"

"I'm going to meet with Mira again tomorrow morning. She's currently being held at the county jail.

"She was driving Ike Morgan home from work. You remember him. Mira met him through a colleague and has been helping him out."

"Right," Michael said. "The bum. A 'professional' relationship." He used finger-quotes around the word *professional*.

Clydene had been staring into her coffee. At this point, she looked up. *Oh God, Ted, you started it now.* Her expression showed nothing.

"I admittedly haven't inquired deeply into their relationship," Ted said. "But I do believe it's currently on a professional level, or semi-professional at least. They don't have a client-counselor relationship, but I don't think they've been... untoward."

"But her feelings are distorting her judgment," Michael said.

Yeah, so what? That has nothing to do with it.

"You don't know that," Ted said. "And even if they were, I don't think it matters in this case. Ike didn't get her arrested."

"Still, she may not be giving you the whole story. She may be giving you the edited version," Michael countered.

Jeez! With friends like this...

"Fine. May I continue now?" Ted seemed annoyed, but Clydene was still wrapped up in her own thoughts.

Of course, she's giving the edited story. So what? She doesn't want anybody to get hurt.

"Sure. Go ahead." Michael prepared to write.

But she's still going to tell the truth.

"The official complaint is that she resisted arrest, aided the attempted escape of a convict in custody, and attempted assault on a police officer."

Instead of writing anything down, however, Michael looked surprised. "Mira?"

"Yes."

"Resisting arrest." Michael was clearly stunned.

"Yes."

Clydene quietly observed the two men. Unfortunately, she had already heard the whole story from her husband. Her teeth were clenched.

"But Mira *likes* to be arrested. It's her thing. Helping the cause and all that."

"Yes, I know."

"And assault? Mira doesn't even like to kill spiders. They're saying she attacked another human being?"

More likely the other way around!

"Based on these accusations, the D.A. has already met with the judge ex parte and she is being held pending a bail hearing tomorrow."

"Wow. Must have been like being assaulted by an ant. Uh..." Michael paused. "Did she do it?"

No, she didn't.

"No, I don't believe she did."

"You don't *believe* she did."

"At this point, I have only my belief, based on the official reports and especially on Mira's side of the story."

And that isn't good enough for you?!

"Okay. What is Mira's side of the story?" Michael made a note in his notebook.

"She was pulled over for driving with an expired registration. Oh, and you should add that to the list of charges."

"Sure. Gotta get those unregistered drivers off the road! Crazy sons of bitches are a danger to all us drunks."

Clydene smiled, a short, angry, evil smile. Her teeth were still clenched.

"It's an arrestable offense, but most officers don't arrest for it. They just demand that you get the car off the road immediately—tow it if necessary—until you get the registration renewed."

"Well, most officers don't work in Abe's Turn. Besides that, the paperwork is a pain." Michael chuckled.

"Yes, and most officers don't have a personal ax to grind with Mira Jayson."

Michael looked up. "What do you mean?"

"Baedes handled this one personally," Ted explained. "He's listed as the arresting officer."

He wanted to make sure it went down without a hitch.

"He's finally been demoted?" Michael joked. "That's great news, right?"

He knew only he would be willing to do whatever it took.

"No, he was just 'getting in some street time.'" Ted's tone changed slightly to indicate these were not his words. "At least that's what he said when I met him in the hallway."

"Street time." Right. Hit the pavement! Jerk.

"Okay, so Beady-eyes tried to arrest Mira. What happened then?"

"He also arrested Ike."

"Well, maybe Beady-eyes isn't all bad," Michael quipped.

Shut up already about it, will ya?

"He claimed Ike was associating with a felon, thus violating his parole."

"He was associating with a felon?" Michael stared quizzically.

"Mira."

"Mira was associating with a felon." That seemed to make more sense to Michael.

Clydene closed her eyes for a moment. She thought she might be getting a headache, because she understood exactly what Ted meant the first time.

"No, Mira is a felon," Ted clarified.

"She is?"

"No, she isn't. But Baedes said she is."

"What?" Michael seemed even more confused than he did before.

No, What's on second. Who is on first. If you were inside of Clydene's head, this joke would have been funny.

Ted started over again. "Baedes claimed Mira was a felon. Therefore, he said, Ike was violating his parole by associating with Mira."

But surely he knew this wouldn't stick.

"Why would he say that?"

He must have something else in mind. A bigger plan. What? Clyde couldn't have told you why she thought there was a bigger plan, but it seemed logical to her.

"He was mistaken." Ted pushed on. "While he was hand-cuffing Ike, a physical conflict ensued. Mira ran to Ike's side, but Baedes must have thought she was— That she had another goal in mind."

"Fine." Michael scrawled on his pad. "So he hasn't been demoted, but he has lost all his marbles."

"Exactly," Ted said.

This is news? Now, that was a funny joke.

"And," Ted added, "I'll try to get you a photo of her with the bruise across her forehead."

"Beg pardon?"

"Where Baedes hit her and knocked her unconscious."

Shithead. Effing shithead jerk. Similar incidents were common-place in Abe's Turn. But Clyde was particular angry about this one. Mira was, after all, her closest and dearest friend, and Clyde knew what it was like to be beat up by a crazy sonofa-bitch, and Mira didn't deserve it. No one did, but Mira especially.

"I think I'm gonna puke," Michael said. "How much of this

can we use?"

Clydene felt ill.

"None of it," Ted said.

"What?!" Michael looked exasperated. "Why did you tell it to me?"

"Firstly, you need to know."

"I do? You're kidding? I don't need to know anything! I know nothing. I see nothing. I hear nothing."

Shut up. You talk too much.

"But this you do need to know, and I'll tell you why."

"This ought'a be good," Michael said.

"Tomorrow, we're going before the judge, and I'm hoping he will dismiss the whole thing as a simple misunderstanding," Ted explained. "I expect it to be a cinch. In that case, we'll need to issue an immediate press release making us sound triumphant and victimized at the same time."

"No problem," Michael said.

Not good enough. Thinking about Beady-eyes, *He deserves a stronger tongue-lashing than that.*

"But if we lose," Ted continued, "we'll need to announce Mira's arrest and trial. I want you to write that one first."

"I thought you said it was a cinch."

"There's a chance that it won't be." Ted paused. "Something feels wrong about this case."

You didn't believe me when I said that.

"What do you mean?" Michael asked.

"I think the D.A. has something hidden up his sleeve, something he got from Baedes."

"Like what?"

"If I knew that, it wouldn't be hidden up his sleeve."

"Voodoo litigation? You gonna argue that in court?" Michael stared at him sideways.

"Let's just be prepared, okay?" Ted said.

"Sure. Just give me more work to do."

"That's Mira's way," Ted said.

"What does that mean?" Michael asked.

"She gets herself into these situations all the time."

You really don't understand, do you?

"Yeah, well, she makes waves," Michael agreed.

Suddenly, Clydene opened her mouth. "Shithead jerks! Even on our side you're shithead jerks!" She stammered for a second. "God!" she shouted. And then she slammed her coffee cup onto the table and stormed out of the house.

— ' c , —

"All rise!"

Ted stood, as did everyone else in the courtroom. Beside him stood Mira, a bruise stretching across her forehead. But she looked smart in her gray suit and skirt, and stood as tall and proud as her stature would allow. When just a few minutes earlier she had wished him a happy birthday, Ted had brushed off the sentiment, because he thought it was stupid. Now, he wondered whether he had hurt her feelings, because things like that seemed to matter to Mira. Ted peeked at her out of the corner of his eye. She looked proud, not hurt.

"Criminal court is now in session, the honorable Nathaniel V. Spiller presiding."

The judge took his seat, as did everyone else in the room. He was wearing a long, dark robe and a long, dark scowl to match.

"Docket number 07233, State versus Jayson—"

Ted stood. "Defendant waives reading and moves for dismissal."

"On what basis?" the judge asked.

"Lack of probable cause, Your Honor. The official police report gives no indication of any plausible aggression by Miss Jayson. She was carrying no weapons, and she is much smaller than the arresting officer; therefore, she posed no credible threat. All we have to go on is the feeling of the arresting officer.

"Furthermore, the official report omits several facts, in favor of my client—"

"Do you mean to say that the report is incomplete?" the Judge asked.

"I do not know whether the arresting officer faithfully reported all that he saw. But I do know that no jury in the state would convict my client based on the evidence."

The judge turned to the prosecutor.

"There is additional evidence, Your Honor. Ike Morgan, who was in the car with her, will testify to the fact that Miss Jayson threatened him, and that she then attempted to assault the officer who was arresting her."

"Ike Morgan was also picked up at the same time Miss Jayson was. As a parolee, he no doubt feels great pressure to back up the government's case," Ted countered.

"A question for a jury, Your Honor," the prosecutor said.

The judge spoke. "I tend to agree, Mr. Jackson. This case is not cut and dry."

"Before you make that determination, we ask for an immediate probable cause hearing. We also ask that Miss Jayson be released on personal recognizance."

"You're kidding!" the prosecutor said. "These are serious charges."

"Miss Jayson is an upstanding member of the communit—"

"With an arrest record a mile long!"

"But always in the context of non-violent protest." Ted knew he was visibly fuming, desperately trying to restrain himself, to keep his mind on track. "She is well known for her political activism and non-violent political protests."

"Well," the prosecutor quipped, "I guess she ran out of non-violent ways to get her point across. Now she's a terrorist with a martyr-complex."

"Fear-mongering and speculation. Ridiculous, because there isn't one shred of evidence to support any of it! More to the point: Miss Jayson poses an extremely low flight risk, because she has always appeared at court when required, and her activism gives her strong ties to the community. "

A sudden quiet fell over the court room. Ted could hear his own heavy, labored breathing. He could feel his heart still pounding inside his chest. His mind was racing, already listing all the points at which he might have gone wrong.

The judge finally spoke. "Let's have a probable cause hearing. Tomorrow morning at 10 o'clock?" He scanned the nods of the attorneys. "Bail is set at one million dollars. Court is in recess." And he banged his gavel.

Later, Ted met Mira at the jail. He sat at a solitary table in the center of a small room, facing a sturdy, windowed door. The place stank the musty smell of a government facility. The door opened and a uniformed guard led Mira in and watched her sit in the vacant chair opposite her lawyer. The guard exited, closing the door on the way out. Ted could see him through the door.

Ted began. "Ike is now saying you bragged about having a weapon and that you threatened Baedes. He also says he relayed this information to Baedes, which is why he reacted the way he did."

Mira gave him a desperate look. It could have been bewilderment. It could have been betrayal. Or maybe it was just anger. "But— I— I didn't have a gun. Are they saying I had a gun?"

"No, you didn't have a gun. And I don't believe Ike. His story has more holes than a colander."

Mira interrupted. "What's he getting out of it?"

"Getting? You mean Ike?"

"Yes, what's Ike getting out of it?"

"Well, I hear they're dropping all charges against him. They're saying it was just a misunderstanding but that you seized the opportunity to attack Baedes."

"They're dropping the charges." Mira stared at the floor. "Ike is desperate," she said.

"I'm sure he is. But we're desperate, too, Mira. Baedes is clearly threatening Ike in order to get to you. And because of the position Ike is in, that's exceedingly easy to do."

"And there's nothing illegal in that?"

Ted scoffed. "What's legal anymore? Anything a person can get away with. And Baedes can get away with this."

"Where do I get a million dollars?"

"We could get you out with $100,000."

Mira nodded.

"Do you have $100,000?" Ted asked.

"No. Can we raise it? Isn't that awful high?"

"For a misdemeanor? Yes, excessively."

"Isn't there anything you can do?"

"Our options are limited. And none of them is likely to work before the weekend."

"I thought as much," Mira said. "He's trying to shut us down, isn't he?"

"It would appear so."

"Michael could stand in for me in a pinch. But it's gonna hurt. I'm afraid the volunteers will be too scared."

"It's an end-run around free speech," Ted said, "and artfully planned and executed, I'm afraid. Baedes is knowledgeable, experienced, and connected, a triple threat." He paused. "I don't know how we're going to get you out of this."

CHAPTER 3

Clyde made her way past the convicts and accused, each seated at a table. All were dressed in orange prison garb. Some conversed with visitors, each seated across from an inmate. Others were waiting for someone like Clyde, someone from the outside, to pay attention to them. None smiled. Old lighting fixtures hung from the cracked ceiling, as did drab, green walls. The room smelled like a government school or a town hall.

Clyde at first didn't recognize her friend. Mira looked battered, her hair, slightly disheveled. Bags hung from her eyes, and her cheeks sagged. She looked beaten down, run down, older. Then she noticed Clyde, and that all changed. Her face lit up like the full moon on a clear night, and Clyde suddenly felt light and energetic. Clyde wanted to run up to her, hug her, and plant a kiss firmly on each cheek. And she would have, too, except she knew it was against the rules.

Instead, Clyde sat and smiled, and she calmly and quietly said, "Hey, you. Weren't we supposed to do this at Bertucci's?"

"Ah, but this place provides much better service," Mira joked. "Bertucci's doesn't frisk you on the way in."

Clyde grinned, but the lightness of the moment had left her.

Her teeth clenched.

"Sorry," Mira said. "Not so funny, I guess."

"It's not your fault."

"Better me than Ike."

"What's going on with him?" Clyde asked. She knew how Mira felt about Ike.

"What do you mean? How much did Ted tell you?"

"Not much. Nothing, really. Only the official version, same as the press release." Clyde wondered what Ted could have told her. What did Ted know about a woman's feelings?

"Any more news on that?"

Clyde was confused for a moment. "The press release. No. It went out, but no one seems to care. The only thing worse than being lambasted is being ignored."

"You'd think we'd be used to it by now," Mira said.

"So what's with Ike? He turns state's evidence on you? You should have seen Michael smoking at the ears!"

"Michael's jealous of Ike's butt," Mira said.

"Hey, *I'm* jealous of Ike's butt!" Clyde giggled.

"What do you mean? Ted's is nice, too," Mira said sweetly.

Clyde was aghast in mock indignation. "You just keep you're eyes where they belong, okay?"

"Oh, that's right. It's almost Wednesday."

Clyde widened her eyes and dropped her jaw. "Well, when was the last time you got any?"

Mira contemplated the question. "Too long ago," she said. "But don't you two have special plans for tonight?"

"Why should we?" Clyde asked.

"Birthday sex," Mira said.

Clyde giggled. "I don't think so. But maybe if throw him a party, I can drive him to sleep on the couch."

"That'll teach him," Mira said. "He can watch all those depressing retrospectives on TV. Why doesn't Ted like birthdays?"

"I don't know. He thinks they're stupid. I think birthdays are just too sentimental for his tastes."

"How old is he?" Mira asked.

"Forty," Clyde answered.

"That's a milestone!" Mira said. "Are you sure you're not going to have birthday sex?"

Clyde wanted to change the subject. "Is that what this thing with Ike is about?"

"What?"

Clyde wondered how she could say it without seeming boorish. "I mean, did you— and Ike? You know..."

"Oh." Realization washed over Mira's face. "You mean, did we have sex?"

"Well..."

Mira smiled sweetly again. "What's with you?"

Clyde just blushed.

"No, nothing like that. It's just..." She paused. "No, nothing."

"But what was with him getting into a fight with Chief Beady-eyes? And now—"

"I wouldn't call it a fight. More like Baedes was beating up on him. That's probably what it was, too. Come on, the guy's as harmless as a fruit fly."

Clyde shook her head. "I still don't get it? Do you think Baedes beat him up into finking?"

Mira's expression turned vacant. She stared off into space.

Now Clyde regretted asking. "He'll never get away with it," she reassured her friend, craning her head to see into Mira's eyes. "I promise."

Mira turned back toward her friend. She spoke cautiously. "Thanks, Clyde. I appreciate what you're trying to do. But please leave Ike alone."

"I meant Beady-eyes," Clyde said.

Mira stared back. She just looked angry and sad.

"He's gotta be behind it," Clyde continued. "We'll figure it out and get him."

Mira's eyes narrowed. "Oh damn. And why don't you repeal the law of gravity while you're at it?"

Clyde said nothing.

Mira continued. "You know, I've never admitted this to anyone before. I've been thinking about this for awhile."

Mira's tone got Clyde's attention.

"You know, this whole thing started with Lando Benitez. Poor guy, wrong ancestry, gets caught sitting in his car in the wrong part of the wrong town. The cops rough him up, arrest him, trash his car, and for the privilege, they stiff him hundreds of dollars he can't afford in bogus fees and fines. You'd think it was just some clueless jerks with uniforms and badges, who need a judge to remind them of the Fourth Amendment, right? After all, there are some of those in every city. But no, they actually get the judge to side with them. And then when poor Lando can't pay, they harass him, arrest him, and charge him again.

"This was back before there were any of us to even help. And Lando was still able to get out within hours. Back then, if I had realized how much higher the stakes were going to get..."

Mira shook her head. "This whole situation is just so screwed up. I don't belong here. I don't even know why I am here. It's not doing any good. I'm not helping anybody, and I... I just feel like a fool." She regarded Clydene. "And now I'm pissing off my best friend."

"Hey, you," Clyde said tenderly. "You're not a fool, and it's not your fault. And you're not pissing off your best friend."

Mira's face remained expressionless.

Clyde said, "Please, continue venting."

"That's okay. The venting is over. Thanks for listening."

"Always, Mira."

— ' C , —

Clyde had collected about a teaspoon of cumin in her palm. Now, she tossed it into the chili pot, muscled a wooden spoon through the thick stew, raised the spoon to her lips, blew on it until it was cool, and tasted.

She stopped a moment to consider the flavor. "Mm. Just about right," she said out loud, to herself. "Just spicy enough, but it's missing a bit of twang."

She stirred in several more grinds of black pepper and a dash of ground mustard seed. All the while, she hummed a tune she made up on the fly, a jazzy number patterned on a 12-bar blues. She tasted again.

"Yes. Perfect," she said.

She lidded the pot, opened the oven, and with two sturdy oven mitts carefully placed the pot into the oven. She always cooked chili—or any type of stew—in the oven, not on the stovetop, because that was the easiest way to control the temperature, to cook it slowly and evenly. In Clydene's hands even this simple peasant stew was gourmet cuisine, a dish to be fine-tuned and pored over. But now that the fine-tuning was done, all that was left to pore over was a sink full of dirty dishes. She would check back every hour or so to peek in and stir. But otherwise, now she just felt like resting.

Clyde turned on the kitchen faucet, squeezed out a dab of soap into one hand, took a splash of water in the other, and scrubbed the two into a thick lather. She thought it was such a fine metaphor, soap and water. Sometimes you can't stop the devil from touching your life. All you can do is to work up a froth of tears and wrath, of drizzle and ooze, of sadness and anger. She rinsed away the slippery, sudsy residue and wished she could do he same in real life.

Clyde plodded into the den, wiping her wet hands on her jeans. She flopped down on the couch. She had hoped cooking would have taken her mind off of her troubles. And it had, but only temporarily. Again, her mind was as stuck as always. She had visited Mira in jail many times but would never get used to it. Seeing her without makeup, without stylish clothes, with that ugly bruise made this proud and beautiful woman seem homely, diminutive. Many people didn't understand the bond between Clyde and Mira. They were like two sides of a coin. One heads, the other tails. One in the limelight, the other in the shadows. One a people person, the other a fact person. One a natural-born leader, the other coming into leadership only now in her late thirties.

But they had more in common than they were different. They were both quick on the draw. When Mira decided to put together this protest, she was making arrangements even before the idea was complete in her head. That was Clydene's life, always deciding at the last minute what to work on next, or what to do, or what to make for dinner. But they were also both perfectionists, always tweaking everything to make it better. You kinda have to be that way when you've only partially thought through what you're doing. That's not to say that Clydene thought quickly on her feet. The phrase "unanticipated situation" to Clydene was terrifying, because it meant "stressed out, stammering, and saying something stupid."

But Mira and Clyde both drew rapid conclusions based on little information. And they were both usually right, at least with anything they knew about. Yes, Clyde had made bum predictions before. Like when she predicted the outcome of the 2000 presidential election; her prediction was not even close to what really happened. But tell her about a software system you'd like her to design, and she understood the architecture of it even before you finished, and long before there were any architectural diagrams on paper. In music, Clyde could tell you exactly what notes to play to make your song sound better, having heard it only once.

Mira was like that, but with people instead of things. Mira did successfully predict the outcome of the 2000 presidential election, right down to the battle over Florida. She didn't predict the hanging chads, but once they had been mentioned in the news, Mira knew immediately what would happen next. Nothing surprised her. Mira could read through a press release and tell you exactly how it would be received, and by which groups of readers. That's why she loved working with Michael; she almost never had to ask him to revise his press releases. Or she could read a news story and immediately see opportunities to leverage it for PR, opportunities that no one else ever saw.

Given the current situation, Clyde didn't feel like thinking about her friend, because it frustrated her and angered her. That's why she felt like cooking. Now, however, she met a giant lull in the cooking process. And she was again thinking of all that bothered her. Maybe it was time to tend to those dirty dishes.

Clyde leaned forward and grabbed the TV remote from the coffee table. *Click.* Within a few seconds, the Mythbusters appeared on the screen, trying to find the fastest way to cool a 6-pack of beer to 40 degrees.

"Ooh! Is this the Baghdad battery episode?" Clyde said to nobody in the room. "That was a nasty trick Tori and those guys played on Adam."

She set the remote back down on the table and picked up a magazine. On the cover was a giant colorized green and orange photo of a retrovirus. The headline read, "Computer Viruses Strike Back: How a new breed of computer virus is terrorizing today's office." She had bought the magazine on a whim, now opened it, and began to read the article. Apparently, hackers were now imbuing their email worms with artificial intelligence, allowing them to hide themselves. *Yeah, right,* she thought. It sounded too fantastic to be accurate.

Besides, she still hated the word "hacker" in that context, even though most of the rest of the world had learned to accept it. Damn it, she herself was a hacker, a computer maestro, a wizard's wizard. She could hack code with the best of them. Yet she had never cracked into a computer system.

Cracker was the correct term, because a cracker was someone who cracked into another computer system. But crackers didn't write worms, and worms aren't viruses. *Two separate things,* Clyde thought. And what this article was talking about was Trojan horses, not "email worms." It was probably old technology, anyhow, easily blocked with any off-the-shelf virus scanner or personal firewall. If they really wanted to talk about computer security threats, they'd talk about cross-site scripting attacks, and XSS viruses.

She tried to read the article, but every time she got through a few sentences, her mind would go off on a tangent. She was just too keyed up, and not actually interested in the article. Still, she struggled to read it, probably because the alternative would be even more uncomfortable, even with the TV to distract her.

In the middle of all this, Gary called to complain about the QX project... Again. She muted the TV before picking up the phone. Gary said the software was malfunctioning. Except that the software was behaving exactly as they had specified. This was just the latest call in a long series of exasperating communiqués. She had repeatedly explained, if the computer wasn't doing what he wanted it to, all he had to do was to tell her what he did want, and she would make the computer do it. And she did. And then he changed his mind without telling her about it. *How can a company run this way?* she thought. *Oh, forgot. Government contract.*

No, he said, it was still not working right. So Clyde stepped into her office and pulled up the latest specification on her computer. Unfortunately, Gary wasn't at his computer. He doesn't have a computer in his office? Where was he calling from? His car? She read him the corresponding part from the spec, but if that isn't what he wants, she can change it to do whatever he wants, as long as he explains what he wants. Yes, he agreed that what she read was all true, but that part of the specification didn't apply in this particular case, and didn't the spec say so? No, it didn't. *And if he had actually read it,* Clyde thought, *he might even know that.* Good thing Clyde had an ongoing hourly contract with them, so she could charge thm for all the time she wasted going around in circles on this project, dancing with the project manager and business analyst. Otherwise, she'd be paying out of her own pocket for all this fun.

She said, "The behavior as it is now is what was specified. As I've explained, I'm happy to make the software do whatever you want. You just have to tell me exactly what you want."

He said he'd have to get back to her. They hung up. This phone call was only the latest volley in a long chain of pointless complaints, and Clyde was beginning to wonder whether she'd be working on the project very much longer, or whether it would be worth it if she did.

The QX project was fun to work on. That is, she got to play with some interesting technology. She even got to meet interesting people, on the few occasions she visited the client's site for meetings. But Clyde began to wonder whether it was turning her into less of a human being. She worked on this project as a sub-contractor for a government contractor. The project itself was a workflow application being deployed in a number of local government offices, including those in Abe's Turn. It helped government employees keep government records and do their jobs.

That was the ultimate irony. Clyde was doing business, indirectly, with the very people against whom she passionately fought. *Fought,* not *hated.* Even in her mind, she avoided the word *hate,* because *hate* was far too weak a word to describe what she felt. She honestly believed these people were going to hell. Not all of them, but a few at least. They surely were not making it to heaven. She knew this, because of the bible story, about the rich, young ruler.

The rich, young ruler comes to Jesus, asks him what he needs to do to make it to heaven. Jesus tells him to follow all the commandments. He replies that he's done that since he was little. Okay, so Jesus tells him the only other thing he needs to do is to sell everything he has, give it to the poor, and then follow him. The guy can't do it and walks away, sad. Jesus turns to his disciples and says, "Verily, I say unto you, it's easier for a camel to squeeze through the eye of a needle than for a politician to get into heaven." Or words to that effect.

But with regard to the QX project, Clyde calmed her conscience by pushing it off to the side. She was not, after all, doing evil. She was merely providing technology that could be used for good or for evil. That some people would use it to execute evil or misguided actions, was that her fault? Occasionally, however, her conscience refused to shut up, and she wondered whether she was fooling herself. Some part of her knew that if God asked, she may not be able to justify herself in good conscience. And isn't that what morality was all about?

Interestingly, these thoughts plagued her most at certain times, those times when what she accomplished were forgotten by the corporate machine, those times when corporate politics took precedence. When Clyde first worked with a larger corporation, she was surprised at how rabid the politics were. She delivered exactly what she was asked to deliver. Unfortunately, the project manager didn't actually sign off on it, in writing. Then when one of the managers at the client complained, they blamed her for reneging on the contract. From then on, she got specifications in writing, and kept written records of all communications with the client. And she used these things as political ammunition. She very quickly learned how to blame someone else, even though it made her feel slimy, dirty, sick to her stomach. And Clyde sometimes felt being in this situation made her less of a human being, because she couldn't trust her co-workers, even though they were all on the same team.

Despite her quiet, reserved demeanor, Clyde enjoyed working with and trusting others. And situations that involved big-company politics tore her in two. On one side, she trusted; on the other, she was logical. The trustworthy side, versus the cold side. The person who stuck up for others and what was right, versus she who was crudely practical about getting the job done. In Clyde's mind one side was not better than the other. She had always lived with both, learned to respect both, to value and admire both equally. And she hated when the two were in disharmony, when she felt she was being forced to choose one or the other.

And too many clients did force her to choose. Big corporations had built-in lethargy and in-fighting that kept them from accomplishing anything. Stupid. And so they hired her to get the job done. Then they put roadblocks in her way and dragged her into their fights. Stupid. Big companies are stupid. As Professor Bernardo de la Paz said in one of Clydene's favorite novels, "More than six people cannot agree on anything, three is better—and one is perfect for a job one can do. This is why parliamentary bodies all through history, when they accomplished anything, owed it to a few strong men who dominated the rest." Or a few strong women.

But Clyde didn't see herself as one of those few strong women. Yes, she had the drive and the initiative. But she was a technology person, not a people person.

Clyde stood from her chair in her office and began to return to the den and her TV show, now almost over.

They really were clueless. You'd think a government project would be constructed with more care. But QX was designed merely according to predominant industry standards, which means what it sounds like: a piece of crap. The software was full of bugs, and the project team just accepted it. There was little oversight over the development process. This caused issues with the project, and any of them could become a problem at any time. And QX was even connected to the Internet. What if some Internet cracker got in? Theoretically, there could even be saboteur on the project team.

Rather than a government project, QX was run more like a government contract, which it was. Naturally, the project was plagued with cost overruns and schedule slips. As a result, corners were cut. The first thing to go was the test plan, because test plans take time. It's much quicker to throw software together and ship it without testing it, without knowing whether it actually works. But at least they peer-inspected the code, right? Are you kidding? That would use up several man-hours a day. Who had time for that? They didn't even do security background checks. After all, this wasn't a stealth bomber they were building.

Good thing, too. Because Clydene had seen the code. The QX project had more holes than a colander. Ironically, all these holes could be plugged easily. But no one was willing even to pay for a security audit and come up with some safety guidelines. As she worked on the project, Clyde did what she could to fix problems and plug security holes. But she was just one engineer, and a mere sub-contractor at that. In order to fix QX, she needed help from the project team. But the project team did not care; Clydene had asked.

At least her mind was no longer dwelling on Mira.

Clyde picked up her magazine again. If only these reporters

knew how bad it really was, what kinds of new-fangled threats there were on the Internet, and how vulnerable most software was to attack, especially corporate software. They would have another issue they could ignore, because it's too complicated, as they claim, for the layman to understand.

— ' c , —

Mira's probable cause hearing went about as Murphy would have predicted. And this depressed Mira even more than she had been before the hearing.

Baedes testified, weaving a tale Stephen King would have admired. It involved a crazed woman, shouting obscenities and reaching for a weapon while she lunged at him. The judge asked almost as many questions as the prosecutor, which was a little odd. Maybe the D.A. was off his game. Baedes's awesome presence on the stand indeed intimidated everyone in the courtroom, except the judge, Ted, and Mira herself. At least that was what Mira thought. Far from intimidating her, Baedes incensed her. Maybe that's why he hated her so, because she was one of the only people he couldn't bully.

Ike also testified for the prosecution, and perjured himself in the process. Mira feared for him for what could happen if it became known that he was lying under oath. Part of her just wanted to give up, in order to keep this truth secret. Ted seemed to have no such fear. He tried to break Ike's story. But someone had thought his story through very carefully. There was no way to prove it was a tall tale. And Ike stoically maintained his version of the tale, even as Ted threw around words like friendship, betrayal, lies, and perjury.

Judge Spiller had no choice but to bind her over for trial. But Mira knew by looking at him that this is what he wanted to do, and he would have found a way to do it, no matter what the evidence was.

CHAPTER 4

Michael started. "We can resurrect Martin Luther King, Jr., get him to do his 'I have a dream' speech."

"If it were possible, someone else would have thought of it first," Ted replied.

"Well, that's it for me. I'm out," Michael said.

Ted paused. "You're kidding."

"Yes, I am." Sometimes Michael joked a little brusquely, but sometimes it was the only way he knew how to cope.

Without missing a beat, Ted continued, "Well, let's wait for Clydene to get back. Maybe she'll have some better ideas."

"How is business for her?" Michael scooted to the edge of the couch so he could reach his coffee on the coffee table.

"Pretty good. She's been putting in a lot of time on the QX project lately."

"Fleecing them pretty good, I hope."

"I imagine so," Ted said. "She's also been working on a new project. I'm not sure what."

"Something top-secret for the CIA?" Another joke.

"I think SD-6. How's your new boss? Still clueless?"

"Always." Michael really enjoyed quick-witted banter. "Today he wigged when my team had a brain-storming session without him."

"Sounds like he might have control issues."

"Definitely. He could actually be pretty good, if he didn't have to be in the middle of everything all the time." Michael actually felt sorry for the poor guy. This single character defect held him back, but boy was it a doozy.

"What are you going to do?" Ted asked.

"No problem. I've dealt with bosses before."

Clydene entered the room. "Hey, you," she greeted Michael.

"Hey, Clyde." Michael saw how hard her friend's incarceration had hit her, and he forgave her for her occasional outbursts of temper. "Ted tells me you have a new client," he remarked.

She looked confused for a second. "No. I've been working on a side-project, just experimenting with a new technology is all. Nothing really interesting, though."

"Well, more for the resume, I guess." Michael said.

"Uh, yeah." She smiled coyly.

Ted interrupted and got the meeting on track. When Mira was unable to make a meeting, he usually took up the reigns.

Their purpose for this meeting was to decide what to do about the upcoming demonstration. Mira's preference was to go on with the event as best as possible, even if she couldn't make it. But Ted, Michael, and Clyde would be in the hot seat. She would back whatever they decided.

The thing was, Mira was the personality behind the protest, and behind the campaign to oust Baedes. It was her cause, her passion. Her petition would be the culmination of this campaign. Mira had given up volunteering for other projects, and had even cut back on her caseload, in order to spend more time on the Committee for a Fairer Future. Yes, it had been a collective idea, as far as Ted could remember. That is, all four of them had come up with the idea of forming an organization to fight Baedes, because he was the driving force behind the

police state that was coming to Abe's Turn, all in the name of
peace and order. All four friends had been incensed and heart-
broken when they realized what had happened to their home-
town. But Mira was the one who had put in her time and
passion, had taken a crash course in politics and law enforcement, had assembled mentors, had devised strategy, had
scoured newspaper articles, had dug up research, collected
statistics, had thought up PR opportunities, had interviewed
victims, amassed personal anecdotes, had gotten them on
board, had drawn volunteers, had kept them fired up. Mira
had spearheaded the project. On top of all that, Mira drilled
herself constantly on tough questions regarding the campaign.
As much as she admitted she hated doing it, she studied and
learned to be an apologist for the campaign. She knew more
about this cause than anyone else involved. And she was who
all the local newspapers called for comments. If she couldn't
make it to her own protest... Well, *that* was going to be the
story.

Ted, Michael, and Clydene went down the list of their
options. They could call off the event, but that would mean
they'd throw away all the effort they'd invested in building up
to it. Besides, it would show Baedes that he could bully them,
and they didn't want to send that message. Another alternative was merely postponing. That was a little better, but not by
much, because they'd still lose momentum, and Baedes would
still get the message that he could bully them. Now, if there
were some other reason for postponing, then they could use it
as an excuse. But none of them could think of such an excuse.
They agreed to postpone only as a last resort and to keep an
eye out for any excuse they could use to rationalize the post-
ponement.

Clyde spoke up. "Okay. We have signs and materials. We
have volunteers. We have permits and equipment and everything else we need. Everything's scheduled. Now... Refresh

my memory again. Why does Mira need to be there?"

Michael answered. "Because she's the personality behind the campaign. She's got to be on hand to give a speech, answer questions, drive the demonstration, and so forth. Besides, it would look really bad for her to miss her own event because she was arrested. The press is going to take Beady-eyes's side and paint her as a criminal."

"Okay. There are other people who could answer questions. Like you, for example."

"Or you," Michael said. He really didn't want to be in the hot seat, even though he was the most qualified. Yes, he loved the limelight, but this kind of publicity was not what he needed.

"I guess so," Clyde said awkwardly. She clearly didn't look forward to the prospect.

"But most of the questions would be hostile questions about Mira's arrest," Michael noted. "I wouldn't want to be in your shoes trying to answer those."

"You'd probably do a better job than me." She was beginning to raise her voice.

"But you believe in the idea more," Michael countered. This wasn't exactly true. They all believed in the idea.

"But you coached Mira. You helped her go through the questions she might be asked. You're the right one for the job. Or instead of a speech, she could issue a prepared statement. One of us could even read it."

"A prepared statement? Like a politician?" Michael hated politicians and had urged Mira to distance herself as much as possible from their double-faced tactics.

Clydene leered at him.

"Let's settle down," Ted interjected.

"Besides, even politicians read their own statements," Michael said. When he got worked up, he just couldn't leave well enough alone.

"You know," Ted interjected, "if we could raise $100,000, we could bail her out."

"Yeah," Michael replied, "and if I were Superman, I could break her out."

"You don't think an urgent phone and Internet campaign could raise the money?" Clyde asked.

"Not likely," said Michael.

"Well, what part of the money could it raise?" Ted said.

"Maybe 5 thou, or 10 if we're lucky." Even that was a stretch, he hated to admit.

"Are there any rich benefactors waiting in the wings?"

"Don't you think I'd be on them already if there were?"

"Maybe. What about prospects? A wealthy lion from whose paw Mira may have pulled a thorn?"

"Not that I know of," Michael said. "But you should ask her next time you see her. She doesn't always share with me all her connections. For all I know, she may have done a favor for Michael Corleone."

"Hmm." Ted nodded. "There's one more option."

"What's that?" Clyde asked.

Ted spoke soberly. "We could disclaim Mira and go forward with Michael as spokesman."

Clyde was livid. "Who's side are you on?"

"I'm on our side—"

"And you, Michael, here you have a perfect opportunity to do something that will show Mira you really care about her, and you won't do it. Sometimes you really make no sense. And you would get to be the center of attention, too! Since when do you turn down a chance to be the center of attention?"

"Ouch," Michael said quietly. That hurt.

Clyde sighed. "Well, I'm sorry to deal from the bottom of the deck, but that's the truth."

Michael thought she was full of anger and bullshit, but he

knew when to talk and when to listen.

"My point is," Clyde said, "Mira's the victim here. We can't let that beat us down. We have to use it for ammunition."

Quiet.

Clyde's dedication for her friend was certainly admirable. And she was right: Mira was the victim. And Beady-eyes was the aggressor. They had to find some way of spinning this to their favor. There was no other option.

"What do you think, Michael?" Ted said.

Michael spoke carefully. "If we have to go in without Mira, then we'll do the best we can. But we'll face a challenge. All the press is going to be looking at the fact that she was arrested for assault. They're going to say that the judge considers her dangerous." He quickly backpedaled as he turned wide eyes to Clyde. "I know she didn't do anything wrong. She couldn't. It's not in her nature. Beady-eyes is a creep. And that judge is full of it. Or full of something.

"The press cares about the drama. They don't give a damn for the truth. So I think our best bet is to work our view into the drama, maybe with a show of solidarity and support. And spin it as example of the kind of abuse we're trying to stop. And then hope for a one-liner."

"Or a sound-bite," Clyde said.

"I don't follow," Michael said.

"A sound-bite on the evening news is worth how many column-inches?"

"A bunch. But there the TV reporters haven't been knocking down our door. Our best bet would be if we had some proof that Beady-eyes had arrested her for personal reasons. That would raise some questions. Or that he manipulated the evidence."

Ted said, "If we had proof that he manipulated the evidence, instead of subjecting it to press scrutiny, I'd introduce it in court. We wouldn't be having this conversation. In fact, any evidence that he was acting improperly could help."

"Well, he surely has been," Clyde said.

Ted looked at the ceiling for a moment. "We're biased."

"What?" Michael said. Yes, they were biased, but only because they were right.

"We think Baedes is up to no good, because we believe he has been up to no good in the past. That has served us, because we've only had to convince fellow activists. Now, we have to convince a judge. That means we need hard evidence."

"What sort of evidence?" Clyde asked.

"Maybe if one of his colleagues came forward with testimony."

"Fat chance of that," said Michael. "We'd do better to bug the place. I'll get some black body-suits, and Clyde can break through the security system." Sometimes when he got upset, Michael's sense of humor ran rampant.

"That's another joke, right?" Ted said.

"Yes," said Michael.

Ted spoke sternly. "Because it would be blatantly illegal. Not only could we not use the evidence, but I wouldn't want to think of what would happen to us if we got caught. As an officer of the court, just telling me about such a plot would be disastrous."

"Ted—" Michael put his hand on his friend's shoulder. "It was a joke, just a bad joke. Sorry. I'm ticked."

Ted nodded. "There's a lot of that going around lately." He took a breath. "You know, the biggest part of examining a witness is knowing what questions to ask. It's not as important as people think, to find a witness who wants to give the right testimony. Because if you can ask the right questions, you can get almost any testimony you want. So we don't actually need anyone to come forward, if I knew who to ask and what to ask him."

Indeed, the four were all under tremendous stress, because

they were trying to pick up the slack in risky and demanding circumstances. But quantifying the problem made it easier to come up with a plan and made Michael feel a little better. They would postpone only if there turned out to be no other option. They could make that decision over the weekend. In the meantime, Michael would send out personalized messages from Mira to each volunteer, including pleas for help. That was a job and a half, but Michael felt the motivation. The goal was to collect pledges toward Mira's bail. This was an emergency, because if they couldn't collect enough pledges before Friday, the event all the volunteers had worked so hard on may never even happen.

However, this was only one side of a two-prong attack. On the other prong, Ted had a court appeal left. He would use that appeal, and any other evidence he could dig up, to try to reverse the bail decision, or at least to reduce it, and to get Mira released.

— ' c , —

By the time they were through and Michael had left, it was late. Clyde made the excuse that she just wanted to check her email before going to bed. She sent Ted upstairs and sat down at her computer. She looked at her email in-box. There were about a dozen new messages, but she didn't do anything with any of them. She didn't read them, delete them, move them to another folder. She didn't even ignore them. Instead, she opened a console window on her computer. As a software developer, she knew all about the internals of her computer, and she frequently used old-style command-line programs that she created herself.

She paused for a long minute, deep in thought. This was the moment of no return. She had been working on this project ever since Mira's arrest. Initially, she couldn't even tell you why, what good it could possibly do. But she had a feeling.

She knew she could uncover something, as long as she didn't get caught. And that was the danger. This was the moment of no return. Beyond this point, she could not undo what she was about to do. And if someone were to discover her, her life would probably be over. Why should she risk it? Simple. Because this is what she had been working toward. Yesterday, she believed this secret project held the answers to Mira's dilemma. What had changed between yesterday and today? Nothing, except Clyde's fear. And she couldn't let mere fear control her life. *There's nothing to it but to do it,* she thought.

With trembling fingers, she typed the cryptic command `pyx_loader`. The letters appeared in green on a black panel, like the old-style green-phosphor monitors. She closed her eyes, took a deep breath, and pressed the enter key. For another few seconds she didn't even breathe. Then computer responded with several lines of equally cryptic response, all in green on black:

```
Logging to pyx.log
Found hole 4 at 172.27.201.183
Administrator access
Attached to EXPLORER
Installed re-attacher, all methods
```

Clyde was dizzy. Pyx had found a security hole in a deployed QX server, a hole which allowed her to break into the system and gain administrator privileges. She didn't know what computer was specifically at the IP address 172.27.201.183, but she knew it was within Abe's Turn. Pyx had installed itself on this server, and now it would begin spreading, like a virus, onto any other government computer it could. And it would begin surreptitiously sending back information, any information it could find, for Clyde to sift through. And if anyone figured out what was happening and that she caused it, yes, it was a federal crime. There was no going back now.

As if in a dream, she entered the follow-up command `pyx_scan`, to which the computer replied:

```
Scanning... Found 5 messages.
```

Suddenly, nervousness grabbed Clyde's heart, as though something had gone wrong. Yes, she had planned to infiltrate a government computer system. But seeing it actually happen brought a reality that freaked Clyde out. But there was no going back, only going forward.

She typed more commands to display the log. It showed records from 5 separate computers, and that Pyx was sending back data. She began looking at this data. Page after page of pointless memorandums, dense documentation, boring emails. But each new one made Clyde more tense, or maybe more excited.

"Oy," Clyde whispered.

"Clyde," Ted said from behind her.

Clyde yelped and spun around in her chair. What the hell was he doing sneaking up on her? He was supposed to be upstairs falling asleep. He was supposed to be an early riser, and late nights were supposed to knock him out. And he was definitely not supposed to see what she was working on! If he did, she feared, he would feel an obligation as an officer of the court to turn her in. He had told similar stories of clients he had defended. And it always upset him, but he always did "the right thing," his words, not Clyde's.

Ted giggled. "I'm pouring myself a glass of wine. Do you want— No. Correction: I'm pouring one for you, too. Stop working and come to bed." He was smiling.

"Sorry, I just got distracted by—"

"Yeah, yeah. I've heard it before. We're going to relax, and we're going to forget all about our problems."

She stared at him blankly. This definitely didn't make sense. It was late. He was tired, or so she thought. And he apparently wasn't noticing anything on the computer monitor.

"It's Wednesday night, remember?" he said.

"Oh, right," she said.

Every Wednesday before bed and every Sunday after church, like clockwork, that was when they got intimate. It was part of their routine, and there were very few exceptions. Clyde would have thought that the regularity of it all would have made sex boring, but Ted always found a way to make it exciting and new, adventurous. In any case, this also explained why Ted cared not a whit what she was doing, only that she wasn't getting ready for bed. She had lucked out.

"Okay, I'm coming. Right now," she said.

Ted went back to the kitchen to pour the wine.

Clyde turned to her computer and closed the console window full of text. She breathed deeply. Then she turned off the computer monitor and went upstairs.

CHAPTER 5

When Clydene was a girl, 9 years old, she wanted to make orange pie. She didn't have a recipe, but she really wanted to make orange pie. She figured she could make an orange-flavored pie crust. And if she substituted oranges for some other fruit, she figured she'd be all set.

Her mother, of course, would never allow it. Clyde had never baked anything before. And she was also known for the clutter she left behind her whenever she did anything in the kitchen. She loved to experiment, loved to create, and absolutely hated to clean up after herself. Truthfully, she didn't even consider whether her mother would allow it or not. All she knew is that she wanted to make orange pie, and she knew how she wanted to do it. So this 9-year-old girl laid out all the ingredients she needed and set about making a pie crust using fresh orange juice instead of water.

Now, making a pie crust from scratch is not trivial. That's why pre-made pie crusts are so popular. There are too many things that can go wrong and spoil the crust. You start by combining flour with a fat, like butter or shortening. You have to make sure the fat is cold, though, or it won't combine correctly with the flour. Then you mix in cold water, or a water-type liquid, until the dough is just sticky enough. Then you refrigerate, and after that you can finally roll it out into a pie crust. Naturally, this all comprises only the start of baking a pie.

Clyde never made it past step one. She used her hands to combine the fat and flour, and overworked it until it resembled a roux. She attempted to save her project by covering the glop with wax paper and popping it in the freezer to chill it— the freezer, because she was too anxious to wait for the refrigerator to do the job. Then she went into the next room and watched TV. But she didn't make it back to the kitchen until her mother walked in to find what she described as "an explosion at the bakery." Ironically, the cookbook Clyde was using specifically said to combine the fat and flour with butter knives or a pastry blender, not your hands, because the heat from your hands would warm up the dough and ruin it. Also ironically, her mother had a pastry blender in the silverware drawer, but Clyde had always thought it was for mashing potatoes.

She finally did come up with a recipe for orange pie, using many other orange pie recipes as references, and after many trials and unsuccessful variations. But that all happened much later, after she had grown to be an adult. Adulthood brings a certain circumspection to one's activities. Still, a person's basic personality, they say, sticks with one from the time one is a child. As we grow older, we add to those simple childish tendencies, we balance them out, but we can never escape them. Who we are is with us always, even unto the grave.

That's why it would be no surprise to someone watching Clydene, now that she was desperate to clear Mira. She also wanted to sock it to the evil monsters who had hurt her friend. Now an adult, she behaved just as she did as a child, with one important addition: This time, she was paranoid about how others would react and careful not to get caught. It was because of this paranoia that she was not excited at her discovery. Rather, it gave her heartburn like a pepperoni and coffee-bean pizza. It was the kitchen table when she was 9, covered with flour and goo and melting margarine, an incriminating scene just waiting for the wrong person to happen upon it. Her discovery came in the form of a computer file, a simple document she was not supposed to have a copy of. She was not even supposed to be able to access it. And yet it was now staring her in the face.

Clyde had been very careful in testing her Pyx virus and injecting it via the QX system. The security hole she exploited was not something she had added to the system. In fact, it was in an area of the system she had never directly worked on. The network connection she used to exploit the hole was neither monitored nor logged. And now that the virus was installed, it sent data back to her, encrypted, over the public Internet. She never had any direct contact with it. There was no realistic way anyone could trace it back to her. Yes, if someone were to discover it, they could shut down Pyx. And if they suspected Clydene of being the receiver of these encrypted Internet transmissions, a security expert could prove it, because only her computer could decode the information. Therefore, they could prove she was the culprit by proving that only she could receive Pyx's transmissions. But at least for now, no one was even looking. And she didn't plan on keeping the jig going long enough to be discovered.

She was actually surprised at how quickly Pyx spread and started sending data. Within several hours it had spread to the police department's computers. And within a day, it had pulled up a gem from Baedes's own hard drive. Clyde found it by searching for "MJ." She had set up a number of other searches, too, that her computer automatically executed, looking for anything about Mira. But this one struck pay dirt, the chief's own notes detailing his plans to arrest Mira, charge her with assault, and keep her in jail. As he had executed each stage of the plan, he had kept track. Baedes appeared to be a compulsive note-taker.

As Clyde pieced together what she learned from the files with what Mira had told her, the whole story began to take shape, like a picture coming into focus. Beady-eyes had been keeping tabs on Mira for a while. He knew her patterns, that she always took the same route home at about the same time each day. He also knew how much work she and her volunteers had been putting into their cause. At first, they came across as just a bunch of crackpots. But all that work was beginning to bear fruit, and this made her a plausible threat, as he saw it. So he figured he'd kill two birds with one stone. He'd shut down the protest and demoralize her troops, all at the same time.

He timed her arrest carefully, close enough to the protest that it would send her organization into panic, but early enough that most people wouldn't connect it with the protest. He could have arrested her on any charge. He could have made up one if he needed to. The expired registration was just a happy coincidence. He planned to charge her with assault and resisting arrest. He didn't originally intend to grab Ike, whose arrest was also fortunate happenstance. The chief was the one who started the scuffle with Ike, in order to provoke Mira. And it worked. Then he extorted testimony from Ike, basically by threatening him with prison. Since Ike was a parolee, that was the easy part, because there was no hard evidence against Baedes, just the word of a criminal and the word of a jailbird. And they weren't even likely to corroborate each other's testimony. Then he asked a sympathetic judge to put Mira away for a while— not in those words, of course. He and the D.A. dressed it up in legal hocus-pocus, but it all amounted to the same thing.

Baedes himself had probably originated the story that Ike told the court. Or maybe he dragged it out of Ike, while making sure Ike told it right. Clydene certainly knew enough about that sort of persuasion. She set her teeth.

Baedes had also shared parts of this plan with "PB." A little research via the other files revealed that PB was Officer Pamela Burns, whom was apparently one of Baedes's protégés, one of his crew that Baedes had taken a personal interest in. In this case, he relied on her to perform research, and he shared with her aspects of his plan, but he made sure she was not a witness to anything that occurred.

Clyde felt like a voyeur, as though she were looking into someone's window, invading his private room, staring at his nakedness, a sight which was holding her, hypnotically. She woke for a moment from her trance, swept her eyes through her office, afraid someone might be looking over her shoulder. But there was no need. She was the only one in the house. All she heard was the hum of the computer's fan and of the refrigerator down the hallway. She was there alone, and only she knew how to access the information she had unearthed. Good thing, too. She shivered to think what Ted might say if he knew what she had been up to.

She also felt like it was too simple to be realistic. If she were in a spy novel, everything would be hopelessly convoluted or involve mysterious technology that couldn't actually exist in real life. But that felt realistic. This truth was stranger than fiction. Baedes had simply written down all of his misdeeds, kept a record, almost as if he were confessing to his priest. And then he left them in an unlocked room with a door big enough for Godzilla to walk through.

All of these thoughts and feelings hit her at once in an eerie blast of mental twilight. But thinking about Ted brought her back to Earth. Indeed, Ted would freak out like only Ted could, angry, upset, betrayed, if he knew what she had done. He would be afraid for her and for himself. He would feel an ethical obligation to turn over all the evidence of her misdeeds, yet a moral obligation to keep her confidence. He would be afraid of losing her and of losing control of the situation, and he hated to lose control. Yet Ted was the man who needed to know what was in the file.

"So how," Clydene said, "do I clue him in, without getting either of us in trouble?"

Yes, she could send him an anonymous email. But she couldn't give specifics, because she didn't know how much this Pamela Burns actually knew. Clyde didn't even want anyone to know that Baedes's files had been compromised, because that would provoke them to seek out the person who had compromised the files. And an anonymous email could still be traced back to her, if a court ordered it. And if Ted thought the sender were someone inside the government, he might just seek such an order.

But what if... Suddenly, the answer was clear.

She had built a feature into Pyx to allow it to upgrade and expand itself, if she told it to do so. She could issue Pyx commands via the same anonymous, secure channels it sent back data. She quickly wrote a script that sent an email. The email claimed to be from an anonymous, inside informant; it was specific enough to identify Burns as a source of information in Mira's case—and so that Ted would know it's not a piece of random spam; and it was vague enough not to give away where the information came from. The email appeared to come from Baedes's email address, but if anyone looked closely, it would clearly have been sent from a public computer terminal in a separate government office, a computer that she noticed was also infected with the Pyx virus, a terminal almost any government employee could have had access to. The email would be almost impossible to trace, if anyone even tried.

Clyde tested the script using a simulator, without actually sending the email. Then she packaged it in a command to Pyx.

She opened up a terminal window and typed `pyx_send` in the green letters on black background she was used to, followed by the name of the command file, `pb_email.pyc`. The computer responded:

```
Logging to pyx.log
Command pb_email.pyc encoded
Posted to alt.test
Transaction id 200709201120A
```

There. It was off. She expected confirmation from the target machine within 12 hours.

— ' c , —

Baedes took a swig from his water bottle. He had been running for almost a half hour, and he was dripping with sweat.

"It's been 30 minutes, and there are people waiting," he said to the younger, short-haired man on the treadmill next to him. He disliked cutting down his run time, but those were the rules. If someone was waiting, use the treadmill for only 30 minutes at a stretch; then give someone else a turn.

"Right." The other man pushed a button to begin the cool-down cycle. Then he checked his pulse and distance. A *Friends* rerun was just starting on the TV. "I don't get this show." He pointed at the television. "I mean, I know it's supposed to be one of the funniest ever made, but it does nothing for me."

"Television is pretty much useless," Baedes said. He wouldn't even have one if it weren't for the sports channels.

"I think you may be right. Though the History Channel has some pretty interesting war documentaries."

"You know I don't have time for that."

"Right. That's why you've watched every single pre-season

NFL game so far this year."

"That's different."

"Sure it is," the man said in a sarcastic tone.

"Yes, it is." Baedes was serious. "Football is a contest of skill and strategy. Twenty-two men go at it, all at once, on the same field. But each with his own unique skills, all for his team. And that team under the direction of a single man, who orchestrates the battle. But only the strongest and smartest team wins. There's no second place." His face, covered with drops of sweat, showed a disturbing excitement. "Why watch a documentary, son, when you can see the war?"

Indeed, to Baedes a football game was a genuine battle, with tactics and strategy and skill. And with a few sacrifices. It was order out of chaos. While most fans just rooted for their team, Baedes usually didn't care who won. But he took pride in being able to understand the intricacies of the game, on multiple levels, from multiple perspectives.

The younger man didn't respond. Either he had nothing to say, or he was searching for words. Regardless of which, before the conversation could continue, a cell phone began to ring. Baedes picked it up, flipped it open, and spoke into the receiver.

"Baedes here," he said.

"This is Officer Burns, Sir. Ted Jackson wants to talk to me about the Mira Jayson case."

"Okay," Baedes said.

"I don't know why he wants to talk to me or what he wants to ask me. But I thought you should know."

"Thank you. I appreciate being informed."

He knew Burns would not betray him, but he wondered what prompted Jackson to talk to her. Still, it wasn't her responsibility to put her neck on the chopping block for him, because he was the boss. It was his job to stand up for and protect his people, and he would do so. Besides, the more she hedged, the more Jackson would keep digging.

Baedes added, "Cooperate fully with him."

"I see. Do you have any guidance on what I should tell him?" she asked.

"I think you should tell him the truth."

Silence.

"Just tell what you saw, but don't interpret the facts, don't repeat hearsay, and don't offer information," Baedes said.

"Yes. I understand," Burns said.

"Call me afterwards, please."

"I'll keep you informed," she said.

After they hung up, Baedes thought about this turn of events. He was in no personal danger from anything she could say. It could mean a short end to Miss Jayson's incarceration, but not until next week at the earliest. Jackson could have gotten Burns's name from the duty schedule or police blotter. Still, it disturbed him that the enemy thought her valuable.

— ' c , —

"Officer Burns," Ted said. He extended his hand and introduced himself.

Ted honestly didn't know what he was doing speaking to this young officer, didn't know what he expected to get from her. A tip from an anonymous inside source, completely unverifiable, yet somehow it felt right. Ted had checked the police blotter and peeked at the duty schedule—Ted had his own inside sources. Indeed, Baedes had taken a car and gone out and had arrested Mira. That's it. The only thing he did was to arrest Mira. He issued no citations, responded to no dispatch calls. It was indeed as if he had planned it. And now that Ted was out of leads, he was desperate.

One of Ted's only hobbies was the study of magic. He loved the intricacies and mysteries of illusion, sleight of hand, mind-reading, psychokinesis, deception and trickery, hypnotic

regression, psychic surgery, mind games of vanishing, levita-
tion, prediction, and the all other products of the magician's
skill and cunning. Ted knew that magic is not real. Magic
happens in the mind, as a result of how the magician presents
it and in how his audience accepts it, a result of what the audience does and does not know. And psychics, they are a special
class of magician. They use surprisingly simple mind tricks to
make their mark believe they have some supernatural source
of information, all the while pulling that information from the
mark himself. Now seated in a private room with young
Officer Burns, Ted started playing psychic.

"Do you know Sam Baedes?" he began.

"Yes, we all do."

"Does he ask you for special favors?" Ted was hoping his
phrasing would rattle her.

She looked askance at the lawyer across the conference-
room table from her.

"No. Well, nothing unusual or inappropriate," she said.

"So when he told you about the Mira Jayson case, that must
have made you feel uncomfortable."

"No," she said, shifting in her seat.

"Really?" Ted raised his eyebrows in mock surprise. "It
would make me uncomfortable to hear one of the other part-
ners at my firm admit to the sort of tactics he admitted to
you."

"He did nothing wrong," Pam insisted, staring off to the
side.

"What he did was akin to falsifying evidence."

"Look," Pam stared at him and spoke adamantly. "The
report says that Miss Jayson charged at him, and that's
completely true."

"But what about the non-existent weapon she supposedly
had?" Ted challenged her.

"Sometimes in the middle of a situation, you have to make

split-second decisions, for your safety and for everyone else's, and you don't have time to gather evidence first. I'm sorry your client got hurt, but she shouldn't have been trying to help."

"But Baedes attacked Ike Morgan, and he did it expressly to create a situation. That's entrapment."

"You have no proof of that," she said. She shifted her weight again in her seat.

"On Monday, September 10," Ted said, "did Sam Baedes take a car and go out to make traffic stops?"

"Yes, you know he did."

"Do you know why he did so?"

"I don't know. Maybe he wanted to get out of the office that day."

"Are those the words he used?"

"Yes—" She cut herself short.

"He said he wanted to get out of the office," he said. No response.

"Did he say why he wanted to get out of the office?"

"No."

"Hmm." He looked into her eyes. "Are you sure?"

Her eyes narrowed. "I'm sure."

"Why do you think he wanted to get out?"

"You'd have to ask him," Pamela said.

"But I want to know what *you* think," Ted said.

"Well, I don't know the answer."

"You don't know what you think?"

"I don't know what he wanted, or that he wanted anything, and I'm unwilling to speculate." She was trying to backpedal.

"Take me through the conversation. From the start."

"What conversation?" she looked confused.

"The conversation where he told you about arresting Mira Jayson."

"Why don't you just ask him what he did instead of

pursuing hearsay?" She grinned slightly.

"Does the chief usually do the job of a duty officer?"

"No."

"So that was atypical."

"Yes, but not unheard of."

"But all he did was to stake out the road Mira was riding home on. That sounds incredibly boring. Why would he want to do that?"

"He said," she explained, "that Mira Jayson was a violent person, that he expected her to be driving in an unregistered car, and that he needed to bring her in. And he wanted to personally make sure it went down without a hitch." She immediately closed her eyes for a moment, as though she didn't mean to say that.

But Ted tried not to appear to notice. "He said that? Just like that? That Miss Jayson was 'a violent person'?"

"No, those weren't the exact words he used, but—"

"What exact words did he use?"

"I don't remember. But that was the sentiment."

Ted took a breath. "Are you familiar with Miss Jayson's reputation?"

"Yes."

"Is her reputation that she is a violent person?"

A pause. "No."

"So did you believe Chief Baedes when he said that she was?"

She paused again. "No."

"So, did you seek any clarification of his statement?"

"Yeah, but..."

Ted waited before saying, "Okay. What was it?"

"I told the chief I had heard that Miss Jayson was a pacifist."

"And what was his explanation?"

"And he said he thought this time she would get in more

trouble than she usually does."

"Sad. Like Ike Morgan, more trouble than he usually gets into."

"Oh, please," she scoffed. "He's got it made. He dodged a bullet, that one. I dug through the files myself. We have so much we could charge him with. He's in such deep shit, he's lucky he's walking the streets."

"Fine then," Ted said. "I won't worry about him."

— ' c , —

Judge Spiller refused to hear any more on the bail issue. Friday afternoon, Ted appeared before a Superior Court justice, with Mira, to argue that Mira's bail should be lifted. He brought up all the same arguments that had not worked before, with two additions:

"Judge Spiller erred in increasing bail," he said. "In the typical case, the court would issue a restraining order, for example, to order Miss Jayson to keep at least 100 feet from Chief Baedes. But a law officer's job is to deal with conflict. What if he needs to arrest her? In fact, that very situation is the one in which Miss Jayson was alleged to have assaulted Chief Baedes. Therefore, a restraining order in this case is silly— ordering Miss Jayson to stay at least 100 feet away from a law officer.

"The very reason it is silly is the same reason the court should discount the argument. In the typical case, if the court had issued a restraining order, and if the defendant were to have violated the restraining order, she would have violated the terms of her bail, and she would need to be taken into custody by a law officer. In this case, however, if Miss Jayson were to commit an arrestable offense, that in itself would violate her bail. Therefore, releasing Miss Jayson in this case has a substantially equivalent effect to issuing a restraining order in the typical case. Therefore, she should be released on her own recognizance without surety.

"Furthermore, Officer Baedes sought to entrap Miss Jayson. Then he used his position to compromise Mr. Ike Morgan, the only witness to that entrapment. The details will need to be hammered out at trial. However, for the purposes of this appeal, this indicates that Mira Jayson was not—and is not—a danger to him. She should therefore be released on her own recognizance without surety."

A lot of legal mumbo-jumbo that basically amounts to: Let Mira go, because it's unfair to keep her in jail.

The Superior Court agreed. Mira was finally free.

— ' c , —

First thing after she stopped at home and cleaned up, she went to see Ike. She found him at a job site, taking a break, standing in the driveway, chewing on a slice of pizza. A haze of clouds covered the sun, casting a cool, fuzzy light over the scene. A light breeze blew through Mira's hair, carrying the scent of new shampoo and fragrant perfume out across the field next door.

"I heard they let you off the hook," she said.

"Yeah, they did," Ike replied.

"I just wanted to make sure..." She faded, then tried again. "I don't know what happened with you after they arrested us."

"Well—" Ike began.

"And I don't want to know."

"Okay," he said.

She gathered that he had been put in an impossible position, and she had turned hero in order to save his skin, and she had already rationalized his innocence in her own mind, and she didn't want to revisit the subject, because she blamed herself for all that had happened. Still, she felt she owed him an explanation, but she had to loosen some words from her brain by shaking her already trembling hands.

"Because," she said, "it would just get me upset all over again."

Ike just nodded.

"At Sam Baedes."

Ike looked inquisitive. "I don't understand," he said.

Mira continued. "I'm so sorry I got you into this. And whatever they did to you... I'm so sorry. I just hope you can forgive me and maybe we can get back to some... normal."

Ike had a pained expression. "I'm afraid you don't realize... what I—"

"Yes, I know all about that. But they forced you to say those things. I don't know how..." And she didn't want to know how they forced him. She didn't want to know what they had on him. She didn't want to know what kind of deep trouble he was in, because she firmly believed in the basic goodness of this man. "I'm just sorry I got you into this."

— ' c , —

Later that day, the District Attorney's office mysteriously dropped the charges against Mira. No one knew why, except Clyde, who noticed an update in Chief Beady-eyes's computer file. Apparently, he was disturbed by "the attack," as he wrote, "on PB." And he was afraid that pursuing this case would be worse for him than if Mira Jayson were simply allowed to continue, for now. So he had gone privately to the prosecutor and persuaded him that the case was no longer worth pursuing. His file didn't indicate what methods he used to persuade a prosecuting attorney that an active case was not worth pursuing. Clyde almost searched through the files for dirt on the D.A., but she changed her mind at the last second. She decided the question was probably better left unresolved.

He had, however, added a final new note to the file. It read: "Information leak. Informant in office? Outside subversive?"

— ' C , —

In his hand, Ted held a tall, thin, stemmed glass half-full of sparkling Brut, as did everyone else seated at the dining room table. He looked out over the collected guests. It was only a small dinner party. Mira brought Ike. Michael brought a woman named Annie, a sultry brunette he knew from somewhere or other. And naturally, the hosts were in attendance.

Clyde had orchestrated the entire menu, a mouth-watering spread: garden salad with homemade lemon vinaigrette; Clydene's garlic-herb chicken and couscous, with a chicken-vegetable gravy; green beans, carrots, and corn; and a couple bottles of Sauvignon Blanc from New Zealand, an economical but wonderful wine, a zesty, straw-colored white that burst with citrus and melon. And on deck, cheesecake and coffee, not burnt this time. As it turned out, the coffee pot just needed to run through a cycle in the dishwasher. As she had told Ted exactly what to do to help her prepare each dish, he happily took a back seat and let her drive. This was her province.

Ted said, "Before we begin, I asked Michael to say a few words."

Michael stood. "Over the past week," he said, "I've had little opportunity to tell Mira how much we appreciate her. It's ironic; usually I have the opportunity, but I don't feel the need. This past week has made me acutely realize the debt we all owe her, and how frequently we each ought to take the time to let her know her how much we appreciate her.

"Working with Mira has taught me more about my craft than any of you know. She brings passion and meaning to every life she touches, and I've aspired to be more like her in that respect, even though I've done a poor job of it.

"Now, she came into our lives when Ted and Clyde were facing a particularly difficult time. And I daresay without her friendship, they wouldn't have the wonderful marriage they do, the envy of husbands and wives everywhere, one of the happiest and most well-adjusted marriages I've ever witnessed. And that includes my own."

Everyone laughed. Ted recalled Michael's story of the one time he was engaged, which ended in disaster.

"And she has of course also graced Ike with many undeserved gifts." Michael paused a moment.

He raised his glass. "Mira, absence is a horrible thing. And it's pitiable that circumstances must beat that truth into my head with a sledgehammer. I miss you, and I'm glad you're back."

"Hear, hear," Clydene softly said as she raised her glass.

"Hear, hear!" repeated Ted.

And there were other murmurs of "hear, hear" from around the table as they all clinked glasses and drank.

Mira blushed. Ted knew enough to notice that, and he knew enough to smile fondly in her direction.

"Well, let's eat," Ted said.

Episode 2: See What You Get for Wearing a Mask?

A man in a black hoodie and black sweatpants stole down the sidewalk, stopped next to the liquor store entrance. Diffused sunlight washed over the scene. The man looked both ways, up and down the street. A blue car idled a few yards away in the direction he had just come. Other than this blue car, the block was empty. A cool, wet breeze blew across the man's yellow-brown face. He raised his hood and tightened it. Then he pulled up from around his neck a black cloth, now obscuring most of his face. The only thing one could see was two dark eyes with dark eyebrows.

He quickly entered the store, a large room with red carpet that flowed around rows of shelves, all stocked with various bottles, some full of wine at $10 a bottle, others containing beer or hard liquor. The store was empty of life, save for a diminutive, portly, balding man reading a magazine behind the counter in the front of the store.

The masked man slid up to the counter and brandished a gun, which he had produced from one of his pockets. "Money, please," he rasped to the clerk.

The clerk spoke with a thin, trembling voice. "I can't open the register without a purchase."

"So buy me a drink." One could see exasperation in his

eyes.

"What, uh, would you—"

"Just do it!" The robber demanded.

So he did it, emptied the register of tens and twenties. Handed them to the bandit, who stuffed them into his pocket. Then they did the same with the ones and fives.

Then, just as quickly as he had come, the masked man slid out of the store. He ran up to the getaway car, opened the passenger's side door, and got in. The car peeled out and disappeared.

— ' c , —

A squirrel, weak and tiny, scampered across the road as Mira barreled rolled down Linden Street. He was three-quarters of the way across, directly in front of Mira's car, when he froze. She slammed on the brakes, but it seemed she could not avoid running over the little guy. Then he suddenly about-faced and shot back in the opposite direction, toward the lane of oncoming traffic., from which an SUV sped toward the hapless creature, who froze again, huddling up on the double yellow line in the center of the road. Despite his hairy situation, it appeared that he was safe. But at the last second, he made a dash for the curb, across the path of the towering SUV. The last thing Mira heard through her open driver-side window was a distinct *crunch*. She winced, as an ache spread through her gut. And then she frowned.

Mira understood—sometimes she felt like she was the only one in the world who understood—how poor Squirrelly had felt. Now, "Squirrelly," always in the past tense, a tradition she had kept to herself since she was a little girl. A tear peeked out from the corner of her eye. Anyone else would have thought she was childish or silly, but that was how she felt. She sympathized with even the lowest of God's creatures. What's more, she understood why the squirrel had gotten run over. The squirrel had been safe huddling in the middle of the road. In fact, if he were to have remained still, he would have remained safe. But tell that to a little squirrel, with 100-foot-tall, 10-ton monsters roaring all around, approaching closer, closer, louder, louder. He had no time to think. It was fight or flight. And when the monsters are coming for you, you run. It matters not that you have nothing to fear, nor that you have nothing to hide, nor that you are completely innocent. You run, even at the risk of a gruesome and ignominious death. Because something deep inside, something that was programmed into you from before you were born, tells you it's your best chance. And you have neither the time nor the energy to figure it out sensibly. So you run. You run as fast as you can. And if you're lucky, the final blow is fast and quick, and you don't see it coming.

Mira found a safe spot to pull her car over to the side of the road. The car came to a stop, and she put it in park. And then she rested her head on her forearms on the steering wheel. And she closed her eyes and frowned, and she breathed deeply. The smell of wet leaves and cool rain filled the air. It had always been a happy smell, because it portended holidays and a break from the hot sticky mess of summer. Now, however, it was a bittersweet smell, like the ending of *Waterloo Bridge*, the one with Vivien Leigh. She got hit by a truck, too.

Images flashed through Mira's memory. A dozen people running for their lives. Protest signs littering the ground. "Due process! Not abuse of process." And "Uphold the law. Fire Baedes." And "How, Chief? ... could you allow this?" A man's hand holding one of these, his other hand in Baedes's face, like a cheap rip-off of the native peoples, shouting "How, Chief!?" Mira shuddered.

A sound interrupted her thoughts, voices. She raised her head to see a family in Halloween garb. It was a little early for Halloween outings, only Saturday, and the holiday fell on a

Wednesday this year, and only late afternoon, not evening.

The family's two daughters looked like genuine Arabian princesses, one in pink, the other in purple. Both wore cute little silver-and-black blouses and a full veil, which didn't quite match the rest of the costume. Like their olive skin, though, the veils only added to the authenticity of the costumes. They giggled as they shuffled along in their poofy pants and long, flowing sleeves.

The little boy, plodded along behind his sisters and over a foot shorter than them, was dressed up as the red Power Ranger, sans helmet, which he held in his hands. He quietly and deliberately, and muscles rippled down his chest and arms. Mira giggled at how cute he was, thinking it would probably be 15 more years before those muscles would actually fit him.

The mother's costume, Mira thought, was the most clever. Her hair was tied up in a bun, with a pink bow. And she wore a pink and red kimono and very authentic looking geisha makeup. Mira knew that she was not Japanese, but her delicate features belied her ancestry. Mira thought she looked beautiful with her regal stature, dark hair, paled face, and bright red lips. What made her costume so clever was that she was the only one of the five whose costume did not include a mask, because she didn't need one. Irony of ironies, her mask covered her face completely; yet, it didn't even exist, to Mira, a profundity.

And the father, who accompanied his wife, wore a ninja outfit, sword at his side, though he had his mask pulled open, to reveal his whole face. There was something about his face, Mira thought, something in his eyes, something that made him strong and noble, the loving and loved protector of his family, a quiet superhero.

The family filed out of their walkway and out onto the side-walk. Mira heard one of the girls say something about playing with someone named Ariel at the party. The other said she was glad they only had to go as far as next door.

Suddenly, the sound of a car engine and squealing tires interrupted the gaiety. As Mira watched in the fading sunlight, a police car quickly pulled up in front of where she was parked. Immediately, two uniformed officers leaped out and brandished their pistols.

"Hands in the air!" they both shouted. "Everyone! Put your hands in the air."

The whole family raised their hands, the little boy holding his helmet over his head.

"Drop the helmet!" one cop shouted at the boy, pointing his gun at the child.

"Habid, put your helmet on the sidewalk," one of his sisters told him.

He did so, then raised his hands high in the air. His eyes began to tear.

The cops clearly hadn't seen Mira sitting in her car, observing all this. One cop ordered the father up against the car, while the other kept his gun trained on the rest of the family. The one with the father put away his weapon and searched the father. He took the father's sword, which was clearly only a prop, and threw it onto the ground several yards away. "No gun," he said to his partner. He pulled out the father's wallet and found in it several $20 bills. "Where's the rest of the money?" he asked the man being searched. "And what did you do with the gun?"

The man was clearly confused. "This is all the money I have." He spoke with a thick middle-eastern accent, not quite Arabic, not quite Hindi. "You can have it. Please don't hurt my family."

"What about the gun?" the cop demanded.

The man stammered, in the same broken English. "I— I have no gun, sir."

The cop turned again to his partner. "We're gonna need backup. I'll call."

The partner nodded. "Okay."

The first cop then pulled the man's hands behind his back and in one well-practiced motion handcuffed him. "You are under arrest for armed robbery of Hammond Street Wines. You have the right to remain silent—"

"What?! I have been here with my family. All day I have been. How could any of us rob anyone? We do not even drink wine."

"Yeah, well then how did you know the robbery was today?" The cop yanked the man away from the car, opened the door, and shoved him in by the head. "You have the right to remain silent," he repeated. "You have the right to an attorney..." He stuck his head into the car as he continued his well-rehearsed speech.

Eventually, he ordered the family to lean against the car, including the little boy, who couldn't have been more than six years old. He began patting them down, starting with the woman. This was especially uncomfortable for her, denigrating even. Anyone else might just have made an educated guess at how the woman felt about it, but Mira knew. As certainly as she knew her own feelings, she knew. Her eyes glued to the scene before her, without look at the seat beside her, Mira reached for her small, black purse on the passenger's seat beside her. She opened it and from within extracted her cell phone. With one eye still on the scene outside and one eye on the phone, she punched several keys. Then she raised the phone to her ear and listened to the line ring through.

"Hello. Ted Jackson, here," said the voice on the other end. In the background sounded white noise like Niagara Falls.

The "hello" part was Mira's idea. She had suggested it to Ted some time ago. He often failed to understand what value words like "hello" and "sorry" had in normal conversation.

But he had been surprisingly open to the change, even though he didn't completely appreciate it.

"Ted," Mira said softly. "I'm witnessing a man being falsely arrested."

"Whoa," Ted said. "Start over. What happened?"

"These two cops charge out with guns and arrest this guy who obviously hasn't done anything wrong. And now they're harassing his family!" She was almost whispering, to avoid drawing attention to herself. Even so, she conveyed emotion through her voice.

"Calm down," Ted said. "Start at the beginning."

The first time Ted had ever asked her to "start at the beginning," it had been very hard for her. She had kept skipping to conclusions instead of simply relaying the facts. And she hadn't understood why Ted was being so picky. It was a frustrating experience. But after many such conversations with him, now, it was old hat. Mira quickly recounted what she had witnessed, so that Ted could draw the same conclusion she had. They went through this exercise frequently, and although he almost always arrived at the same conclusion she did, she never understood how he got there. Now, Mira finished her story by telling Ted how troubled the cop was, because he was convinced there was a gun hidden in a six-year-old boy's muscle-suit.

"Where are you?" Ted asked.

"On Linden Street, right off of Washington."

"I'm about 10 minutes away. Stay put." He emphasized that point. "If the officers want your statement, let *them* ask *you*. Don't you offer to help. Meanwhile, if you have a pen and paper, write down everything you see."

"Okay." With one hand, she began rifling through her purse for her small notebook and pencil.

Ted added, "And remember what I told you before."

"Okay." Mira didn't think about it, because she didn't want

to remember.

"You're up to this?" Ted asked, uncharacteristic.

Mira breathed. "Yes, I've got it," she said confidently.

"I'll see you in a few minutes," Ted said.

"Thanks, Ted."

They hung up. All the while the cops had been badgering the family for information. Either these people, including the six-year-old, were all trained spies, or else there wasn't any information to be had. And they weren't trained spies.

Mira opened her notebook and caused her pencil to scribble furiously on the page. But she had only written half of the story when she heard a new noise, a storm door opening and closing. A man emerged from the house next door. He stood at an average height, with an average build, appeared an average color, with brown eyes and hair. Probably had a wife and 1.85 children. And he approached the police officers, both now interrogating the family. One of the daughters was openly crying, along with her brother. The approaching man wore gray pants, a beige sweater, and a scowl. Suddenly, Mira felt sick to her stomach.

One of the cops whispered something to his cohort then went off to meet the newcomer. Mira could only hear bits and pieces of the conversation, because the repeated interrogation of the other cop, who was closer, drowned out most of it.

The cop said something, then the man.

"Nothing..." the cop replied.

"... my friends," replied the man.

"... robbery... arrested..."

More discussion.

"That's ridiculous," said the man.

The cop responded with something Mira couldn't hear. He was clearly trying to handle the man.

Then the man said something and tried to walk around the cop.

"Stay here, sir!" the cop warned.

The other cop paused his interrogation.

"If they're not under arrest, they're free to come with me," the man said.

"No they're not, sir!"

Now the man shouted at his friends. "Fatima! Are you alright?"

No response. Mira knew the woman was crying, even though Mira could only partially see her face. The kids were all probably also. A wave of nausea washed through Mira's gut, and she felt her teeth grind in her mouth. A tear trickled from her right eye, but she forced herself to write in her notebook. The black lines dug deeply into the paper, and the pencil point snapped off.

Mira's phone rang, and she saw on the phone's display that Ted was calling. Mira flipped opened the phone's clamshell case and hastily took the call.

— ' c , —

Clydene pulled a Pyrex pot from the refrigerator. Inside sloshed a brine, dark brown in color, in which soaked two large pork chops.

Ted had worked late at the office every day all week, and Clyde had hardly seen him. He had left home before she awoke and had come home exhausted, going straight to bed. And now he had worked Saturday, too, and evening was approaching. All their friends were preparing for dates or had other plans, and Clyde herself was looking forward to dinner and a movie, alone with her husband. The dining table was already set, and the candles were out, ready to be lit.

Clydene set the pot on the counter. She took a quick detour to the stove to turn down the potatoes, which were begin to boil over. She removed each chop from the brine, patting it down with a paper towel and laying it on a plate. Flames were already streaming from the burner under the heavy, iron skillet. She wet her hand from the sink faucet, dropped a few drops of water onto the skillet, saw it fizzle gently.

"Perfect," Clyde said to no one.

She picked up the pork chops, one at a time, each between two fingers, and laid them gently in the skillet. As each one touched the hot surface, it fizzled up, and Clyde drew in the wonderful aroma of pork and thyme.

The phone rang that familiar electronic jingle. Clydene quickly washed her hands and dried them on the fluffy kitchen towel before striding to the wall where the phone hung and answering it.

"Hello," she said.

"Hi. Ted here."

"Hey, you," Clyde cooed as she smiled. "Will you be home soon?"

"I'm going to be delayed."

Clyde's gut tensed up, but she resolved to hear him out. Nothing more from her husband.

"Whatever it is," she suggested, "can't you bring it home?" Clyde heard car noises in the background, and Ted was sounding cell-phone-y. "Are you in the car?"

"Yes. I'm in Abe's Turn. But I'm going to be delayed."

Her heart skipped a beat. "Is everything alright?"

"I think so. Mira called in a panic. Apparently, it's Lando Benitez all over again."

"Oh." Clyde didn't know what to say next, or even how to interpret Ted's last comment. Was he being sarcastic? She knew Mira's passionate sympathy sometimes got on his nerves. Or was there really a situation? And was Mira alright? In any case, Clyde thought she might not mind it if a terrorist blew up the Abe's Turn police station, because she missed her husband and lover. *Why don't terrorists ever blow up the right buildings?* she wondered "Okay. I'll keep dinner," into the phone. "Call me as soon as you can, okay?"

"I will, as soon as I know something new."

"Bye-bye, Love," she lamented.

They hung up.

Clyde leaned against the kitchen counter and sighed. She stared at the table, dark and empty of human company. Then she set about her next task, to figure out what she was going to do with two half-cooked pork chops that weren't going to be eaten until God knows when.

— 'c, —

Ted had been driving home at the end of an interminably long week. While most lawyers worked long after the sun went down, Ted was in the office almost every morning before the sun rose. Even though this day the sun had not yet set, and even though it was Saturday, he had been going for over 12 hours at the office and was looking forward to a quiet evening with his wife. That's when his cell phone rang.

He almost didn't take the call. There were some very good reasons to let it ring through to voice mail. One, he was tired. Two, he was driving. Three, it was Mira, and Mira often meant work. On the other hand, when Mira meant work, it was always work he was proud of. Besides, she was a friend. And Ted secretly admired Mira more than anyone else he knew, admired her for reasons that were also secret.

Ted donned his hands-free set and answered the phone.

Mira spoke in a panic. "I'm sitting in my car, witnessing a man being falsely arrested. What should I do?"

"Hold on," Ted said. "I need more information. Take it from the beginning. What happened?"

"These two cops charge out with guns and arrest an innocent man, and now they're harassing his family!"

Ted was afraid Mira was going to lose it and break down, and then he'd never figure out what was going on. He was too tired for this, too angry at the jackasses that had set Mira off, and too frustrated. "Calm down," he said, more to himself than to her. He breathed and slowed his speech. "Start over, please. Tell me, step by step, what happened: from the beginning."

Mira then told him a story similar to those he'd heard before, but raising enough questions to make him suspicious of foul play. Firstly, this was happening in Abe's Turn. Dramatic arrests happened, yes, but usually in the city, not in Abe's Turn. The residents of Abe's Turn engaged in white-collar crime, if they dared commit any crime at all. Dramatic arrests occurred when an officer approached a suspect who had a guilty conscience, and the suspect bolted. Frequently, drugs were involved. None of those factors came into play here.

Other questions, more of them than Ted could keep track of. Why didn't the officers question the suspect? If he had an alibi, why didn't they look into it? His alibi seemed pretty convincing on its face, because the whole family was dressed up and only heading next door. And if this was about a robbery that had just occurred, which Mira's story seemed to indicate, then where was the evidence? The very fact that they felt the need to badger a six-year-old about a hidden gun, that fact alone showed that there was something wrong with their case.

Or maybe Mira was exaggerating. She said it was "Lando Benitez all over again," whatever that meant. Yes, the situation had some superficial similarities, visitors from another country, victims whose skin happened to be the wrong color for the local prejudices. But Ted knew, these factors occurred more commonly than anyone would like to admit. Most of those poor people fortunately did not end up like Lando Benitez. Ted didn't see any reason to think this situation was that bad, yet.

As it turns out, Ted was only a few minutes away from the action. He told Mira to stay where she was but to create a written record of everything she saw. Her written notes could be useful if he needed her testimony. Then he hung up and called his beloved Clydene to let her know he would be late to dinner. When he explained why, she understood completely. Ted didn't understand the depth of affection those two had for each other. He took a moment to chuckle that if he ever wanted to have an affair, all he'd have to do was to say it was with Mira, and Clyde would go along with it.

He stopped at a red light on Washington Street, only one intersection away from Linden. He called Mira back.

"I'm right around the corner. What's the situation?"

There was much blathering in her explanation, but he got the gist of it. The accused man's neighbor, clearly a friend, was causing a ruckus with his upset.

Excellent, Ted thought. *Already fighting on multiple fronts.* That would make it easier for Ted to sneak in as a lawyer and get information.

The friend had also revealed the name of the accused: Hashim Osama.

With a name like that... Ever since Ted's 34'th birthday, it was more likely a man named Hashim Osama would get struck by lightning than that he would get a fair shake. The thought enraged Ted, and suddenly he no longer needed to depend on Mira's compassion and empathy as a reason to fight. Suddenly, he had his own reason to fight, a passion that forced him to commit to the fight, to commit to win.

Ted squealed around the corner and pulled up to the curb. He hadn't realized, he had been pushing down hard on the accelerator, as if he were driving a bullet.

"Okay, Mira. I'm here. Sit tight," he said. He hung up, pulled off his hands-free set, and popped his cell phone in his suit pocket.

With the mannerisms of a Man in Black, he stood from the car, confidently closed the door, straightened his tie. Hands in plain site, he approached quickly but carefully, exuding authority.

"I'm an attorney," he said. "May I speak to Mr. Osama?"

"At the station," the cop said.

"What about his wife? Is she under arrest?"

"How did you know to come here?" said the cop.

Ted ignored the question. There were several ways he might have known, and Ted didn't need to explain himself.

"May I speak with her?" Ted asked.

The cop glanced at the still anxious friend, who was temporarily dumbfounded. "How do I know you're really a lawyer?" he asked.

The guy was a twerp. Ted was ready to show identification, to rub it in his face. But before he could, the other cop spoke up. "He is. I've seen him around."

At that time, another police car pulled up, lights flashing. Two more cops got out, and the first walked over to meet them. Ted approached Fatima and whispered in her ear. "My name is Ted Jackson. I'm an attorney. A friend called me when she saw what was happening to you. Would you like me to represent you?"

No answer.

"Alright. Just sit tight."

He went up to the cop. "Do you have any more questions for the family?"

"I think we're done for now."

Ted's presence had clearly changed the situation. They no longer appeared panicked about missing booty, hidden guns, violent superhuman six-year-olds in red muscle suits, or any other such thing.

Ted turned back to Fatima. "You and your children can go now," he said.

She remained mute and frozen.

He approached her again. "Fatima," he repeated, "you and the kids can go back home. Or maybe you can visit with your neighbors."

She looked right at him. There were long tear-streaks running down her cheeks. She spoke through thick layers of mucus and tears and accent. "What about my husband?"

"We'll get that straightened out." Then he lowered his voice. "But you and the kids should get away."

She still didn't move.

Then a bang emanated from the police car, and a muted voice shouted something unintelligible in a non-English language.

Every eye stared on in horror.

She went.

CHAPTER 2

Sam Baedes took a keen interest in the Hammond Street case from the moment it became a case. He was in his garage when the call came in. In the foreground, a grinding wheel scraping against a welding joint; tiny, glowing, splaying shards, showering onto the floor; ozone and hot steel and burnt flux. In the background, as always, a police scanner interjecting intermittent reports.

Baedes did not have what people called an artistic personality. His art was not designed to please art lovers, even though it was special to him, unique to him. He worked with diamond-edge saw blades, grinding wheels, blow torch, solder, arc welder, and other tools of the metal worker's trade. His medium was scrap metal, culled from the riches of the junkyard. His sculptures did not represent machinery. Nor did they make statements about life in the industrial age. Nor did they dwell on the high concepts of love and enmity, of time and eternity, of peace and war. Baedes simply took what had been junk and transformed it into meaning. He took what was chaos and turned it into order.

Baedes released the trigger of his hand drill and listened to the grinding wheel spin down. With his other hand, through heavy work glove, he adjusted his thick protective goggles and inspected his work. The welds that had previously bulged from each joint now could nigh be noticed. The police scanner came to life, dispatching an officer to investigate a 211S, a silent robbery alarm, at a location on Hammond Street. Baedes quietly ambled to his workbench and set down his tools, but inside he was burning. He hated criminals with a passion that made him insane. He hated bullies and thieves and aggressors and anyone else who abused his neighbor.

If there was anything his art represented, it was this, his life's work, taking the raw material of evil man, cutting it, shaping it, fitting it into ordered society. It created civilization out of barbarism, safety out of danger.

Baedes washed up, changed his clothes, and drove out to the station. As he walked in, he saw the man they had picked up and charged with the robbery, being handcuffed to a bench. He strode up to the arresting officer.

"What do you got?" Baedes asked him.

"Arrested this guy for robbing the liquor store over on Hammond Street."

"Right. Heard about it on the radio. What evidence?"

"He was in the immediate area at the time, and meets the description of the perp, right down to the costume."

"Did you find the gun?"

"He must have stashed it somewhere."

"What about the money?"

"Ditto."

"The D.A.," Baedes noted, "will need that evidence to convict him. Find it."

The cop shook his head and was about to speak, when the chief continued.

"And just before Trick-or-Treat day?"

"It's the right guy," the cop said.

"You sound sure."

"I am."

"Good," Baedes said. "Convince the D.A. Do whatever it takes."

"By the way," the cop interjected, "Ted Jackson is in on this. I think Jayson tipped him off."

That got Baedes's attention. He thought for a moment. *This is the first time she's poked her nose into my business since the leak. This guy might know something. And if she's involved, she'll make it personal. And political. It doesn't matter the merits of the case.*

Then Baedes asked, "Did you let Jackson talk to the prisoner?"

"No. He wanted to. I told him to wait until we processed him."

"Hmm. Think carefully. Who's Jackson representing?"

"I assume this guy."

"Don't assume. What did he say? Did he tell you this guy was under representation?"

"No, he didn't. He just wanted to talk to him, called him by name, even. 'Osama,' by the way, if you can believe it."

"So no one's asked this guy any questions?"

"No. I was just—"

"Thank you," Baedes said.

Before he disappeared, he ordered that husband, father of three, and falsely-accused prisoner Hashim Osama be brought to an interrogation room. Then Baedes quietly stopped by the armory for a stun gun and joined him.

— ' c , —

Ted rushed over to the police station, making only a brief stop to check in with Hashim's wife and children and another brief stop to pick up some cash.

As it turned out, Hashim's family had sincere friends in the neighbors, those to whose home the Hashims had been heading when terror struck, a family whose father had the unlikely but real name of Marvin Kelton Mooney. He had been named after his father and grandfather, and he was the man who had so adamantly intervened in the Hashims' plight. Ted's head filled with silly visions of Mr. Mooney's tenaciousness and of angry antagonists shouting, "Will you please go, *now!*"

Funny, Ted thought, *how the stories you hear in childhood stay with you for your entire life.*

If this was a costume party, however, the two things conspicuously missing were the costumes and the party. Aside from Fatima's daughters, no one was any longer wearing celebratory garb of any sort.

Hashim and his kin had moved from Pakistan only a few months earlier, when Hashim's employer had offered him a position in the U.S. Ted met his son Habid, his daughters Atiya and Salma, and his wife Fatima, whom he made the mistake of calling "Mrs. Osama." She explained that they took her husband's first name as their family name, because they are part of his family, a common naming convention in her country. So she is Fatima Hashim, even though he is Hashim Osama.

As Ted expected, they didn't have any legal representation. But since Ted had proven himself by sorting out the situation, and after talking for a few minutes and hearing his story, they all accepted him, at least tentatively. And of course, Mira fell right in with the group, as though she were a part of the family. Ted explained that he would arrange bail. It could take several hours, but he would call when he knew more.

Little Habid looked up at him and said, "Tell daddy to come home quick."

Ted said, "I'll do that."

And Fatima added, "And tell him we love him."

Ted nodded.

From there, he drove straight home, because that's where the safe was, and the cash. He could smell dinner as he approached the house, from all the way down the walk. It was a shame he wouldn't get a chance to enjoy his wife's stupendous cooking.

As he opened the front door, Clyde came to meet him. He had just barely gotten through it when she thrust her arms around him, planted a long, wet kiss on his lips, sighed, and said, "I missed you."

"I'm here for bail," he said.

Her countenance fell. "Anyone we know?"

"I just met him," Ted said, "but Mira has a feeling about him."

"Okay. Do you want a pork chop and some potatoes to go?"

Ted suddenly realized how hungry he was. "Yes, actually, I think I would."

"I'll put it together. You grab the money."

Ted walked all the way to the back of the office. Under a stack of papers was a free-standing safe with a combination lock. He worked the combination for a minute, then opened the door. From one of the shelves inside he pulled an envelope and a ledger. Moving to the desk, he counted out a thousand dollars from the envelope. He picked up a pen and recorded the withdrawal in the ledger. Then he inserted the thousand into another envelope, which he had extracted from a desk drawer, and stashed it in his suit breast pocket. He returned the remaining materials to the safe, closed it up, and returned to the kitchen to meet Clydene.

She had prepared two segmented Tupperware containers full of food: pork chops (already cut into bite-sized pieces) and applesauce, red and yellow mashed potatoes with pan gravy, and green beans. She also carried two forks and was wearing her jacket.

Ted looked at her. "You're going somewhere?"

"I'm going with you."

"You'll be waiting around, probably for hours."

"I don't care."

"It's a long, boring process."

"Hey, you," she cooed, "I've been cooped up here all day without my husband, and I'm at least going to enjoy the 10-minute ride to the police station with him." She thrust both dinners at him.

"I only need one," he said.

"Yeah, but I need free hands to carry my book and my purse."

"Right. I guess I should have known that." He took the dinners. They were warm on his hands. "What are you reading?"

She showed him. "*Dancing on the Edge of the Roof*, by Sheila Williams." She was about half done.

"Another recommendation from Mira? Is it any good?"

"Yeah, it is. I don't know where she finds all these obscure gems."

Ted thought a second. Mira was always encountering obscure gems of every sort in every life category. "Maybe they find her," he said.

The two drove together to the police station. Or more accurately, Clyde drove while Ted ate. And inbetween bites, he told Clyde the entire story, from beginning to end, in as much detail as he could remember.

As he finished the story, Clyde remarked, "You were right. It is Lando Benitez all over again."

Ted still didn't understand what that meant.

— ' c , —

To Mira it was one of those moments in which time slows, like in the movies. Her senses became more acute. For a few horrifying minutes, she lived to make her heart bleed. She had been scribbling furiously, sitting in her car, for what seemed like a week. In reality, it was only a few minutes. But in those few minutes, she had filled her notebook with page after page of first-hand testimony of events she loathed to witness, much less to recount. She was greatly relieved when Ted finally showed up and she could think again.

I'd better call Ike.

She needed to devise a suitable story for why she would not be meeting him as planned. She didn't feel like going into the real story with him. Then she opened her cell phone and dialed Ike's number. He answered.

"I'm running a little late," she said.

"Is everything alright?" He sounded concerned.

"I just got distracted. Committee business." That wasn't a lie.

"Oh," he said. "Nothing serious I hope."

"No. I'll see you in 15 or 20 minutes?"

"So you're not at home?"

"Uh, no— What do you mean?"

"If you were just getting ready to leave," he joshed, "it would take you another hour to get ready."

"Very funny," she said.

"Where are you?" he asked.

"I, uh— I'm on my way. I got a phone call in the car."

"You answered the phone while you were driving?"

"Well..."

"You know, that's dangerous. Not to mention illegal."

"Well, I pulled over."

"You pulled over to answer the phone while you were driving?" He made it sound like it was a silly thing to do.

"No, I— Well— I just thought it might be important."

"You know, sometimes you let committee business take over your life. How can you do that? How?"

How? Mira remembered the strong, worn hand of a man thrust into Baedes's face, like a poorly staged native greeting.

Baedes seized it with one hand, twisting it around in a well-practiced motion, grabbing his handcuffs with the other. Mira looked on in terror.

She shook her head to clear it of the memory.

"Mira?" Ike said through the phone. "You there?"

"Yeah, I'm here."

"I'm just saying that maybe you should take it easy sometimes, throttle it back. You can't save the world. You'll burn yourself out trying."

Mira was silent. She knew Ike was only saying this out of his own frustration. Now she not only had heartburn, from all that she had been witnessing, she also felt like crying. Because someone needed to save the world. Or at least someone needed to do the right thing. And it was she.

Mira just sat there and breathed heavily.

Ike broke the silence. "So, if you still want to hang out, you can meet me at home. Okay?"

"Yeah, okay." Her voice squeaked a little. She cleared her throat. "Yeah. I'll see you in a few minutes."

Mira was hungry and tired and depressed. She rested her head on the steering wheel again and breathed deeply. She tried to think happy thoughts, to go to a happy place like the yoga people do. Mira didn't know anything about yoga. But this is something her father used to say to her as a little girl when she couldn't get to sleep at night, to go to a happy place. Her mind churning with thoughts and ideas, she could barely sleep. And her father would pad into her room and sit next to her on her bed and speak to her tenderly.

"What's wrong, Little One?" he'd ask.

"I can't sleep," she'd say.

"Are you scared?"

"No," she'd say.

"Are you sad?"

"Maybe," she'd answer.

"What are you sad about?"

"Just nothing."

"Well, you know, happy thoughts chase away the sad thoughts, if you think of happy things. What happy things would you like to think about?"

They'd compile a list of happy things that Mira could think about. And before they would finish the list, Mira would roll over and fall fast asleep.

Mira loved her father very, very much.

That was not a happy thought, was it?

Mira's thoughts were interrupted when someone touched her shoulder. She started.

"I want you to meet these people," Ted said, as if nothing was wrong.

"Uh... Yeah, okay."

Mira collected herself as best she could. Much of what transpired next she immediately forgot. Only a few key pieces. Ted introduced her to the family and neighbors. Five minutes later, Mira wouldn't be able to remember anyone's name, except those of Fatima and the children.

Fatima slouched on the couch, her son in one arm, her daughter in the other. The little boy wore a T-shirt and tights. His mother had washed off her makeup. The elder daughter sat at attention beside her sister. Mira stared at the girls' outfits. *That* was a happy thought.

"Why did you both decide to dress up like princesses?" she asked the two sisters.

The taller, elder sister shrugged. "Because we wanted to."

"No other reason?"

"No. We just both like to be princesses."

"Well, it looks like you put a lot of work into your outfits. They're wonderful." Mira smiled.

The younger daughter said, "I wanted green, but we could only find pink and purple and blue."

"Well," said Mira, "pink is a nice color, too. Pink is my favorite color." She sat down on the floor.

"Pink is nice," the little girl said. "But I like green better."

"Like grass?"

"Like trees," she replied.

The neighbor's wife and two sons entered, carrying refreshments.

Mira nodded. "Trees are nice." She looked at the younger sister. "Your name is Salma?"

The little girl nodded.

"And yours is Atiya." she turned to the elder.

"Where's my daddy?" Salma asked.

Mira glanced at the little girl's mother, who carefully and subtly shook her head.

"Well," Mira said, "he just has to talk to some people. It's an emergency." Then she changed the subject.

"Do you know how much I like trees? When I was a little girl, about your age"—she pointed to the elder sister—"I really wanted to climb the tree in our back yard. But my daddy told me not to, because the third branch was too thin. That's what he said. He told me it was too thin for me to climb on, and it wouldn't hold me up, and I'd fall and get hurt. But you know what? I really wanted to climb that tree, and I thought I could grab onto the third branch close to the tree, where it was thicker, so I wouldn't fall.

"So one summer afternoon, when no one was looking, I started to climb that tree. Do you think that was a good idea?"

Salma, wide-eyed, said, "No."

"So what happened?" asked Atiya.

"Well," Mira continued, grinning, "I actually made it most of the way up the tree. I held on to the third branch, just as I had planned, and pulled myself up. I was excited, because I was actually making it. Then when I tried to reach higher, that tiny branch slipped out from under my foot, and I fell all the way to the bottom. I broke my wrist." She held out her right arm, as though it were wrapped in a cast. "The doctor had to put a wire in my bone to keep it from healing the wrong way." She pointed up and down her wrist. "I had to wear a big cast for months." She mimed stroking the cast with her left hand. "And my wrist hurt all through the summer and almost until the next summer, even after the doctor took the cast off."

"Did you cry?" asked Salma.

Mira nodded. "Yes, I did. I cried a lot. My daddy was inside the house, and he heard me fall, and he heard me crying. So he rushed out, and I was afraid he was going to yell at me. But do you know what he did?"

The girls were speechless.

"He put a splint on my arm, and then he carried me to the car and drove me to the hospital. And in the car, while he was driving, he told me about how when he was a boy, he tried to climb a tree just like that, and he fell the same way I had, and he broke his leg."

"I bet you never climbed that tree again!" one of the Mooney boys interjected.

Mira paused. "Actually, years later, after college, I did climb that tree."

Now everyone paid attention.

"One of my friends helped me, and I actually made it almost to the very top. But that's a different story. I was much older then."

"Maybe your daddy will try to climb his tree now," said Salma.

Mira paused. "Well, years ago my mommy and daddy had an accident, and they died."

Throughout all this, little Habid had been holding onto his mother, but listening to every word. Now to everyone's surprise, out of him came a tiny voice.

"Were you scared?" he said.

Mira looked at him. "Oh, honey," she said passionately. "No, it's not like that. Your daddy is just fine. He just had to —" She took a breath. "He'll be right back. I promise."

— ' C , —

Clydene awoke in a stupor. She reached around with her left hand and massaged her crooked-feeling neck on the right side. For a moment, she wondered where she was. Then she remembered. She had fallen asleep on her husband's shoulder, waiting for Godot, or someone.

She had apparently awoken when Ted shifted her off of him and stood. He walked up to a man with olive skin.

"Hashim, I'm Ted Jackson."

The man seemed not to hear him.

"Hashim Osama?"

He looked at Ted knowingly, but said nothing.

"I paid your bail, and I can give you a ride back home."

He began to pass Ted by.

"We need to talk," Ted said sternly.

Hashim swung around, and right in Ted's face, he whispered angrily, "Why do you talk to me?" He seemed more scared than upset.

"Because you need me to help you."

"I do not want your help." He walked toward the door.

"Fatima sends word that she loves you," Ted said.

Hashim stopped in his tracks for a moment.

Ted continued, "And little Habid says to come home soon."

The man paused for a few seconds, then he nodded and continued out the door.

Clyde approached her husband. "Nice client you got there," she whispered.

"I don't get it," he replied.

"He's scared," she said. "He's scared to talk to anyone, to do anything. Must have been a horrifying experience for him, getting arrested. God only knows what police in his country do." She scoffed, then lowered her voice. "They might even be as bad as here."

There was a moment's pause. Clyde wondered what Ted was thinking.

Clyde said, "I bet Michael's having more fun than this on a Saturday night. Want to share some of your angst with him?"

"No. Let's let him enjoy his evening," Ted replied. "I'll call him tomorrow afternoon."

Clyde finished the thought. "Maybe by then, Hashim will feel more like talking."

CHAPTER 3

Eleven thirty-five! Talk about sleeping in! Michael's head was aching. He flopped back on the pillow. Something was missing. He had forgotten something. What day was it? Sunday? Nothing happening on Sunday. He dragged himself out of bed and worked his way to the bathroom. Beholding in the mirror a round, unshaven face, half-closed, blue eyes, disheveled, black hair, stocky build with a slight paunch, and that sticky, chalky taste in your mouth first thing in the morning, he suddenly felt singularly alone.

Wasn't alone last night. Or was that a dream?

He finally decided that it was not a dream but that the woman with whom he had danced also did not now make him less singularly alone.

Having completed his morning ablutions, Michael felt awake and refreshed, relatively speaking. But he still needed coffee. He donned a bathrobe and plodded down the hall toward the kitchen. He made it through the living room and into the kitchen, before he noticed a sultry brunette wearing a little black dress, sprawled out on the couch, reading a book that Michael had left on the coffee table.

"Ah, that's what I forgot," he said. And what a night for him forget! He must really have been hammered. *There must be something wrong with my brain,* he thought.

"Good morning, Sleepyhead," she said. "Or actually, good afternoon by now."

"I didn't know you were still here. Have you had lunch?" he said.

"Yup. Made myself at home. Hope you don't mind."

"That's a good book. There are DVD's in the cabinet there if you want to watch a movie. You just have to jiggle the handle sometimes to get it to open."

While they were talking, she had slid up next to him. And she now gave him a peck on the lips, which he returned hesitantly. She considered him a moment. Then her eyes took on a flirtatious expression.

"Michael," she said from behind hungry eyes, "you forgot something? What did you forget?"

He regarded her. No reason to let her know he had forgotten all about her, and now couldn't even remember her name. "Oh, nothing."

"You don't mean me, do you? And what we had last night?" she said playfully.

"Uh, no." Michael felt like a deer staring down a pair of headlights. He didn't want to reject her, but he also didn't want a relationship. And frankly, the way she was talking was beginning to scare him. "I forgot that I'm out of coffee cake."

"Good." She smiled coquettishly. "I don't know what I'd do if you forgot what we had. I mean, what we *have*."

She cuddled up to his arm, fixed her big brown eyes onto his baby blues, and cooed in pouty tones. "Would you like me to make you some coffee, Mikey-Pooh?"

Mikey-Pooh? This was definitely not what he expected—or wanted—from a one-night stand. How drunk was he last night? Michael didn't know what to say. But he knew he had to say something. "Uh. I don't want—" he began. Then he tried again. "That is, maybe we can—"

She snuggled up to Michael's cheek, brought her lips close to his ear, and she whispered softly and passionately, "Gotcha."

Michael was still figuring out what was going on, while the woman broke out laughing.

"Aw, I had you goin', didn't I, *Mikey-Pooh*?" she mocked.

"Good one," Michael said. He did his best to laugh at himself, even though he was finding it quite difficult to appreciate the humor. Still, he knew this would make a great story to tell at parties.

"God! I didn't know you had that much to drink!" she said.

"Only of your sweetness, my dear."

"Do you even remember my name?"

"Janine, right?" The name just came out of his mouth. Yes, that was right, he thought.

"Give that man a cigar." She popped open the coffee maker.

"No thanks, I don't smoke."

"I dunno. You were pretty smokin' last night." She was cooing again.

He slid up behind her and put his arms around her waist. "It's easy to dance with the right partner."

Janine turned around to face him, their bodies so close. "You doin' anything today?"

"No way. Sunday is the day of rest."

His fingers lightly caressed the small of her back through the thin fabric of her dress. He hovered his lips over hers and breathed deeply her perfume, still noticeable from the night before, a sweet, light scent that excited him like no other. He had frequently noticed it on another woman, also a raven-haired goddess, and one who excited him like no other. He gently kissed Janine, their lips delicately melding.

— ' c , —

"Let's open our bibles to Romans, chapter 13."

Clydene grabbed a house bible from the pew and opened to the index.

Ted put his right arm around her shoulder and nuzzled into her cheek.

"What are you doing?" she whispered.

"I'm reading along with you."

"I haven't found it yet."

Having noted the number of the page on which Romans started, she flipped to it.

His arm still around her shoulder, Ted put his other hand on her bare knee.

The pastor began reading. "Everyone must submit himself to the governing authorities, for there is no authority except that which God has established..."

Ted started moving his hand under her skirt, up the inside of her thigh.

"Ted!" she whispered at his ear, trying to remain as inconspicuous as possible.

"You forgot to keep your knees together."

She put her knees together. "Well, they're together now." She glanced around the sanctuary. No one was looking. That didn't mean no one noticed.

"No one can see," Ted said.

"Pastor Bob can see. And I want to hear this."

"... Do you want to be free from fear of the one in authority? Then do what is right and he will commend you..."

She felt a knot in her stomach. Maybe she didn't want to hear it after all. Ever since she had cracked into Baedes's government computer, she had been wrestling with the moral implications. Yes, what she did was for a good cause, for Mira's sake, to preserve her freedom and the freedom of everyone in Abe's Turn. And the end result was for the good. But did any of that justify her? Clyde wrestled with the moral implications, and Baedes himself was "the authority," and he surely would not appreciate what she had done to thwart his plans.

Ted's hand was still on her thigh as he continued to protest. "But you never wear skirts during the week, and you have such sexy legs."

Since Clyde worked as a consultant, from her home office, she rarely dressed up to go to work. Only when she visited a client site did she don the business-wear, usually a pants-suit, so she could look at least something like the other programmers, but a little more classy. On weekends, however, when Ted and Clydene went out, she liked to look like a woman. It made her feel feminine. Maybe a little black dress if they went out Saturday night, and something a little more respectable for Sunday morning church.

"Okay, I'll wear the skirt this afternoon," she said. "Just calm down. And stop distracting me."

Ted was obviously getting horny, and a little early in the day. They usually didn't get hot and heavy until after Sunday dinner, which is why they always ate Sunday dinner alone, just the two of them, at home.

Ted leaned his head against hers.

"... not only because of possible punishment but also because of conscience. This is also why you pay taxes..."

Conscience. That was it. Clydene's conscience had been nagging at her, an unresolved conflict in her spirit, whether what she had done was the right thing to do for her friends, and whether she would ever do it again.

Ted whispered into her ear. "I guess it would inappropriate for me to grope you."

"Yes, it would," she replied. "What's with you today? Daylight savings doesn't end for another week. What, you can't wait an hour until church is over?" *Talk about premature,* she thought.

"What's with me is you look good," he said. "And smell good." He kissed her on top of the head.

Pastor Bob had completed reading his text. At this point, he stepped from the behind the podium and leaned himself against the empty communion table. If they were having communion that day, the table would be set, ready from which to administer the sacrament. As it was, the table was bare, without even a tablecloth. Its ornate woodwork belied its surroundings: a simple, wooden podium; a stained, red carpet; worn pews with hard, wooden seats. As a tiny, seed church, they were lucky to have found a building with an air conditioner, though they didn't need it today.

They were not struggling as a church. Or at least Clyde did not think being small was a bad thing. The tiny, informal, small-town atmosphere was one of the things that drew the Jacksons—and particularly Clydene—to this particular church and its congregation. The other draw was Pastor Bob's conversational speaking style and his straightforward, open-minded approach.

And he was no more straightforward and open-minded than now, as he leaned informally against the sacramental table, almost sat on it, hands in his pockets, and said, "I'm about to say something politically controversial and very unpopular. I'd actually rather avoid it, because this could get me into trouble. Most preachers avoid it, or just spout the party line. But I can't avoid it, because we've been studying Romans, and we can't skip chapter 13 just because we don't like it or it makes us uncomfortable or it could get us into trouble.

"On the other hand, I can't just spout the party line, because I don't actually believe in it.

"Most theologians take this passage at face value. Now, that's not so unreasonable, is it? 'Governing authorities' are what makes civil society. Without the police to protect us, crime would run rampant. Without the judge to adjudicate disputes, everyone would take the law into his own hands..."

Clyde re-read the pastor's text, or rather, read it fully through for the first time. Two sentences in particular jumped out at her:

He who rebels against the authority is rebelling against what God has instituted, and those who do so will bring judgment on themselves. For rulers hold no terror for those who do right, but for those who do wrong.

Clyde felt sick. *What was God smoking when he came up with that one?* she thought. *Or maybe God just never lived in Abe's Turn.*

Pastor Bob was still talking. "... And so, Paul says here we should always submit to the governing authorities, and never rebel against them. Because these authorities are God's servants in a civil society. Some commentators have even gone so far as to say that the law defines the difference between right and wrong. If something is illegal, it's also immoral. And if something is legal, it must be alright. And if something is legally required—"

He folded his hands and took a breath.

"There is a man named Władysław Bartoszewski. Don't worry if you can't pronounce that. I had to practice it for an hour before I got it right."

He paused to let the chuckles subside.

"Anyhow, Mr. Bartoszewski is 85 years old. He's a Roman Catholic. He's been a journalist, an activist, even a politician. Now, he's Minister of Foreign Affairs in Poland. But in 1940, he was a prisoner at Auschwitz, the Nazi death camp. Inmate number 4427. He was picked up by the Nazis as part of a massive manhunt in Warsaw, and they kept him at Auschwitz for over 7 months, until the Polish Red Cross convinced them to let him go."

Pastor walked back to the podium. "I want to quote you

something he said about his experiences at Auschwitz:

"'I lost consciousness on December 12, while cleaning bricks,' he says, 'I was exhausted, injured, and in pain. That was normal for Auschwitz. Just as it would have been normal if I had died under a blow from a club, or from having my throat crushed by a capo's boot. The strange thing was that prisoners carried me to the Krankenbau and laid me out next to the stairs. They could do nothing more, because they had to return immediately to work. They saved my life.'

"At the time, he was 18 years old. He almost never made it to 19.

"He was just getting his life started, and you'd think after a traumatic experience like that, Mr. Bartoszewski would keep a low profile. Having been dealt the hand of grace by the Red Cross, you'd think he'd do as little as possible to anger the Nazis. Yes?

"But after he was released from Auschwitz, one of the first things he did was to join Żegota. Now, this was the codename for an underground organization, operated by the Polish government in exile. Its purpose was to help Jews in Nazi-occupied Poland. This was blatantly illegal, of course. Treasonous, even. Żegota were subversives against the Nazi state. Being involved with them was a serious crime. The penalties were severe.

"If you got caught hiding a Jew, here's what would happen to you. You were to be immediately shot, or taken out to be publicly hanged."

Bob leaned close to the microphone and in hushed tone enunciated the next sentence. "You didn't even get a trial."

At some point, Ted had removed his hand from Clydene's thigh and his arm from her shoulders. She didn't remember when. He was now staring intently at the man behind the podium. She felt sick inside, vulnerable, helpless. She wrapped her hands around her husband's strong, right arm, cuddled up next to it. He wrapped his arm around her, pulled her close, kissed her again.

Pastor Bob continued, "How does this relate to our text? The Nazis were the governing authorities in Poland at the time. Now, you could argue that they had invaded Poland. So maybe they didn't have a legitimate claim to rule Poland... if that makes you feel better. The practical result, however, was that the Nazis occupied Poland, and they did set the rules.

"The Nazis also did have a rightful claim to govern in Germany. Not many Americans realize this today, but Hitler was elected in a democratic election. How can you get more legitimate than that? But the Nazis in Germany were just as horrendous as in the rest of the world.

"So the question we have to ask is: Why would Władysław Bartoszewski, being a good Roman Catholic and a moral Christian— Why would he jeopardize his life, not to mention his very soul, by going up against God's servant, the governing authorities?

"Despite our text, there's only one answer I can come up with. He did it, because it was the right thing to do. It was the only thing to do."

There was much more to Pastor Bob's sermon. He summarized the atrocities committed by Stalin, Mao Tse Tung, Pol Pot, and others; the religious persecution currently going on in Indonesia, Africa, and elsewhere; all with the support or consent of the governing authorities, and many times being fought by illegal, underground, Christian movements led by people ready to go to jail but skilled in evading the police.

Much to Clydene's dismay, Pastor had no answers. He posed several interpretations. And as he explained each in turn, he also explained why that interpretation is probably incorrect.

Faith is sometimes a hard thing.

Another hard thing is forcing yourself to wait until after church, all hot and horny, after the sermon, after the concluding prayer, after pushing a cursory goodbye at anyone you meet in the hall, on the way from the pew to the coat rack, from the coat rack to the car, after the seemingly interminable drive home. For Clydene and Ted, it was like you see in the movies, the two lovers plastered all over each other, faces rubbing together, stumbling up the walkway, fumbling with the keys, thrusting open the door, pushing each other's jacket to the floor, unbuttoning her top, unzipping his pants, hands where they don't belong in polite company.

"Oh shit!" Ted shouted.

"What? What did I do?" Clydene asked. She thought she must have accidentally pinched him in the wrong place.

Ted quickly zipped up his pants. This baffled her, until he motioned to the living room behind her. She turned around to see a black-haired woman reclined on the couch, holding a book, her sleek, compact purse resting on the coffee table.

Clyde felt her face flush. That must mean it was as red as a beet, because she usually didn't feel embarrassed, even when she was. She usually just got nervous instead. But this time, she felt red hot, as if she had just committed some sort of unspeakable act for which she was now bearing the ultimate humiliation.

"I'm sorry?" Mira said tentatively, with that facial expression that says: Yeah, if you think you're embarrassed, you should be where I'm sitting, because I'm positively freaked out; and yeah, maybe I should have called first, and it's so my fault, but I couldn't call you, because you were at church, and you *did* give me a key; besides, I *really* need a friend right now.

Suddenly, Clyde felt sympathy. "Oh no. I'm sorry. I just— I didn't know you were there." She re-buttoned her blouse as she walked into the living room. "Are you okay?"

Ted sighed.

Clyde was suddenly divided between her friend and her husband. "Oh— Uh... Ted— Ted and I were just, uh..." Her gaze darted from Mira to Ted and back again.

Mira broke in. "I know. It's okay. I should have known— Uh, I should have called first. I'll go." She sat up and started stuffing the book into her purse. She looked sad.

"Isn't that the same outfit you were wearing yesterday?" Ted asked.

Mira paused a moment. "Yeah, it is."

"Hey, you," Clyde said tenderly, sitting down next to her friend, resting a hand on Mira's shoulder. "Did something happen?"

"Well, I kind of spent the night at Ike's."

Clyde didn't know what to say to that.

"And..." Ted prompted.

Mira continued. "And we had breakfast this morning, and then I drove around for a little while, and then I came over here."

"And what's wrong? What happened last night?" Ted asked.

"Nothing," she answered. "I mean, nothing happened. We just hung out last night, watched a couple movies, ate some popcorn, that sort of thing. It was late, and I crashed on his couch. Nothing bad happened. We hung out. It's fun, that's all."

Clyde said, "Yeah, okay. Well, you two have been hanging out together for a while now. If it's so much fun, why do look like a puppy just died?"

Mira stared at the blank screen of the TV for a minute, as if she were watching a gut-wrenching scene from a sad movie.

Ted asked, "Has he even kissed you yet?"

"No," Mira eked out.

"Held your hand?"

No response.

"Made a pass at you? Bumped into you? Tried to feel you up? Anything?"

Clyde turned to him in horror.

"You know, Mira, maybe he's just not interested," Ted continued, apparently oblivious.

"Okay," Clyde said to him, scowling. "You said you needed to call Michael this afternoon. Why don't you go upstairs, change into something more comfortable, and make your phone call?"

He agreed, then kissed her, sneaking a hand in to pat her butt.

"We have company!" she whispered.

Now that Ted was gone, Clyde got down to business. "Okay, Girlfriend, now that the children have left the room: What's really going on?"

"See? Is that too much to ask?" Mira said.

"What?"

"That's all I really want. Someone who will pat me on the behind once in a while."

Clyde thought about this. Or rather, she already knew exactly what she thought, but she had not yet worked up the courage to say it. She hated to see Mira sad, and as much as she loved her friend, she was getting frustrated. So she decided to out with her thoughts. But before Clyde could put her thoughts into words, Mira interjected something new.

"The thing is," Mira said, "I think he's actually interested. But he's..." Her voice trailed off.

"Maybe you should just tell him how you feel."

Mira shook her head, terrified. "No, no. I can't do that."

"But if he's into you, maybe he just doesn't know how you feel."

"No. It's more complicated than that."

"I don't understand." Clyde shook her head. "Please explain it to me."

Mira just stared at the floor.

Clyde decided to take another approach. "How about some piping hot *chocolat*?" she asked. "Good for what ails the soul."

Mira smiled a little and nodded. She followed Clyde into the kitchen. Clyde made homemade hot cocoa with just a pinch of red pepper, while the two girls chatted about the weather, Clyde's Sunday outfit, makeup, and other mundane things. Finally, they were seated at the kitchen table, a steaming cup of dark, brown cocoa, with a puff of whipped cream on top, between each pair of hands.

Clyde sipped from her cup, breathing in the rich aroma, sensing the tang of the pepper on her tongue. She closed her eyes and basked in the full experience.

Mira said, "I'm thinking of giving up work on the Committee."

Clyde almost spewed hot cocoa out her nose. But because this would have been such a horrifying experience, her body instead opted to choke on what was in her throat. She began to cough, managed to set her cup back on the table, spilling some in the process. She clapped her hand to her chest, as if to dislodge a stuck piece of food. Red-faced, she finally was able to breathe again.

"Are you alright?" Mira asked, clearly concerned.

"Am *I* alright?!" Clyde almost screamed. She felt like screaming. "What have you done with my friend, Mira?"

Mira looked and sounded hurt. "I'm not your friend anymore if I don't want to be an activist anymore?"

Clyde rolled her eyes. "No, of course you're my friend. You'll always be my friend. But this is your— *thing*. This is your baby. You got into it because you couldn't stand— I've never known you to do anything else. I've never known you to *be* anyone else." She was exaggerating, she knew, but she still meant every word. She stared at Mira, awestruck, not knowing what to say, not knowing what to think.

"It was just an idea," Mira said. "I probably won't."

Clyde was still flabbergasted. "Why would you even consider it?"

Mira seemed to have trouble putting her thoughts into words. "I'm— I'm just tired. I'm tired."

Clyde rubbed her eyes, as if she was just waking up from a bizarre dream. "Well, then... I'm floored."

"Don't tell anyone else, okay?"

"Our secret," Clyde intoned somberly.

But Clyde couldn't get it out of her mind. Mira's heart was one of those few brilliant filled with a burning passion for what mattered. "Tired" might cause her to slow down. It causes everyone to slow down once in a while. But to give up what she loved? Even in Mira's full-time job as a counselor, she didn't show the same passion that she did for her political activism. They had discussed it many times before. Mira had often raved at the idea of quitting counseling and devoting herself full-time to the Committee. The only reason she didn't is that she couldn't afford it. Like everyone, she needed to pay the bills. But the message was clear. Yes, her job made her happy. She got to help people and achieve real accomplishments that mattered. But the Committee was something Mira believed in. This was her destiny, and she knew it. So what, Clyde wondered, had happened to make Mira suddenly question her own destiny?

"Mira, what's going on?"

Mira just sat and stared.

"Is this about Ike?"

Nothing.

"Is this about what happened last month?"

Still nothing.

"You know, what happened wasn't your fault. And you not being there isn't going to make anything any better."

Mira's eyes began to water, and her voice cracked. "But my being there can make things a lot worse."

"Okay, now that's just crazy."

"It's not crazy," Mira choked out. "Baedes has a personal vendetta against me and against anyone who dares to associate with me. You know that."

Clyde dwelled on that thought, during the pause before Mira continued.

"When you believe in something, you think you can change the world." Mira waxed philosophic. "You think nothing can stop you, that you can overcome any obstacle, find a way over it, under it, around it, or through it, whatever. But then you run into reality. Because no one can change the world, Clydene. The world is too big and too powerful. The world is always going to do exactly what it wants, and it doesn't care what you believe in. The world always wins."

Clyde knew Mira was talking to herself, about herself. And she had a feeling if Mira continued in this vein, she would depress herself into psychosis. But Clyde didn't know how to respond, so she changed the subject.

Clyde sighed and said, "How do you think your new friends from yesterday might like a world-famous chicken-mushroom casserole?"

Mira wiped her eyes. "Yeah, I think they might. Is that complicated to make?"

"Nope. I was going to make one for dinner. It takes less than an hour. We should make two, one for here, one to deliver."

— ' c , —

"Bastards!"

"Now, Michael, not all of them are the epitome of evil," Ted replied to the speakerphone.

He had untied his tie, carefully unknotting it using exactly the opposite motions he had originally used in tying it. Now he hung it in the closet and began to unbutton his shirt.

"That's bull, and you know it!" the speakerphone continued. "They humiliated that man, right in front of his wife and kids! The sleaze oozes from the top."

Even through the phone, Ted could feel Michael's eyes like blue flames burning a hole through time and space, staring right into his. That's one thing about Michael. He always looked you straight in the eye. And despite the fact that they weren't face-to-face, Ted knew Michael was even now looking him straight in the eye. Yes, for all of Michael's faults, at least he always gave you that much.

Ted said, "Okay, I understand that you're upset—"

"Puleeze! You have no idea how I feel!"

That was true enough.

"Okay, so explain it to me," Ted replied. "If you're not upset, why do you keep yelling at me?"

Michael paused a moment. Then he spoke more calmly. "You just don't understand, Ted. You'll probably never understand. It's just how you are. You're an excellent logician, but..."

"But what?" Ted smiled. He really wanted to hear what came next.

"We work better as a team."

Ted stared for a moment out the window. "So you're saying I'm a lousy activist."

"I wouldn't put it that way."

Ted looked back at phone. "Please, do."

Michael nodded. "Okay. You're a lousy activist. But we need your skills and talents."

Ted sighed. "I'm too old for this."

Michael finished a sip of something and gulped.

"How old are you, anyhow?" Michael asked. Then he quickly added, "If you don't mind my asking."

"Ted doesn't talk about his age," Clydene said from the bedroom doorway.

"How long have you been eavesdropping?" Michael asked.

"Eavesdropping?" Clyde said. "The way Michael was hollering, they could hear him in Texas."

"Sorry," Michael said. "It's just that Beady-eyes really gets my goat."

Ted found himself staring hotly at his wife, and ignoring his friend on the other end of the line. He said, "Michael, I'll call you a little later."

"Are you kidding? Is that the end of the story? What happened to the poor guy? You can't just leave me hanging."

Clyde talked at the phone, "Why don't you come over and join us for dinner? We're having a chicken casserole."

"Well, I kind of have a guest of my own."

Ted continued. "There's more to the story, Michael, but I have something I have to take care of."

After a second, Michael said, "Oh. I'll expect your call in a half-hour or so. Bye!" And he hung up.

Clydene had her mouth open. "Do you tell him everything about our personal business?"

"You tell Mira everything."

"But that's just girl talk," she said.

Ted never understood what "girl talk" actually was, and he uncharacteristically didn't want to argue the point. So he segued into a different subject.

"Talking about girls..." He swept his eyes up her figure and breathed deeply. "Oh my God, you're sexy." He stepped up to kiss her, but as he approached, she turned her head, and he ended up sucking at her neck. He didn't care one way or the other.

"Uh..." Clyde said. "That's not girl talk. And Mira's still downstairs."

"That's nice," Ted said.

"We want to make a casserole for the Hashims. And for dinner. One for dinner and another for the Hashims."

"Uh huh." Ted kept going. His hands had been caressing her back. Now he moved them up her sides.

"I invited her to stay and eat with us."

"Fine with me," he said, only having half heard her.

"I need to get back downstairs to make dinner."

"You have time for a quickie." He sucked on her ear.

"She'll wonder where I am."

"Tell her you had to use the bathroom." Ted knew that Mira would figure out the truth anyhow.

"She'll hear us."

He whispered softly into her ear, "Not if we're very, very quiet."

She whispered back, "Sometimes a quickie can be fun."

"Bing bang boom," he replied.

"No way. Forget the bing and the bang!" Suddenly, she shoved him onto the bed and was straddling him like a tiger.

— ' c , —

The two friends approached the front door of the house on Linden Street, where only yesterday Mira had felt angered, helpless, stunned. Since then, the sky had cleared, and the wind had died, and now the rays of the setting sun cast elongated shadows across the ground and onto the buildings. Mira no longer felt stunned or helpless. She felt a trepidation, though, and she didn't know why or about what. With each step, the clear Pyrex cover jiggled on the casserole dish Clyde carried, small, square, and white, with flowers painted on the sides. Mira held her purse more tightly. She stepped up to the door and rang the bell.

"Did you have any special plans for Halloween?" Mira asked her friend. Maybe engaging in small talk would clear her head.

"No. Ted and I have both been busy. Plus, we're not really party animals. We'll probably just spend a quiet Wednesday at home."

"Right, Wednesday." Mira knew Wednesdays Ted and Clyde got romantic. Every Sunday afternoon and Wednesday night. For a moment, she wondered what it would be like to have regularly scheduled sex with someone she deeply loved.

"Do you have any plans?" Clyde's words interrupted Mira's thoughts.

"What's that?"

"Going to any parties?"

"No. I don't think so—" Mira wondered whether Ike was doing anything Wednesday and why he hadn't asked her to come along. Then she remembered that he might take someone else, assuming he's planning anything. He had no obligation to Mira. "I don't know," she said.

Clyde seemed to become concerned. "What is it? What's the matter?"

Mira shook her head. "Nothing."

"Ike again?"

"I don't want to talk about it right now." She stared at the door jamb.

"Okay."

"There's nothing new to say anyhow." Mira felt a lump in her throat.

"You really have to talk to him, Mira."

Mira rang the doorbell again. She needed to find some way to distract her thoughts, to focus them on something else. "I wonder why no one's answered the door. Maybe they're not home?"

A voice came from a distance to their left. "They're home. But they haven't been answering."

Mira looked over. It was the next-door neighbor, calling from her front porch.

"Hi, Jane," Mira called back, smiling. Mira didn't know how she knew the woman's name, but it turned out to be the correct name. She remembered meeting Jane Mooney, but the whole incident was a blur. If you had asked her to recall specific details, she wouldn't be able to, but somehow the right words came out when she wasn't really thinking.

"Ever since Hashim got back last night, the whole family has gone into hiding. The kids haven't been out to play. No one has answered the door, and they haven't been returning calls."

The woman looked like a stay-at-home mom with plain features and an ordinary, medium-length haircut. She looked like a soccer mom, now a concerned soccer mom; no, a worried soccer mom.

"I wonder what happened," Clyde said. "He seemed pretty scared when we went to pick him up from the police station. Wouldn't talk to us at all. I mean, sometimes Ted can be a little intimidating. But this time, he was actually personable."

Mira chuckled. And so did Mrs. Mooney.

Since no one was coming to the door, Jane invited the two over for tea. Her husband Marvin had taken the kids to the park, and that gave Jane ample opportunity to tidy up the house. It was a perfect time to have company over. As it turned out, Jane was not a stay-at-home mom, but a working mom. Still, she had motherly tendencies, as most working moms do, as Mira had often discovered. And even a fair number of working dads, for that matter. However, the few hours each day the kids spent at home were enough for them to leave a trail of destruction in their wake, and that irked Jane Mooney.

Mira nodded. "I can sympathize," she said.

"Oh, do you have kids?" Jane asked.

"Uh, no. But— What I mean is..." What she meant was that she sympathized with the kids. She was the one who always left a trail of destruction in her wake. But this was not a subject she wanted to get into with an almost-stranger.

"Mira's a certified personal counselor by profession," Clyde interjected. "She's always cleaning up other people's messes."

"Yeah," Mira said. "I guess that's one way to put it."

— ' c , —

Clyde was a virtual pack rat. She was always starting new projects, finishing them halfway or using them once, then abandoning them on her computer's hard drive, folders upon folders full of files she just could not bear to delete, because she was sure she would need them again someday. She couldn't even archive them to disc, because when she needed them, she wouldn't be able to find the disc on which she had put the files.

She did the same with the dozens of half-abandoned web accounts she had all over the Internet. Each seemed useful at the time. And in each case, Clyde kept the account active, just in case. She filed away the login information in a file on her computer so she could come back to it later if she needed to. She almost never needed to.

So it was with Pyx. Pyx was a small program, a virus Clyde had created to target Baedes and to protect Mira from him. It didn't do anything malicious or disruptive. But it did surreptitiously infiltrate his computer and siphon off files, which it then transmitted securely and anonymously to Clyde's computer. Clyde had set it up over a month ago, used it once, and then kept it going, just in case she needed it again.

In keeping Pyx around, Clyde took a risk. She should have disabled the virus as soon as she was done using it, because if Baedes or his minions were to discover that their computers were transmitting information to the Internet, they could investigate. And if they suspected, for whatever reason, that Clyde was involved, a properly trained investigator could link her computer to the purloined data.

But unlike most viruses, as it turned out, Pyx did nothing to tip its hand. It did not cause unwanted advertisements to pop up on the user's screen. It did not delete files or display cryptic messages. And it was well designed and well tested, so it did not produce unwanted side-effects, like slowing down the computer or its network connection. Additionally, it was specifically targeted at only certain computers, certain government computers. It was designed not to spread outside of that network. It was caged, not out in the wild. That meant it was unlikely to be detected by the experts, those who hunt down viruses for a living, because virus hunters don't generally hunt caged viruses.

Pyx was basically invisible. And for the past month and a half, Pyx had been quietly collecting information, encrypting it, and posting it anonymously in public forums, disguised as "test" posts, lost amongst the countless myriad of test posts floating around the Internet. Then on her computer, Clyde had set up an automated program to go out to these public forums, look for the information Pyx had posted, and download it. All this happened automatically. Clyde didn't even have to think about it, once she started the process.

Now, however, she had a reason to peek into these files

that her computer had been downloading from the department's computers. She wanted to know what had happened to Hashim Osama to turn his family to sudden recluse. The official records showed that he was arrested for armed robbery and that he claimed an alibi. This was all information readily available to Ted, or to whomever ended up defending him. Baedes's unofficial records, however, showed something more startling.

As usual, Baedes was a prolific note-taker. Clyde gathered it must be in his nature, because she knew no one else who so anally recorded significant facts. Clyde found on Baedes's computer a file all about Hashim, a recent file. Baedes had created it only the day before. It recorded only one entry, a long one, in which Baedes referenced the official record. But the chief also noted that it was doubtful that Hashim was the gunman. Then a long series of admissions and denials, of a most peculiar nature. Hashim apparently "admitted" that he knew Ted and Mira, but "denied" that Ted was his lawyer. He "admitted" that they were "friends," but "failed to provide any additional information."

Funny, Clyde thought, since she thought that none of her friends knew anything about this guy, especially Mira, who said she had just met his family and neighbors. Mira also seemed to know very little about Hashim himself. Furthermore, Jane was close to Hashim's wife, and their kids were all close, and she had just met Ted and Mira, too. Unless he meant, "friends" as opposed to "lawyer and client." Or unless he was stretching the truth.

But there was much more. Hashim apparently "denied" knowing a number of names, including several that Clyde recognized as being connected with the Committee. Finally, there was a note that he "had no knowledge of any plot against the government of Abe's Turn." Not that he *denied* having such knowledge, Clyde noted, but that he specifically *had* no such knowledge. The difference, Clydene noticed seemed significant when it came to Baedes's notes. This statement stood in stark contrast to the others in the file. And being married to a lawyer, she recognized the difference. This was a conclusion, not a statement of fact as were the other notes in the file. But how had Baedes drawn such a conclusion? And why had he not recorded the facts leading up to that conclusion, as he consistently did elsewhere?

Hashim was also referenced in another document, a list of names of people, with a summary of each person's association to Mira Jayson. Some of these names also had files of their own. Some Clyde recognized, but others she didn't.

Clydene herself had a file, she was mortified to discover. Her file mentioned her work as a software development contractor, a personal friend of Mira, and a "low-level volunteer" for the Committee. But it did not mention her connection with government contracts or her work on the QX project. The final note concluded that she was "quasi-political, with high ideals, but unwilling to get hands dirty. Possible source of information, but tread carefully."

It became clear to Clyde that Baedes was on an unofficial witch hunt. He clearly didn't have access to the Committee's mailing list, or else he would be targeting everyone on it, and Clyde would have heard about it. In fact, it puzzled Clyde as to why she had not heard of him targeting anyone before now. Ted surely would have heard, as would every other criminal defense lawyer in the county. Looking deeper into the files revealed why, at least partially.

Take the case of Howard Crane. Everyone called him Hal. Clyde was only acquainted with him and only recognized his name because she had met him several times at envelope-stuffing parties and other volunteer events. Baedes had known Hal volunteered for the Committee when Hal was picked up on a DUI a couple weeks ago. It was a stupid thing for Hal to do, and he knew better. Clyde remembered the event, because of Hal's good luck in the matter. She remembered thinking that if he were guilty, then yeah, they should throw the book at him. And she remembered thinking that she did not want to be associated with reckless individuals who would endanger other peoples' lives with their drunk driving. And she remembered being incensed that, even though he was clearly guilty, his lawyer got the charge thrown out for insufficient evidence.

In Hal's file, Baedes had a summary of all this, plus a note that the DUI charge was "dismissed without prejudice," fancy legal jargon that meant that they could bring the charge again if new evidence surfaced. Then there was the name and address of a witness. A quick check confirmed Clyde's suspicion, that this name was not in the official files. It represented new evidence that had not yet officially surfaced. Maybe not enough for a conviction, but probably enough to bring a little hell to Hal's life.

Also in Hal's file, page upon page of names, dates, observations, reports, all connected with Mira.

Baedes was buying secret informants with botched would-be convictions. Or maybe he was extorting information. It depended on how you looked at it. And the information he was seeking was not about the Committee, but about Mira, including her personal life.

This didn't explain how he got away with it without the lawyers finding out. Or maybe they were finding out. Hal's lawyer, Clydene knew, was obligated ethically to keep secret the details of Hal's case, unless Hal wanted him to tell, and Clyde was sure Hal wouldn't. But what happens when the squeeze play doesn't work? What happens when Baedes threatens someone who has too much pride to give in? Clyde clearly didn't have all the pieces to the puzzle. She put the thought to the side, promising to take note of anything that might explain what's happening.

For a moment, Clyde wondered how far Baedes would go in his quest. His beachhead had always been the law and his position as an enforcer of it. But if he were willing to step outside the law in order to get information about Mira, how far outside the law would he be willing to go to hurt her? How far would he be willing to go in general? Or a better question: How much could he get away with?

It was then that Clyde realized the one thing that would explain Hashim's inconsistent testimony, why it was unofficial, and why he clammed up. And she realized why it had taken so long to process his bail, something she had not thought too hard about at the time. And why it was so important to Hashim that she and Ted had been sitting there, counting the minutes, waiting for him to be released, important in a way Ted himself did not realize.

C lydene knew three things about physical abuse. The first thing Clyde knew about physical abuse is that the victim blames herself for the abuse. She does not blame the abuser. Secondly, she feels helpless and fearful. And lastly, the victim will tell the abuser anything he wants to hear, do anything he wants her to do, even believe anything he wants her to believe, if she thinks it will spare her further torment. Clyde also knew one more thing, that it didn't take a pattern of abuse to produce these effects. A single attack could do it. How she knew these things is a subject she didn't like to talk about, or even to think about. Suffice it to say that Clyde had personal experience in this area, personal memories, and she had spent long hours with professional counselors and psychologists overcoming the symptoms of it. But Clyde still hated to talk about it. She hated to think about it. And Ted agreed. There weren't many things Clyde and Ted couldn't talk about in their marriage. This was one of them.

But that evening, as Clyde went through the files she had stolen, these memories kicked in. It was a like Thomas Magnum's little voice, telling her that something was wrong. At least that was how Mira always described it. Clyde's little voice encouraged her to keep looking. Then it told her what had happened to Hashim Osama, not in gory detail, but concretely enough that she didn't want to believe it. She told her little voice that they were missing something and that if they kept looking, they would find another explanation. But the further they looked, the more adamantly her little voice insisted that it was right. Finally, she stopped arguing and just sat, staring at her computer screen, stupefied.

She asked herself why this was so important to her. Why did she even care? She didn't even know this guy. Did it really matter what happened to him? But Mira cared, and Mira was Clyde's best friend. And that was also why—Clyde told herself—she didn't want to admit what she thought had happened to Hashim, because she didn't think Mira would be able to handle it. But in the corner of her mind, her thoughts told her that was bull. Mira would handle it just fine. Rather, Clydene Jackson was the woman too sensitive to handle this particular tragedy. She shuddered.

Clyde's memories of the afternoon came flooding back over her. She remembered the photos Jane had shown her, the stories she had told, how close the two families were, how their lives clicked together when Hashim's family had moved in, like pieces of a snap-together, plastic model, despite all their differences, stories of family outings and of dinners over each others' homes and of friendly get-togethers. And Clyde marveled at the sympathy she felt for these people she had never actually met.

Then, from somewhere deep inside, their attacker became as hers had been on her own fateful night, the horror that had carried her to the edge of death itself, had brought out the best and the worst in love, had made her question her very right to be happy. An evil man had robbed her of a piece of her own soul. Now, Baedes was the attacker, who in her mind had so clearly perpetrated the same torture on another human being. A hidden fury burned her heart, and this sweet, rational

woman suddenly envisioned Baedes tied naked in a dungeon.
She wanted to lash out at him. No, that wasn't good enough.
She wanted to point a .45 between his eyes, grin an evil grin,
and blow his brains out. What she felt was not mere anger; her
mind had been taken over by furious rage, unsullied by even
the tiniest speck of restraint.

Hold on, she reminded herself, *I don't actually know that
Baedes personally did this. Or even that it really happened.* There
was certainly enough corruption among his lackeys. The
whole department reeked of violence, when it suited them.
But did it matter whether he personally was involved? Beady-
fucking-eyes knew about it. His files prove that. He was a
systematic abuser, bullying everyone he could control, on a
personal campaign of terror. Mira once commented that he
didn't know how to take honest criticism. She was probably
right.

Clyde hurt, physically hurt. She started reading the file
again, and with every word, it built up her worst memories,
terror upon terror, horror upon horror. Her imagination ran
rampant, and she forcibly shoved it back into its box. And
then it exploded. It was neither gradual nor subtle nor quiet.
No tear came to her eye. There was no time for that. She cried,
wretched, wailed.

And she finally understood what Mira had been talking
about. Clydene wanted to stop the world and get off. It was no
fun anymore.

— ' c , —

Mira rarely drank to excess. But tonight was an exception to
the rule. This first day of the work week, she had seen over a
dozen clients, and all of them had personal emergencies of one
sort or another that they expected Mira to solve magically.
Toward the end of the day, she had to bite her tongue to keep
from yelling at people.

On top of that, her stomach was still reeling from the weekend. Every moment her mind couldn't focus on work, it started to dwell on the people she loved and how she had hurt them. She knew that Baedes had been after her, had been fishing for information he could use against her, had been threatening anyone associated with her, had been bending the rules, "making deals" to sell her out in exchange for leniency, had been digging up every suspect she had ever helped, had probably even gotten to a few of them. What's more, she could not talk to anyone about this, because she had promised Ted, because if anyone found out he had told her, he could lose his bar card. He had twisted the rules for her, just as Baedes had twisted them against her, and she had to do the right thing; she had to keep Ted's secret, for now. But the secret weighed heavily on her heart, and her mind kept going to all the people who were now at risk, because of her.

That was a lie. There was only one person her mind kept going to, the man who started Baedes's fishing expedition of terror, who right now represented all the people in her life, and represented all her love and fear, vision and uncertainty, conviction and doubt. The doubt had been building steadily for over a month. And while she couldn't explain it in words, there was a definite feeling, a new feeling she felt about herself, not a pleasant feeling, but a wretched melancholy, a depression about to turn into self-loathing, kept at bay only by Mira's singular ability, ironically, to see the glass half full.

You can't always control who you fall in love with. Mira thought. She didn't talk about it, but she had strong feelings for this man who—unknown to him—had made her fall in love with him. She was in love with him, because he made her feel happy. He was her giver of pleasure and of pain. She loved how his eyes made her feel when he smiled. She loved how he smelled. She loved how rugged he looked in his five o'clock shadow. She loved how he loved life. She loved how he penetrated her soul, divining by some hidden sorcery exactly what she thought and felt, like no one else could. Sometimes, not even Clydene knew her as well as Ike did. Clydene, one of the only people in the world who truly understood her. And Mira loved the greatness within him, the way he inspired others. She wanted him on her team. More importantly, she wanted him in her life.

But she didn't know whether he wanted her in his, at least not in the same way she wanted him in hers. And she couldn't figure out whether it could work, or even if it was the right thing to do. When it came to Ike, Mira was a ship without a compass.

She knew that others saw the way she felt, even though she tried not to talk about it. But she tried not to hide it from Clydene, because they shared everything with each other. Still, she had not been able to talk with her best friend about how deep her depression went and how deeply she had it buried. It was just as well. How could she hope to communicate these feelings to Clyde when she couldn't describe them to herself? Too many feelings were swirling around in Mira's stomach, and at the time she couldn't make sense of any of them.

Part of her didn't want to make sense of them. She just wanted to lose herself in a movie, the movie she always ran to when she felt lonely and tired and aching inside. So she curled up on the couch in her rose-covered jammies, with a bottle of California Zinfandel, and she popped *Moonstruck* into the DVD player. Before the film was over, she had put away more than half the bottle.

Meanwhile, Mira watched Loretta Castorini fall in love with her own man she couldn't be with. Mira could see it in Loretta's eyes, right there in Cammareri's Bakery. Mira reached her hand to her neck and fingered the necklace Ike had bought for her those months ago. The necklace was tacky; it was cheap; it was costume jewelry. But she had seen it one day at the mall, and she said she liked it, and so he bought it for her, just like that. She was sure, at the time, he didn't have the money. She smiled at the memory, a passionate, painful smile, and a single tear dripped from her left eye. She dropped the necklace, letting it hang again from her neck, and wiped the tear away with her fingers.

But it was too late to stop crying. Piece by piece, moment by moment, the memories Mira had been avoiding began to intrude into her psyche, forming a complete story. After she had been released from jail, the march on Town Hall went on as planned. Ike joined them in picketing and chanting, which had made Mira feel elated. Now, curled up on her couch, she longed to remember that feeling, but the memory was too distant. Events piled up to form a mountain that separated her from that feeling. But she still knew that feeling had been real. It had been a perfect feeling, now decimated. And it was all her fault.

If Mira had not urged Ike to march with her, if she had not told him it would release his frustration, if she had not blindly leaped into the fray dragging Ike along with her, if he had not been the straw that broke Baedes's camel's back... Ike had indeed let his frustrations out. As the protesters marched, signs held high, Ike's seemed to be held just a little higher than the rest. His chants had a passion behind them that infected both demonstrator and onlooker alike. And when they asked, "How, Chief?!" Ike raised his hand in a mock native greeting. Yes, it was corny, and it was racially insensitive. But it made Mira laugh.

The press gawked on, and there was even a blogger or two with a digital camcorder. Mira and Michael excitedly answered questions of anyone who asked. Clydene and Ted stood by, not taking active part, as previously agreed. In case Mira encountered trouble, Ted and Clyde would be her people on the outside. But there would be no trouble. This event was coming off more perfect than she could have imagined.

Then the devil himself arrived. Mira wasn't sure what Baedes was doing at Town Hall. It didn't matter. He strode past the demonstrators, who glared at him from beyond a chorus of "How, Chief?!" And when Baedes paused to glare back, Ike shoved his mock-native hand in his face.

"How! Chief?!" he shouted.

It took only a few seconds for the chief to react. He grabbed Ike's outstretched arm and yanked it around, forcing it behind Ike's back. The chief pulled out his handcuffs and proceeded to arrest Ike. Mire knew he didn't need an actual charge, because it didn't matter. He could make something up if he needed to.

Demonstrators began bugging out like cockroaches. Some ran. Others set down their signs and nonchalantly blended in with the surrounding crowd. But Baedes had no intention of arresting anyone other than Ike, not the other demonstrators, not the sign-litterers, not even Mira.

Oh that he would have arrested her! For a moment, she wondered whether she should charge to Ike's rescue, so that they could go to jail together. But she couldn't bring herself to do it. It wasn't the same as being arrested for peaceful action. In Mira's mind, those incidents were easy to deal with, even though they angered her, because she knew she was in the right. But interfering with the law, even when the law wrenched her heart as it was doing at that moment... Mira gawked in horror, until it was over.

She hadn't noticed that not everyone had deserted her. Mira had true friend in those who had remained with her and would for all time. Michael placed his hand on her shoulder. He rubbed her back gently. She felt him, but she didn't feel like noticing. Without a word, she stooped down and began picking up the signs and tracts that were littering the ground. Ted was already tidying up the area.

Clydene put her arm around Mira and whispered in her ear, "Leave those, honey. Ted and Michael can take care of that."

She took the objects from Mira's hands, grabbed Mira by the shoulders, and lifted her to standing. Somehow, Clyde fended off the crowd and the press, as she led Mira to her blue Camry. Leave it to Clyde to come through in a crisis, even if she would be feeling the full weight of it later. Once safely in the passenger's seat, Mira brought her knees to her chest and held them there. Her face contorted, and wails and tears flowed from her heart. Clydene touched her shoulder, but Mira refused to be consoled. It had been her fault, all her fault.

Since then, Baedes had been adding a new element to his interrogations, a fishing trip for damaging information about Mira and her legal counsel. Ted told her this was happening. He knew about it not only from his own clients but also from the grapevine. Naturally, some of the people Baedes badgered were both innocent and ignorant, and Ted and Mira were getting a bad rap in criminal defense circles. But other sharks were trolling for chum to feed the monster, to get their guiltier clients a better rap. Ted warned Mira not to tell anyone else about this, not even Clydene, for now, because this information was gained partially through privilege, and Ted's telling it to Mira could possibly be breaking privilege, and Mira knew how dangerous a minefield that could be. Besides, telling wouldn't do any good, and once told, the story cannot be untold. Reluctantly, Mira agreed to keep it a secret.

But the secret weighed heavily on her. There was a time she would have been happy to hear that Baedes was so upset because of the fight she was fighting against him. But that was before she had faced in her mind the unsuspecting innocents that would end up in the middle. She wasn't sure she could come to terms with that, and she wished she could talk it out with Clyde, to get herself centered. Intellectually, she knew she was doing the right thing, but such knowledge was little comfort to her.

Mira had a feeling Ike was one of those who had been compromised, maybe the first. She didn't know what he had told Baedes, or what he was telling Baedes, and she didn't want to get him into any deeper trouble. So she avoided him. But he still managed to call her once every couple of weeks.

Wracked with guilt, Loretta found a way to get past her problems and to live happily ever after. Mira, on the other hand, was drunk from misery and wine.

Even as memories and thoughts and feelings poked at her psyche, all she could truly remember was that she was guilty and inconsolable. Mira herself had pushed Baedes over the edge and sent him on a manhunt for her, mowing down anyone who got in his way. Mira had been prepared for him to come after her. She had been prepared to make sacrifices for the cause. She clearly had not prepared herself to watch while those sacrifices were systematically exacted from the lives of the innocent and the beloved.

She curled up on her couch in her flowered, cotton pajamas, pulling her knees to her chest, and wept.

— ' c , —

Monday came and went and turned into Tuesday morning, and all this time, Clydene's conscience had been struggling with her newfound knowledge. Her first thought was that she was stupid for not paying better attention in the first place. For over a month, Baedes had been searching for her (though he didn't know it), blaming Mira, and playing dirty. And all the time, Clyde had not known anything about it, and she could have.

Her second thought was that she had to do something. Her third, fourth, and fifth thoughts were that there was nothing she could do. She couldn't go to Mira, because Mira was already teetering on the edge of giving up. This new news would push her over the edge. She couldn't go to Ted, because she loved her husband, and if Ted found out she had committed a felony... She feared even to let her mind go there, even to think that Ted could allow her to go on breaking the law, no matter the result, no matter what was just or fair. Ted was too good for that. He played too close to the rules, was part of the system, believed in the system. Ted would turn her in—she was certain of it—or would insist that she turn herself in. This fear was the reason why she had not been keeping better tabs on Baedes, the fear of being caught. It was why she had been so secretive about her discoveries. It was why she did not trust Michael, because Michael was more Ted's friend than hers. But even if she could have told any of her friends, none of her friends could do anything to help.

She felt powerless. She couldn't even help the Hashim family, because they didn't know her or trust her, and they were still not talking, to anyone. She wasn't a stalker, anyhow. There was only one person who might be able to help them, and that was Jane. Clyde had a good feeling about Jane, and more importantly, Mira expressed good feelings about her. Even so, Clyde didn't know if she could trust Jane with her secret. Not that it mattered, because Clyde really didn't know anything, not when it came to Hashim. Yes, she had a list of strange questions and answers, and a more horrifying list of suspicions, but no real evidence. Likely, the only testimony of whatever happened in that police station was locked inside Hashim's own tormented mind.

So on one level, it felt strange to Clyde that she was meeting her new friend Jane for lunch. Even as they sat down in the green and brown booth at the hole-in-the-wall diner, where Clyde normally wouldn't be caught dead, even as they browsed the menu, ordered breakfast fare similar to that whose aroma permeated the air they sniffed, even as they

sipped their watered-down coffee, even as Clydene prepared
to broach the subject, she didn't really know what she was
going to say. That probably meant she was going to say something stupid.

Oh well, here goes nothing, Clyde thought.

"I can't tell you how I know this," Clyde began. "In fact, I
don't really know anything. And even if I did know it, I
couldn't admit that I knew it or tell you how I knew it. Can
you keep a secret?"

Already Clyde knew she was screwing this up.

"Yes," Jane said straight-faced. "I can keep a secret, if it's
important."

Clyde spoke softly. "What I'm saying is, if anybody asks,
you and I just had lunch and chatted. In fact, we didn't even
have lunch. Because if anyone finds out that I know what I
know, people will get hurt."

"Are you with the CIA?" Jane said, just above a whisper.

Clyde was confused for a second. Then she laughed. "No.
Nothing like that... Actually..." A couple had been seated in
the table next to them, and Clyde started to think it was a little
too cramped for this discussion. "I have to use the ladies room.
Want to come with?"

Safe from the eyes and ears of the crowd, Clyde started
telling Jane about her suspicions, about abuse of process,
about taking advantage of a visitor on American soil, about
threats, about torture, about officials extracting information in
the color of law.

Jane was incredulous. She couldn't believe such a thing
could happen, not here, not in the twenty-first century. So
Clyde piece by piece revealed to her the entire secret. She
didn't mean to, but once she started talking, it all came out,
and fast. Clyde had revealed the entire story before she knew
what she was doing, cracking into the government computer
network, discovering Baedes's secret files, his quest for infor-

mation, his mission of terror, his notes on his interrogation of Hashim. She suddenly feared Jane might not keep the secret. Then she feared Jane might blame her. Or that Jane might think Clydene was delusional. Pick whichever fear you wish: Clyde feared for her life.

But Jane didn't seem angry. Nor did she seem suspicious. She didn't seem anything. The two women quietly strode back to the table. Their coffee was still sitting there, undisturbed. They sat. Jane sipped.

"What do you want me to do?" Jane asked.

"I thought you might be able to talk to Hashim or his wife. Find out whether I'm out of my mind."

"You're not." Jane choked on the words, her eyes squinted, and Clyde could see wetness in them.

"I'm so sorry," Clyde said. She touched Jane's hand. Then she reached into her purse for a tissue and handed it across the table.

Jane explained that she had talked to Fatima going out to the market. But Fatima had been distant, and when Jane probed her on the subject, she brought Fatima to the verge of tears. Jane could not repeat what they talked about, because she was sworn to secrecy. But with the details that Clydene provided, she said, everything started clicking into place.

"Are you mad?" Clyde asked.

"Livid," Jane said.

Clyde didn't know what to say. "I'm sorry," she eked out.

"Thanks." Jane buried her nose in the tissue.

"You won't tell anyone about me," Clyde said, more a question than a statement.

Jane shook her head. "No."

"Can you do anything for Hashim?"

"I can ask them—" Jane choked on her words again. She breathed. "I can try to get them to talk to a lawyer."

A new voice interrupted their conversation.

"Clyde?"

Clyde turned to look at the newcomer. She was an average-looking woman, in her thirties, medium hair, brown eyes.

The woman rephrased. "Are you Clydene Hobbes?"

Clyde stared back at her, doing her best to look concerned, upset, confused— anything except what she really felt, which was scared. She didn't know why she should feel scared. She wasn't doing anything wrong. There wasn't any reason she shouldn't befriend Jane, or that Jane shouldn't befriend her.

The woman continued. "I'm Julie. We went to school together at Springfield High?"

Clyde immediately remembered, but her mind was too full to think through all the facts right now. Clyde shook her head. Clyde lied. "Sorry. I never lived in Springfield."

— ' c , —

Mira pulled herself up each stair, with each step contemplating the words she planned to speak to Ike. She secretly wished that he was not home, so that she wouldn't have to face him. But as she approached his apartment door, she heard a man speaking indistinct words over soundtrack music playing through a television speaker inside, and she knew Ike would come to the door if she knocked. Maybe she should have buzzed him from the front instead of sneaking into Ike's building as the pizza guy left. But she didn't want to talk to Ike unless it was face-to-face, or maybe even at all.

Mira stared at the gold, plastic numbering on the flat, wooden door. Apartment 4B. For a moment, she stood listening to some fictional nighttime drama being played out within. It couldn't hold a candle to the real-life drama playing out in the hallway, within her own heart. She stood staring at the door, then the door jamb, then the little table Ike had set in the hallway. It held some minor knickknacks, a wooden bowl of candy, a matching wooden cup, hand-painted, an empty, blue bottle once filled with white wine, markers of his personality, his taste, his vision. She breathed in the scent of fallen leaves mingled with the bad cologne and old cigarette smoke of the people who lived across the hall.

She wondered whether she should have stopped at home first, to change and freshen up. It had been another long day at the office. Even though she looked sharp in a dark business suit, she felt hot and sweaty and dirty.

This was silly. She was making excuses. She knew what she had come to do. She was committed. In half-consciousness and half-daze, Mira reached out her hand, held her breath, and pounded several times on the door with her knuckles.

Then she waited. It seemed an interminable wait, and Mira thought she heard some voices superimposed over those of the characters on the TV.

Oh no! Mira thought. *What if he has company over?*

But no one answered her knock. Maybe it was Mira's good fortune that no one heard her. She had decided to slip away and forget the whole thing, when the door swung open. Mira stood face-to-face with a woman, dirty blonde, long hair, buxom but fit, a little taller than Mira herself, wearing a large T-shirt and little else.

"Can I help you?" the woman asked.

For a moment Mira was stunned. She wondered whether she had accidentally knocked at the wrong door.

"I— I'm sorry," Mira stammered. "I think I must have the wrong apartment."

"Who is it?" Ike said from inside.

Suddenly, Mira felt as if she were in a B-rated horror flick, as if she were one of those stupid females in skimpy clothing who had just ventured into the monster-infested dark tunnel after having been sternly warned against it by the delusional paranoiac.

"I don't know yet," the woman answered Ike.

Ike peeked around the corner. "Oh. Hi, Mira. What can I do for you? Come in. We were just making Piña Coladas. You want one?"

"Uh... No... Actually, uh—"

"Sorry. Where are my manners?" Ike said. "Soph, this is Mira Jayson. Mira, this is my girlfriend, Sophie Marcum."

The breath left Mira's body.

"Mira!" Sophie said. "I've heard so much about you. I understand you've been a real friend to Ike."

"Uh, I guess so." Mira could see that the woman did not appreciate her friendship with Ike as much as she was trying to make it seem.

"So," Ike said, "are you coming in? Or should we bring the party outside?"

"I'm, uh—" She shifted gears. "I'm sorry." She tried to speak cheerfully. "I didn't know you were seeing anyone."

"Well, it all happened kind of fast."

"Oh, I see. You know what? It can wait. I need to go, anyhow."

"I'm sorry to hear that," Sophie said with a tinge of sardonicism.

As the outside door wheezed to a close, Mira stood for a moment on the outside step and breathed deeply.

— ' c , —

Clyde lay on the couch in her living room, in the dark. Ted was working late, which was good, because she didn't feel like talking to him or to anybody. There was nothing on TV, and she didn't feel like cooking. She didn't even feel like playing her guitar. She just sat in the dark and gazed at the vague shadows on the ceiling.

Her cell phone rang. She didn't feel like talking to anyone right now. But it might be Ted, and it might be important. She picked up the phone and peered into the small display. It was from a phone number she didn't know. Curiosity got the better of her, and she flipped open the phone and answered. It was Jane.

"I thought you might like to know," she said, "I talked to Fatima tonight."

It was Clyde's good fortune that she had taken the phone call. She needed some good news to lift her spirits.

Jane continued. "I couldn't convince them to talk to a lawyer."

Clyde was mystified. "But what about the criminal charges? Why would he go with a public defender? Is he going to plead guilty? He didn't do anything."

"The charges have been dropped."

"Huh?" Clyde shook her head. "What do you mean, 'The charges have been dropped'? Just like that?" Clyde asked.

"Yes, the charges have been dropped. Just like that."

"Oh." Clydene didn't know how to process that information. "Well, that's good news, I guess," she finally said.

"I'm not sure," Jane said. "Fatima says they're moving back to Pakistan, this week. They've already made arrangements."

Clyde said nothing.

"... just like that." Jane finished her story.

"I'm so sorry. I feel responsible."

"Why? It's not your fault."

"Yes, but I—"

"Clydene, you did nothing wrong. We just have to make sure this doesn't happen again, to anyone else."

Clydene nodded her head, not thinking that Jane couldn't see her over the telephone.

"At least, that's what I think," Jane said.

Clyde had to get her bearings. "Uh, yeah. I don't know how, though."

"Let's have lunch again," Jane suggested.

And so they made lunch plans for the next week, though

Clyde didn't see what the point was. The two were just about to say their goodbyes when Clyde's doorbell rang. She hurriedly hung up and answered the door, wondering what new cruelty this day could deliver.

Mira stood outside in the chilly, night air. Clyde couldn't really see her in the dark. Without a word, Mira stepped inside and cried bitter tears on Clyde's shoulder. So Clyde wrapped arms around her and consoled her.

Episode 3: Home for the Holidays

Clyde wrapped her arms around her weeping friend. Mira mumbled something about "Ike." Then they stood there without saying a word. They stood for a long time, while Clyde's thoughts wandered from worry to worry, then from sorrow to sorrow, then from anger to anger.

She worried about her friends, because she had brought Baedes's suspicions down upon them. She worried about Mira, because Baedes thought Mira was at the center of a conspiracy against him. She worried about herself, because she didn't want to get caught. And she worried, because she knew that if she ever wanted to turn herself in, the easiest way would be simply to tell her beloved, her own husband. And after Ted got over his rage at what she had done, and called the feds to take her away at gunpoint, he would represent her and defend her in court, with a passion borne out of love. But she worried, most of all, because all the clever legal defenses in the world could not repair the damage this will have done to their relationship.

She sorrowed at how powerless she was, and how helpless. She knew she had acted with the best of intentions. But intentions didn't mean a thing if all she accomplished was to bring pain upon those she loved. She sorrowed for Mira and for her pain. She sorrowed that she could do nothing to help, because Mira felt a longing of the heart, which could only be solved by Mira's heart itself. She sorrowed for Hashim Osama and his family, innocents caught in the crossfire of an ugly political battle. Who said politics was only about words? Words have consequences.

And was that her fault? What had she ever done to Hashim, or to Jane, or to Mira? Clyde knew three things about being abused, and the first was that the victim blames herself for the abuse, even though it's the abuser's fault. And Clyde was not the one toting a gun, waving it in people's faces, disrupting the lives of innocent families, or hurting her friends.

In her mind, Clyde heard the words, "See what you made me do?" They sounded as loudly as if they had been spoken.

Rage began to boil in Clyde's heart, because she had only fought an evil. Her attacker's free choice made him hurt her. She had no obligation to feel anything but hate and revulsion for him. It was *not* her fault, and it was wrong for him to blame her for any of this.

Clyde was pissed at Mira, too. Because Mira had lost sight of the prize. Not only did Mira blame herself, she was letting her feelings compromise her judgment. Clyde wanted to snap Mira out of it.

"Hey, you!" Clyde barked. The words did not come out tenderly and sweet, as they did when Clydene said them.

Mira had stopped crying, but was still resting her head on Clyde's shoulder, like a little girl cuddling up to her mother. Now, Mira looked up, and Clyde could see fear in her eyes.

Clyde softened her voice and tried again. "Hey, you." Then as she stared into Mira's sad, puppy-dog eyes, she forgot what she was mad about.

"Come in and sit down," Clyde said.

— ' C , —

A man stood in the doorway of his townhouse. He seemed to be observing the crowd of children gathering in the lot. In reality there was only one child he was interested in, the 12-year-old boy sitting on the stair of the neighbor's apartment. The man, whose name was Damian, noticed that the boy too was only watching the commotion. But Damian kept an eye on him nonetheless to make sure he didn't get too close.

The children crowded in as though they were the electrons of a giant atom, their autumn coats pressing in on each other as they shifted in and out, back and forth, up and down, around a central nucleus, each one straining to see what was happening inside. Occasionally, a catcall or a collective cheer interrupted the din, but mostly they made a steady noise of indistinct voices. It looked like just a assembly of middle school students getting ready for a neighborhood, after-school ball game. But if you were paying attention, you could tell that the gathering was more serious. Too many kids. Too loud a din. Too focused on the action at the nucleus of the atom.

Someone must have been paying attention, because the disturbance lasted only a few minutes. A new kid joined the crowd. Then, suddenly, a girl broke free from the mass of bodies and shot out across the parking lot, like a subatomic particle escaping the atom's nucleus. The rest of the atom immediately split, one half toward Summer Street, the other toward Lyman Avenue. Three seconds later, police officers swooped down upon the scene.

The blonde policewoman, tall and athletic, navy jacket and pants, with a black leather belt and an official-looking insignia on her badge, hair tightly wrapped in a bun, approached the 12-year-old boy and two of his friends, who were now standing and talking. Damian stood back, but strained to hear the conversation between her and the boys. The 12-year-old boy motioned in Damian's direction, and the policewoman glanced over. That was more than he could take. He stepped down from his perch and ambled toward the boys and their interlocutor. The cold air bit at his hands, but he dared not warm them in his pockets, because he preferred to leave them in plain sight.

As he approached, Damian heard part of the conversation.

"I know one," the 12-year-old boy said with a thick, Hispanic accent. "Her name is Kay. She ran over there." The boy pointed in the direction the girl had run.

"Is that what all of you saw?"

One of the other kids said, "Yeah, I guess so. I didn't see much. We just got here. But I saw Kay running away."

She turned to Damian. "And you were over there?" She pointed to their apartment.

"Yes." Damian spoke perfect, American English. "I was primarily watching my son there"—he indicated the 12-year-old boy—"you know, to make sure he wasn't involved in it."

"Okay." She asked the boy, "Do you know where this girl lives?"

He paused.

Damian gave him the "Yes, it's okay" look and nodded slightly.

"Yeah. I think she went home."

"Which apartment does she live in?"

"She lives down there." The boy pointed down the street.

"Do you know what number?"

"Uh. I think it's... next to the corner, not Summer Street, on the next street."

"Can you show me?"

"Yeah."

Another cop approached.

"Hold on a second," the policewoman said, and she had a quick conversation with the other cop. Damian couldn't hear any of what they said, until she said, "No. They're witnesses. He's a witness," indicating the boy; "he's a witness," indicating Damian. "But they were about to..." and her voice trailed off again.

When she was done talking to the other cop, she said, "Okay. You can show me where she lives now."

Damian accompanied the 12-year-old boy as they showed the cop where Kay lived. Kay was one of those unfortunate kids whose father didn't live with her and whose mother didn't care about her. She was about 12, like Damian's boy. The two children went to the same school. She and her friends had been known to pick on the younger kids, and police reports had been filed by several parents. Kay also made up her face and dressed like a hooker, even at the age of 12. It was well known in the neighborhood that she slept around. Once, she was even caught having sex in a public place with a young, teenage boy. Damian and his wife had forbidden their kids from hanging around with Kay or with any of her friends.

While they were walking, the policewoman got a call on her walkie-talkie. She took it, then she said to Damian, "You go ahead I'll catch up."

They did, and once they were out of earshot, Damian asked the boy, "How are you doing?"

"Okay. I don't think Kay wanted to fight. She was being bullied by some other kids."

"Serves her right," Damian said.

"She's not as bad a kid as you think she is."

"You're kidding, right?"

— ' c , —

Clydene was honestly looking forward to meeting Jane for lunch, because Jane was the only person in the world she could talk openly with. Over the past week, Clyde had been receiving ongoing, automated reports from the Pyx virus on

Baedes's unofficial files, as well as official files, emails, and other files. At first, Clyde didn't believe how much junk email was shuffled around the Abe's Turn governmental network. But then she remembered that it was essentially like any big corporation. Clyde desired to talk to someone about what she was doing. She wanted to mull it over with another human being. Normally, she would talk with Mira, but in this case Mira could not know, because knowing that Baedes was on the warpath would devastate Mira. So Clydene looked forward to her lunch with Jane, the only person who knew about Pyx.

Clyde arrived at the restaurant early. She had driven all the way out to Stafford Springs so that no one would recognize her, though she didn't know why, or at least couldn't put it into words. And she chose a restaurant that served real food that she could palate. Having parked her blue Camry, she stood at the entrance and squinted out across the lot. Even though the sun was still bright, the air was beginning to get colder, a gentle reminder that it was no longer Summer. Occasionally, a chill breeze blew her fiery red hair into her eyes. She brushed it back with her hand. And whenever a passerby entered the restaurant, she caught a whiff of garlic and fresh Italian bread from inside. Finally, Clyde noticed Jane, with genuine happiness at the sight of her.

Inside, a waitress led them to a nondescript booth somewhere within the maze of tables. The overhead speakers resonated with a classic soft-rock love song. At a nearby table a good-looking young man and woman ate ravioli from the same plate while they made goo-goo eyes at each other. Clyde sighed. She would always be a romantic at heart.

"Remember that?" Jane asked, nudging her eyes in their direction.

"Romance? Yeah, I guess so," Clyde said. "I don't know. Being married is different, but I wouldn't say being single was any better." All Clydene could remember about her life before Ted was the loneliness and the mood swings.

"You don't have kids."

"No."

"Children change everything." Jane gazed longingly at the lovebirds. "I remember that, but I don't remember the last time I looked at Marvin like that."

Clyde suddenly realized she was staring at the lovebirds, and she snapped her head back. The lovebirds didn't seem to notice either way.

Jane continued. "They become your whole life." Her voice became serious. "This is kind of heavy, isn't it?"

"A little," Clyde said.

"Guess what happened at work? They scheduled me to work tomorrow afternoon, and I have to be home to pick up the boys from the bus after school. That's the way it is every day. They don't seem to get it."

"So what are you going to do?"

"I told them I had to leave at 2, no matter what the schedule said," Jane stated matter-of-factly. "They can fire me if they want, but you have to have your priorities straight."

"Couldn't you leave them with someone for a few hours until you got back? Maybe a neighbor—" The words left Clydene's mouth before she could stop them. "Uh, I mean... Uh..."

"Yeah, I know what you mean." In some ways, Jane was a thick-skinned broad. "But if I was going to leave them with someone else so I could work, I might as well let someone else raise them. Because that's what I'd be doing anyways."

"I can understand that." Clyde did understand, even though she didn't have children of her own. Her own submerged maternal instinct peeked out occasionally from within her. She and Ted had no kids not because they didn't want kids. It just never seemed to be the right time. For a moment, Clyde realized that her biological clock was ticking away, and she felt just a little bit empty and a little bit envious of Jane.

"I'd love to have a job like yours," Jane said. "Work at home. I could have the kids home with me and earn money at the same time."

"Yeah, but you'd have the same problem." Clyde thought of all the times she had neglected Ted because she was working on a project. "You'd have to set aside time for them, or you'd end up ignoring them."

"We should probably figure out what we want to eat." Jane picked up a menu. "I've never been here before. What's good on the menu?"

"The rosemary chicken luncheon special looks good."

"Yeah?"

"Yeah. With a glass of the house Pinot Grigio."

"A glass of what?"

Clyde looked up over the top of her menu at Jane's face. "White wine."

"Oh." Jane returned to her menu.

"Sorry about that," Clyde said. "One of my hobbies is gourmet cooking. And part of that is being a wine snob."

Clyde returned to her menu. She was eying the shrimp primavera, but the talk about rosemary chicken made her want that, too.

"Fatima is probably back in Pakistan by now," Jane said apropos of nothing.

Clyde knew, there was no "probably" about it.

Jane continued. "What can we do to help?"

Clyde set down her menu. Jane was staring across the table at her. "To help Fatima?"

"To stop this kind of thing from happening again." Jane whispered. "I don't mind telling you, I'm scared."

"Why? You're not Pakistani?"

"Yeah, but they were really sweet people. They never hurt anyone else. And they— If it could happen to them, it could happen to any of us. I don't want my kids to go through that."

"This is true," Clyde said.

"So just let me know. I know you follow that whole thing."

Clydene's mind suddenly went blank. She had come prepared to chat about Baedes, longing to talk about it, and now that Jane had brought up the subject, Clyde didn't have any practical answers.

"Who do you like for town council?" Jane asked, before Clyde could formulate a response.

"Me?" Clyde said. "I'm not voting for any of them."

— ' c , —

Michael ushered his guest down the green wall of the office cube farm. Other walls were blue, orange, yellow, and other colors, each colored wall identifying a known location in the otherwise indistinguishable maze of cubicles. Ergonomically calibrated artificial light beamed down from the high ceiling. All around them, computer keyboards clacked, and subdued voices melded in an indecipherable drone.

Michael loved the hustle and bustle of office life. It felt a little like being at a party, and he loved parties. He loved meeting people, being around people, talking to people. And he loved showing off to his friends and acquaintances.

Michael and his visitor stopped to examine one of the posters placarding the green wall.

"Yeah, I'm really proud of this one. This ad out-pulled our previous control by 70 percent!" Michael said. His baby blues beamed like little flashlights.

"You should become a freelance consultant, my friend." The visitor's dark skin and eyes betrayed his Hispanic descent, but his voice rang with the educated tones of a confident, wealthy executive. As he grinned, tiny crow's-feet appeared at his temples, and his smile lines deepened. Wearing a clean, white polo shirt, he belonged on the golf course, not as an honored guest being conducted through one of the biggest ad agencies in the city.

"No thanks," Michael said. "Not everyone is cut out to be an entrepreneur— No offense."

"None taken."

"At heart, I'm one of those creative types who'd rather leave running the business to someone else. Besides, in an organization this size, I get to talk to lots of interesting people I'd never get to meet otherwise."

"Creative type? I thought you were the head of your department. A director?"

"Yes, Creative Director. But that's still a creative position. I manage the project, make sure it gets done right. But other people handle the business end of things. It's like being a film director, as opposed to a producer, if that makes sense."

"Yes, it does." The visitor nodded.

"And speaking of producers, here's my boss."

Another man approached, a nondescript, no-nonsense type with a fake smile. He wore a short, business-like haircut and a white, button-down shirt.

Michael turned to him. "Paul, this is a friend of mine, Joaquin Alvarez, but we call him Jay. Jay, Paul Cr—"

Paul interrupted him. "It's good to meet you." He reached out and shook the visitor's hand. Then he said to Michael, "I didn't know you were having a meeting today."

"It's nothing formal. I was just showing him around."

"Excuse me," he said to the visitor, and took Michael off to the side. He whispered, "Is this a potential client?'

"Yes," Michael whispered back.

"Then you should have gone through me."

"Relax," Michael said in his normal speaking voice. "I'm not going to reveal anything top-secret. Because you know,

I'm too smart for that. And we're just talking preliminary, informal. Nothing set in stone."

"Why don't I join you then?" The manager had also returned to his normal speaking voice.

"Well..." Michael glanced back at Jay. "We had planned to meet— uh— sit down in my office, and I don't know if there's a conference room available."

"I'll check the schedule." He headed back to his cubicle.

Michael returned to Jay, who was staring agape at Paul.

"If you want to escape, now's the time," Michael said in a humorous, hushed tone.

"Wow, you weren't exaggerating, were you?" Jay said.

"Well you weren't surprised, were you?"

"Hell, yes!" Jay checked himself and lowered his voice again. "I mean, it's one thing to hear about— someone like that, another thing to experience him."

Michael chuckled. "Really, he's harmless, though."

Jay faced Michael. "You know, you really could run your own business."

Michael sneered with the left half of his face.

"Seriously," Jay continued, "you're good with people, and that's the most important part of doing business. I mean, yes, there's accounting and legal crap and plenty of paperwork. But you can hire people to take care of all that stuff, or take on a partner."

"Well, that's nice of you to say," Michael politely intoned.

"And you wouldn't have to deal with Señior Pointy-hair, anymore."

Michael chuckled again. "But I *like* Pointy-hair. Every ad needs a villain, and where do you think I get inspiration for my best ones? Besides which, it's fun to poke him. He's like the Pillsbury Doughboy, if the Pillsbury Doughboy were a crack addict."

A pause.

Michael took a breath. "That didn't come out as funny as I thought it would."

"No, I guess not," Jay said.

The boss returned and ushered them to an empty conference room. As they sat, Jay explained his situation, more for Paul's benefit than for Michael's, because Michael already knew most of the background. Jay and his brother owned and ran a home heating oil business, J&D Heating Oil, in the town of Abe's Turn. That's how he and Michael knew each other, because Michael also lived and had contacts in Abe's Turn, and they had met at a local Chamber of Commerce event.

"What I'm concerned about," Jay said, "is this new competitor, World's Best Heating. They recently started up in the area, and some of my customers are going with them, because they're undercutting us. They must be losing money on the deal. Not unheard of, to dump lots of money in and undercut the competition, just to get established. They probably have mob investors backing the operation."

Paul chuckled.

Jay continued. "Seriously, though, the owner of the company, Freddy Carrillo, his relatives have been associated with organized crime. I'm not worried about that, though. Mob bosses don't open up one-horse home-heating outlets.

"In any case, this is a critical time in our annual cycle. The weather is getting colder, and people are thinking about preparing for winter and about high heating costs. That makes them likely to switch to a lower-priced offer. And after they switch, it's going to be that much harder to get them back later in the season, even if WBH raises its rates.

"Personally, I wonder if they're doing a bait and switch, luring new customers with rock-bottom prices, under-delivering on service, and then knowing that they'll need to raise prices half-way through the winter. And probably will blame it on Iraq or something."

"So you need to undercut their prices," Paul said.

"No," Michael said. "He needs to come up with a winning offer that springboards off his unique abilities. I have a few ideas—"

"But if people care about price, you have to cut your price."

"But we can't cut our prices," Jay said.

"You have to find a way—"

Michael interrupted with a dismissive wave of his hand. "You don't have to compete on price. And you don't want to. That's the worst thing you could do."

Paul glared at him from across the table.

Michael ignored him. "You have a list of your customers right?"

"Yes," Jay said.

"Of course you do. Otherwise, how could you deliver their oil and bill them? You can put together a direct mail campaign. That's relatively inexpensive. Talk about the relationship you've had with them and the reliable service you've given.

"If they're concerned about price, we can come up with creative offers that ease their fears, like a monthly plan."

"Yes, we already offer something like that. We distribute the cost of the winter season over the whole year."

"Exactly. We can market that as a way to manage winter heating costs. Or you could offer a guaranteed maximum price, a ceiling on the winter heating bills, even for those who didn't lock in their rates last June. The price ceiling doesn't even have to be low, just something to make customers feel better.

"Better yet, offer a premium plan that includes free emergency deliveries, or other free heating services, like repairs to their furnace. It's like being on retainer."

"That's all well and good," Paul said, "but—"

"Don't stop me. I'm on a roll.

"You can talk about how you never leave a loyal customer in the cold. Remember that guy you told me about? He lost his job, and you kept deliveries coming to his family all through the winter, even though he couldn't pay at the time? And then you billed them over the next year?"

Jay nodded.

"That's one powerful story. You don't even have to make any guarantees for a story like that to work.

"And you don't have to offer special deals to just anyone. You can make these offers only to your best and and most loyal customers, because you know they won't take advantage of you. Besides which, you want to reward them, which will just increase their loyalty. Or maybe you could offer special guarantees to your most loyal customers.

"And maybe to one or two new customers that *they personally recommend*." Michael punctuated each word with a pointed finger. "That would be a good way to build your customer base. And use the revenue from the premium plans to pay for special introductory offers to new customers."

Jay was grinning now.

"Whoa, whoa, whoa," Paul said. "We need to make sure we have the resources in the department."

"Let me put together a proposal, then," Michael said, "and we'll allocate the resources."

"But I don't know if we can accept the liability for deals like that."

Jay was clearly confused. "What liability?"

Michael interjected. "There's no liability, Paul. He approves all the copy, and there's an indemnity clause in the standard contract."

"That doesn't always cover the bases."

"Besides which, we commonly do similar campaigns for other clients. This is no different."

"It's different because I haven't approved it yet," Paul said.

"Okay. So approve it!" Michael thought a moment. "What's stopping you?"

"I need to see more first."

"Fine, we'll start on the campaign, but nothing goes to press without your approval."

"That will do," Paul eked out.

Jay stared straight through Michael's eyes. "Business issues," he said.

Michael chuckled at the thought that Jay was secretly trying to lure him away, right under his boss's nose.

CHAPTER 2

Seated at the office desk, Damian stared at the piles of papers before him. Yeah, Jay was a genius. Or rather, he had hired a genius to help them. Only a couple weeks ago, they were looking at one of the coldest financial winters since they got into the home heating business, all because an aggressive, new competitor started stealing their customers away. Now, thanks to a brilliant marketing campaign, not only were they no longer losing customers, they had more new customers than they could comfortably handle.

Unfortunately, there was a downside. Jay was always out having business meetings now, making deals with local retail businesses, doing radio and television interviews. And this left Damian alone to pick up the slack, to run the office and make deliveries. They were already looking for part-time help. And Damian had agreed to interview a prospective employee. But there was no reason, he thought, he shouldn't get a little paperwork done while he was waiting. He picked up a pile of delivery receipts and started entering them into the computer.

He only got a few sheets into the stack when the office door jingled open and a large man entered. He wore his dark hair short, like an ex-marine. A slick, brown, leather jacket defined his broad shoulders. Underneath, he wore a dark shirt and slacks, and black shoes.

Damian rose to shake the man's hand, stepped from behind the desk. "Hi. You must be Craig." He reached out his hand. The man grabbed Damian's hand and squeezed, hard. He crowded Damian and forced him back against the desk. Damian stared in horror, puzzled over what was happening, feared for his safety.

"I ain't Craig," the man sneered at Damian. "I'm your enemy." He released Damian's hand, took a step back, began to saunter around the room. He picked up a small, plastic snow globe from the desk and examined it. Then with the other hand, he flipped open a manila file folder and turned his attention to the papers therein. The snow globe had been a gift from Damian's eldest son. The papers were customer files.

Damian rubbed his hand, still tender. "I think you really hurt my hand," he said.

The man slammed the snow globe down on the desk and snarled, "I can do more than that."

Damian stared at the snow globe.

The man picked it up again and inspected it. "Is this special?" he asked.

Damian nodded nervously.

"Do you know who I am?" the man asked.

Damian neither said nor did anything.

The man continued. "I'm here on behalf o' your new competition. Now, we try to be reasonable. We play nice. You know, fair competition. But you don't give us a chance. You were here first. You have an unfair advantage. So you step in and undercut us, even before we can get started." He looked questioningly at Damian. "You know what I mean?"

"We charge more than you," Damian replied. "And you stole our customers away first."

"What?" The man looked more angry than inquisitive.

Damian repeated himself matter-of-factly. "You tried to

undercut us, not the other way around."

In response, the man wound up and pitched the globe across the room, hard and fast. It crashed into the wall with a loud thunk. Damian whipped around and saw it in three pieces, spilled on the floor.

The man marched up to Damian, grabbed his shirt with one hand, and waved his other fist in his face. "You're not getting it. I'm asking you nicely." He dropped his fist, grinned haughtily, and shook his head. "You see, my boss, he's a reasonable guy, not the sort that comes into a town and takes over. He knows how to share, just like everybody else in this town. But my boss, he don't like to be bullied. So you got to learn how to share, too. *Capisce?*"

He paused a moment. "Besides, what you're doing is illegal."

The accusation disturbed Damian, in his gut, put him on the defensive. "If you think we're doing something wrong, why don't you sue us? Why all the mob mentality?"

"Because proper channels takes too long. It costs too much. Even if we win, we still lose."

He continued. "This is the only way. And we only warn you one time. Lighten up. Or else I'll do whatever it takes to make sure you stop... uh, throwin' your weight around."

Damian wondered what kind of demented, twisted logic it took to embrace such a bizarre incongruity. He also wondered what made him think he could get away with it. But the man stood a foot taller than Damian, and Damian could see his muscles bulge even underneath the leather jacket. He sneered in Damian's face and his fist was still clenched. And Damian had a bad, bad feeling about this. If this bully were to mess up Damian's face, no one would bring him to justice. Because Damian knew he couldn't go to the cops, because of his son. For a moment, Damian wondered if the man knew this as well.

Then before Damian could work out what to do next, the man stood tall, nonchalantly brushed the wrinkles out of Damian's shirt where he had ruffled it.

He said, "Think about it. Because next time I won't be so nice."

And he left.

— ' C , —

Ted couldn't believe it, once the news reached his desk. True, Jerry was only human, and humans made mistakes. And Ted had made mistakes of his own over the years, and some of those were doozies. But mistakes tend to backfire on you, and now was not the time for mistakes. Still, Ted knew that if he could breathe deeply for a few minutes and not think about Jerry or his blunder—

Ted tried to unclench his teeth. Instead, he slammed his fist down on the desk, rattling the pens and pencils in his pen-and-pencil holder. Then he did relax his jaw. He took a deep breath. If he could distract himself for a few minutes, he knew he'd be able to think clearly afterward.

A knock sounded from the door, which opened to reveal a young man in a dark suit and red tie. A layer of sandy hair sat atop his head, and a pair of delicate glasses framed his brown eyes.

"It's not a good time, Jerry," Ted said.

"I'm sorry to hear that," Jerry replied. "I still need to speak with you urgently."

"It's not a good time, because I've already heard." Ted was desperately trying to remain calm.

"Oh." Jerry stared off to the side for a moment, into the air. Then he took a few steps forward. "Don't you want to debrief me?"

Ted stood from his chair. He raised his voice. "Now are telling me how to do my job? Huh? Is that how it's going to be? After you..." Ted could feel adrenaline pumping through his veins, undiluted rage like a bomb ready to detonate, being held in check only by sheer force of will.

He slammed his fists on the desk again, and Jerry took a shocked step back.

Ted closed his eyes and breathed deeply. "I just need a few minutes to get my mind around this," he intoned without opening his eyes.

"Unfortunately, we have a meeting set up in an hour, and I think there's more here to go over than we have time for."

"Are you kidding?" Ted was raising his voice again. "I think it's all pretty cut and dry! *You lose!*" Ted stabbed at the air between them to enunciate his point. "You lose. I lose. We all fucking lose!"

Ted stepped out from behind his desk. "Damn it!" He shouted. "I trusted you. I stuck up for you. I put myself on the line for you. And this is how you repay me?"

"It was a mistake," Jerry said.

"A mistake?! Is that all you can say? Do you have *any* idea how *stupid* a mistake that was?"

"I know exactly how silly it seems, but it's still a very common contract provision."

"Do you think I care—"

"Most lawyers don't even pay any attention to it, because it's boilerplate."

"Wonderful! I could have hired anyone if I wanted fucking boilerplate! I could have hired a fucking legal secretary!"

"This happened years ago, years before I made partner. I realize this is a youthful indiscretion. But it *was* youthful."

"Indiscretion?! You think you got caught in bed with a married woman? *That* I could deal with!" Ted put his hands on either side of his head, clenched his teeth again, and writhed. "God!"

"Besides," Jerry continued, "it does mean more business for

us."

Ted suddenly stopped. He stared at Jerry, mouth open. His voice quieted, but it sounded just as angry. And it increased in volume as he continued talking, louder and louder, until he was shouting again. "I don't believe it. You have the unmitigated gall to come in here and try to *defend* yourself? As though your incompetence is just par for the course? And might even be *good* for us? What kind of a fucking screw-up are you?!" And then he screamed in disgust and fury.

Michael knocked at the door. "Excuse me. I don't think you realize how far your voice carries."

Ted looked at his friend and suddenly felt very ashamed. But his face didn't move a muscle. As a litigator, he knew how to reveal feelings that weren't there and, more importantly, how to conceal feelings that were eating him alive— when he needed to.

Michael turned to Jerry. "Hi, Jerry." Michael smiled at him. "Good to see you again."

Jerry nodded a hello.

"Can you give us a few minutes?" Michael asked.

Jerry paused for a moment before he nodded again. "Sure," he said.

After he left, Michael closed the door. In one hand, he was carrying a paper bag. He reached into it and lifted out a can of cola, set it on the desk in front of Ted's chair. He reached back into the bag and pulled out a sandwich.

"Do you want to tell me what's really bothering you?" Michael asked.

Ted shook his head. "Young lawyers are so incompetent," he said. Truthfully, he didn't want to think about what had been bothering him.

"That's not what I mean," Michael said. Out from the bag came another cola and a second sandwich. "I brought lunch, and you need food."

Ted nodded. "Yes, I think you're right." He walked around to his side of the desk, sat, and opened his sandwich just as Michael was taking a bite of his.

"I haven't seen you like this in a long, long time, my friend." Michael reclined in Ted's guest chair.

"I'm just tired. Stressed."

Michael nodded. "You want to hear about someone else's problems for a change?"

"I'd love to," Ted said.

"A client fired me today."

Ted stopped mid-bite and said, "Well, you probably had it coming."

"Seriously," Michael said. "No joke. He fired me."

"What did you do to him?"

"Made him a million dollars."

"That's a joke, right?" Ted said. Sometimes he couldn't tell.

"No, I'm afraid not. I put together a campaign that is earning him a million dollars over the next year, and in gratitude, he fired me."

"I'm still waiting for the punchline."

"Get ready for a long wait," Michael said, and he resumed chewing.

Ted thought of his inability to help Hashim and his family, a memory still fresh in his mind. He knew Baedes must have threatened him, but he also knew that they could have fought Baedes and won. "Sometimes you can't make people do what's best for them," he remarked.

"True," Michael said. "But that's because their mind is somewhere else, not on what you have to offer.

"But these guys, these clients, they came to me. I didn't go to them. I didn't have to convince them of anything. And I gave them exactly what they wanted. And they were ecstatic about it. Until this morning. Then, suddenly, I'm fired. They don't even tell me personally. I get the news from my boss,

Señor Pointy-hair, and you can imagine how enjoyable that was. Then they won't answer their phones, won't return my calls. If I didn't know any better, I'd swear they dropped off the edge of the earth."

"Hmm." Ted asked himself what reason might have caused a happy business client to desert a consultant who was making him so much money, and how to find out which reason it actually was. He took another bite of his sandwich.

Michael swigged his cola. "You know," he said in a casual tone, "you need to apologize to Jerry."

"I know," was Ted's reply.

— ' c , —

Jane gave the only excuse she could think of.

Her husband had caught up to her in the living room, while she was bending over the the coffee table, tidying it up. He sidled up behind her, patted her on the rear, and said, "Tomorrow's your day off this week. Do you have any special plans?"

Now she replied, simply, "No. Just housework and taking it easy."

That was a lie, of course. She had planned to meet Clydene Jackson again for lunch. Or maybe brunch. They had also kicked around the idea of going shopping. And Jane was looking forward to the get-together. But when asked about it, she knew she shouldn't say anything.

Clyde was involved in some pretty shady activities. And Jane supported her, because despite how nefarious her methods may have looked to an outsider, Clyde was one of the good guys. Jane felt a rapport with Clydene, because Clyde had sincerely tried to help Jane, even when they had hardly known each other. And now Jane's grief had turned to anger, and Clyde was one of the only people in the world who could understand that anger. Perhaps she even felt it, too. And no matter what else, there was one thing Jane simply could not do. It was part of her innate being, a habit bred from the time she was very little. Jane could not betray a confidence. And this was a confidence. So Jane and Clyde's relationship had to remain on the QT.

Now, when Marvin asked whether she had plans for her day off from work, she said what she needed to. She lied.

"Let's spend the day together," he said. "I'll take a vacation day, and we'll do something, just the two of us. Like it was before the boys were born."

Jane was taken aback. She straightened up suddenly. "Uh, I don't know if that would work."

"Are you kidding? Why in the world not?"

"Well—" Jane searched for an explanation. "You can't just call in and say, 'Hi. I'm taking a vacation.' Don't you have to tell them, like, two weeks ahead of time?"

Marvin kissed her forehead. "It's slow at work this week, dear. It's the best time for me to take a day off."

"Okay," Jane said, but she was secretly thinking that she would have to rearrange her schedule, sneak in a call to Clyde's cellphone.

"What?" asked Marvin. "Don't you want to spend the day with me?" He must have detected something in her demeanor.

"Uh, no, I'm good."

"So what's with the funny look?"

"Uh, I was just thinking about something else."

He paused a moment. "You had plans."

"No, no plans," she said.

"If you have plans, just say so."

"I don't have any plans," she insisted. She looked directly into his eyes and intoned, "I'm looking forward to it."

He searched her eyes as if digging for the truth. "Fine, then," he said. "It's a date."

But he didn't go on to the next subject. Instead, he said,

"Who did you have plans with?"

And that's when the fight started.

— ' c , —

Sunlight streamed through the tall windows onto Clyde's kitchen table. Seated under it, she opened up to a blank leaf in her notepad. At the top, she wrote the word, "Guests." Then she listed the obvious: "Mira," followed by "Michael." Besides Ted and herself, that would be six people, assuming Mira and Michael each brought a plus-one. That meant, if they put the leaf in the dining-room table, they could invite two more couples, make it an even ten.

Personally, Clyde doubted Mira would invite anyone, nor that she would want to. And Clyde knew that Mira would hate to be set up. So that left a spare place at the table, or an odd number. Clydene didn't mind having an odd number. It was more important to her that her friends have a good time together at Thanksgiving. And that was what bugged her about Mira. Clyde had a feeling Mira was going to have a miserable, lonely time, no matter what anyone did. And that really sucked.

So four, possibly five, open spots. Clyde knew at least one more person she wanted to invite.

Ted had been watching television in the next room. Now, he entered the kitchen and opened the refrigerator.

"Hey, Ted," Clyde said. "Remember those people we met a few weeks ago out on Linden Street?"

"You mean the Hashim family?" He pulled a bottle of water from the refrigerator.

"No, their neighbors, Marvin and Jane Mooney."

Ted considered for a moment, as he took a gulp of water. "Yes. I remember them."

"I'd like to invite them to Thanksgiving dinner."

Ted looked surprised. "Really? What makes you think

they'd accept?"

"I don't know that they would. Do you have any objection to my asking?"

"No objections. Knock yourself out."

"We still have 2, possibly 3, spaces open. Do you have anyone you want to invite?"

"Not particularly. I might know someone from the office."

"Okay."

"Or you could ask Michael. He always knows someone."

Michael did indeed know someone, several people, in fact, and he was very anxious to offer them these spots. He finally caught up with Jay and his brother Damian at the J&D corporate office, which consisted of a single room, paint peeling from the walls. As Michael entered, a bell jingled cheaply. His shoes clacked on the worn, wooden floor. Jay was sitting on, leaning against a cluttered desk near the opposite wall. Filing cabinets lined another wall. And Damian balanced himself on a ladder above a large-leafed plant in the corner, next to the room's sole window, which looked out onto the street. Damian was fiddling with something on the ceiling, something that looked like a small security camera.

Meanwhile, Clyde reached Jane on her cell phone. But when Clyde asked if it was a good time to talk, Jane hemmed and hawed. Suddenly, Clyde heard a man's voice yelling directly into the phone. Something about "it's over" and "never want you to call my wife again, do you understand?"

"No, I don't understand," Clyde said.

There was a pause, then the man said, "Are you gay?"

"Ugh! God, no!" Clyde said, disgusted and embarrassed. "Who the hell is this!?"

"So, you're *not* having an affair with my wife?"

Back at J&D, Michael asked Jay, "Have you had a break-in."

"No," Jay said. "We're just shoring up security."

"Who'd want to steal anything around here?" Michael asked.

Jay scoffed and said, "You'd be surprised."

On the phone, Clyde felt and sounded angry. "No, I'm not having an affair with anyone. And certainly not another woman. Who is this? Is this Marvin?"

"I don't think I would be surprised," Michael said. He knew something was amiss, even though he didn't know what it was. And he absolutely hated the feeling of knowing something but not being able to figure out what it was. "What's going on?"

"I don't know why you think anything is going on," Jay said.

"Because you cut off an award-winning campaign, and now you're tightening security in this little two-man office. You afraid Damian's going to rip you off?"

Clyde did her best to smile, because she had read somewhere that it made you seem friendlier and more likable, even on the phone. Even so, her words came out in sharp, harsh bursts. "This is Clydene Jackson, Ted Jackson's wife. I believe you met my husband." She waited for a reply.

"Yes, briefly."

Clyde softened her voice. "Each year, we have a Thanksgiving Day party. If you'd like, you're welcome to come." Then she backtracked a beat. "I'd like you to come. That is, I'd like it if you could come. It's completely family-friendly. So bring the boys. We have some close friends over, and... That's about it."

Michael told them a story. He hated to reveal so much of what lay beneath his skin, but it was what he always advised his clients to do. And so it was only fair that when the chips were down, he should come clean as well. He leaned up against the wall and began:

"I fell in love in college, to a beautiful, wonderful, smart girl. The problem was, I wasn't doing so well in my classes. Academics just don't agree with me. The only reason I was there was because my parents wanted me to go. But that's another story.

"So I was in love with a straight-A student, and I was just barely passing. And she didn't know any of this. Because I was afraid to tell her the trouble I was having. I was afraid to tell her how much I hated it. I thought she would look down on me and that would be the end of it. So I kept it a secret."

Jay interrupted. "This has nothing to do with the price of eggs."

Michael put his hand up to calm him and continued. "But things got so bad for me, I finally had to tell her. And do you know what she did?"

"What?" Jay asked blandly.

"She thought it was no big deal, and she introduced me to her Uncle John, a self-made millionaire who felt exactly as I did about school. Actually, he was more crass about it. I believe his exact words were, 'I don't know why anyone would ever want to waste their money on college.'"

Jay and Damian both chuckled.

"Anyhow, it wasn't the end of our relationship, and I became John's protégé. Completely changed my life."

Jay said, "And what's the moral of the story? That I should tell you what you think is going on, because you'll probably surprise me and be understanding and solve all the problems you think I have?"

Michael smiled lightly and nodded. "Something like that."

Jay shook his head. "You're a marketing genius, but you can't solve everyone's problems."

"If I'm such a marketing genius, why did you drop me like plague-infested vermin, without even a word?"

"That had nothing to do with you," Jay said.

Damian finished his task and began to descend the ladder.

Jay and Michael were each leaning, one against the desk, one against the wall, each at the same angle.

"So you were happy with how the campaign was going?" Michael asked.

"Very happy," Jay said.

"So that's why you stopped it."

"No, the reason we stopped it—" Jay apparently couldn't find the words to express what he needed to say next.

Marvin apparently couldn't find the words to express what he wanted to say next. He told Clyde they'd have to get back to her. Then he hung up.

Clyde stood, staring out into her back yard. The wind rustled the leaves of the trees, producing a small shower of red and orange confetti each time it blew.

She sighed and wondered what it all meant.

CHAPTER 3

Michael stared across the table at a sad face, a young, fair face, turned suddenly old, framed by dark, smooth hair, turned suddenly gray, a face which in turn stared out the dining room window. Her face looked darker than it ought to have. Under her eyes swung dark, tired bags of exhaustion. Her cheeks drooped like a dog's jowls. He was sure she had been a decade younger only a few weeks ago. They were all growing old, too old, too fast. Life was so short, and it was impossible to be happy. In the end, as the Preacher wrote, all is vanity. Michael didn't remember much from the Bible, but that he remembered. *Vanity of vanities, saith the Preacher, vanity of vanities; all is vanity.*

"I'm sorry, Mira," he said. Every word felt tired.

Mira peered at him through a confused expression. "What for?" she asked.

He stopped for a moment. He really didn't remember why he felt sorry, but he did. "Whatever's making you so miserable." His voice sounded tender and inviting.

Clyde raised her eyes, which had previously been examining the designs etched into the edge of her plate. Now she scrutinized Michael's face. Even though his attention was still on Mira, Michael saw Clyde out the corner of his eye. And

Ted, from the head of the table, momentarily stopped carving the Thanksgiving ham. He too inspected his friend's face, just for a moment. Then he returned to the ham before him.

Mira looked like she was about to say something, but in the end, she kept quiet.

"That's okay, you don't have to talk about it," Michael said. "I was just trying to make conversation."

Clyde spoke up. "It was still a sweet sentiment."

Ted paused his carving again.

It may have sounded sweet, but it was really just mental exhaustion. He didn't feel like being the star of the show tonight. And he would never be sweet enough to earn the affections of the small, sensitive woman with sleek, black hair and dark eyes.

"See," Ted said. "Now, why was that sweet?"

"Because I'm too tired tonight to be an asshole," Michael said.

The two women giggled, and Michael felt his spirits lift a smidge.

Ted resumed carving. He had sliced up about a third of the ham, and he was close to having enough for everyone to eat.

Michael sighed. He breathed in rich aromas of about ten different recipes, ably prepared. Clyde had done it as usual, a wonderful spread, even if only the four of them had showed up to the party. *Yeah, some party,* Michael thought. *If this is the party, I'd hate to see the funeral.*

"This sucks," Michael said.

"Well, thank you," Clyde said. "I love you too, Michael."

"No, I mean, we're supposed to be partying. We should be laughing it up and having fun."

Then he added, "The food is the only part that doesn't suck."

Mira snorted and grimaced and resumed staring out the window.

Clyde said, "I don't think many of us much feel like laughing right now."

Ted set down the carving knife.

Michael leaned back in his chair. "Yeah, I don't much feel like it myself, to tell the truth."

Silence permeated the room for a moment.

"That sucks, too," Mira said.

— ' c , —

Damian was alone in the office when the big man in the brown leather jacket returned. This time, he was accompanied by a pair of companion ruffians. They three barged in, and without a word the two grabbed Damian by the arms and yanked him to his feet, almost pulled his arms out of their sockets, dragged him to the wall, held him there, while the big man shouted at him. It all happened so fast, Damian only caught bunches of words.

"I told you... still in my way... interfering with business... asked nicely... not anymore..."

Damian protested. He had done what was asked. He had tried. Indeed that was the truth, but it was too late. Their campaign had been too good.

The man wound up and punched him in the gut, and Damian thought his insides were going to come out his mouth. He heaved in pain. The two men yanked him up, and the big man slugged him again, in the same spot. Damian wailed. The man hit him again.

Then the man grabbed Damian by the face with one hand. "Look at me!" the man yelled.

Damian did his best to see between tears. The man spoke through clenched teeth, just inches from Damian's eyes.

"So innocent. You ever had your face messed up?"

He was still holding Damian's face with one hand while the man's other fist, clenched, hovered inches from Damian's nose. It began to pull back, and Damian braced himself.

The experience was not what Damian expected. There was pain, yes. But mostly he felt his head jostle with an odd jarring sensation, followed by dizziness.

Through the haze, a gun cocked.

"Stop right there," Jay said from the entrance, "unless you want to lose the use of that arm."

Damian could see nothing, but he could sense every word and every action. Jay was aiming his black, semi-automatic pistol at the big man. It was Jay's favorite gun. He took it to the range at least one a month.

"Except that I'm not as good a shot as I probably should be," Jay continued. "There's no telling what I might hit."

The man slowly turned around.

"Is that gun registered?" he asked, coolly.

"Yes," Jay said. "What about these goons? Are they registered?"

"Hey," the man said, "there's no need to let this get out of control."

"Too late," Jay said, teeth clenched.

The big man gave a signal to his cohorts, who released Damian. Damian staggered in his brother's direction and collapsed against a wall.

"Now we're going to call the police," Jay said.

"No," Damian rasped, weakly. He could feel his senses beginning to return.

"Yes," Jay said. "This ends here."

With the gun still pointed, Jay reached into his pocket and pulled out his cell phone. He flipped it open and started to key "911" with one hand. As if by magic, the three assailants had disappeared through the inconspicuous door in the far corner of the room, which led to a utility-and-storage area, and to the emergency exit.

— ' C , —

The man in the brown leather jacket drove a black luxury
vehicle into the office park on 3rd Avenue, pulling up to the left
of a more humble, gray sedan with its window rolled down.
The man seated in the passenger's seat beside Brown Leather
rolled down his window.

"Everything is all set," said the man within the gray sedan.

"What about the security camera footage?" asked Brown
Leather's passenger, who wore dark sunglasses and dressed in
an expensive business suit.

"It appears to have been mis-filed," replied the gray sedan.
"What's even worse, no one seems to remember that it ever
existed. So it doesn't look like we'll be able to track down
whoever attacked Mr. Alvarez. At least not until we discover
more evidence."

"Excellent," replied the man in the suit.

"In fact," the gray sedan continued, "it seems Mr. Alvarez
may have been involved in another altercation in his neighborhood. We suspect he may be involved in other criminal activities. We'll know more this afternoon."

"An unexpected development, I'm sure," said the suit.

"Let's just say," sneered the gray sedan, "once the papers
and television news reports on his arrest, it will likely foul up
their operation. I recommend you let us handle this for now.
After all, that is what you're paying us for."

— ' C , —

Jane rolled effortlessly down the road in her dark green
minivan. She had finished work for the day, and she was now
looking forward to meeting her kids after school. Her heart
felt relieved and carefree, until she saw a car pulled over on
the side of the road. The car had been pulled over by a cop,
whose flashing lights still warned of danger. The car's driver

stood, spread-eagle, with his hands flat on the car's roof, while a tall, athletic, uniformed officer stood nearby.

Jane didn't know the specifics of the situation. She didn't know why the man was pulled over. She didn't know why he was ordered out of his car or whether he would be arrested. And none of that mattered. Because ever since October, ever since her close friends and next-door neighbors had been harassed and arrested for something they had not done, she had felt a growing fear. The experience had hit too close to home. What she felt wasn't a rational fear, nor was it a healthy respect, as people sometimes say fear is. What Jane felt was terror, helplessness. Her gut tightened, and she couldn't breathe. She saw herself as the driver who was pulled over, harassed, humiliated, and abused.

— ' c , —

"I'm incompetent," Ted said, in an uncharacteristic moment of inner confession.

Michael squinted his eyes at him from across the table of the hole-in-the-wall café. "You're one of the best litigators I know," he said.

"Thank you for the complement, but I already know I'm a competent litigator." Ted sipped his coffee.

Michael did get it. Ted was a litigator, and arguer, not a people person. He loved being right, loved arguing arguments, loved winning them. But a people person needs to lose arguments sometimes. Ted was no good at that. Michael didn't care. It took all kinds, was Michael's philosophy, and he got along with Ted just fine.

"Don't worry about it," Michael said. "Everyone's incompetent at something. That's what I'm here for."

"To be incompetent at something?"

"Right." Michael went along with the joke, but after a second, he thought maybe Ted didn't get the joke. "No, what

I'm here for is to be incompetent at different things than you, because it takes all kinds of people to make the world complete. I'm yin to your yang."

Ted took a breath. "Actually, you're yang to my yin. And I would like to be the yang once in a while."

Michael needed to get at the bottom of this if he was going to help his friend. Ted was normally confident and head-strong, even when he was clueless, and Michael had no idea what triggered Ted's newfound self-doubt.

"Where is this coming from?" Michael asked.

Ted took another sip of coffee and savored it.

Michael backpedaled, as he leaned back in his chair, fearing that he may have crossed a line, probed too deeply, asked too much. "You don't have to talk about it if you don't want to. It just seemed like you wanted to."

Ted swallowed and nodded. "I don't know how to analyze this problem."

"What problem is that?" Michael realized he was letting his own coffee get cold. He picked it up and sipped. It was no longer piping hot, but not lukewarm yet, either.

"Every day," Ted said, "I gain a new appreciation of what you do for a living."

Michael sipped his coffee again, and listened.

"Your expertise is in getting inside the heads of the multi-tudinous idiots in the world and pushing them in the right direction."

Michael chuckled. "I'm with you so far."

Ted continued, "I fear it's a skill I will never master."

Michael closed his eyes for a moment and sighed. Then he looked straight into Ted's eyes and said, "How many jury trials have you done?"

Ted looked surprised. "I don't know."

"A bunch?"

Ted nodded. "Yes, a fair number."

"And how many did you win?"

"But that's different."

Michael ignored Ted's objection and continued. "And how many judges have you appeared before?"

"Judges aren't people. They care about facts."

Michael chuckled again. "You think so?"

Ted paused a moment. Then he said, "No, I don't. Judges don't care about facts any more than anyone else."

"That courtroom is your domain," Michael said. "You just need to bring it out here into the real world— No, scratch that. You need to get over this mental block you have that's getting you down. It's all in your head."

From the instant the words left Michael's lips, he knew how stupid and condescending they sounded. Still, they were what he really believed. And he had learned through countless hours of conversation that Ted responded best when he shot straight. So he said what he thought.

"There are two problems with that," Ted said. "Firstly, you can't argue with results. You constantly tell me that. And my performance in my personal life is measurably less than my performance in the courtroom.

"Secondly, what I do in court is different than what you do. I can't make a judge or jury do I what I want them to? The law gives them limited options, and all I can do is to find out what their values are and to tailor my presentation to take advantage of those values. I only give them an excuse to act on their own prejudices. But I can't implant an idea in their heads, like you do. Every time I try, I fail."

"So stop trying," Michael said.

"Very funny, my friend."

"I'm serious," Michael continued. "Do you actually think I somehow manipulate people's minds?"

"Yes, I do," Ted said.

Before Michael could object, Ted continued, "And if I had

that skill, I wouldn't be in such a slump right now."

Michael peered quizzically at his friend. "What happened?"

"Halloween happened."

Confusion overtook Michael. "That was over a month ago."

Ted nodded. "Yes, it was."

"Where have I been?"

Ted stared back at him. "You've been right there."

Ted continued. "Remember the man who was arrested for holding up a liquor store?"

"And they dropped the charges because they arrested the wrong guy," Michael said.

"Yes, him."

"That was weird," Michael interjected.

"I've seen stranger," Ted said. "I paid his bail, never got a dime of that money back, and when I tried to talk to him, he wouldn't even say hello."

"Sounds like an ungrateful bastard," Michael said.

"I couldn't get through to him."

"Yeah, so?" Michael's coffee had cooled substantially now, and he took a large gulp. "Clyde said he was frightened. And maybe he was, coming from Pakistan. I don't know what he expects from the legal system." Michael glanced at Ted's coffee. "Your coffee is cold."

"Yes, I know," Ted said. "That was not the first time I couldn't get through to someone who needed me. And he was short-changed because of it."

"I thought you said the charges were dropped."

"They were," Ted said. "But he still got the short end of the stick."

"That's not your fault. Besides, everything worked out alright in the end."

"He picked up and moved back to Pakistan," Ted said.

"Who's complaining about it, besides you?"

"You see?" Ted said. "This is why I don't like to talk about these things. No one gets it. I'm not—"

Ted cut short what he clearly wanted to say.

"You're not what?" Michael said.

"Nothing," Ted said, shaking his head.

"Uh. Yes. Something!" Michael said this in a sing-song voice, as though he were taunting his friend. And in a way, maybe he was. He was tired of getting the official run-around, and now he didn't care what the fallout would be. If Ted was going to drag him out for coffee and talk, he was going to talk. Michael was sick of beating around the bush.

Ted did talk. He struggled with each word, measuring it carefully before uttering it, as though each one was laced with nitroglycerin, and he needed to carefully package each word individually before he could say it.

"I'm... not... sure... I... get... it... myself."

Michael looked him straight in the eye again. "You wanted to help him for your own benefit, not for his. You don't actually know that he got short-changed, because you don't really know what he's thinking and feeling. You just want to feel connected, and you don't."

Ted just stared back, uncharacteristic. Michael thought he might be getting through.

"Theodore, my friend, you can't depend on other people for your self-esteem, because you can't control their thoughts. How you feel about yourself comes from within, regardless of what anyone else thinks. And the sooner you admit that, the sooner you'll be able to change how you feel about yourself."

Michael examined Ted's face, but he couldn't tell what he was thinking. "Does any of this make any sense?" he asked.

Ted shook his head. "No, I don't think it does."

Michael couldn't help but chuckle.

— ' c , —

Damian was sitting at home reading a book when they

knocked on his door. The radio was playing a jazzy rendition of *God Rest Ye Merry Gentlemen*. The two children were playing downstairs in the basement. No one else was home, because his wife was still at work.

As he answered the door, he felt self-conscious about the bruise on his face. He apparently had no broken bones, but his head and body still ached. Damian didn't want anyone to see him this way, even though he knew in his head that he had nothing to be ashamed of.

Damian thought it strange that the police could not find the men who had beat him up, even though they all but identified themselves, on camera. Damian wondered if maybe he would continue to feel ashamed until the situation was resolved. He did know he would continue to feel uneasy until it was.

He swung the front door open and shivered at the cold, dry breeze that wafted over his body. Greeting him just outside were two uniformed police officers. He recognized one from the day there had been an after-school fight outside his apartment. She was the officer whom he had talked to.

"Hello," he said, and he smiled at her.

"Mr. Alvarez?" said the man standing next to her. He was taller than she, and tougher looking.

"Yes," Damian acknowledged.

"We're talking with families in this neighborhood about the fights around here lately."

He eyed Damian's face.

Damian said, "I only saw the one. That was the day we talked to you," and he motioned toward the lady cop. "That's all I know."

"Hey, what's that?" the man pointed into Damian's apartment.

As Damian turned to look, the man shoved past. He strode in two steps to an end table and picked up something. He held up a baggie in which hung two marijuana cigarettes.

"Those aren't mine," Damian said. They really weren't. In fact, he was sure they weren't even there on that table a moment ago, and he didn't understand how they had been found there.

"Yeah, sure. I haven't heard that one before," the cop said sardonically. He ordered Damian to the floor, face-down, handcuffed him, and began to read him his rights.

"What about my children?" Damian said. "I can't leave my children at home alone."

"We'll have them taken to Social Services."

Damian shook his head. "No. Please. I can call my brother. He can be here in a few minutes."

The lady cop spoke. "I can stay with them until he arrives."

Damian gazed longingly at her.

The man cop began to protest. "Standard procedure is—"

She interrupted. "We don't need to get Social Services involved."

"But that was—" he started to object. "That is the rule."

"Social Services is too... complicated," she said, as though it were an explanation or a defense.

He shook his head and chuckled with incredulity. "You don't know what you're getting yourself into, Pam. The fit's gonna hit the shan."

"Don't worry," she intoned sternly. "I've got it covered."

— ' c , —

Damian never got a chance to make his phone call from jail. Officer Pamela Burns called his brother Jay, who immediately called Michael, because Michael had once told him about a good criminal lawyer he knew, who immediately called Ted.

Michael's version of the story was more than Jay had told him. It included a scene in which Baedes himself personally planted the false evidence, in order to misdirect investigation and further victimize Jay and Damian.

Ted refused to just accept Michael's version of events, brushing it off as silly. But after Ted spoke to Jay and Damian, he did agree that it was time for another special meeting of the Committee.

Michael bit into his coffee cake and sipped his coffee. He reclined on the big, comfy couch in Ted and Clydene's reception room. Usually, they met in the living room—or "den," as Clyde sometimes called it. But for special guests, they pulled out the reception room. Tucked into a corner of the house, just off the main foyer, the Jacksons' reception room welcomed guests with light hues and plush chairs and sofas.

Michael was surprised at how good the coffee was today.

"Wow, that's good!" he said to Clyde, the only other person in the room.

"Incredible what you can accomplish by cleaning the pot," Clyde replied.

"You should do that more often." Then he added, "I always wondered how you could be such a wonderful cook and have your coffee turn out so... uh..."

"Pukey?" Clyde said.

"Yeah, pukey," Michael agreed with a large grin.

Mira, Ted, Jay, and Damian entered.

"Okay, let's call the meeting to order," Mira said. She was clearly in executive mode, as Michael called it, not the soft, timid creature she was most of the time. "As you know, Jay and Damian have been having some trouble with Baedes and his department. I'm going to ask them to tell us their story, all together here, so we can hear it from them. But first, we should ratify spending on their bail and legal fees."

Ted interrupted her. "Point of order," he said. "I've already worked out payment for legal expenses."

Mira looked confused and a little disturbed. "What do you mean?"

"We've worked it all out. We don't need the Committee's money."

"Okay," she said, slowly, as though she weren't sure how to pronounce the word. "Then I'll hand the floor over to Jay and Damian."

Jay thanked Mira, and he told the group his story and the story of his brother.

When he got to the part where WBH's henchmen beat up Damian, Clyde interjected bitterly, "I'm not an expert, but I'm pretty sure that falls within the realm of unfair competition."

That elicited a chuckle from those gathered, even Damian himself, who was sitting quietly, listening, as Jay spoke.

Most of the crew had already heard pieces of the story. But they had never had the opportunity to hear the whole thing told by the men to whom is was happening, to see Damian's bruised face in quiet witness, and to ask questions.

The first question came, interestingly enough, from Clyde. "So, they're just misdemeanor drug-possession charges. Probably not even any jail time. Why don't you just plead out?"

Damian suddenly spoke. "Because I need to fight," he said. When no one seemed to understand, he continued. "I am not a criminal," he said. "What I do, I do for my family, and for my community. And I do not bring drugs into my house, and I don't allow anyone else to." He paused and shook his head. "And these charges hurt you. Business associates stop working with you. The government denies you benefits. Even this little thing would ruin me. It would ruin my family, and it would ruin my business. So I have to fight it."

Clyde nodded. "I understand," she said.

Mira asked, "Okay. I know you've been threatened and attacked by mob thugs. What does that have to do with your arrest?"

Clyde answered for the two brothers. "Baedes is dragging his feet on finding the thugs, because he hates bullies and favors the underdog. And he thinks Jay and Damian are the bullies. He says they have a monopoly, and that they're conducting unfair business. And that's why he had Damian set up, because he wants to damage their reputation."

Mira stared and thought. Jay looked confused. Damian sat quietly. Ted looked embarrassed.

Michael said, "I think you're giving Baedes too much credit." But secretly, what she said felt right to him.

Ted took an opposite view. "You don't know what you're talking about, Clyde. You're jumping to conclusions just because you feel sorry for these men."

Clyde said, "I've never felt sorry for anyone. I'm saying that because it's the truth."

"Fine, then. How do you know it's the truth?" Ted asked.

The next thing Clyde did both disappointed and amazed Michael. Instead of laying out reasons for her belief, she clammed up. She said nothing. She looked like she was about to say something, wanted to say something, and maybe even had something to say. But she didn't say it. Michael stared at Clyde intently. And for an instant, he thought he saw a secret hiding behind her eyes. He glanced at Mira, to see if she noticed the same thing—Michael admired Mira's ability to see into peoples' souls. But Mira was involved in her own thoughts, whatever they might be.

"See," Ted said. "I didn't think there was anything there. Besides, Baedes wouldn't look the other way and let the mob take over the town. He'd tell them to stay in line, contact the

Attorney General, and file an antitrust suit."

Now, that really was giving Baedes too much credit. Michael didn't think Baedes even knew the word *antitrust*.

"A lawsuit would take forever, and by the time the smoke cleared, WBH would have lost their business."

Ted looked at her as though she had two heads. "That's not true. The court can issue a preliminary injunction to prevent irreparable harm, like the business going under. And I'm sure they have enough funding to sustain a legal challenge. There's no reason they would resort to bribery and violence just to promote competition."

Clyde was livid. "So what are you saying? Damian's making it up? He didn't really get beat up? Baedes didn't back-shelf his case? What? Our city's finest are as on the ball as ever with this one? Well," Clyde backtracked, "I guess they are, but that's beside the point—"

"I don't see what we can do to help," Mira interrupted, with an edge in her voice.

Ted explained. "The fact that no arrests have been made, even with the abundance of evidence available, is interesting, and perhaps further investigation will find something there we can use. But the significance of this case is as follows..."

"Ted, you need to get to the point," Clydene said.

Ted continued. "Most people who are brought up on drug charges—especially drug possession charges—never get the chance to challenge those charges, even if they're innocent, because the drug laws themselves are stacked against the accused. That's why it's so easy for the police and district attorney to distort the evidence to get a conviction, or even to manufacture evidence.

"That's why many defense lawyers won't touch these cases, or they just recommend a plea bargain. Even if the accused is demonstrably innocent, most of them can't afford the legal fees to bring these cases to trial. Therefore, most such cases never see a jury. Most people arrested on drug charges simply admit to being guilty, even if the evidence itself is circumstantial or shoddy.

"Now, we have someone who not only maintains his innocence, but is willing and able to defend it. Furthermore, my preliminary investigations indicate— This is off the record, by the way."

"Of course," Mira said.

"—indicate that the evidence against Damian was handled shoddily. Because of the way the physical evidence was handled, there may not be any physical evidence to directly implicate my client. All that's left is the testimony of two police officers."

There was a moment's silence while those gathered mulled over Ted's words.

"And I think I can sell the possibility," Ted concluded, "that the evidence was planted."

Michael asked Mira, "Does that sound interesting yet?"

— ' c , —

In some places in the world, people don't believe in snow. They believe snow doesn't exist, that it is merely stuff of fairy tales and legends. Even in some parts of the United States, the people don't believe in snow. Jane remembered one friend from her youth, couldn't remember her name. What Jane did remember was that this friend grew up in southern California, where palm trees grow and the weather is moderate. But when she moved away from home to go to college in New England, the weather amazed her. The people of New England did not live with earthquakes and tsunamis. They lived with snow—and to a lesser extent hurricanes.

Jane remembered the conversation, or part of it anyway.

"I didn't even believe in snow until I moved here," her friend said.

Jane giggled.

"No, I'm serious," the friend continued. "We never had snow in Los Angeles, and I thought it didn't actually exist. I thought it was something you only hear about in stories and fairy tales."

Jane remembered being amazed at how much a person's past affects her, how much preconceptions can shape how she views the world. The first time this friend drove in snow, she was probably terrified. Jane, however, grew up with it.

She barreled along comfortably in her SUV, despite the fact that large white flakes were falling faster than she had expected. Yes, the weather man had warned her. But she needed to get home, and she didn't want to wait for terrified drivers like her old, half-forgotten friend. Fortunately, the road was wide enough to make travel safe, even if she started to slide. It was wide enough for two lanes, though it was only marked for one. Cars frequently formed two lanes along this road during rush hour.

Jane approached a blue compact, putting along as though it were struggling to push through. There was less than an inch of fluff on the ground, and the surface provided plenty of traction, enough to go faster than 10 miles an hour.

"*¡Hijole!*" Jane said. "I could walk faster than this!"

She glanced in her rear-view mirror, then carefully pulled off to the right and began passing the little, blue car.

Suddenly, she saw the flashing red and blue lights in her rear-view mirror. For most people, it probably would not be a big deal. But recent events had set Jane on edge, terrified her even. And now a cop car was following her, coming from out of nowhere, into the here, pulling her over.

Her heart felt as if it had stopped.

— ' c , —

Michael followed Ted down the old, courthouse hallway. The

plaster walls, cracked in places, shone a simple off-white. The clean, black and white floor tiles alternated in a chess-board pattern. And a musty scent pervaded the air, the smell of old building.

"The trial is in Courtroom 2," Ted said, "right up here to the right. Just grab a seat in the gallery. I need to meet with my client."

"Knock 'em dead," Michael said.

Before entering the courtroom, however, he found a men's room. He was about to open the door when he heard a voice he knew from inside, a voice he could never forget, the voice of a large, crew-cut, beady-eyed bully.

"You're all set for you testimony?" Baedes said.

"No problem," said another voice.

"And if he accuses you of planting the evidence?"

"I'll appear mildly flustered, but I'll stand my ground, and our guy will handle it on cross."

"Right," the chief confirmed.

"Do you think he knows?" the other voice asked.

"About the evidence?"

"Yeah."

"No. I think they're expecting to lose. There's a reason these cases never go to trial, in a sane world," said the chief.

"It almost makes you wonder what's the point."

Michael heard them walking, and he quickly ducked to the side and sat on a nearby bench. Baedes exited the room, a younger officer next to him, turning away from Michael, walking down the hallway. They apparently did not even see him. But before they were out of earshot, Michael heard the chief say:

"The top dog can always use a little humiliation."

Michael's first thought was, *That stupid, fucking jerk. I'd love to take that top dog down a notch.* But he said nothing, did nothing to intervene or to challenge them. That would only have gotten him in trouble. No one would believe his story, anyhow, even if he were to call upon all his powers of persuasion to tell it. No one would believe the story, because the man in uniform and his boss would claim Michael made it up.

Michael entered the courtroom as the jury was being empaneled. What he noticed next fascinated him and horrified him at the same time. Already seated in the courtroom was Beady-eyes himself, and seated next to him, his henchman in uniform.

Michael thought, *Clyde was right. Beady-eyes is involved. Lucky guess?*

Clyde had indeed been right, not just about a cop planting evidence for a drug bust— That was a big enough cliché by itself; it required no leap of logic or insight, or even truth or evidence. But *why* would he plant evidence? What was his motive? Did Clyde nail it on the head? As an ad man, Michael knew all about human nature, because it was part of his job, and he had learned to be an observer of human nature. For example, Mira had an almost astounding ability sometimes to sense what others were thinking, an ability that both endeared her to him and scared him. But Mira had not come up with Clyde's crazy theory. Clyde had come up with this theory on her own, and everyone had thought it was outlandish, everyone including Mira.

Michael's thoughts were cut short by the action in the courtroom.

The prosecutor gave his opening statement. Then Ted gave his, in which he claimed he would demonstrate that "the evidence against Mr. Alvarez was so shoddily handled that no one can know for certain if he's guilty or innocent. That's reasonable doubt." Ted also said he would reveal an astounding fact: that the arresting officer himself had means, motive, and opportunity to plant the evidence. The prosecutor asked Dietrich—that was the officer's name—to describe what had happened that day. He admitted the baggie of marijuana cigarettes into evidence. It was everything one would expect from watching courtroom television dramas.

But Ted's cross-examination surprised everyone. Rather than scrutinizing the officer's account of the events, Ted asked about fingerprints. "Are you aware of any forensic tests performed on the baggie or its contents?"

"Yes," replied Dietrich. "The crime lab fingerprinted the baggie and its contents."

"Objection," said the prosecutor, matter-of-factly. "Hearsay."

"I have here the forensics report, and I am prepared to call to the stand the technician who wrote this report." He picked up several papers from his table and handed them to the prosecutor.

The prosecutor looked over the papers and said, "Objection withdrawn, and the state stipulates as to the content of this report."

Ted handed the report to Dietrich.

"Please look on the second page," Ted said with an air of smugness, "at the top of the page, and tell me if there were any fingerprints found on the baggie or its contents."

He flipped to the second page and said, "Yes there were."

"Whose?" Ted asked.

Dietrich hesitated.

"Whose fingerprints?" Ted repeated.

"Mine," Dietrich said. "But that makes sense. I was the one who found it."

"Were your fingerprints found only on the outside of the bag?"

"No," Dietrich intoned.

"Were they found on the cigarettes as well?"

"I guess I touched them," Dietrich said.

"Yes, I guess you did," Ted said. "Were any other fingerprints found anywhere on the inside or outside of the bag, or on its contents?"

"No," Dietrich replied.

"So were Mr. Alverez's fingerprints anywhere on the evidence?"

"That doesn't mean anything. He could have wiped them off."

"He also could have left them somewhere less conspicuous. Didn't you stop to think that if he had had the foresight to remove his fingerprints from the evidence, he would have had the foresight to put the evidence somewhere where a passing police officer couldn't see it?"

"Objection," the prosecutor replied.

"I withdraw the question," Ted said. He looked a little taller than normal.

"One more thing," Ted said. He picked up the sealed baggie and examined it. "Hey, one of the cigarettes is missing!" he said.

He showed the baggie to the jury and to the judge. The judge started to say something, when Ted exclaimed with great flair, "Oh, here it is!" And he reached behind Dietrich's ear and pulled out a thin, white object. Then without opening the baggie, he pushed the object into the plastic, and magically, the cigarette returned to the inside of the bag. He showed it to everyone, as a giggle rustled throughout the courtroom.

"Very entertaining, Mr. Jackson," said the judge. "I trust you have a point to make."

"Yes, your honor." Ted turned to Dietrich. "Do you think that's a clever trick?"

"Well..." Dietrich hesitated. His eyes darted back and forth for a moment.

"Here's a better question. Do you know how I did that particular trick?"

"I can imagine how you might have done it."

"Because you're an amateur magician yourself."

"Yes," Dietrich replied.

"You sometimes perform at kid's birthday parties."

"Uh..."

"... because it's fun and a nice treat for the kids," Ted said.

"Yes."

"Indeed," Ted said. "You could even perform a trick with an object like, oh, say, this," and he held up the baggie of marijuana cigarettes. "You could make it look like you picked it up, even if you had planted it there yourself."

"Objection," said the prosecutor.

"Overruled," said the judge.

"Yes, I guess so," said Dietrich. "if I really *wanted* to." He stressed the word "wanted."

Ted continued. "And this type of sleight of hand is in fact very basic. Even an amateur like yourself could perform it convincingly."

"With practice, I could. But I *didn't*."

"Thank you, Mr. Dietrich." Ted strutted back to his seat.

Ted noticed the tall, burly police chief, dressed in a business suit and seated in the gallery. Far from intimidating the lawyer, his presence made Ted even more determined to nail him and his department to the wall. Ted knew that Baedes was interested in the case. Baedes was even involved, Ted knew, because he was on the prosecution's witness list. Ted wanted to nail him to the wall, because Ted hated to lose. Even more than that, beyond even Baedes's extreme approach to law enforcement—and the fact that he was biologically incapable of admitting that he'd ever been wrong—Baedes was after Ted and Mira, personally, and Ted knew that he had taken some of his fear and frustration out on Ted's clients. Questions, threats, lies, all without counsel present. Damian hadn't told him anything, because Damian hadn't known anything, because there wasn't anything to know. That seemed just to make Baedes more upset, more angry.

Ted hated to lose, but he hated even more to be bullied.

As Damian put it, "You didn't know which was worse: the man in the blue uniform, or the man in the brown jacket."

"That's easy," Ted said. "The blue uniform didn't actually hit you, did he."

"Yeah, but I thought he was going to."

As for Damian Alvarez, it normally made sense that he would fight tooth and nail over such a minor charge. True, if he pled guilty, nothing would likely happen to him, except for a fine that he was more than able to pay. But there were a host of so-called collateral punishments he could be subjected to. Even a trivial offense like possession, if he were convicted, might mean he couldn't adopt a child, might cost him business clients, could interfere with his getting a job, if he needed to.

It would also mean he couldn't own a firearm. And ever since the man in the brown jacket threatened Damian, Jay insisted he keep a gun in the office, just in case. Because these competitors, they were militant, they were dangerous, and— mob ties or no—they were crazy. And with all the evidence of that assault, the cops still had not yet identified the man in the brown leather jacket. Damian had gotten a call from the investigator on the case, a Harris Kemp, who had asked him a bunch of questions. And that was the last Damian had heard. One more reason for Ted to nail Baedes to the wall.

Whatever other reasons for following his defense through to the end, Damian was determined to see it through, and he had the money and means to fight. And the case could be great publicity for the Committee. Michael would no doubt see to that. Ted wasn't sure that his client was strictly innocent. But he thought there was a chance he could get Damian off. So Ted took his client's lead. He argued tooth and nail.

And he was winning.

Truthfully, the prosecution had flubbed their case. The prosecutor was a newbie. They probably threw him on this case as an easy win, something to break his teeth in on. As a result, he didn't do his homework. The evidence was suspect. And he made numerous mistakes in his execution.

The other officer at the scene, a Pamela Burns—whom Ted had previously had dealings with—testified for the prosecution. She confirmed Dietrich's story. And the prosecutor added some stuff in about how she and Dietrich had always been honest, disciplined, and only in search of the truth. But Ted got her to admit that she had not noticed the evidence at first. It was only after the other officer had pointed it out to her that she noticed it.

Then he asked her, "You have a degree in Criminal Justice."

"Objection," said the prosecutor.

Ted stared quizzically at him. The judge must have been, too, because he added, "Irrelevant."

Ted responded, "Judge, I have the right to question this witness."

"Agreed," said the judge. "Overruled." And then he looked at the prosecuting attorney and said, "Please try to be more selective with your objections."

Ted repeated himself, "You have a degree in Criminal Justice."

"Yes," she replied.

"In fact, you have a master's degree."

"Yes."

"And you attained this degree while working for the Boston police department."

"Yes, I attended Boston University while employed at the Boston police department, under the PCIPP."

"The PCIPP is an incentive program," Ted said.

"Right, the way it works is—"

"That's okay, we don't need to know that. But we would like to know, did you like working in Boston?"

"Yes," she said.

"Why did you move to Abe's Turn?"

"It's a smaller department, a chance for career advancement."

"But Boston still has a good police force."

"Yes, absolutely!" she said.

The prosecutor apparently couldn't hold his tongue any

longer. "Your honor, what does this have to do with anything?"

"I'll allow the question," the judge said, "but move it along."

Ted continued. "You worked there for how many years?"

"Three," Pam said.

"While you were working in Boston, did you ever encounter anyone using marijuana?"

"Yes."

"In fact, you encountered many who had small amounts of marijuana in their possession."

"Yes," she confirmed again.

"Out of the many people you encountered with this amount of the drug," and Ted held up the baggie, "how many did you arrest?"

Pam hesitated, and she looked at the chief, who had glued his gaze on her from the gallery. "I don't recall," she said.

"Well, I dug through the arrest records in Boston in order to find out the answer. Care to guess what number I came up with?"

"No," she said, to chuckles from the jury and gallery.

"Would you believe three?"

"Yes," she said.

"Only a few arrests. Did you just ignore most of the offenders?"

"No," she protested. "Most of the time, we found more than that, and we did arrest them. But sometimes with trivial cases, we just confiscated the contraband and let them off with a warning, because it wasn't worth all the trouble of prosecuting them all. If we had to arrest every pot smoker in the city, we wouldn't be able to fight more serious crimes."

"You wouldn't be able to fight more serious crimes." Ted grinned.

"Uh—"

"So why did you and Officer Dietrich take the time and effort to file an arrest in this case?"

"Objection," said the prosecutor. "He's putting the law on trial."

"Not with that question, I'm not," Ted interjected. "I have a right to impeach this witness."

The judge agreed. "He has the right to question the integrity of the prosecutorial witnesses. Objection overruled."

Pam said nothing. She stared at Baedes again, who was resting his face in his hands.

"Who told you to arrest Damian Alvarez?" Ted glared at her and added, "Remember that you're under oath."

Pam still said nothing.

The judge said, "Answer the question."

"We were ordered to," Pam squeaked.

A murmur rippled through the room. Ted strutted back to his seat, as if that was the answer he had expected, and he did not try to push any further. In reality, he had taken a chance on that last question, because he didn't really know the answer. And the first rule of cross-examination is never to ask a question unless you can already prove what the correct answer is. She could have lied outright, and there wouldn't have been anything Ted could have done to contradict her. She could have said that they they had simply *chosen* to arrest Damian Alvarez, on a whim. But Ted had led up to his finale with strong questions. And when the time came, it looked like he knew more than he actually did. He got more than he had bargained for.

The prosecutor called Baedes to the stand. He established the chief as a law enforcement expert and basically allowed him to make a speech, while asking him questions.

Baedes said, "People don't realize that marijuana is the number one drug that sends teenagers to emergency rooms today. That shocks people. They think pot is some sort of a safe drug, but it isn't. It's the number two cause of car crashes. It's a much worse drug than people know.

"Maybe they *were* ordered to arrest Damian Alvarez. So what? The standing order in Abe's Turn is to arrest *all* drug criminals, *all* the time.

"That's just tough love, which is not a bad way to go. It's done a lot to make us safer. Since the War on Drugs, we've significantly reduced drug use in the United States. Teenage drug use is way down. And crime is way down. We have a record low crime rate in Abe's Turn, and one of the reasons we do is that we've taken a lot of the slime off the streets and put them into prison. I'm glad that our cops are tough on drugs.

"The reason crime has gone down is very simple, more people are in jail for longer periods of time. If we didn't prosecute these crimes, everybody would start using it, because there wouldn't be any penalty to it. They'd start thinking, I'll go drive my car high on this or that. Imagine your brain surgeon toking up before your operation. Oh, that would be good for you, wouldn't it? These drugs are not good for you. Fortunately, it's against the law.

"By the way," he added, "it's against the law in Boston, too."

Meanwhile, Damian sat looking innocent, his wife and kids staring angrily behind him. On cross-examination, Ted pointed out that studies show drug use is up, not down. He challenged the chief's crazy scenarios, like a brain surgeon toking up before an operation. (Is that why brain surgeons operate drunk? Because alcohol is legal?) Ted also cited statistics that show that Baedes's toking brain surgeon probably would not have gotten caught anyhow, at least not under the drug laws, no matter what the law said and no matter what the police did.

The prosecution had done most of the hard work for Ted. They had all but given the jury a reason to acquit, by letting

Ted impeach every single one of their witnesses. Ted additionally had witnesses who would testify that Dietrich was
crooked. All that was left was to make Damian likable enough
to make the jury *want* to acquit. And that, Ted was sure, Damian's wife and brother would accomplish.

The prosecution rested its case. Court broke for lunch. As
Ted as Michael walked down the hallway, they encountered
Baedes and Dietrich chatting. Baedes suddenly stopped
talking and glared at Ted.

"I guess you're pretty upset about my winning this case,
huh, Sam?" Ted said.

Baedes's face betrayed his agitation, even to Ted. "You
shouldn't have gotten involved."

This perplexed Ted, and he formed his face into a mock
pout. "Not get involved? With my own client?"

"He wasn't your client before we arrested him."

"Bull. You don't know that."

"I do know that your client would have been better off
without you."

"That almost sounds like a threat." Ted smiled, taunting the
chief. But inside, he was concerned.

"Just a statement of fact," Baedes replied. "You appreciate
facts, don't you? Like the fact that you just attacked two fine
officers in there. And all to get a druggie off the hook."

"Yeah, well, you have no proof, and fortunately, in this
country, we have a little thing called *reasonable doubt*. It
protects the rights of the innocent."

"You mean, the *guilty*," Baedes growled.

"Fortunately, the jury sees things differently."

"You think so."

"Yes," Ted replied. "I think so. Otherwise..." Ted lowered
his voice and grinned. "Otherwise, you wouldn't be so upset."

Baedes's face turned red, and he underscored his words
with stabs of his finger. "I hope you realize who you're

helping. That's a druggie and a bully. He's crossed the wrong people. And that puts you in as much danger as him."

Ted chuckled and his eyebrows moved as he talked. "I think I'll manage," he said.

In reality, Ted thought that last comment felt like a threat, and it worried him.

He suddenly noticed that Michael had been standing quietly and listening, wearing a scowl.

Baedes breathed deeply. "I'm just saying."

— ' c , —

Clyde was planning Christmas dinner when she heard a knock at the front door. She opened it, revealing Michael's big, round, blue-flashlight eyes staring at her with a strange look on them, a look she couldn't identify.

"Hey, you," she said sweetly. Then she considered for a moment. "What's wrong?" she said.

"Can I come in?"

"Sure," Clyde said, and she showed him into the living room. "Is Ted alright?"

"Oh, yes," Michael said comfortingly. "They're waiting for the jury. He doesn't expect to be too late, because he's sure the jurors have weekend plans." He paused for Clyde to giggle. "He suggested the three of us eat out tonight."

"Sure, I guess so," she said. "Yeah, I think going out would be fun. Do you know if Mira has any plans?"

Clyde cringed as soon as the words came out of her mouth. She shouldn't be asking Michael whether Mira has plans, because he wouldn't know. And she didn't even know how he might feel about the four of them going out together socially. They hadn't gone out as a group in a long time. What's more, Clyde knew how Michael felt about Mira, and she knew that Mira did not return his feelings. Michael acted as though it didn't matter to him, and they had been able to keep their relationship professional. But to Clyde, the two had both seemed to be distant, for a long time now, as if they were just shells of their former selves. Clyde missed Michael's witty repartee, of which she saw much less. Somehow, he seemed too serious and businesslike to be Michael. And Clyde missed connecting with Mira, which was as much Clyde's fault as it was Mira's. Clyde had already decided not to share her secret, not even with her closest friend. And the only person who knew her secret, Jane, seemed to be avoiding her calls. That worried Clyde in itself. But the thing that bothered her most was that she had no one to talk to about what she knew, and that there was very little she could do to help. She couldn't even tell her beloved, her husband. All she could do was to gently suggest to him that he could consider using her so-called crazy theory to nourish that seed of reasonable doubt in the minds of Damian Alvarez's jurors.

Michael didn't seem to notice Clyde's mention of Mira. "I wouldn't know," he simply said. He seemed to be thinking about something else.

"Oh," Clyde said, relieved. Then she cautiously proffered, "Do you mind if I give her a call?"

"Sure, go right ahead." Then he came back to life. "Hey, we haven't gone out for a long time. The last time we got together socially was, what? Thanksgiving?"

"That was social?" Clyde joked. "That was painful," she said.

"The food was good!" Michael said.

"Oh would I that the food could have saved the day."

Michael sighed and looked at her tenderly. "Hey, don't feel bad. It wasn't your fault. I shouldn't have been so wrapped up in myself. I'm sorry."

Clyde was genuinely surprised. "Wha— It wasn't your fault. We were all upset about something." Then she added, "The problem is that we weren't talking about what we were upset about." She hardly believed those words had come out of her mouth, and she didn't really know why she had said them.

"Well, I think we talk just fine. But..."

Michael's words trailed off mid-sentence. He seemed to be solving a deep problem in his mind. This was something Michael almost never did. Michael was always talking, always listening, always observing, always doing. He seemed to just know what he wanted to do, and he rarely planned anything, much less thought about it.

"What is it?" Clyde asked.

Michael thought for a moment longer, as if he were formulating his next words, very much unlike Michael.

"How did you know?" he said.

"How did I know... what?"

"How did you know that Baedes has a thing against Jay and Damian, because he thinks they're the top dogs? And how did you know that he wants to take them down a notch? And how did you know that he was the one who orchestrated the trumped-up drug bust, with the sole purpose of damaging Damian's reputation and his business?"

Clyde immediately went into fight-or-flight mode. She didn't even think about it. *Danger,* her mind thought. *Must lie.*

"I didn't know," she said, "not for sure. That was just a crazy theory. Ted's just playing lawyer games, that's all."

"You're lying," Michael said. "That was too specific to be just a lucky guess. And this has nothing to do with Ted."

"What's your damage, Michael?" Clyde looked at him as though she thought he was crazy.

"Firstly, I can tell you're lying, because I can see it in your eyes."

"What, are you a mind-reader now?" Clyde retorted. She didn't care now whether he was upset by her brusqueness. In fact, she would have preferred him to become upset, because maybe it would distract him and get him off track.

Michael ignored her. "Secondly, I overheard Beady-eyes himself discussing the matter with one of his ego-inflated minions."

"Oh." Clyde nodded.

"You don't seem surprised."

"Huh?"

"You don't seem surprised that your 'crazy theory' is actually correct." He used air quotes around the words "crazy theory."

He continued. "See, now, I haven't told anyone about this, not even Ted. I know the truth, because I happened to be in the right place at the right time—and because Beady-eyes is an idiot... But that's another subject altogether.

"What confuses me is, how did *you* know the truth, and before anyone else did?"

Clyde squinted her eyes and shook her head. "I didn't *know*. I just guessed. It was just a crazy guess, a crazy theory. A fluke. That's all. It was just a fluke that I happened to be right. I can't explain it. These things happen sometimes, you know?"

Michael paused a moment, and he nodded. "Okay. You don't feel you can tell me. That's okay. Maybe you don't feel I can be trusted to keep your secret. But just think about this: I haven't told anyone what I know. And I'm not going to tell. Because this is big, Clydene. And if you knew something, I know how we could have done something about it. But not if you don't trust me."

Clyde pshawed at him. "What could you have done?"

"I know people," he simply replied.

Clyde just stared at him, not knowing what to think, not knowing how to feel, not knowing how to respond.

Her voice cracked as she said, "I'd better call Mira."

Michael nodded, and Clyde picked up the phone from the

living room coffee table. She was about to dial, when Michael said, "I don't know if I should tell you this, but..."

Clyde waited a moment before she said, "But what?"

Michael continued. "You should know something."

She hung up the phone receiver. Her impatience grew.

"Ted and I ran into Baedes at the courthouse." Michael looked worried.

Clyde's imagination ran wild. Was Ted okay? Was their marriage still okay? Was Ted going to yell at her? Was he going to have her arrested? Or was he going to come home with bad news that would change their lives forever? Or even worse, would he come home and say nothing about it, while their relationship changed from under her?

Michael still did not continue.

"Well," Clyde said, "you can't just leave me hanging!"

Michael chuckled. "I guess not." He became somber again. "But it's not good news. And I don't think Ted realizes it's serious. But I'm beginning to think it is serious."

Clyde glued her eyes to Michael's.

"We ran into Beady-eyes at the courthouse, and he threatened Ted."

Clyde was nonplussed. She was not aware of any plan Baedes had against her husband, other than to bully Ted's clients more than he bullied anyone else.

"What did he say he was going to do?" Clyde asked.

"He didn't say. He didn't make any direct threat, nothing that would stand up in court, even if we *could* prove that he actually said it. But I took it as a threat, against Ted and against Jay and Damian. Beady-eyes is looking for revenge. To him, it's personal."

In her mind, Clyde scanned through the facts she knew. Beady-eyes knew who the thug was who had assaulted Damian. He knew that this thug was associated with WBH, and with organized crime, because the thug had told him so.

But he let the thug go free, because in his view, J&D were even worse. And he believed in fighting fire with fire, as long as he could get away with it. Yes, that sounds like it could be a personal crusade. And the level of harassment they'd already received did not yet accomplish their enemies' goals.

She looked back at Michael's face.

Quietly, he said, "What should I do?"

"Jay and Damian should go on vacation. Or failing that, they should step up security at their offices. It's likely that they may get another visit from their friendly neighborhood goons."

"I see," Michael said.

Clyde continued. "And don't expect any help from the police in assisting you, or in catching the creeps who have been terrorizing them. The cops could be parked across the street, and you couldn't pull them away from their donuts."

Michael chortled, but his teeth appeared to be clenched.

"In fact, the only reason they wouldn't join in the terror-izing is because they don't want to get their hands dirty." Then she corrected herself. "Baedes doesn't want to get *his* hands dirty."

Michael seemed to contemplate this for a moment. "Fuck," he whispered.

Clyde considered for a moment whether she should say more. After all, everything she had said could be chalked up to mere theory and coincidence. But it was some coincidence, because it would all turn out to be true.

"I know the name of the head thug," she said.

Michael looked surprised to hear this. But he said nothing.

"One more thing," Clyde said.

"What's that?"

"We didn't have this conversation."

Without missing a beat, and dead serious, Michael said, "You mean about inviting Mira to dinner tonight? Why not?

Because that's the only conversation I remember having."

Clyde hammered the point home. "I mean it," she said. "You can't even talk to Ted— *especially* not Ted. He wouldn't understand." She felt sick to her stomach.

"One of the rules," Michael explained, "is that I don't tell you who I talk to. And you don't tell me. And I don't tell anyone that I talked to you, and you don't tell anyone that you talked to me."

He continued, "I'll make sure Jay and Damian get the help they need."

— 'c, —

Jay Alvarez returned home with his wife and kids, returned home from his brother's victory dinner—it appears the jury believed either in official corruption or in jury nullification—to find the house lights on and a strange car just barely visible in the dark of the driveway.

Mrs. Alvarez gawked at the scene and said, "Who's that?"

"I don't know," Jay said, as he drove right by.

He hadn't told the rest of the family about Michael's call. Michael had poured out his heart-felt congratulations to them. As always, Jay could tell he was sincere, even over the phone. But Michael had sounded disturbed, fearful, in what he said next. He suggested Jay and Damian get in touch with a private investigator friend of his, "to keep those creeps from harassing you any more." Michael said he had already briefly discussed the situation with his friend the private-eye, who went by the unlikely name of "Samson."

Now, Jay turned his car down a side street opposite the house, and pulled over to the side of the road. He could still see his home behind him. There was activity within, which he could discern from the moving shadow on the window shades, but he couldn't tell what it was. He pulled from his breast pocket the scrap of paper he had scrawled on: "Samson,

Private Investigator," followed by 10 digits in groups of 3, 3, and 4, each separated by dashes.

Screw this, he thought. He told his wife to stay in the car with the kids, and to call the police and tell them their house was being robbed. Jay sneaked across the street and around to the basement entrance. Inside, he could hear above him heavy steps, interspersed with the loud crashes of destruction. He pulled his safe out from under the basement steps, fumbled with his keys for a moment in the dark before he found the right one, unlocked the box, flipped it open, dug under papers and removed a semi-automatic pistol and magazine, loaded the magazine into the pistol, cocked the loading mechanism.

He breathed in the cold, dry air and carefully ascended the staircase. With each step, he feared a rattle or creak that might betray his approach. But the stairs did not creak, and he had no reason to fear giving up the advantage of surprise. The feeble sounds of his careful footfalls simply could not match the booms of the demolition of his personal property, the violation of his home, the invasion of his sacred castle.

Now at the top step, he listened. He needn't have done so. He had been listening with each step on each stair. The wrecking had clearly finished in the living room to his right and had moved into his den, on the left. This was perfect.

Jay carefully turned the handle and nudged the door open a fraction of an inch. Then grasping his gun with both hands, at the ready, he pushed open the door. He pointed the gun at his attacker, whom he immediately recognized, whom he had half expected to be there.

Jay stood in the over-sized hallway, from a vantage point that allowed him to see most of the den. Half the room was in shambles, knickknacks shattered, furniture in pieces, his home theater system partially dismantled, and not the proper way. Jay stared down his brother's attacker, a large, muscular man in brown leather, from the safe end of the barrel of his .45, just as he had done weeks before.

But this time, the attacker could not escape out the back exit. The large man continued swinging a bat at the objects in the room. He probably could have made a pig's breakfast of things in a matter of seconds. But he seemed bent on utter decimation, and he was taking his time, going over everything thoroughly. His back to Jay, he did not notice the loaded pistol pointing at him.

Adrenaline rushed through Jay's body, his senses acute, his objective within reach. Surprisingly, he wasn't out for revenge. He didn't want a mess. His mind was on automatic, instantly accessing the many hours he had spent training, practicing, studying for a situation just as this, what he had originally justified as caution and mere sport. What happened next passed in only a few seconds.

Jay ordered the man to drop his weapon.

The man turned to face Jay and said, "Okay. I don't want any trouble." Then he dropped his worn, wooden bat on the floor. It was scratched and even chipped in a few places, and it generated a heavy *kerthunk* as it hit the floor.

Jay glanced at the bat. Then he saw the man reach under his jacket. Jay's next move was pure reflex. He didn't even think about it. He aimed and fired. Maybe he missed his intended target. Maybe he didn't. The attacker's gun fell to the floor as his head flung forward. The gunshot rang in Jay's ears for what seemed a full minute, as splotches of blood splattered against the opposite wall.

— ' C , —

As it turns out, the FBI had been after this thug, who went by the name "the Ripper"—many people speculated because he had a lack of imagination, but only God truly knows why—for felonies reported in three states. Apparently, he had been semi-freelance muscle with his own ties to organized crime.

No link was ever proven between him and J&D's competitors, but WBH coincidentally changed ownership shortly thereafter. One of the more controversial radio talk-show hosts even speculated that WBH owner had been called back by "his mob boss" for so totally flubbing the operation.

Jay's story hit the TV news, complete with footage of Damian's assault from the J&D security camera. (It was a digital camera, and Damian had kept a copy of the footage on disc.) Commentators argued whether Jay was justified in shooting the intruder in the head as he did, or whether he even was aiming at the man's head or at some other part of his body. In any case, it was hard for anyone to garner any sympathy for the thug. And because the Ripper was armed, the law after much hemming and hawing eventually came down on Jay's side, and even Baedes couldn't fix it (though he did promise to keep a close eye on the Alvarez brothers).

Ted and Clyde held off on Christmas dinner, until December 31. That night, they had a grand New Year's party: Michael, Mira, Jay and Damian and their families, and numerous others whom Ted and Michael knew. All left 10 pounds heavier than when they arrived.

The only person missing, from Clydene's perspective, was Jane. Weeks earlier, Clyde had quietly called Jane and invited her and hers to New Year's 2008. Jane just as quietly had replied that she didn't think they should see each other any more. Clyde didn't remember the last time she had been dumped.

Clyde carried her glass of merlot, meandered back to her office. Without turning on the light, she shuffled through the room, to the window. In the dark, the room felt cramped, closed in. But at the window, she met a bright half-moon that sent flashes glinting off the dark liquid in her glass. She sipped. Through pursed lips, she breathed in its aroma and flavor. She closed her eyes as she savored undertones of cherry and oak.

"Not enjoying the party?" Michael said from behind her. "You made it possible, as usual."

She turned to face him. "Oh, I was just thinking." She slid her index finger around the rim of her wine glass.

"About what?" Michael asked.

Clyde paused a moment, to put her thoughts into words. "Did you ever dream about moving somewhere else? Somewhere far, far away?"

"Somewhere where everything is simpler?" He seemed to know exactly what she was feeling.

"Yeah," she said. "Why do we stay here?"

Michael looked out the window for a moment. Then he said, "Each of us is who he is. And you're going to be the same person you are, no matter where you live. You're going to act the same way, and you're going to feel the same way. You can't escape who you are.

"But somewhere else, you may not be in a position to do anything about it. That might make things simpler. But it doesn't make anything any better."

Clyde nodded, and the two stared out the window a while longer.

When Clyde turned around, Ted was watching her from the hallway.

EPISODE 4: FOR WHAT AILS YOU

The morning of Valentine's Day, 2008, Ted pushed open the glass entrance of Rico's flower shop. The little bell fastened to the top of the door jingled, and Rico looked up from behind the counter.

"Hey, Mister Jackson!" Rico exclaimed with a twinkle in his eye. "I knew you would be here today."

Rico was a stout, balding, little man with dark gray hair, whose voice lilted with an Italian-American accent. He was one of the few people whose presence filled up a room so fully that it could challenge Ted's.

"Look here," he continued.

He stepped out onto the floor of the shop, past two islands packed with prearranged flowers on display, and hobbled up to a wall case.

"I have beautiful, colorful roses. Perfect, eh? What do you think?"

"No," said Ted lightheartedly. "I'd rather go with something simple this year. Have any red tulips?"

"Yeah," Rico said. "A dozen?"

"Ten," Ted said.

"Ten red tulips," Rico repeated. "That's it? Just tulips?"

"Yes. And a card."

"Ah!" Rico grinned. "Something romantic!"

"A blossom for each year I've been in love."

"That's what's on the card?" came a voice from a woman, as short and as stout and as gray-haired and as Italian-American as her husband. She had just entered from the back room, lugging a bucket full of blossoms.

Ted sighed. "Yes, that's what's on the card."

"Eh, did you two marry in '01?" Rico asked. "Yeah, I remember, you were still on your honeymoon... Oh, that was awful—"

"No, that was his birthday, Rico," the woman interrupted. "And you forget, they met earlier."

"Oh, right. So ten red tulips. Got it. Good as done. Clyde's gonna love 'em." He turned to a young man just coming up from the back room. "Hey, Anthony, come make Mister Jackson here a bouquet of tulips. Ten red ones, okay?"

"Sure thing," replied the young man, tall, dark, and handsome. Then he asked, "Hey, Ted, how's the wife?"

"She's fine."

Rico added, "You just make sure she doesn't leave him over the wrong flowers, okay?"

Anthony chuckled. "Sure thing, Uncle Rico."

Unfortunately, he had barely picked the stems out from the display case when the door bell jingled again, and into the shop barged three large men, armed, arrayed in crisply pressed blue uniforms and intimidating blue jackets.

They strode up to Anthony, and one of them said, "Anthony Giordano?" more as a demand than as a question.

"Yeah?" Anthony said.

"You're under arrest."

The woman gasped, bringing her hands to her cheeks. She looked like she was going to faint.

Rico whispered to himself, "*Signore del cielo!*" Then he quickly said, "This is our lawyer."

But Ted was already on it. "What's he charged with?"

The cop said, "So, he's already been talking to his lawyer." Then he pulled a piece of paper from the inside pocket of his jacket. "Here's the warrant."

Ted took it and read it as the other two cops muscled Anthony into handcuffs.

"Ow," Anthony complained.

"Quit being a baby," said the cop who did all the talking. Then he began to quote Miranda to the young man.

Ted interrupted. "This man is represented by council."

"Yeah, I get it," said the cop.

"Don't ask him anything, not even his name, got it?" And without waiting for an answer, he faced Anthony. "Say nothing. Not a word! I'll meet you there."

Anthony nodded as they dragged him out of the shop.

Ted turned back to Rico and saw that his poor, old wife was silently sobbing. He walked up to Rico and whispered, "This warrant indicates that the police think Anthony raped the Williams girl, the one that's been on the news. Do you know anything about that?"

"No, I don't believe it. He doesn't even know her. And even if he did know her... No... You got to understand. Anthony's a little bit... uncivilized. Blame it on his mother. Black sheep of the family, you know? But he's still a good kid. But there's no way Anthony could have done that. I don't believe it, not even if I live to be 500 years old. Never!

"God! This is wrong, Mister Jackson. They come into my place of business and assault my family? And with what? You have to fix this. You *capite*?"

Rico's voice was raising steadily, and Rico's bride, now partially recovered, said, "Calm down, Rico."

"Yes," Ted agreed. "Calm down. *Capisco*. I'll meet him at the station. Okay?"

— ‘ C , —

The morning of Valentine's Day, 2006, Saddam Hussein announced that he was on a hunger strike, along with his cohorts. They were protesting their treatment by the international tribunal. And news commentators were still absorbing themselves with Dick Cheney's hunting accident the previous Saturday. Ted noted these things in passing, as he prepared for his closing before the jury that afternoon.

"Miss Williams never saw her attacker's face. So she couldn't actually identify him. She said she knew him, that she recognized him by his voice. But you saw in this very courtroom that she *failed* to point out Mr. Hill's voice from among just three men. As you heard yourself, his voice sounds quite average. How many men are there out there who might have been the actual attacker?

"Officer Simmons also could not identify the attacker. All he saw was a figure running from the scene, in the dark. No distinguishing characteristics. No distinguishing behaviors. Except that Mr. Hill does have distinguishing characteristics. As you yourself have seen, he walks with a limp. How could he have run as the attacker had? Yes, the officer later upgraded his story. After he saw Mr. Hill walk with a limp, he began to say the attacker 'hobbled' away from the scene. But that was not his original, unbiased statement!

"The prosecutor also failed to show how Mr. Hill could have gotten his hands on sevoflurane, the anesthetic that the perpetrator used to knock out his victim. This is a highly controlled drug, only available to anesthetists in operating rooms. Mr. Hill is an English teacher. How would he have gotten his hands on sevoflurane? It's not even available on the street, because there are cheaper drugs that common criminals use to knock out unsuspecting victims. Yet, we know for a fact that that Miss Williams' attacker used sevoflurane. The prosecutions own lab experts confirmed that.

"How convenient it was that this attacker never revealed his face. The prosecution is desperate, so desperate they even went so far as to suggest that he hid his face because he had a distinguishing scar that he wanted to hide.

"In logic, there is a fallacy called Appeal to Ignorance. In an Appeal to Ignorance, one side"—and he pointed to the prosecutor—"claims that they have no evidence to prove Mr. Hill did *not* hide his face; therefore, he must be. Does anyone besides me see the insanity in that? He hid his face; therefore, it must be him? By that logic, any of us could be suspects. Because *I* would be afraid to show *my* face if I had committed this horrific act. Look, no scar!" He pointed to his right cheek, where Gordon Hill was permanently marked.

"How about you?" Ted continued, sweeping his hand across the jury. He pointed to a dignified gentleman in the front row. "How about you? Would you show *your* face, if you had committed this act?" He pointed at another jury member. "How about you?" He continued. "How about you? Or you? Would any of us *not* hide his face? Just for fear of being caught?

"That's why in our system of justice, it's up the the prosecution to *prove* beyond all reasonable doubt that they have the right man.

"Please, ladies and gentlemen, let's be reasonable. The only reason the police have to suspect my client is that he happened to be walking down the street, *five* whole blocks away. Let me be clear about this. Walking down the street is *not* a crime! At least not in the America I live in, the country I'm proud of.

"Beyond all reasonable doubt, that's the standard of proof upon which rests the integrity of our system of justice. We do *not* just go throwing innocent people in jail, just because they have a visible scar, or walk with a limp. Or even if they don't! We demand that prosecutors *prove* beyond *all reasonable doubt* that they have the right man. This is the honor of the law you swore to uphold.

"And in this case, we cannot know beyond all reasonable doubt. Frankly, I shouldn't have to get up before you at all, today. I should have to say anything to you, because the prosecution has failed to meet its burden of proof. The fact that I am here, speaking to you, makes the point all the stronger. And that's why I stand before you today, asking you to carry out your promise, and to return a verdict of not guilty."

— ' c , —

"I can help you," Baedes told the young man, "but only if you help me."

For a moment, Baedes wondered what the young man on the other side of the table was thinking beneath the tuft of neatly combed, black curls on his head. But in the final analysis, it didn't really matter what the young man was thinking. It only mattered what he did and what he said and whose side he was on.

Anthony Giordano stared up at the burly police chief with dark, soulful eyes. Yeah, Miranda was a pain in the ass, a stupid legal theory 5 crazy judges came up with over 40 years ago, and it's been hampering law enforcement ever since. Fortunately, there were ways to end-run around Miranda. Baedes knew he wasn't supposed to be talking to the perp. But only one officer knew that he knew, and that officer Baedes could trust not to talk. Besides, the perp had been Mirandized, and if he chose to waive his rights, that was his business. And if he was like most perps, he wouldn't be able to keep his big mouth shut; they all wanted to tell their story, with or without a lawyer. In any case, the worst that could happen is that the information Baedes learned would be disqualified as evidence against Giordano. And Baedes was not after evidence against Giordano. The perp's right to keep his mouth shut didn't extend to other people.

"You know Ted Jackson, don't you?" the chief continued.

"Yeah."

"How do you know him?"

"He's a customer. What does it matter to you?"

"What does he buy?"

The young man peered through thin slits under a furrowed brow. "Flowers. What else would it be?"

"Information, maybe?"

No response.

"You also know Mira Jayson," Baedes said.

"No, not exactly," came the response.

"Come on, Anthony. It can't go like this. You have to come clean, or I can't do anything for you."

Anthony grunted and rolled his eyes. "How stupid do you think I am? You're trying to distract me. You just want to trick me into saying I did something, so you can pin it—"

"Anthony." The chief spoke calmly but deliberately. "Don't fool yourself, Anthony. We don't need any confession from you, because we already have you dead to rights. You followed that girl to her apartment, and you forced yourself inside, and you beat her up, and you raped her. She told us exactly how it happened, and we have a mountain of physical evidence to convict you. Make no mistake. You're going away, my son, for a long, long time." He let that sink in. "What I'm talking about is a deal. You help me, and I help you."

Baedes continued. "We think Ted Jackson has been selling government secrets. And I think you're one of his couriers." Baedes could see the whites of the young man's eyes, splashes of fear peeking out from around each iris. He grinned. "What's it going to be, Anthony? Start by telling me about who you work with."

Anthony hesitated. He finally said, with an edge of his voice, "No thanks. I think I'll wait for my law—"

"Unless you come clean, you're going to go to prison for the rest of your life, young man. Don't be a fool. I can help you. Come on, you probably didn't rape that girl, right? Maybe it was consensual. And maybe you didn't rough her up, either. There's probably some evidence of that, too. And I can help you find it. But unless you come clean with me, you're going to go away for a long, long time."

Anthony sat, stone cold silent.

Baedes nodded and swallowed. "You'll be sorry, you know."

"Yeah, well, we'll see, won't we."

Baedes stooped over the table. He rested his hands on the tabletop, hanging his face close over the young man's. "Oh yes," he said without blinking. "You will."

Anthony looked up, but he neither moved nor breathed. Nor did he say a word.

Finally, the chief said, "Well, at least you can tell you friends not to cross me, because they'll see what happens to those who do."

He stepped through the door in the small room, leaving the young man behind. In the hallway, he met a diminutive, balding man in a dark suit and tie.

"Ted Jackson is here," said the dark suit in a edgy, nasally tone.

"This one's not going to talk, for now. Might talk after he thinks about it for a while. Too bad there's no evidence to exculpate him. He could use some."

"Unfortunately not." The dark-suited man held up a nondescript Manila folder. "Here are some papers that were delivered to my office by mistake. I think they were meant to go to you."

Baedes took the folder and glanced at the lab report inside. An unidentified sample of blood from the Williams rape kit. What did he just say about exculpatory evidence? Baedes had been waiting for an opportunity like the Williams case, and he was glad this report had into the right hands. He couldn't allow the perp's guilt to be clouded by misleading evidence.

"Thanks," Baedes remarked. "I have paperwork to do. Tell Mr. Jackson his client has already been sent to lock-up. He can catch him at the arraignment."

The dark-suited man nodded.

— ' c , —

Mira had agreed to meet in a cozy coffee shop on the corner of Main and Commons, and she had promised herself she wouldn't get her hopes up, because the last time she did that, she ended up hurt. Even still, she drove in from the city to meet him for just a casual lunch at the Commons Café. The atmosphere smelled of coffee, and in the background, Mira heard the clanking of glassware. The shop's several rooms were arrayed around a central counter. Small tables dotted the floor plan, and comfy green-patterned couches and wicker chairs with flowered cushions lined its boundaries.

Black purse in hand, she crept timidly toward the counter, scanning the faces of the patrons. It didn't look like Ike had arrived yet. But it had been months since she had seen him, months which seemed like years, and she wasn't sure she would recognize him. He had been calling her once in a while, but she had been making excuses why she couldn't see him. She didn't want to see him. She didn't want to get him into deeper trouble than he already was. More on the nose, she didn't want to feel the way she felt about him. She needed time away from him, time to recover, time to calm down.

Mira's heart was beating faster than normal, and her breaths fell heavily upon her chest. She felt as if she were in a dream, as if everything were not quite real. She studied the menu, neatly printed in colored chalk on a large, slate black-board overhead. It described a selection of coffees, baked goods, and sandwiches. She finally decided on a coffee and a ham-and-cheese bagel sandwich.

"Hello, Mira," said a sweet, soft, masculine voice just behind her.

Mira swung around and gazed up at the smooth face of the man she had been waiting for. His sandy hair had grown out a little, and he had parted it neatly to one side. His presence smelled like mild aftershave, and his dark eyes looked like chocolate. He wore a thick sweater of blue and beige and burgundy and green, and Mira wanted to squeeze it to see how soft it was, or rather, how soft he felt in it. And if it were anyone else, she probably would have. But right here, right now, she wasn't sure of herself. Mira didn't know whether a hug would be merely friendly or whether it would betray feelings she had promised herself she would not feel.

So instead she said, "Aren't you cold out without a coat?"

He grinned. "I don't know. Aren't you hot dressed as the Michelin Man?"

Mira suddenly noticed the bulging, blue winter coat she was wearing, and she felt her face flush hot red.

Ike said, "Can I hang up your coat for you?"

She unzipped it and slid it off, revealing a tight-fitting salmon sweater over a white blouse. She felt sheepish under Ike's radiant gaze.

He took the garment. "Get whatever you like. It's on me."

They brought their food to a table and sat and ate. They eased into conversation. Had she ever eaten here before? No, she hadn't, but she was enjoying herself. Was he still working? Yes, and things were going well for him. But the roofing business was slow over the cold winter months, and he had arranged to take a vacation day. Because once spring hit, with its melting snow, driving rain, and abundant roofing emergencies, there would be far too much work and not enough manpower, and he would not be able to get time off. How was work for Mira? Fine, but she couldn't talk about details, because of counselor-client confidentiality. How was the Committee? Slow. They were working toward a ballot question for the 2008 November election, but that work would not begin in earnest until April. The big part of that was to form a separate committee just for the ballot question. They called this the Committee to Replace Sam Baedes, which just happened to be run by and consist of the same people behind the Committee for a Fairer Future. Yeah, politics makes no sense sometimes. This process had actually begun some months ago.

Then Mira asked the question she had been dying to ask, but had no interest in asking, because she was too ashamed to ask. "How's your girlfriend?"

"Sophie?" Ike said. "She's fine." Then he added, "And she's not my girlfriend anymore."

"Oh," said Mira. "I'm sorry to hear that." She held her breath for a moment, involuntarily.

"Don't be. It was good while it lasted."

"What happened?"

"Well... I guess she just wasn't the right one." Then he asked, "Are you seeing anyone?"

"Not really," she replied.

Not really? That was a deceptive way to put it. The truthful answer was an unequivocal *No!* She had been depressed about men in general, and she was beginning to wonder whether she should try lesbianism. If she had been one of her own clients, she would have told herself that you can't "try" being gay. Life doesn't work that way, because sexual experimentation can't resolve deep-seated emotional issues. She would have advised herself to focus on the things in life that make her happy. And she would have worked with herself to adjust her image of romance to be more in line with reality, so that she could steer herself in a more positive direction. All this she would do if she were one of her own clients. Unfortunately, there's no one more neurotic than a psych major. Doctor, heal thyself.

After lunch, Ike walked Mira to her car, which she had parked in one of the metered spaces on Main Street. Mira felt self-conscious about her unassuming, puffy coat, which left everything to the imagination. She told herself it didn't matter, but for some reason, she cared nonetheless that she look attractive. So she put her arms through the jacket's sleeves, but left the front unzipped. The air outside was nippy, but calm, and a strong, clear afternoon sun warmed everything it touched. Ike remarked how good the weather turned out, and how romantic the sun was. In response, Mira relayed a joke she had heard about a blonde who wanted to visit the sun. (You can't visit the sun, because you'd burn up, to which the blonde replied, "Duh, not if you go at night!") Ike laughed a polite laugh.

"Sorry," she said. "I guess it wasn't that funny."

Ike smiled warmly. "Are you kidding? That's a great joke. I have to remember that one."

Mira reached her car and stopped walking, and without thinking about it, with her left hand she brushed her hair behind her ear on one side. "Uh, this is me," she said, pointing to a bright red Nissan hatchback.

"Nice," Ike said, peering through the passenger-side window. "When did you get this?"

"A couple months ago."

"Well, it fits you."

"Thanks," Mira said.

Ike turned back to her and stared into her eyes. "Hey," he said, with a sweet, tender voice. "It was really good to see you again."

"You too," she replied.

"I missed you."

Mira hesitated. Then she squeaked, "Me too."

She regretted those words as soon as she uttered them, but she couldn't remember why. She felt more than ever as though she were in a dream, as though things were happening to her inside her mind and she couldn't control them. It was as if part of her mind had shut down, the part that directs her conscious thoughts, and her subconscious had taken over.

Ike took a step forward and ran his fingers through her hair where she had brushed it back. Cradling her head gently in his hand he brought his lips to hers. Carefully, tenderly, their lips touched. Mira felt a slight suction, and she closed her eyes and responded in kind. With his other hand, he reached inside her jacket. It ruffled as he pushed past, behind her, across her sweater, and caressed the small of her back with the tips of his fingers. With delicate motions, his tongue stroked the inside of her lips. His breath rushed across her face, smelling of coffee. His mouth tasted of sugar. For a moment, Mira's whole body felt on fire, not with pain, but with satiated longing. Her nipples felt tender, her body, enraptured, her being, at peace. She groaned softly. Then, as seamlessly as it had started, it was over.

Mira breathed out a deep, heavy breath. She stared at the sidewalk. A sudden fear and guilt embraced her, deep in her gut, but she couldn't remember why that would happen.

"This is wrong," she said.

Ike was mute. She looked back at him. He looked dumb-founded.

"I'm sorry." She shook her head. "I have to go."

She ran around to the driver's side of the car, rifling through her purse. By the time she reached the door, she had come up with her keys and opened the door. Ike might have been asking something. She couldn't hear him. She just got in the car, started it, and drove off.

— ' C , —

Clyde watched the jury file into the courtroom. The judge, a stout man with very little hair on his head, leaned back in his chair and said, "Foreman, have you reached a unanimous verdict?"

"Yes, your honor," the jury foreman said.

The judge continued, "Defendant, please rise."

Mr. Hill, and Ted beside him, stood up.

"What say you?" the judge asked.

The head juror read from his note, "In the matter of the Commonwealth versus Gordon Hill, on the charges of aggravated rape and battery, we find the defendant *not* guilty."

Unlike the courtroom TV shows, the entire room remained silent, until the judge spoke. "So say you all?"

Each juror nodded.

"Very well. The jury is discharged. Jurors, we thank you for your service. The defendant is free to go. Court is adjourned." The judge banged his gavel.

Clyde slid off of the bench and slunk up behind Ted. She snuggled up to his arm. "Congratulations," she cooed.

Ted turned and pecked her on the lips.

"Well, well," said Mr. Gordon Hill. "Who's this pretty lady?"

On top of his head, short hairs shone bright red, even more so than Clyde's, like a field of tiny flames. Freckles spotted his pale complexion, from which gazed large, piercing, green eyes. From just under his left eye, a scar trickled down his cheek like a river. And when he said the word *ladeeee*, he accentuated each vowel, and he drew out the last syllable with a suggestive leer.

Frankly, he creeped Clyde out.

Ted nonchalantly answered. "This is my beautiful bride. Clyde, meet Gordon Hill. Gordon, this is my wife, Clydene."

"Clyde, eh?" He held out his hand. And when out of politeness she returned the favor, he took her hand and kissed it, all the while gazing into her eyes.

Clyde was desperate to get out of there. "It was nice to meet you, Mr. Hill," she said. Then turning to her husband, "Ted, romantic dinner reservations." She eyed him.

She immediately regretted using the word *romantic*, considering the third wheel currently eavesdropping. But Ted so frequently worked late. Even Clyde's late nights at the office didn't compare to Ted's. So whenever she had the opportunity to go out with her husband, it didn't have to be fancy to be romantic. Even hamburgers and fries were a special occasion.

"I have to cancel," Ted said. "I have a mountain of research to finish for a meeting tomorrow morning."

Clyde felt her countenance physically fall.

"Don't wait up for me," Ted continued. "Hey, why don't you take Gordon?"

"No," Clyde said as pleasantly as she could muster. "I think I'll just whip something up at home."

Chapter 2

Ted had of course lost his share of cases. That didn't mean
he was used to it. Because Ted hated losing, more than
anything else. And to keep from losing, Ted had a three-part
strategy: preparation, preparation, and preparation. Now, Ted
was to depose J. Gill's accountant in the morning. That is, the
man was his accountant until he accused Gill of financial
malfeasance, and Gill's wife, the only other shareholder in
Gill's corporation, sued him. Ted needed to devise a ques-
tioning strategy that would uncover the accountant's motives
as well as nail his feet to the floor, so he can't backpedal at
trial. And he needed to accomplish this without cluing the
witness, at least not until it's too late. Ted needed to anticipate
what the witness might say, and what Ted might ask in
response, and what the witness might answer. Planning for a
deposition is like playing a game of chess, except that you
don't know where the pieces are until after you've made your
move. Clyde would forgive him, he was sure, for reneging on
their dinner plans.

Before he left the courthouse, however, his now vindicated
client had asked him for a quick word in private.

"So, that's it?" Gordon Hill asked once they were in a
witness room.

"That's it," Ted confirmed.

"It's all over?"

"It's all over."

"They can't do anything else to me."

"Right," Ted said. "You've been found not guilty."

"Even if they got additional evidence, they couldn't do anything about it."

"That's correct." Ted mentally went through the list of loopholes the government sometimes uses to get around double-jeopardy. None seemed significant here.

"But I can still tell you something and have it be covered by lawyer-client privilege, right?"

"Of course." Ted gathered that Gordon wanted to ask him a deeper legal question, and now he waited for it.

"I'm not... not guilty," he said. "I was guilty. I did it."

Ted had experienced this before, a client declared "not guilty" who now wanted to make restitution, felt his conscience pinging at him, to be absolved of his misdeeds. Ted nodded and explained matter-of-factly, "Even though the government can't prosecute you again for the same crime, you still probably want to keep that quiet. For example, the victim could still sue you under civil law, and that has a whole different set of rules. There are also many who unfortunately would take it upon themselves to punish you, any way they can think of. So you need to lay low and stay out of trouble."

"I've done this before, you know."

"Done what?"

"Other... similar crimes."

Ted thought a moment, then he asked, "You weren't tried on any of those charges?"

"No. Was never even arrested."

"Those crimes could still be prosecuted, up to 15 years after the events occurred, under the same charges, if someone files charges and there's enough evidence. And a confession would count as evidence. So you don't want to go around talking about them. As I said, you want to keep quiet, lay low, stay out of trouble."

Gordon seemed to consider these words. Then he said, "I want to stop. I just don't know how."

"I have a list of criminal psychiatrists who can—"

"N— uh... No, no, no." Gordon was shaking his head. "Psychologists freak me out."

"These gentlemen are medical doctors. They'll keep your secret as safe as I will. You'll enjoy complete privilege with them, just as you do with me. Now, I can't recommend or refer you to any doctor in particular. But call my office first thing in the morning, and my assistant will get you a list of names, okay?"

Gordon waited a moment, then smiled. "Okay. I'll do that. Thanks." Then he added, "It's not my place to say, but... You should go home, be with your wife. She deserves to have someone with her tonight."

Ted chuckled. "Well, I'll think about that." This was Ted's version of diplomatic. He had already made up his mind.

— ' c , —

Clyde didn't feel like going home to an empty house. She drove around for untold minutes—or was it hours?—feeling sorry for herself, listening to the radio, a long string of nondescript pop love songs bombarding her ears. Occasionally, the DJ took a call from a sickening woman gushing about true love, or an infuriating man dedicating a very special song to it. Finally, Clyde had heard enough of this parade of affection, and she wended her way back home. *Even an empty, lonely house has to be more fun than this.* She never considered turning off the radio.

The blue Camry parked in the driveway, a gentle tick-tick resonating under the hood, Clydene sulked as she fiddled with her keys in the dark. She paused at the foot of the walkway. The gentle breeze felt like Winter but smelled like Spring. She looked up into the clear sky and identified Orion, the archer, keeping watch over her from directly overhead. It was the only constellation she had ever learned to locate in the chill, Winter, night sky. She sighed a deep, sad sigh and felt her lower lip involuntarily collapse under the weight of her cheeks.

"Well, my friend," she said to the picture in the stars, "at least we have each other."

Clyde trudged the remainder of the way to the doorway, pulled open the storm door, inserted her key in the lock, turned the knob. She pushed the door into darkness, listening to it creak on its hinges.

"I'll have to do something about that," she said to herself, knowing she would forget all about it in five or ten minutes.

Stepped up the little step into the foyer, dropped her keys into her purse, closed the door, debated for a moment whether she should lock it and force Ted to use his own key when he finally arrived home, God-knows-when. She elected to leave the door unlocked, just in case Ted got home before she went to bed. She didn't want to feel guilty about forcing him to fiddle with the lock when she was right there.

Into the kitchen, up to the refrigerator, swung open the door. *There must be something in here. Leftovers?* She scanned the shelves of the chill chest, empty except for some raw vegetables and staples like milk and butter. She opened the deli drawer. Some sliced turkey and cheese, which she swiped up. Grabbed a loaf of bread from the counter, lumbered over to the kitchen table, and set about making a sandwich.

"Damn! Forgot the mustard," she said. Back to the fridge.

Having procured a plate from the cabinet and assembled her dinner thereon, she brought it into the living room, collapsed on the sofa, grabbed the television remote, clicked on, bit into her sandwich, chewed thoroughly.

On screen, Alan Shore passed around a self-portrait of an expressionless, nine-year-old girl, a picture entitled "Happy Girl." Marissa could not smile, and no one wanted her. Somehow, Clyde could sympathize. She took another bite of sandwich. If she closed her eyes, Alan Shore reminded her a little of Ted, except that Ted wasn't so passive-aggressive. Just misunderstood. And missed.

A commercial came on. Clyde couldn't tell what they were advertising. This was not the exciting evening she had planned. This was the lonely night she had thought she had avoided, upon her now, and nothing she could do would fix it. Her anger stewed.

I don't ask for much, do I? I don't want him to give up his career. Hell! I just want a little time, that's all. Is that unreasonable? God! I'm his wife, for crying out loud. Damn it! That little bastard! He can't find just a couple hours for me? For us!? Just once a year?

She felt angry, not only because of Ted, but also because she had doubted herself, that she was entitled to his affection. She knew this wasn't his fault, but she was hurt and upset. And she wanted to blame him for anything she could think of.

Commercial over, at trial, another lawyer slapped down a copy of the national protocol for treating victims of sexual assault. Apparently, a raped woman had become pregnant with her attacker's baby, because the hospital wouldn't provide emergency contraception. Already angry, Clyde set her teeth. Even though it was make-believe, somehow she couldn't help but become part of the drama.

A knock sounded at the door, jolting her from her thoughts. *Strange,* Clyde thought. *Who could that be, this late at night?*

Without leaving the couch, she pulled back the curtain behind her. She had to push herself up a little to see through the window, holding her sandwich and plate in her lap so that it wouldn't slide to the floor. She couldn't see anything, because it was dark outside.

"Damn," she said. *Forgot to turn on the outside light.*

She set the plate on the couch and strode up to the front door, flicked the switch for the outside light, peered through the peephole. Nothing there, as far as she could see.

She pulled open the door. Still nothing. Pushed open the storm door and craned her head through the gap, sweeping it from side to side in order to take in the whole yard. Still nothing. No one there.

"Hmm," Clyde said, puzzled. *I did hear a knock, right? Maybe it was the TV.* Yes, she was sure it had been the TV. She had just been so deep in her own thoughts, she wasn't paying attention to what was going on in the room, on the tube. Rewinding the experience in her memory, she now remembered the scene that was on. One of the characters had come through a door, and he must have knocked first.

Clyde shook her head at herself, thinking she was going to need a shrink if she kept this up. She stepped back into the foyer, letting the storm door wheeze shut, and she swung the creaky front door closed, pushing it until the latch clicked. Clyde paused a moment, thought about her sanity, shook her head again at herself, snorted, and turned back toward the living room.

From nowhere, something soft and mildly sweet-smelling hit her in the face. She had run into it, and now she couldn't get it off her. She gasped for breath, choked, coughed, pushed at the thing. Someone was behind her, pressing himself to her back, smothering her with his hand. She knew she should do... What was it she should do? She couldn't remember. Even if she were able to remember what she should do, she couldn't think of it. Or something like that. Her mind was a blurred jumble of thoughts, sounds, and images. Or was the room actually dissolving into chaos? She continued hacking under the thick, empty smell that was suffocating her, struggling against it, ever more desperate, ever weaker.

She didn't remember what happened next.

— ' c , —

The air smacked of dirt, sweat, and stale urine. The guard slid open the cage door, and Ted entered the cell. Anthony was sitting on a bench physically attached to the structure. Ted sat across from him.

"Anthony." He spoke softly. "We have a probable cause hearing tomorrow morning."

"Okay," he said.

"That means the prosecution will set forth their evidence, or rather, just enough to show that they can make a case at trial. The hearing poses little risk to us, because even if they win, we get a sneak peek at what their case will be at trial. Does that make sense?"

"Yes."

"However, if we win at probable cause, we won't go to trial."

"Yeah," said Anthony with a grin, "That's what I want."

"It's by no means guaranteed..." Then Ted saw the grin on Anthony's face. "That was a joke, wasn't it?"

"Please just try your best. I don't want to wait in jail for God knows how long while you get a trial ready. I hate it here. Whatever I can do. If you want me testify—"

"I don't think so. It's very unusual for a defendant to testify at his own probable cause hearing, because it usually doesn't do any good, and it could give the prosecution more ammunition that they use against you." Ted took a breath. "And as far as rotting in this cell, your father's already working on raising bail."

"Bail or no, I hate the idea of this hanging over my head even one hour longer than necessary. You know just having these accusations being reported in the press is ruining my reputation, and my father's. What's it going to do for his business?"

"I don't know. But what you *can* do is to tell me what happened."

"I don't know what happened. I wasn't there. I didn't do what they say I did." His words began spilling out faster than usual.

"Okay. Do you know Nona Williams?"

Anthony hesitated.

"I'll take that as a 'Yes.' A jury surely would."

"You're not the jury," Anthony objected, angry.

"Correct. I'm not the jury. I'm your lawyer, and that means whatever you tell me, I will only use it to help you. That's my job. So please tell me what happened."

Anthony stared at the steel bars for several seconds. "Yes, I know Nona. But we've kept our relationship a secret."

"I have a feeling the truth will out."

"There's no way to keep it a secret?"

"Not if she's telling the police about it," Ted replied. "Just how deep did this relationship go?"

Anthony stared into Ted's eyes. "We were having an affair."

This puzzled Ted. "Why have an affair? Neither of you is married. If you want to be together, why not just be together?"

"Because she has a boyfriend, Paul Randolph."

Ted took out a notepad and pen, and he wrote down the name. "And she didn't want to break up with him?"

Anthony stared at the ceiling for a moment. "Look at me. She's out of my league." He looked back at Ted. "I don't think she wanted to be embarrassed. So we kept it a secret."

"I see. Let's talk about Tuesday night. I understand that someone raped her and beat her up pretty badly."

"It wasn't me."

"Okay. Did you see Nona on Tuesday?"

"Yes, that evening."

"Tell me about it," Ted said.

"We met at a place called China Gardens, out in Palmer."

"So, someplace where no one would recognize you." Ted made another note.

"Yeah. We ate at about seven o'clock. We were done by about eight-thirty or nine."

"Okay. Then what happened?" Ted kept writing.

"Then I rented a room, at the Park Street Inn. I brought Nona up the back entrance." He paused. "After a while, she went home. I stayed the night."

"What time did she leave?"

"I'm not sure. I was pretty out of it. But it must have been before 11."

"Could it have been closer to 10?"

"Yes."

"And did you have sex?" Ted asked pointedly.

Anthony nodded, with that body language that says, "I'm supposed to be adult about this, but I'm really uncomfortable."

"Then what happened?"

"Then I woke up early the next morning, took a shower, and went to work."

"You wore the same clothes?" Ted asked.

"Huh?"

"Your clothes. Did you bring a change of clothes to the hotel? Or did you wear the same clothes two days in a row?"

"Uh. Same clothes."

"Who did you see yesterday? Or rather, did anyone see you wear the same clothes yesterday, the same clothes you were wearing on Tuesday?"

"I saw my uncle, but he doesn't notice what I'm wearing."

"Still couldn't hurt to ask him. One more thing: If what you're telling me is true, someone attacked Nona after she left you."

Anthony nodded sadly.

"And she's covering up for him," Ted continued.

"I guess so."

"Do you have any idea who it might be?"

Anthony thought for a minute. "No, I don't know."

— ' c , —

Clydene paced across the kitchen floor, down the back
hallway, through her tiny office, up to the window. She caught
a glimpse of the picket fence dividing their property from the
neighbors' as she whipped her body around and headed back
to the kitchen. As she made this round trip again and again,
she had a conversation with the air around her.

"Don't tell me not to take it personally. Beady-eyes made it
personal! He comes after innocent people, because he hates *us*.
Anything he can get away with, he just does it. It doesn't
matter whether you're innocent. But if you're not on his side,
God help you! God help us all! 'But we promise never to abuse
this power!'? God! He tortures the innocent, locks them up
without council, without sleep, badgers them until they give
in. He punishes his enemies at will. He is lawless, a criminal in
uniform.

"And they support him! Don't they realize that anyone
who approves of him approves of what he does? Don't they
know we will all be held accountable for the things of which
we approve? And if you vote for him, you have signed your
own warrant. I would not choose to face the Great and Mighty
with that record on my account.

"Eventually, he'll come after us all, hunt you down." She
set her teeth. "And there won't be anything you can do."

She was stomping by now. A tear streamed down the side
of her nose. She felt angry and hurt, helpless and victimized.

"Damn it! I did this... But if I had not, how much worse off would we be?"

The doorbell rang. Clyde wiped the tears from her eyes and sniffled. She reached the door, paused, breathed, then opened it. Cold air wafted over her body, mixed with a hint of perfume. On the landing just outside stood small, dark-haired woman, bundled in a puffy, blue, winter coat. Because the landing was a step lower than the house proper, she looked even shorter than she actually was. Her head came up to Clyde's chest. Despite that, the woman stood tall and proud. Clyde reminisced for a moment, noticing for the first time in a long time how big her friend made her feel, regardless of her physical stature.

"Mira," Clyde said. "What's up?"

"I need your advice." Then a look of concern spread across her face. "What's wrong?"

"Come in," Clyde said. "Don't mind me." Then she made an excuse. "Sad movie. What's up?"

"I had lunch with Ike."

"I thought you couldn't be around him."

"Yeah, I know," Mira said.

"You changed your mind?"

"Kinda." Mira paused, then blurted out, "He kissed me."

Clyde stood, nonplussed, mouth gaping wide. That reaction just seemed right for the occasion. But truthfully, Clyde wasn't surprised.

Mira beamed, radiated, as though she had just had sex.

"Are you sure it was just a kiss?" Clyde asked salaciously.

"No, it was just... He just kissed me. He put his arm around me and ran his fingers through my hair, and we kissed, just like that."

"At lunch."

"Well..." Mira giggled like a teenager.

So Mira told Clyde all that had happened that afternoon. Clyde interjected occasionally with comments like "It would be like hugging Poppin' Fresh," or "Was he wearing tight jeans?" or "So, on a scale of 1 to 10..." Clyde knew she could be crude, sometimes inappropriately so. As long as they didn't actually say the word *sex* or any of its synonyms. But Mira kept talking. It felt like they were having a slumber party.

"So, what do you think I should do?" Mira asked.

That sobered Clyde. She thought about it. There was a good reason Mira had stopped calling Ike, had stopped carpooling with him, had stopped talking to him, had cut him out of her life. When Mira was around Ike, something happened to her. His presence made her lose control of her feelings. Mira had fallen in love with this man, this man who had shown so little interest in her, and she had drenched Clyde's shoulder with her tears. That had been months ago, and Mira was just beginning to get back on her feet. Clyde shuddered.

Clydene understood how her friend felt. Which one of us hasn't fallen inexplicably for someone? Mira never lost that adolescent innocence. Mira was a visionary, and she felt deep feelings. Both sometimes got her into trouble.

"Clyde?" Mira interrupted.

"Yeah... What was the question again?"

"I'm too close to it to think straight. What should I do?"

Well, she could do as Nancy Reagan and just say no. But what if things would have worked out? Mira lived in loneliness, and Clyde had often felt lonely for her friend. Clyde glanced at the tulips Ted had sent, now displayed on the coffee table. She remembered what it was like in the beginning, before Ted, before the end of loneliness.

On the other hand, she would hate for Mira to get hurt again. Yes, to love and be loved entails a certain risk. You risk getting hurt, just as surely as you risk living happily ever after. Still, why allow yourself to fall in love with the wrong guy? It would be a shame if Mira allowed herself to fall in love again, only to be hurt again...

That is, if she hadn't already fallen in love.

"Do you love him?" Clyde asked.

Mira blushed. "No. That's silly."

"But it's *Ike*," Clyde protested.

"So? How much can you fall in love during lunch? It wasn't even a real date." Mira's eyes seemed to light up at the thought of a date with Ike.

The next words came out of Clyde's mouth almost without a thought. "Does he love you?"

Mira's face froze for a few seconds. Then it fell. The color seemed to drain out of Mira's cheeks. Then she forced a smile and said, "I don't know. What does it matter? We can figure that out later."

"You asked me what I thought you should do. I think you should find out how he really feels about you and how far he's willing to take this relationship."

— ' c , —

Ted arrived home well after midnight. He pulled into the driveway, in the same spot he always parked, noticing the empty spot where Clyde's car usually sat. Approaching the front door, he noticed flashes cast by the television onto the living room curtains. He tried the knob. It opened easily. Peeking around the corner, he made out the couch, empty except for a half-eaten sandwich on a plate.

"Clyde?" Ted called.

No answer. Just some guy on TV interviewing some comedienne.

He tried again. "Clyde!"

Still no answer.

Must have gone out, he thought. *Leaving the door open and the television on?*

Maybe she was asleep. Ted bounded up the stairs. "Clyde!" he called into the darkness. He didn't know why he was so anxious to hear her voice.

No answer.

He dashed into the master bedroom, flipped the light on.
The bed had not been slept in. Darted over to the guest
bedroom, flipped on the switch. Still nothing.

He rushed back downstairs, dodged into the spare downstairs room. Switched on a lamp, illuminating the big comfy
couch and armchair, stacked with papers and miscellaneous
nicknacks.

"Clyde?" he begged, even though he could see the room
clearly devoid of life.

Then he canvassed the rest of the house: the office, the
kitchen, even the basement. Clyde was nowhere to be found.
Neither was any indication of where she went, and why in
such a hurry. He knew it had been in a hurry, because she left
the door unlocked and the TV on. No note. No message on the
answering machine.

Ted picked up the cordless telephone and dialed Clyde's
cellphone. He heard first, then he saw it, sitting on the living
room coffee table, Clyde's purse. Her phone was ringing from
within, audible even through the layers of fabric. Ted walked
over to it, flipped open the top, looked inside, and saw the cell.
He pulled it out. By that time, Clyde's cellphone had switched
over to voice-mail. Through the cordless receiver, Ted heard
his wife's voice invite him to leave a message.

Strange, that after so desperately desiring to hear her voice,
he should be so horrified by it. Ted pushed the feeling away.
With his thumb, he pressed the "off" button on the cordless.

He paused. Something else wasn't right. Something in the
purse. Something he had seen. Ted peered inside again, and
he immediately realized what was wrong. He set down the
cellphone, reached into the bag, and pulled out a ruffled,
white handkerchief.

This isn't Clyde's.

Then he brought the white cloth near his face and sniffed it. Ted had no good reason for doing so. But he did so nonetheless, maybe in hopes of some clue. Maybe because this was his only clue. Or maybe because his brain was only half in control of his mind. He was operating on automatic pilot. The cloth smelled mildly sweet. Ted felt suddenly dizzy. It could have been the stress of the situation taking away his balance. But what his mind was telling him was something different, the worst thing that could have happened. He loathed to admit it, but he knew the truth and knew that he couldn't escape it.

Ted dropped the handkerchief back into the open purse, and with the thumb of his other hand he simultaneously pushed the "on" button on the phone. In court, he always referred to his opponent as "the prosecutor." But now, Ted couldn't punch the man's home phone number fast enough.

He brought the phone to his ear and listened to it ring.

Pick up! Damn it! Pick up!

"Hello?" said a groggy voice on the other end.

"Brian," Ted bellowed. "I need you. Now!"

— ' c , —

Clyde half woke up, groggy. She was moving, subtly jouncing, a steady hum droning in her ears. She groaned. A heavy strap was digging into her clavicle. She opened her eyes—or were they already open? She couldn't see.

"Where am I?" she said.

"I thought you should be with someone you love on Valentine's day," a voice said.

"Ted?" she asked.

She now realized something was covering her eyes, and she could not move her hands.

"No, Ted's at work, *honeeee*." The word had an eerie quality. The man speaking it drew out the last syllable like a vocal exercise. She had heard something like that before, but in her stupor, she couldn't place it.

Not only was something covering her eyes, it was covering her face, too. She sighed deeply.

CHAPTER 3

Groggy, Clydene opened her eyes a slit, squinting at an unfinished plywood wall. In the center of it, large, metal hinges fastened a make-shift door of thick plywood. Mismatched cardboard boxes lay stacked in irregular piles on the plain concrete floor. A dingy, yellow light alone illuminated the space, clearly a basement storage room of some sort.

She asked "Where am I?" but heavy, sticky tape held her mouth shut, and all that came out was "Hmmm *hm* hmm." Now she noticed heavy duct tape binding her hands to the chair in which she was sitting. And she couldn't move her legs, because something—probably the same heavy, sticky tape—also bound her ankles to the legs of the chair.

Something touched her cheek from behind, brushed her hair back. She whipped her head around to see, and there he stood, towering, hanging over her, wearing a jack-o-lantern grin, flames of titian hair lapping the space above his head, a grotesque scar mutilating his left cheek.

"You finally woke up. You had a nice, long nap, *honeeee.*"

He ran his finger, lightly, down her neck. Clyde felt its touch deep within her, poking nausea into her gut. She did not move, but she felt her teeth fight to gnash under the heavy, cloth tape. He continued down, across her clavicle, and over her white blouse. He stopped to hover at her right breast. Clyde froze.

"I felt it," the man continued. "There was a connection between us. It was spiritual. You felt it too, right?"

Clyde said nothing, just stared. But inside, she wanted to get out of there. She wanted Ted to storm through that door, bust it off its hinges, put this psychopath in his place. But if Ted had been with her, none of this would have happened.

"Oh, silly me." The psychopath giggled. "You can't talk with this, can you?" And in one motion he grabbed the tape and ripped it from her face, leaving a stinging on her cheek, and a feeling as though Clyde's upper lip had been pulled apart. She ignored the feeling, stared at her attacker, as though by the sheer power of her glare she could do what her absentee husband had not been available to accomplish.

The man knelt down next to her and petted her cheek and forehead, running his fingers through her hair.

Clyde shuddered. *No,* she thought. *I will not give him the satisfaction. I will not give in, and I will not cry. No matter what he does, I will not cry...* She gritted her teeth.

"Don't worry," he said. "It will be our little secret. No one will find out how we feel about each other."

All at once, without thinking, Clyde lashed out with the only part of her body that was unbound, her teeth. She grabbed onto his hand or forearm, she wasn't sure which, and she sunk into his flesh as though she were biting into a juicy, red apple. But the texture was chewy, and the juice was salty. Still the feeling was just as sweet. She grabbed onto him with the tenacity of a pit bull. She thrashed her head from side to side, like a shark hungry for a snack.

He may have cried out in pain. She wasn't listening. He may have begged her to stop, may have even threatened her. But Clyde's ears were closed.

Suddenly, something whacked her her on the right side of

her head. Then again. Clyde released her hold on her prey.

"Bitch!" he screamed at her. He examined his right arm where Clyde had bit him. Blood trickled from the wound.

She couldn't tell how deep it was, but it was bleeding pretty profusely. Clyde felt a twinge of malevolent satisfaction, and she grinned slightly.

"Why did you do that?" the man asked.

Clyde saw that he looked sincerely sad, and she began to think that maybe his psychological problems were more complicated. Clyde couldn't believe it herself, but she actually felt a little sorry for the guy.

"Should have that looked into," she said. Maybe she was sorry, just a little, for hurting him. After all, he hadn't physically harmed her, but it looked like he might need stitches. Or maybe she just wanted to find some way to connect with him, maybe get him talking about himself, find out what makes him tick, figure out some way to convince him to let her go.

He glared at her. "What's that supposed to mean?" he demanded.

His tone did not set Clyde at ease. On the contrary, she felt apprehensive about saying anything. Clearly, whatever this guy's problems were, they were too much for Clyde to understand or to handle.

"I just meant that if you don't have it treated, you'll end up with another scar."

Clyde immediately felt as if she had said something wrong, although she didn't know what, how, or why.

He snarled, "You're one of those, aren't you?"

Clyde was on the verge of panic.

His demeanor became suddenly calm, almost Zen-like. "No one ever mentions my scar unless they're making fun of me. To normal people, it's invisible. That's only polite, after all." He shook his head. "I thought you were nicer than that."

Without another word, he lumbered over to the door,

pulled it open, and left. He had left the light on, and Clyde heard a clacking through the door that could have been a padlock being latched shut. Clyde worked at her bonds, but the tape was firmly wound around her wrists and ankles, and she made only modest gains. She thought heard people walking on a wooden floor nearby. Maybe she was in a public building. Clyde shouted as loudly as she could, hoping someone would hear her and come to her rescue, but all she accomplished was to make her throat hoarse.

Innumerable minutes or hours passed, and Clyde heard another clacking at the storage room door. The man entered, a white bandage wrapped around his arm. He closed the door and latched it. In all that time, Clyde had only slightly loosened her bonds. Her arms felt tired from struggling, and her wrists felt raw from rubbing against the duct tape.

Without preamble, he said, "Let's start with something simple. What's your name?"

Clyde said nothing, not wanting to cooperate. If he couldn't remember the name of his victim, she wasn't going to help.

He peered at her. "Did you understand the question?"

Clyde stared at her interrogator, not knowing what would come next, but knowing now more than ever that she should never have felt sorry for him. And that she must never give him the satisfaction of thinking that she ever did.

"Okay," he said. "Let's try again." He strode over to her, and for the first time, she noticed that he decidedly did *not* walk with a limp. Without warning he raised his hand and brought it down across her face, hard.

Clyde felt the sting of his handprint across her cheek. She flinched. Then she glared back at her attacker.

He calmly strolled to the other side of the room and began to remove his belt. Clyde only half imagined what this meant, but she refused to let herself be intimidated.

"Let me show you," he said, "what will happen if I don't

get the right answer." He folded the belt in half. Holding the ends in one hand, the fold in the other, he pulled his hands rapidly apart, causing the belt to let out a sharp snap. The interrogator walked up to Clyde and snapped the belt again, this time right in front of her face.

The sound rang in her ears, and she blinked. She hissed, "You can't intimidate me."

"We'll see," he said. Then he enunciated each word: "What is your name?"

— ' c , —

Ted stared at the linoleum of the kitchen floor. He followed a line in the tiled pattern up, over to the right, then diagonally until it met its mirror image, over some more, and up, another diagonal jaunt, and the journey started all over again.

"Ted, I need to you focus," a diminutive, balding man said. He wore a white polo shirt and blue jeans, and he spoke with a thin drawl that made him sound like he had something to hide.

"Hrm," Ted grunted. He desperately needed to distract himself, from the interrogation in which he was currently engaged, from the numerous investigators stomping through the house, from the fear and fury building within his gut.

"Do you know where he might have taken her?"

Ted felt his blood pressure rising. "If I knew that, don't you think I would be there right now?" He suddenly realized he was shouting.

"Okay," the man said, "you don't need to bite my head off."

Ted grunted again. "Nothing else seems to work," he muttered.

The little man either didn't hear or didn't care. He said, "I hope you aren't trying to protect your client, because you know you can break privilege for this."

"Only if I have actual or constructive knowledge that he intends to harm someone." Ted immersed himself in legal jargon, because it allowed him to distance himself from the situation he was in.

"We found fingerprints. We have the rag. How much more 'constructive' do you want?"

Rage took Ted's words and turned them into inarticulate sounds. With great effort, he unclenched his teeth. "Brian, I called you, because you know his habits better than I do. Until tonight, I didn't even know..." Ted rubbed his eyes with the fingers and thumb of one hand. "You're the expert. You tell *me* where he is."

"Okay." Brian stood up and began to head toward the next room, where investigators were still scouring the house for trace evidence.

"And then I want you to take me to him," Ted added.

"I don't think—"

"I want to be there," Ted repeated.

Brian simply sighed.

"Hey," said a familiar voice.

Ted looked up to see Michael entering the room.

"This better be good," Michael continued, clearly annoyed.

Brian interjected before exiting, "Oh, I think it is. You see if you can do anything with him."

"What are you doing here?" Ted spoke with an edginess that reflected his anger, anger first at the situation, and anger now at the fact that someone had brought Michael into it.

Michael began. "I was in the middle of the best date of my life—"

"Every date is the best date of your life," Ted scoffed. "Brunette or blonde?"

"Redhead, with freckles. And some guy with a pole up his butt and a starched shirt so stiff I could hear it ruffling on the other end of the phone calls me and says I need to get myself down here as fast as I can before you get yourself arrested."

Ted breathed. "Let me get you some coffee." He rose and marched to the other side of the kitchen, where the coffee maker sat on a counter. If only he kept busy, he could distract himself.

"Where's Clyde?" Michael asked.

"She's not home right now." Ted gritted his teeth, breathed again, removed the carafe from the machine, brought it to the sink, and began to rinse it out.

"Well, maybe we should call her?" Michael said tentatively.

Ted suddenly, involuntarily, brought the carafe smashing into the bottom of the sink. It boomed and crashed, as shards of tempered glass went flying.

"Okay, that's enough," Michael intoned firmly. "You are going to sit down and tell me what's going on."

Ted didn't move. In an uncharacteristic moment, he neither moved nor thought. He saw the fragments of glass in the sink, on the counter. He knew some lay on the floor, too. He didn't care. His conscious mind had shut down.

"Do it now," Michael instructed. "Walk to the table, and sit. Or else." He left the thought unfinished.

Ted complied, sat in the chair next to the window. As he sat, Michael took the carafe handle from his hand. Ted hadn't even realized he was still holding it.

Michael sat across from him. "Where's Clyde?" he asked, his voice remaining firm.

"I don't know."

"Okay, what *do* you know?"

"She's..." Ted couldn't make himself say the word.

"Go on," Michael urged.

Ted breathed again, and he forced his mouth to move. "... kidnapped."

Michael didn't even seem to blink. "Why do I get the idea that you know who the kidnapper is?"

Ted nodded and swallowed. He breathed again, refusing himself the right to worry. "A client of mine—*former* client."

"Where does he hang out? Who does he know?"

Ted shook his head and swallowed again. He refused to feel sad. He looked into Michael's captivating eyes, and it suddenly struck him how very blue those eyes were. "I don't know anything about him," Ted replied. "Only the case."

Michael regarded Ted for a moment. Then he nodded. "Okay, maybe something will occur to you. I want you to sit here and try to remember people or places he might have mentioned, who might know where he is. Can you do that?"

Ted's conscious mind shut down again. He just stared at his friend.

"Can you do that?" Michael repeated.

Ted nodded slowly. "Yes," he said.

— ' c , —

At the sound of the doorbell, Clyde glanced at the clock.

"Oh no," she said.

"What's the matter," Mira asked.

"I didn't realize the time. It's getting late." Her whole face felt tight.

"I'm sorry," Mira said.

Clyde relaxed her expression. "Don't apologize," she said sweetly. "You did nothing wrong."

The doorbell sounded again. After a moment's pause, Mira said, "Maybe you should get that."

"Right," Clyde said. She strode to the front door and pulled it open.

Michael entered. "Oh," he said noticing Mira sitting in the living room.

"Yeah," Clyde said. "We were just chatting about Ike."

Mira glared at her. She immediately regretted mentioning Ike.

Michael rolled his eyes and sang, "He's baaaack."

Mira shook her head. "Okay, whatever. I have to get back to work." She grabbed her coat, and Clyde chased her out the door.

"I'm sorry, Mira. I didn't mean—"

"It's okay, Clyde. I'm not mad at you. I promise."

"You know he's only that way because—"

"Because I refuse to be one of his bimbos."

"That's not fair," Clyde said.

Mira spoke sharply. "Clydene, when it comes to relationships, Michael lives a life Aristippus would have envied."

Clyde didn't know what that meant.

Mira closed her eyes a moment. "In other words, he's a self-centered, hedonist."

"Oh."

"Don't you ever wonder why he's still a bachelor, at his age?"

"You're almost the same age," Clyde reminded her.

"Okay, but at least I'm trying to do something about it."

Suddenly, Clyde saw it in her friends eyes. "You are in love."

Mira didn't answer.

"Just find out how he feels," Clyde reiterated.

Mira grunted and marched off without looking back.

Back inside, Clyde found Michael browsing the books on the coffee table, and she tore into him. "'He's back'?! What were you thinking?"

"That guy is trouble. And he always gets Mira into trouble."

"So you came over here to make some trouble of your own?"

"No, I came over because you asked me to."

Clyde didn't feel like talking anymore, but she needed to. She breathed deeply and exhaled slowly. "You said I could tell you if I got another tip about Baedes, and you might be able to help?"

"You've heard something?"

Clyde nodded. "Baedes is holding back evidence in one of Ted's cases."

"What do you mean?" Michael looked confused.

"I mean, he has a forensics report the D.A. doesn't know exists. He's keeping it a secret, and it would exonerate one of Ted's clients."

Clyde added, "Baedes is after us."

"Okay. This is not news."

"No, I mean, he's been interrogating suspects, fishing for leads on Ted and Mira, corrupting the process to make life difficult for them and anyone connected with them."

Michael smirked. "More ammunition for the publicity machine."

That remark horrified Clyde. "No, I don't think you understand. He only started doing this after I leaked information that got Mira out, last Fall."

Michael regarded her. "*You* were the source of the leak?"

"Yes."

"So you have an inside contact."

"No," Clyde said. She waited a moment, because part of her didn't want to go on, but she was already committed, so she might as well reveal all. "I cracked into their computer systems."

Michael nodded. "Brilliant," he said.

Clyde continued, "Baedes keeps notes on everything he does. He's a compulsive note-taker. I get copies. He's been looking for *me*, and blaming everyone else..." Clyde felt the corners of her mouth turn involuntarily downward.

Michael said, "And how do you feel about that?"

Clydene held back the flood of tears she felt pressing from inside of her eyes. She didn't really know where it came from.

"I don't know," she said. "How should I feel? Angry?

Guilty? Sorry?— I don't know how to feel." Then she asked, "How should I feel?" She heard her voice distorted by her facial muscles, involuntarily contorting.

"Beady-eyes is not the first bully I've had to face," Michael said. "And there's only one way to deal with a bully. You have to make him believe that you can beat him up, and that you will if you need to. No wonder the jerk is freaked. You've made him vulnerable. So how should you feel? You should feel like you're making a difference. He tramples everyone, and will continue to, no matter what you do. But you have it within your hands to give the innocent a chance."

Something about these words touched Clyde deep within, and sudden wailing tears mapped rivers on her cheeks. Michael sidled up next to her, wrapped his arm around her shoulders. She rested her cheek against the rough fabric of his denim jacket, and for a few minutes drenched it with her tears. She convulsed in irregular bursts of sorrow she herself didn't completely understand, a flood of pure emotion pent up, agitated, like a can of seltzer, then finally released, and now it was spewing everywhere. She finally got out the words, "I just don't know what to do."

"Here's what you do," Michael said. "You keep an eye on what's happening. You do what you can without getting caught. And you *never* let anyone else know what you're up to. Does Ted know?"

Clyde shook her head. She was still sniffling, but paying attention to every word Michael uttered.

"Then don't tell him. He doesn't need to know, so keep him out of it. We don't want to make him complicit, because that would just compromise him.

"Besides," Michael added, "you know how he feels about following the rules."

Clyde nodded.

"Unfortunately, in this case, the rules are useless. Get any information you can. I'll make a few inquiries— I can't go into details—and neither should you, unless you actually need to— but I'll find out what I can. Whatever we uncover, maybe we can get it to Ted. But the first rule has to be secrecy. Don't tell anyone what you're up to. Only reveal information on a need-to-know basis, okay?"

Clyde nodded quietly. Her head was floating in fluid, but for some reason, she felt better.

"How are you at making up cover stories on the fly?"

Clyde was no good at thinking up lies, especially not under pressure. She was as transparent as a piece of glass.

Michael seemed to know the answer to his question. "You should always have a cover story prepared, in case you're discovered doing something you're not supposed to. It doesn't have to be perfect. It usually only has to be good enough to confuse the person you're talking to until you can escape or change the subject."

With the word *escape,* the enormity of what Clyde had gotten herself into hit her.

At that moment, the front door opened, and Ted, staring at Clydene and Michael, Michael's arm still wrapped around her shoulder.

Michael looked over and said, "Hey, Ted. Good that you're here." He patted Clyde on the back and stood.

"What's going on?" Ted asked.

"I dropped by to see you," Michael explained. "But Clyde and I got to talking." He continued, "You should talk to her."

"Why? What's this about?"

Michael ignored the question. "What I wanted to talk to about can wait. So I should let you guys talk." He began walking toward the door.

"What made you think I would be here?" Ted asked.

"I called your office, and they said you were out."

"So what? That doesn't mean I would be home."

"Where else would you be?" Michael said.

"I had a meeting," Ted explained.

"Oh. Well, I guess I assumed you'd be home." Michael eyed him carefully before they said their final goodbyes.

During all this, Clyde was desperately trying to think up a story that would jibe with Michael's *and* would explain why her eyes were puffy and read and why she had been obviously crying on Michael's shoulder.

After Michael had left, Ted turned to his wife. His voice was suddenly concerned, as if he had just noticed she had been crying. "What's wrong? What happened?"

"I think I'm pregnant," Clyde heard herself say.

CHAPTER 4

From the defendant's table, Ted watched Nona Williams take the stand. A tailored jacket showed off her well proportioned figure, and a gray, tweed, mid-length skirt showed off her shapely legs. A bailiff swore her in, and in response to the oath, she intoned, "I do." She took a moment before being seated. Her straight, yellow hair flowed around lightly freckled, porcelain cheeks. Pale eyebrows hung over eyes of brown, looking down a simple, straight nose at Ted and the Italian-American seated next to him. Despite her snobbish vibe, Ted understood what young Anthony saw in her. Even marred, her beauty filled the room. A butterfly bandage held together the skin above her right eyebrow, and a purple bruise covered her chin and left jaw. Still, her natural radiance shone through. Neither did her upper lip, still swollen, affect her speech. She spoke elegantly, with grace and authority, as a woman of class and etiquette.

Press packed the gallery, which Ted had expected. Nona Williams was the daughter of town selectman Gerald Williams, who had built a real-estate management empire before getting into politics. It was said that the Williams family owned half the town. As a result, the story of Nona's assault and Anthony's arrest remained discrete only not even until the day that charges were filed.

Next to Ted sat Anthony Giordano. Anthony's parents occupied gallery seats just behind them. Ted had explained to them all that Miss Williams would take the stand, would look and sound sympathetic, would tear into Anthony, might even lie. But Ted would have his say, and they had to trust Ted to deal with the situation. Ted knew that Rico had a short temper and loved his son, and Ted needed him to keep control.

The Assistant District Attorney trying the case was a short, balding man named Brian Chambers. He and Ted used to be cordial, if not friendly. But over the years, their cordiality had morphed into antagonism. Brian's boss constantly pressured him to put suspected criminals away for longer and longer sentences, an objective that Ted took great satisfaction in thwarting, even if they were guilty. Meanwhile, Brian's cozy relationship with Baedes made Ted sometimes angry and always suspicious. Now, whenever Ted and Brian went head to head, the case was no longer just a job. They both took the battle personally, and both took losing personally.

Brian Chambers asked Miss Williams to describe the events of two nights ago. She began:

"I was at home, reading. At between ten-thirty and eleven o'clock, someone rang my apartment, from the front door of my building." She looked for approval from the prosecutor.

"Go on," he said.

"Well, I suppose it was a stupid thing to do, but I was expecting a visit from my suitor, Paul Randolph, sitting over there." She pointed to a well dressed, grim-faced, young man seated in the gallery.

Brian Chambers prompted her, "You were expecting a visit from Mr. Randolph, so what did you do when you heard the buzzing from the front door?"

"I pushed the button to open the front door. I didn't first ask who was there, because I assumed it was Paul."

"Then what happened?"

"I opened the door to my apartment so that he could get in, and I sat back down on the couch to continue with a book I had been reading. I was deeply involved in reading when someone entered the room. Naturally, I thought it was Paul." She paused at this point in the story.

"But it wasn't Paul, was it?"

"No," she said.

"Who had entered your apartment?"

She delayed before answering. She inhaled, a short, sharp breath. "He did," pointing at Anthony. "The defendant."

Brian Chambers spoke with sympathy. "What did you do when you realized who was there?"

"I began to run to the phone to call the police."

"You didn't ask the man who he was or what he wanted?"

"Well, he was coming at me, and he grabbed me before I could get to the phone. And then—" She choked up.

The prosecutor placed his hand on her forearm. "When you're ready, tell us, what then?"

The young woman took a deep, uneven breath. She swallowed and stared at the ceiling, to her left, away from Anthony and his lawyer.

"He grabbed my hair and threw me against the table. Then he pulled me up and threw me against the wall."

She returned her gaze to the prosecutor.

"I screamed, but he punched me in the face. I thought he was going to kill me."

She was visibly weeping now.

"I begged him to stop, told him it wasn't my fault. But he wouldn't listen. He hit me repeatedly."

The girl seemed about to bawl. Tears, genuine tears, flowed freely down her cheeks. But she didn't stop. Rather, her words became faster, louder, more intense. She looked to the ceiling again.

"I tried to fall. I tried to curl up, to cover myself. But he yanked me— He struck me again."

She brought her red-stained eyes square with the sad eyes of the prosecutor.

"He continued to strike me, pummeled me."

Brian said nothing. He simply waited.

She looked back up at the ceiling, this time at the opposite corner, above where Ted and Anthony were seated.

"He pushed me to the floor. He pulled down his pants, and he got on top of me. And he pushed his way up under my skirt. And he—" She swallowed. "He went inside me."

She closed her eyes for a moment, then returned her gaze to Brian Chambers. "I don't really remember what happened after that. The next thing I remember, Paul talking on the phone to an emergency operator, and then an ambulance arrived and took me to the hospital."

Brian nodded, patted her on the arm, said, "Thank you, Miss Williams." Then he sat down.

Ted rose. "Your Honor, I suggest we take a short break."

"No. I'm ready now," she interrupted. She was patting her eye with a tissue.

"Your Honor," Ted pleaded.

Judge Spiller, who had been quietly observing the proceedings, now spoke. "We'll recess until after lunch. Reconvene at 1:30." He banged his gavel.

Ted ushered Anthony and his parents toward a witness room. On the way, several reporters tried unsuccessfully to get a quote, and several cameras did get a shot. Ted silently held the door, as the family entered the private room.

Rico began the discussion. "She's lying."

His wife, clearly upset, seemed to doubt. "But those things," she said. "Those things happened."

Rico gazed warmly at her. "But Anthony didn't do them."

"You're right of course," Ted said.

Rico eyeballed Ted hopefully. "You believe me, then?"

Ted explained. "I believe that she made up the part about her being raped. Because of her eyes. It wasn't recorded in the record, but I noticed her eyes. While she was telling her story, her eyes looked off in the same direction, toward the ceiling. But when she got to the part about Anthony, she looked in the opposite direction." Now he addressed Anthony. "We know that you and she were lovers, but we also know that you didn't do this to her. She's covering up for someone."

Before Anthony and his parents could process Ted's chain of logic, however, he commented, "Unfortunately, as far as the court is concerned, we would have more luck with pixie dust."

"So how do you prove it?" Anthony asked, his eyes so full of worry that even Ted could see it.

"I had a private investigator check out your story," Ted said confidently. "Don't worry. We can prove it."

— ' c , —

After lunch, Ted stood, buttoned his suit, casually approached the witness stand, in which Nona Williams once again sat.

"Miss Williams, you testified that when you saw my client in your apartment, you immediately ran for the phone."

"Yes," she replied confidently.

"So then, you didn't know who he was."

"No." She shook her head as she said it.

"You didn't know him?"

"I didn't know him," she reaffirmed.

"You had never seen him before?"

"No."

"Never?"

"Objection," said the prosecutor. "Asked and answered."

Ted explained. "I just want to make sure we're crystal clear on this point, judge."

"I get the point, Mr. Jackson. Objection sustained. Please,

move it along," said the judge.

Ted pursed his lips and nodded. "Now, you see, that's funny."

"How so?" she asked. Even Ted could detect the smugness in her voice.

"At least three different people can place you with my client, in a restaurant in Palmer, earlier that very evening, between 7 and 8 o'clock."

Ted waited for a response, but she seemed tongue-tied.

Ted continued. "Perhaps you would like to amend your testimony."

"Well..." And then nothing.

"You do know that lying under oath is perjury."

"I'm not lying!" she suddenly exclaimed. "I don't know who they think they saw, but it wasn't me! Maybe he found someone who looked like me so he could stalk me and say I knew him, the pervert." She glared at Anthony.

Anthony remained stoic.

Ted continued. "I don't think so. But maybe if several eyewitnesses confused you and this mystery woman, maybe you mistook some other man for Mr. Giordano? Because he certainly wasn't at your apartment that night."

"I know what I saw," she insisted. "You don't forget—"

"How can you be so sure, if you had never seen him before?"

"You don't forget," she said. "And you're ignoring the DNA evidence. And if that all weren't enough, you can identify him from his scar."

"Beg pardon?" Ted asked.

"His scar," she repeated. "He has a scar on... on his *thing*."

A chuckle rippled through the room.

Frowning, she looked down her nose sideways at Ted, as though that were code for what she had just tried to say.

But Ted was unperturbed. "Hmm..." He shook his head

slowly. "The problem is, it seems your recent fame has gotten the better of you. As it turns out, everyone loves to talk about the famous. And if it involves a scandal..." Ted raised his eyebrows at her, as though he were speaking code right back at her.

"Objection," moaned the Assistant District Attorney, who had been sitting quietly, taking notes.

The judge said, "Sustained. Mr. Jackson, if you have a question, please ask it."

"If that wasn't you in the restaurant, I guess that also wasn't you who was seen waiting in a car at a nearby hotel later that night?"

"No!" She stared, aghast, back at Ted. "Do you mean to imply— How dare you?! You take that back!"

Now it was Ted's turn to glare smugly back at her. Or rather, he felt like glaring smugly, and he thought he had a right to. However, he had one more point, and he needed to look sympathetic to make it stick with the judge and the press.

"Nona," Ted said softly. "Who really did this to you?"

"He did!"

"No he didn't. Who are you covering for?"

"No one! He— I don't know."

"Miss Williams," Ted said, "we know that you and the defendant had sex that night. You're right: The DNA is in evidence. But we also know that it didn't happen in your apartment."

"No," she protested. "It happened just as I said."

"Someone hurt you, and once you were at the hospital, you had to claim that it wasn't consensual in order to cover up the fact that you and he were having an affair."

"No!" she repeated.

"Nona..." Ted sighed. "Nona,"—with his most compassionate face—"no one could blame you for wanting to cover that up, but an innocent man's future is at stake."

"Please don't call me Nona."

"Nona, how did this really happen to you?"

"Please call me 'Miss Williams.'" She frowned sternly and glared even more steeply down her nose. Once beautiful, now it appeared pointy.

Ted wasn't one for sentiment. But even he had to admit, this was sad.

— ' c , —

Mira lowered herself onto her chair, as Ike held it, brushing the back of her little black dress forward as she sat. The air smelled of garlic and Parmesan cheese. And candlelight cast flickering shadows on the white tablecloth and ceramic dishes. Ike sat across from her, modern gray suit, peach shirt, red-orange striped silk tie. A waiter named Giovanni arrived, asking if they would like to start with wine or an appetizer.

"Have you ever had escargot?" Ike asked.

"No." Mira was mildly amused. She didn't actually believe that snails were an aphrodisiac, but she felt feisty and enjoyed playing along.

Ike grinned handsomely. "Do you trust me?"

Mira grinned back. "Implicitly," she breathed, as seductively as she could muster.

Ike turned to the waiter. "Please bring us escargot for two, and a bottle Pinot Noir."

Mira was worried about the bill. Who was bankrolling this fancy dinner? Was Ike suddenly irresponsible with money? Or did he have an unknown source of cash? *Oh my God!* Mira thought. *I hope he didn't steal it.*

She spoke up. "I, uh, don't want to spoil the mood."

"Okay," Ike said. "So don't, then." He chuckled.

Mira sighed. "Where are you getting the money to pay for this— *this?*" She opened her hands as if to wrap them around the table, to indicate what *this* was.

"I have a job," Ike said, clearly perturbed.

"Yeah, I know." Mira began to feel a tightness in her chest. "I just meant... This is really extravagant. Are you sure it's alright?" Her countenance reflected her distress.

Ike's expression relaxed. "Yes, it's fine. It's a special occasion with a special woman. I've got it covered." Then he added, "Trust me. You said you did, right?"

"Yes," Mira agreed. "Okay, but just promise me you haven't done anything that will get you into trouble."

He chuckled again. "I promise," he replied sweetly.

The wine was smooth, soft, earthy, and full. The escargot tasted like garlic-and-butter gummy worms. Mira gathered, that was how snails were supposed to taste, at least when they were cooked in garlic and butter. For an entrée, they each had the Chicken Parmesan with ziti. They talked about other strange foods, table manners, people who annoy you at parties, embarrassing episodes from their pasts, and anything else that could deepen Mira's feelings without forcing her to ask about Ike's. Mira told herself that she didn't want to plunge into that discussion until later, even though she had promised herself that before the night was over, she would ask him how he really felt. Therefore, "later" couldn't last forever.

Clyde had elicited that promise from her. Mira needed to promise Clyde, because she was terrified of the answer. She was terrified that Ike would see in her eyes how deeply he had won her, and that he would freak out and bolt. She was terrified that he might say they were just having fun and that they shouldn't get too attached. She was afraid that if she didn't ask, he would decide later that they were "just having fun," and she would get hurt. She had been here before. She had been here before with Ike, though he didn't know it. Most of all, she feared he would shun the danger she represented, because anyone who got involved with her was in danger of being charged with a crime, and Ike was still technically on probation, still vulnerable to threats Baedes could make.

Mira was terrified, so she put off the uncomfortable subject as long as she could. But by the time they were each sipping a cappuccino and sharing a tiramisù, Mira knew she needed to address the issue.

"Something wrong with the tiramisù?" Ike interrupted her thoughts, and Mira suddenly realized she had been daydreaming.

"No, everything's wonderful." She forced herself to smile.

"You look sad," Ike said.

"I'm sorry. I just—" Mira searched for words.

"You wish it didn't have to end?" Ike gazed hopefully.

"Yes, kind of, but—"

"It doesn't have to end," Ike said. He reached across the table and caressed the back of Mira's hand with his fingers.

"Do you love me?" Mira blurted, suddenly overcome.

If Mira didn't have Ike's full attention, she had it now. He pulled his hand back, and a look of dismay covered his face.

"I'm sorry," Mira said. "I shouldn't have... Forget it."

Ike said, "I like you, Mira. I like you a lot. I want to spend time with you. I—" He paused. "I don't know if—"

"That's okay," Mira said. "I get it." She could feel her face burning red. She began to stand.

"Wait," Ike said, and touched her hand again. "Please."

His cavernous eyes pleaded with her.

Ike continued. "Can't we take it slow? Just get to know each other? At least for a short while? It's important to me."

Mira could see that he was sincere, desperate even.

"I— I'm afraid," Mira admitted.

Ike considered this. "Is that why you were so upset about kissing me yesterday?"

Mira nodded.

"I don't want to hurt you," he said.

"I know." But Mira knew that didn't change anything.

"At least let me drive you home."

Mira hesitated. But when she stared into his desperate eyes, she finally consented.

Ike paid the bill, helped Mira on with her coat, walked her out to his car, opened the passenger's door. He placed his hand on her upper back as she was about to step into the car. She stopped, felt the pressure of his hand through her coat. His touch. A simple touch. How could such a simple thing evoke such powerful emotions? Mira felt her eyes begin to well up. Ike wrapped his arms around her and pulled her to his chest. She tried to push away, but he tenderly shushed her, caressed her hair. She could feel him weeping, too, deep inside his chest.

"If you only knew, Mira," he said. Then he whispered, "But I'm trouble, I've always been trouble. You don't want to be with me." He was crying. "You should leave, just leave, and save yourself."

— ' c , —

When the evil man threatened Clyde again, threatened to strike her unless she told him her name, she grumbled, "You already know my name," which was true.

Unfortunately, that was not the answer he was looking for.

Still reeling from the sting of his strap on her left forearm, she heard him ask again, "What's your name?"

"My name is Justice," she scoffed. It sounded stupid coming out of her mouth, but she was on a roll and unwilling to admit she sounded stupid. "I'm going to come after you and tear you to shreds, you little bug."

He just sneered, with a maniacal laugh that said he thought he was beyond the reach of anything so puny and insignificant as her. "Do you think I've never done this before? I know exactly what I'm doing. That's why they can't catch me. I even leave them little clues. But they'll never catch up to me. And you won't catch up to me either, my *deeeer*."

Clyde snarled, "I bet that's how you got that gash across your face. Someone caught up to you. Am I right?!"

That was also not the answer he wanted. Clyde clenched her teeth, her fists, panted against repeated stings of his strap. A tear ran down her cheek.

He wiped away the tear. "My *Deeeer*, please don't do this. I don't you to get hurt. But you must admit what you feel and what you want. And this is the only way. Please make it easy on yourself. Cooperate. Answer my question. A simple question. Your name. That's all I want. What is it?"

Why should she hold out for this? He already knew her name. If she answered, she would not actually be revealing anything to him. The information would not profit him any. Why should she not tell him what he wanted to hear?

"Clyde," she said. That was her first mistake.

It was also not the answer he wanted to hear.

"Clydene." She tried again, desperately wanting to ignore the stinging in her right arm now.

Still the wrong answer. She got the strap across her face.

What the hell is wrong with this pervert? Clyde seethed.

"Go to hell!" she yelled through clenched teethe.

That was definitely not the right answer.

The blows continued. The strike across the left side of her neck was the first that made her scream. And to avoid crying, she began to fume. She spat at him. With renewed strength she pulled at her bonds. She imagined that if she only tried hard enough, she could bite him again, this time for good. She conjured up every one of the basest obscenities a good Christian girl might ever have heard and blasted them at his ugly, scar-marred face.

None of it did any good.

A brief respite. Still seething, Clyde ached, burned. Her heart beat fast and hard. She breathed as fast as she could.

Anger gave way to panic. She had worked herself into a tizzy, and she needed to calm herself down. But she didn't want to be calm. She wanted to be angry. It was the only way she knew to fight back.

The assaulter grabbed her hair with one hand and pulled back her head until she could reach neither to the right nor left. So she spat at him. She felt her heart go thump-thump through her scalp.

With his other hand he ripped her blouse open at the front.

Her chest heaved up and down with each hyperventilating breath.

He let go, strolled behind her, came back with a pocket knife, which he pulled open. The sharp edge of the blade traced a smooth, menacing arc from the pinpoint tip down to its base. He pointed the knife at Clyde's throat. "Let's try this *agayyyyn*," he said.

She breathed quickly and heavily. Panic set fully in now, and she struggled to calm herself.

"Okay," she said as soothingly as she could muster. "If you tell me what you want to know, I'll do my best to tell you."

He grinned, brushed the knife softly up Clyde's throat. She dared not move. She tried to hold her breath, but to little avail.

"Don't make me slip," he warned, still in that same cool, menacing voice. Holding the knife still to her throat with one hand, with the other, he caressed her torso.

Clyde closed her eyes and winced, but did not struggle, felt her heart thump-thump, thump-thump, like Poe at 78 RPM.

Gently, tenderly, the knife still pressed to her throat, his arm embracing her, his hand at her back. She had been arching her back, without realizing, leaving enough room for his hand between her and the back of the chair. Still, eyes closed, she dared not move, even as he unhooked her brassiere, even as she felt the cool air upon her naked breasts, even as she heard him sigh with pleasure. She fought nausea, but she dared not move. She felt seasick. Indeed, worse than seasick.

Once, when she was in college, a date took her on a tour of Boston Harbor. He was an awful date, rich kid and proud of it, more interested in impressing her with his immense means than in being with her, and most interested in how she made him look. Fortunately, Clydene, who had never been on a ship before, developed acute nausea. She spent almost the entire tour hunched over, dizzy, holding in the bile, all of which gave her an excellent excuse to ignore her date.

Now, strapped to this chair, Clyde would have loved to have felt that good.

The knife left her throat, but Clyde still didn't want to open her eyes. She feared the shame and embarrassment she knew she would feel. She prayed a silent, desperate prayer for hope, and a lone tear trickled from her right eye.

"Let's try this again," he said calmly, no creepy drawl, as if he were a normal person. "You know what will happen if I don't get the answer I need. I don't want to hurt you. But unless you cooperate, you force me to do things I don't want to do."

"Just please tell me what you want me to say," Clyde managed, between breaths and quiet sobs.

"I need to know your full name," he said.

Clyde thought carefully, then spoke each word carefully. "Clydene Patrice Hobbes-Jackson," she said.

This was still not the correct answer.

— ' c , —

"You don't realize what this guy does," Ted told Michael. "If her story was true..."

Ted didn't want to consider the brave testimony of young Stacie Williams in Hill's rape trial. Fortunately for Hill's case, she had been confused. She had not seen his face, or couldn't recall it, yet couldn't remember whether he was wearing a mask or had drugged her. She couldn't clearly identify his voice or any of his physical characteristics. Her psychiatrist said she was suffering from post-traumatic stress disorder and that her mind had blocked out certain memories. This was convenient for his defense, because her testimony turned out to be the only evidence linking the crime to Ted's client. It was wonderful for him as a lawyer. But if even only a fraction of her story were true—

Ted couldn't think about that. He knew he didn't always show Clyde the appreciation or attention she deserved. But he also knew she was the only woman in the world who could put up with him and sympathize with him. And she was the only person to whom he'd ever truly opened himself. When he decided that he wanted to get married, there was only one—

He couldn't think about that right now, either. He told himself he needed to focus, to wrack his brain for some piece of information that would bring the police closer to where she had been taken. That's why, Ted told himself, he couldn't be distracted by sentiment. In reality, however, sentiment made Ted feel helpless, and Ted knew this.

"If her story was true... we need to get Clyde back."

He had been staring at the kitchen table. Ted wondered whether Michael was even still in the room, still listening to him, so quietly. All Ted could hear was an occasional footstep in the house, or an occasional voice, indistinct and distant. He looked up. His friend was indeed still there, still sitting across from him, eyes transfixed on him.

Michael, the man could be a wiseass sometimes, but sometimes he knew exactly how to listen.

Footsteps entered the kitchen, the footsteps of Brian Chambers. "Any more thoughts?" he asked.

Ted shook his head.

"Okay," Brian continued. "We're searching his apartment, and we're also checking out other places he's been known to frequent."

Ted nodded slowly, serenely.

"There's one more thing," Brian said kindly. "We discovered your wife's car abandoned a few miles down route 39. We think he transferred her to another vehicle and drove off. We've collected forensics, but we'd like you to take a look at the car, see if there's anything that looks out of place or missing."

Ted blew up at him. "What the hell is that supposed to accomplish?! How am *I* supposed to know if something is missing? I couldn't pick my wife's car out of a police line-up! And even if I could, so what? What we need to do is find out where *he* is, not where she left her groceries, or whatever she uses that car for." Ted felt sheepish, but he suppressed it. "I don't have time to be going out on useless excursions!"

Ted was standing, waving his arms around like a madman. When had he stood up?

"Ted," Michael said calmly. "If you find nothing, no harm done. But even if you find the littlest piece of evidence, it might help Clyde faster. And isn't that what you want?"

Ted remained silent.

"And the trip might also help jog your memory. Memories are like that. It's when you distract yourself with useless trivia, that's when something important pops up to the surface."

Ted stared at his friend, expressionless. He wanted to ignore all the evidence, didn't want to be involved unless it was to grab Gordon Hill by the neck and rip his head from his body with his bare hands.

"Let's go," he said.

CHAPTER 5

When Clydene awoke again, she didn't open her eyes. And she couldn't open her mouth. Nor could she move her arms. She had been clenching her teeth, it seemed, and struggling against her bonds so vigorously that there was no strength left in either her jaw or her arms. Or her legs, she now discovered. Her feet were tired. Toes, hands, fingers, all refused to move except with great effort. Frigid air rested on her hands, on her arms, on her feet and shins, on her chest, her torso, her calves. The chill touched every undisclosed crevice on her body, even those surfaces that still burned, and those that still bled. She left her eyelids down and tried to relax, tried to slow her breathing, even while she still struggled for oxygen in small, swift bursts, in-out, in-out, in-out. But bile churned from the bottom of her stomach. She was suffocating in her own panic, and despite her best efforts, she could do nothing to stop it.

The man was still there. Clyde felt his presence in the room, felt him staring, intruding into the intimate.

He said, "I've always loved freckles." He sighed.

Clyde felt his finger, or something—if it was anything but a finger, she didn't want to know—caress her shoulder, her chest, following the trail to where the freckles disappeared.

The man chuckled. "I'm sorry about the cold. In a moment, you'll be warm, and your purple lips will turn bright red again." He ran his finger across her lips. It smelled like sex. "Soon, everything will be all better. Trust me."

Wishing the things she felt were all part of a bad dream, yet knowing they were all real, Clyde begged, "Please," as best she could. "Need... doctor... Please." The words came out mumbled, because her jaw refused to flex.

"*Sweeteeee*, only one doctor can fix what you've got wrong. This is the only way to get you better."

Clyde began to sob helplessness. "*Naaw...*" she wailed. She tried to shake her head, but it just flopped from side to side.

"Let's review, shall we," he said.

Clyde heard his footfalls on the concrete floor.

"Open your eyes," he ordered, calmly.

Clyde didn't want to. She hoped that if she just relaxed her eyelids and breathed as deeply as she could and brought her sobs under control that he would just leave her alone.

Smack! She heard him snap his belt at her, a warning slap.

She squinted in the brightness around her, beheld blurry shapes in the spacious room.

"All the way," he said.

She tried the best she could. The image was getting clearer. He still wore clothes, and his wounded arm was still bandaged. He still stood before her wielding a belt. And his open pocket knife was still lying on a nearby box, to remind her that he could use it any time he needed to.

"Let's review," he continued. "What is your name." He paced back and forth before her like an interrogator in a Nazi prison camp.

She struggled with the words. "Miss Clydene Patrice Hobbes, Sir."

"Good," he said. "And how old are you?"

Between pants and gasps of air, she managed, "Thirty-eight, Sir."

"Excellent!" he exclaimed with joyful enthusiasm. "See how easy this is?"

Clyde saw neither the joy nor the ease of any of it.

"And do you like it when I touch you?"

Clyde shuddered, involuntarily sobbing again. But she feared the consequences, so she lied. She managed to nod and moan a tearful assent.

"How long have you been alone?" he asked.

She knew the right answer: *Always*. Was this to be the summary of her life? To die alone, neglected, helpless, at the hands of a tormentor, an assaulter, a rapist, at the mercy of his twisted, psychotic fantasy? Where was law and justice? Where was her husband, her protector? Where was her savior?

She recalled to her mind the only thing she could think of that had kept her sane, allowed her to believe she was not alone, nor would ever be alone. A little Bible verse she had memorized when she was a teenager, as a result of those deep emotional upheavals all adolescents endure. Whenever it had seemed her life had been falling apart, she chanted it to herself to comfort herself. And now she recalled it to her mind, recited it with her lips, huffing and puffing and mumbling the words through tears, between gasps for air.

"Peace I leave with you, My peace I give to you; not as the world gives do I give to you. Let not your heart be troubled, neither let it be afraid."

She had not completed even the first sentence before she heard the first swish of the tormentor's strap. But she continued to recite it, repeatedly, even through sobs and tears.

— ' c , —

The cyclops eye of a bright, full moon stared down at Ted from halfway up the nighttime sky, illuminating the pavement, the gravel, the trees, the hubcaps of Clyde's blue Camry.

Brian had parked outside the perimeter, and Ted reluctantly regarded the vehicle, from a distance, Michael still by his side.

A police detective in a suit and tie handed Ted a pair of latex gloves, led them to the car, and opened the driver's side door. He scowled silently in Ted's direction as he motioned with his hand for Ted to enter.

Ted didn't want to look inside, though he neither knew nor cared why. He wanted to kick in the window, to rip the upholstery, to destroy, to burn. He set his teeth, walked up to the open door, stooped, and peered through. The overhead light lit up the passenger compartment. There was a steering wheel, two bucket seats, automatic shift stick between, everything one would expect to see. What exactly did they expect him to find, anyhow? Stolen jewelry? Missing unmentionables? Were they just trying to occupy him with useless hoo-ha? Or were they really that desperate for clues?

Ted donned the gloves, sat in the driver's seat, held the steering wheel, stretched out, scanned the dash. Nothing, nothing, and nothing, not that Ted would know the difference, because he never sat here.

"I never sit here," voicing the thought as soon as it occurred to him. "I shouldn't fit."

The unnamed police detective spoke. "You mean the seat should be moved up closer to the steering wheel?"

"Right." Ted nodded.

"That's consistent with the other evidence we've uncovered. He drove the car. What about the keys?"

"What about them?" Ted pawed at the ignition switch.

"They're in evidence," the detective answered. "But they were found in the ignition. Does she usually leave her keys in the ignition?"

"No. She usually keeps them in her purse."

At this point, the detective excused himself for a moment and went off to the side to talk to another officer.

Ted opened the glove compartment. He didn't know what he was looking for. He scanned the contents. Registration. Owner's manual. Miscellaneous papers. An old, portable CD player. For how long had that been collecting dust in there?

"Ted," Brian said.

He sat up and looked out of the car. The detective had returned.

Brian continued. "He drove off from here in another car. We've identified the car, and we located it."

Ted's eyes perked up at that news.

"It's parked at his apartment complex. But he's not in the apartment. We believe he's nearby."

Ted immediately knew where the perp had taken her. But he had to work out how to proceed. He couldn't just reveal that Scarface had once opined that the perfect place to bring a woman was his apartment storage area, that it was secure and remote, in a separate utility building. And no one ever went down there after dark. At the time, Ted discounted it, because it sounded like a joke in poor taste. But now...

In any case, Ted couldn't just tell Brian that he had known all along, somewhere in the back of his stress-wracked mind, what the answer always had been. Besides, Ted had to be there when the arrest went down. He owed that to Clyde, to be there to help her, and to see the perp, to stare him down, to let him know who had caught him. But the police were not going to let Ted in on the bust, not even with Brian's influence —and Brian would not even go along with the idea. It was just too ethically questionable.

Even Ted himself knew that he couldn't allow himself to compromise his reputation in that way. But he also couldn't allow himself to appear inept or stupid. And he couldn't violate attorney-client privilege, he told himself. So he needed to lead the cops personally to the right place without letting them know what his ultimate goal was.

"I'd like to look over the apartment site."

— ' c , —

In-between Saturday-morning coffee and email, Clyde
sneaked away with her cell phone. Ted had brought a suitcase
worth of work home with him the previous night, and he was
reclining in the den reading reports. On the bright side, she
and Ted got to spend Saturday morning together. The down
side was that Clyde needed to find an excuse to get away if
she wanted to be out of Ted's earshot.

"I'm going out for a little walk," she announced.

Ted glanced out the window. "The weather report said it
was going to be cold today."

"Yeah, I know." She lied. "But I just really feel like taking a
walk. Don't worry, I'll bundle up," she said as she lifted her
thick, winter jacket from the hook beside the front door.

Having donned the coat, she pecked Ted on the lips and
began opening the door. "I'll be back in 10 or 15 minutes."

"Hold on," he interrupted. "I think I'll join you."

"Uh— But it's cold out."

"Yes, but it's also sunny and clear, and I enjoy the
company." He grinned, shimmying by her in the hallway, and
grabbed his own coat from the hook.

"Um..." She was searching desperately for an excuse to
convince him to stay so that she could call Michael. "I was
going to make a business call, and I'd feel bad about ignoring
you."

"A business call on Saturday, Gracie?"

"Oh yes." Clyde thought for a moment. "Well, there's a
chance the person I need to talk to is available on Saturday."

"Alright," Ted said. "I won't be offended if you talk on the
phone." He brushed the hair from her ear.

"Right." Clyde gathered that he had won. She would have
to revise her plans to call Michael. But for now, she needed to

keep up the appearance that she needed to talk to a client. So she walked along with Ted, pretended to try to make a call, and discovered that she didn't have the phone number. She must have forgotten to add it to her cell phone.

The two walked along for a few minutes, down the private road they shared with several other homeowners, stepping through potholes the size of the Grand Canyon. A brisk, gentle breeze ruffled the trees, casting eerie, moving shadows across their path. Clyde thought it was silly that their road should be in such a state of disrepair, and that she should do some research to see what it would take to get the road resurfaced.

When they reached the end of the road, at Washington, across from the industrial park, Ted said, "I know you didn't need to make a business call. Why didn't you want me to walk with you? Who were you planning on talking to? Or who were you planning on meeting?"

Fear seized Clydene by the stomach. She hurriedly explained that indeed she did have a new client, Big Rose Shipping. They were in the process of deploying a new shipment tracking system, and she needed to get in touch with Jadon Biggs to go over a couple issues with the project. This story had the benefit of being completely true.

Ted didn't seem to notice, however. He said, "I've known about your clandestine rendezvous with my best friend, since November." He breathed in. "And I don't appreciate being lied to."

Clyde stared at him, confounded.

"At first I thought you were planning a surprise for the holidays. And when that came to naught, I assumed it was for New Years. But when the meetings continued and you both kept denying them, I knew something was up."

Still standing at the side of the road, on Washington Street, Clyde suddenly felt angry. "You hired a private detective!"

"That I did," Ted said.

Speechless with indignation, she faced him now and sputtered at his face, "How— could you?— I don't believe it!"

"I hardly believed it myself," Ted coolly remarked.

Now Clyde found her words. She pointed her finger in his face. "Look, you. How could you think that little of me?" She waved her hand at him. "God! After all we've been through, how could you even think that I—" Clyde felt sick to her stomach at the thought that anyone, must less her own husband, would entertain the thought of her in an illicit affair.

Ted was calmly listening.

Clyde had to pause, to regain her mental footing again, because of her outrage. She continued, "Yes, I've been meeting with Michael, and no, it has nothing to do with you, but I promised to love you and you only, and I've kept that promise. That you could even *think*, could even *consider* that I might— cheat? Oh my God! You're kidding! Right?"

Clyde's face was contorted into the shape of a pretzel.

Ted pursed his lips. "Everyone can see you."

Clyde didn't care. She flipped her middle finger at him, shouted one more epithet at him, and stormed back toward the house. Maybe, she thought, he actually was too much like Alan Shore.

— ' c , —

Clydene's whole body felt hot, even as the cool basement air wafted over it. Sweat rippled down her forehead and dripped from her nose. Nausea churned through her stomach. Dryness scorched her throat. Her head spun and pounded, and her thoughts phased into and out of sobriety. Breath continued to rush in and out. She couldn't stop breathing.

A hand wiped sweat and tears from her eye. It caressed her cheek and her lips.

"I know you don't want to admit the truth about how you feel," a voice said.

Clyde couldn't see who it was who spoke. The colors of the room blurred together into an intense, whirling whiteness. She could make out the words, however. And she recognized the touch on her lips, a touch that made her cry.

"It doesn't have to be like this," the voice continued. "I told you before, you can get out, if you just show me your good intentions. And you'll get some water to drink, too."

He ran his fingers across her lips.

"Kiss," he said. "Show me affection."

Clyde hesitated, not knowing how to process what her senses told her.

"It's the only way," the voice said. "Come on. I've never lied to you. Kiss me. Repair the damage you've done. You know how you feel about me."

Clyde's hands, feet, face were frozen from the inside.

"Shh," the voice whispered sweetly. "We don't want anyone to hear us. Suckle my finger, and they'll go away."

Like an automaton, Clydene obeyed, pursed her lips as the room imploded around her. A voice shouted an obscenity, and her lover was brutally wrenched from her.

"No," Clyde whimpered. She squeezed tears from her eyes. "Clyde! Clyde!"

Hands caressing her bruised, bleeding, once beautiful face.

A roar, like that of a lion.

A repeated pounding echoing in her ears.

A rough cloth covering her nakedness.

A tugging at her hands and feet.

A hand on her forehead.

A familiar voice: "Oh my God! She's burning up!"

Chuff. "Yeah, we need an ambulance..."

Meanwhile, Clyde collapsed in a puddle of her own sweat.

— ' c , —

Ted sat and watched his beloved sleep and listened to the now familiar *beep, beep, beep, beep* of the heart monitor.

When she had first arrived at the hospital, the monitor had been beeping twice as fast. The doctor had asked Ted a hundred questions, which Ted loathed to answer. But answer them he did, as best he could. She wasn't getting enough oxygen, the doctor explained using some 25-cent medical term with the word "malignant" in it. If that was supposed to ease Ted's stress level, it didn't work. But Ted was too tired to argue, and the doctor assured him that they had the situation under control and that she was going to be okay. It had been lucky, in fact, that they had gotten to her when they did.

Lucky. What an ironic choice of words.

Ted silently promised himself he would never again let himself be so distant—and clueless.

He admired Clydene's hand, a beautiful and delicate hand, now scratched and bruised. Her wrists were rubbed raw from her bonds. Almost every inch of the front of her body had been battered. He tenderly touched one of the only places still unmarred, her thumb.

Still asleep, she stole it away.

That's was good sign, Ted reminded himself. It meant she could move. When she had first arrived at the hospital, she had been almost paralyzed.

"She may not want you to touch her for awhile," a soft, woman's voice said.

He looked up to see a short but attractive young woman with raven hair, shoulder-length. She wore a white blouse and tan skirt, stylish and unpretentious, and she exuded confidence and authority as she walked.

She continued, "But she still needs you."

"And who are you?" Ted said, annoyed.

"I'm from the Sexual Assault Crisis Center."

"You have an answer to this crisis?" Ted stood, still annoyed, and stared down at her.

"No, I don't," she replied matter-of-factly.

"So why are you here?" Ted felt like shouting, but he was trying to keep his voice down. One moment, he had resolved to turn his life around, never to make the same mistakes again; the next moment, he sank deeply into depression; lather; rinse; repeat. But he could always resort to anger in order to maintain control over his feelings.

"Because," the woman said, "when she wakes up, she's going to think this was her fault, and she's going to be as angry at herself as you are at yourself."

Ted was nonplussed. He had never considered such an outlandish possibility, that Clyde would blame anyone other but him. In a split second, Ted listed all the reasons why it was his fault Clyde was in the hospital right now. He knew he did not deserve her, but he needed her, and he didn't know what to do to fix it, and he didn't like to feel helpless.

The woman continued. "You wouldn't think it, but believe it or not, that's the most likely outcome." She stared Ted in the eye. "That Clydene will think it's her fault."

Ted shook his head. "It's not her fault." He sat back down.

"Who's fault is it?" the woman asked.

Ted paused. "I don't know you well enough to answer that question, Miss—"

"Jayson. But please call me Mira."

— 'c, —

Ike waited in his gray coup in one corner of an empty parking lot of an empty shopping plaza. Another car drove up, a conservative blue sedan, and pulled up beside him, on his driver's side. Ike opened his door, got out, and then entered the passenger's side of the blue sedan. He shut the door.

"What do you have to report," said the close-cut, burly police chief from the driver's seat beside him.

"We've dated. She likes me, but she hasn't shared any

details with me. I don't know if she trusts me."

"Whether or not she trusts you, she's attached to you. Note how she was crying on your shoulder."

Ike now felt even more violated than he had been feeling. "You've been spying on me."

"Only to confirm that your reports are truthful."

"You don't trust me?"

"Only to a point. I've offered you a lot. I've offered you your freedom. And that would be very painful for you to lose. But Miss Jayson has some benefits she can offer you, that no man could counter-offer." Baedes looked knowingly at Ike and nodded slightly. "You know what I mean?"

Ike glared at him.

Baedes returned to looking out the windshield. "Anyhow, I needed insurance."

Ike felt violated, but there was nothing he could do about it. Baedes had him trapped, already had proof, contrived or not, that he had violated parole. And if Ike didn't do as the chief asked, Baedes would have him arrested, charged, convicted, and sentenced, all faster than he could defend himself.

"I'll help you get in, but I won't hurt her." That was Ike's version of having a backbone.

"This is bigger than her," the chief said. "It's bigger than you, bigger than me, bigger than all of us."

"What is?" Ike said.

"The specifics are unimportant," he said, Cancerman-style. "All I need from you is a little information. That's all. And you can have your life back."

— 'c , —

Ted and Anthony, Rico and his wife, Brian Chambers, Miss Nona Williams and her boyfriend, numerous reporters and onlookers, all listened as Judge Spiller spoke.

"The state's case is certainly very weak. The physical

evidence is neither contested nor conclusive. The primary prosecution witness has impeachable testimony and questionable motives. And we certainly have every reason to avoid putting the friends and families of the victim and the accused through any greater an ordeal than absolutely necessary, since their lives will be under the spotlight, the whole city watching, everyone on the edge of their seats, wondering how it will play out.

"I myself wonder how it will play out. And that perhaps is best reason to let this case go to trial, because if no one knows how it will play out, then the case is not cut and dry. And that indicates there is sufficient doubt as to the facts of this case that a jury must decide them. Furthermore, the evidence and testimony as presented would clearly ensure a conviction under the law, unless the defense can muster significant evidence against them.

"I therefore find that the prosecution's case does meet probable cause. Trial is scheduled for April 21."

The judge banged his gavel, as Anthony's mother began to tear up, as Anthony himself stared with a blank expression, as Ted began talking of next steps. And Nona Williams grinned with satisfaction, as her boyfriend scowled, ushering her past the reporters, into the hallway.

Privately, Ted thought, *My God, Anthony. You are so screwed.*

— ' c , —

One evening, many days later, the computer system that ran the police HQ security cameras crashed, bringing down the visual security system. No one even realized that it had crashed, which was not a problem, because the computer itself had a so-called watchdog circuit, which monitored the health of the software and rebooted the computer if it ever crashed. And that is indeed what happened.

But the process took one minute and 47 seconds. And there

was a nondescript gentleman who had been waiting for his friend, a cop called Dietrich. He was nondescript in that he could have been any young man, and no one would have been able to identify him. He had no outstanding features. He stood at an average height, had average hair and eyes, and had a face that instantly made you want to like him. If he had any distinguishing characteristic, it was how he was dressed. He wore jeans and a plain, navy T-shirt, and over his shirt he had donned a blue denim jacket. If anyone had to describe him, he would simply be known as "the man in blue."

This young man who was waiting for Dietrich, in the blue denim jacket and jeans, went by the name of Quincy Schneider, and he also happened to know a hard-boiled private investigator by the name of Corey Samson, who himself just happened to know Michael Kelley, Ted's friend, not only knew Michael, but also owed him a favor.

In the space of that one minute and 47 seconds, while the cameras were out, while everyone happened to be occupied with the last things they needed to finish before getting out of the office, Quincy Schneider stole away from the men's room, where he had been supposedly using the facilities, to nearby Sam Baedes's office. The office was clearly deserted and locked. While glancing to his left, to make sure no one could see him, Quincy Schneider deftly inserted a lock pick and tension wrench, gently twisting the wrench, sweeping the pick across the inside of the tumbler, poking at the lock pins. Within seconds, the door popped open.

Inside the office, the only light came from a partially blinded window looking out over the street. Quincy Schneider scanned the stacks of file cabinets. Donning a pair of latex gloves, which he had pulled from a pocket of his coat, he opened a drawer with the letter 'G' on it, for *Giordano*, but he found nothing he was looking for. He also tried 'W' for *Williams*. He tried another drawer, one that appeared to have case files in it, but again came up dry. He finally opened a nondescript, unlabeled drawer of a nondescript, unlabeled cabinet in the corner. It contained miscellaneous clutter and what appeared to be someone's dirty gym shorts. But behind the clutter were several file folders, miscellaneous receipts, some pages of hand-scrawled notes, field surveillance reports, and a suppressed report on the test results of some unidentified blood taken from the Nona Williams crime scene.

He quickly folded these pages and hid them in a pocket deep inside his jacket. From another pocket, he pulled a card, akin to a business calling card. In one corner was emblazoned a logo: an engraved, red letter, 'C'; and circling it, two tadpoles, one black, one white, or maybe spermatozoa, or more likely the yin and yang. On the rest of the face of the card, no name, no address, no phone number, only one simple but confusing sentence, printed in simple black ink a sans-serif font:

Your Conscience was here.

Bonus Extras

Movie and television studios have long taken to stuffing DVD's with interviews, behind-the-scenes featurettes, extra scenes, writer commentary, on-screen games, and every other piece of trivia that might possibly spark a fan's interest.

Why don't book publishers provide additional chapters, with the same idea? Yes, occasionally a volume will contain an extended preface, in which the author reveals the biographical significance of the work. That's hardly what I'm talking about.

Yes, pages cost money. Printing a book is not like stamping a DVD. Whether you have 2 hours of video or 5, a DVD still costs the same. I'm oversimplifying, but if you can fit it on a DVD, whether you fill it up or leave it empty, a DVD costs $X to make. So yeah, movie studios would fill up that extra, free space with whatever footage they can find. Books, not so. Each extra page makes the book more expensive. And neither readers nor publishers want to pay for needless pages. But that argument underestimates the value of those extra pages. Because most of the cost is in setting up and binding the book. Extra pages cost relatively little. And fans *love* extra stuff.

Therefore, in the spirit of the DVD, I've included two Bonus Extras. The first is a behind-the-scenes essay, entitled "Whatever Happened to Zorro?" about the inspiration and motivation behind the story of *Abe's Turn*. The second is a short story, a minisode if you will, "Recovery, Relapse, Relationship," in which Mira meets Clydene, just after the events of episode 4.

Granted, *Zorro* was neither a crime nor an espionage drama. *Zorro* was an action-adventure story. That's not the point. The point is that Zorro is more than just "a guy in a cape and a mask," as one reviewer gushed regarding the 1998 film *The Mask of Zorro*.

A guy in a cape and a mask? Oy vey!

I'm not talking about just the character Zorro. I'm talking about the *character type*, the concept of Zorro. Zorro is more than just a guy in a cape and a mask. Zorro is the great righter of wrongs, the outlaw who fights for justice against the corrupt with authority and power, the corrupt who abuses it to the detriment of the poor and weak.

By contrast, popular fiction of today—in prose, in film, on video—seems to have forgotten the character type. Gone are the Robin Hoods who steal from Prince John in order to feed the over-taxed masses, the television private-eyes who spend more time circumventing the police than they do working with them, the Huckleberry Finns who sneak runaway slaves past so-called justice to freedom, the Winston Smiths who reject the Newspeak of The Party and challenge the Thought Police, the Guy Montags who secretly circumvent those unfair laws they themselves have sworn to uphold, the Hawkeye Peirces who openly ridicule the government insanity in which they themselves have been violently forced to participate.

Because they are gone, I've found *Abe's Turn* exceedingly hard to categorize. I originally thought of it as a crime drama, but it doesn't fit the mold. Modern crime dramas revolve around the infallible cop and the evil suspect. The infallible cop jumps to conclusions, torments suspects to get information, and cuts corners, because he *just knows* who's guilty. He examines suspects through a microscope under which no one could look good. But he's never wrong. Or at least if he is, he says something profound, so that we all know he realizes how fallible he is, even though it never mitigates the brutality with which he does his job.

In too many modern crime dramas, the innocent person never needs to hide, never needs to run, never needs to lie, and never needs to talk to his lawyer first. The infallible cop, on the other hand, gets a "feeling" about a person's guilt or innocence, and he never arrests the wrong guy. Or if he does, at least he's sorry afterward, and everything is forgiven. Even so, if a suspect has ever been arrested before, for anything, even on bogus charges, it still proves his guilt.

Most disgraceful of all, in the modern crime drama, the infallible cop always digs up incontrovertible proof of the suspect's guilt, and that justifies the fact that he cut corners elsewhere. It makes me feel ill.

The modern crime drama feeds off of the worst of human nature: our hatred, our fear, our prejudice.

Other story genres also don't fit. The pattern in espionage stories, for example, is that either the hero is an agent of the CIA or the villain is a rogue that the CIA fears (or else is a drug lord). (See me roll my eyes?) Political fiction, on the other hand, assumes that the system itself works. (Yeah, right.) And adventures anymore are so often about just another guy in a mask and a cape. Even the more recent "Zorro" movies seem to have lost the sparkle of the classic character, at least as I remember him.

Zorro seems to have died.

Or maybe he's just gone into hiding. We still see him peek out from time to time, for example, in the body of Alan Shore, as he defends a straight man falsely accused of soliciting gay sex in a men's room, or tries to help a man imprisoned by the feds without due process. But Alan Shore isn't Zorro. Alan has his own brand of justice, which he is only too happy to impose on others, as long as he can make it legal.

Whatever happened to Zorro? This question, I think, first inspired the idea of Abe's Turn. The question itself, not its answer, because I don't really know the answer. The best I can say is that maybe Zorro has been in hiding, and now he's coming to Abe's Turn.

May I Feel Your Pain?

I tell people, I miss Bill Clinton. I mean, yeah, people accused him of being a liar and a philanderer and a cheat, and he certainly was a dickhead and a jerk and—worst of all—a *politician*. But despite all that, Bill Clinton was so much fun to laugh at:

> I did *not have sexual* relations with that woman... I *never* told anybody to lie, not a *single* time, *never*. These allegations are *false*. And I need to *go back to work* for the American people.[1]

Years later, that speech is *still* being posted to YouTube. And it still sets me rolling on the floor, laughing! I firmly believe that G.W. Bush would make a better president, if only

---

1 The emphasis is in the original; however, the meaning of this speech still depends on what the definition of *is* is.

he had one good intern.

And the laughs continue. Even James Bovard's scathing treatise on Clinton-era government abuses, *Feeling Your Pain: The Explosion and Abuse of Government Power in the Clinton-Gore Years*, makes me guffaw. And not all the humor, I think, Bovard intended. Consider the following snippets (one or two of which I have admittedly taken a little out of context):

> In reality, AmeriCorps looks more like a federal relief program for nightclub comics... [list of examples] Clinton said in 1994 that AmeriCorps "may have the most lasting legacy of anything I am able to do as your President, because it has the chance to embody all the things I ran for President to do." [Well, yeah, I think it kinda succeeded.] (p. 7-8)

> Clinton bragged in 1994 that AmeriCorps is "the least bureaucratic, least nationally directed program I have been associated with." [And you wouldn't believe how easy that is when all you have to do is just make shit up.] In practice, this means the feds shovel out the money and ask few, if any, questions about how recipients spend the windfall. [I am *so* in the wrong line of work!] (p. 20)

> In February 1996, Al Gore prepared to roll out a plan for a new clean-up tax on sugar growers [to help pay to repair damage to the Everglades]. [Alfy] Fanjul [the biggest sugar producer in Florida] called and harangued Clinton for 22 minutes on February 19, 1996—interrupting a two-hour mentoring session Clinton was having with Monica Lewinsky... [Nudge, nudge, wink, wink.]

Sugar is cheaper in Canada than in the United
States primarily because Canada has almost no
sugar growers... [or maybe no interns.] (p. 191-192)

Ralph Clark [mastermind of the Freemen]... had
received over $650,000 in farm subsidy payments
since 1985... [plus] almost $2 million in federal
farm loans... [plus] annual payments of $50,000 to
reward him for not growing crops on land he had
bought with government loans—long after he
effectively defaulted on those loans. Why did
Clark receive so many government loans? Because
he was uncreditworthy. [Duh! If he were credit-
worthy he could have probably gotten a loan
anywhere, and then what would we do with the
government subsidy?!] (p. 194)

But Bovard ruins all the humor and starts talking about
Waco, Ruby Ridge, Columbine, the Brady Act, Kosovo,
Bosnia, Yugoslavia, the CDA (shot down by the Supreme
Court), the Clipper Chip (and Clipper II, and Clipper III),
Echelon, Waldemar and Loretta Watzlaff, Anna Ward, Ralph
Garrison (may he rest in peace), Mario Paz (may he rest in
peace), Willy Heard (may he rest in peace), Ismeal Mena (may
he rest in peace)... and Bovard doesn't even get to the COPA
(a.k.a. the CDA II, recently ruled unconstitutional yet again,
still being battled in the courts via "ACLU v. Reno II"—How's
that for a legacy?), the DMCA (which led to the arrest of
Dmitry Sklyarov, later acquitted), Steve Jackson Games v. the
Secret Service (which began during the preceding Bush years),
the Amateur Action BBS raids (also crossing administrations),
the Pensacola BBS raids, the Wiretap Bill, Jake Baker, Randal
Schwartz (not federal, but during Clinton-Gore), Daniel Bern-
stein, Peter McWilliams (who finally died in 2000)...

The Bridge to the 21st Century.

Of all these names, events, programs, and laws, you probably recognize only a portion. For every stupid and despicable thing our government does with our tax money *that you've heard about*, there are dozens that you probably haven't.

Clinton was well out of office before I even made a first cut at *The Conscience of Abe's Turn*, but I can't help think that these events shaped the primordial inspiration for the story.

The bullshit continued after Clinton, of course. The federal government thugs' no-knock, midnight raid against Elian Gonzalez. The USA PATRIOT Act. Osama bin Laden. Afghanistan. Iraq. Off-shore torture. *Habeas corpus*.

But Bush hasn't provided the comedic folly of the Clinton years. Let's face it: National paranoia and U.S. bombings and arrest and torture just aren't funny. Even Hawkeye never joked about them, just about the incompetence that caused them. And I find myself unable to bring myself even to that. How does one put a funny face on pure evil?

(It becomes Batman's Joker, that's how.)

And then dissent became "unpatriotic" and even effectively illegal in some settings.

And so I faded from politics. I just couldn't handle it anymore. My problem is that I'm not a politician. I don't have that psychopathy gene that allows one to stand passionately on a subject and not really mean it, to violently change millions of personal lives without regret because it's just part of the job, to denigrate one's opponents and then figure it's just politics. My problem is that I actually care.

My spirit prevented me from following Bush's follies the same way I did Clinton's, because I needed the light absurdity to distract me from the utter seriousness of it all, the fact that some innocent people do indeed get caught in the pitiless gears of the government machine.

However, *Abe's Turn* provides an outlet for my disapproval, my sadness, and my fears. It provides an outlet for my disapproval, because I get to say, in the voices of my characters, what I really think about the police state. It provides an outlet for my sadness, because these characters feel the same sadness. And it provides an outlet for my fears, because anyone who has been following police-loophole bullshit legislation over the past 20 years, the villain of *Abe's Turn*, Sam Baedes, does and will commit the same abuses, if *he* deems it necessary to "maintain order." Still I will resist employing Michael's sardonic pun. I will not call him "Beady-eyes."

Moreover—perhaps more importantly—*Abe's Turn* provides hope. It says, maybe the good guys can win. True, the story of *Abe's Turn* is implausible, impractical fiction. So what? I'm sick and tired of popular stories in which we the proletariat are forever doomed to a life of subservience to the political will. I need hope, even if a vain hope.

Abe's Turn enables me to expose myself to politics again. In recent weeks, I've even found that I like it again, that I can even stand reading about Bush's wars, and I am able to feel wretched sickness, hot anger, despondent sadness, and still not be driven to insanity by it.

During the Clinton years, I discovered Harry Browne, running for president on the Libertarian Party ticket. Harry Browne didn't get to see liberty in his lifetime, even though he believed in it. But I don't want that hope to die. Hence, *The Conscience of Abe's Turn*.

TANSTAAFL!

During the Clinton years, I also discovered Robert Heinlein's classic libertarian novel, *The Moon is a Harsh Mistress*, which became one of my all-time favorite novels (maybe even my most favorite novel of all time). It clearly influences and inspires *Abe's Turn*, although my story treats different themes and will reach a different destination than Heinlein's did.

A recent issue of the *Liberator Online,* an online newsletter published by the Advocates for Self-Government, reported that the Appellate Court for the second district of California ruled that "parents do not have a constitutional right to educate their children in their own home."[2] The court then quoted from a 1961 court case, saying that the government schools are there to train children in "loyalty to the state and the nation as a means of protecting the public welfare."

The Liberator goes on to quote from Adam Schaeffer of the Cato Institute: "Seldom do the defenders of the government education monopoly reveal in such forthright language the true purpose of their position; they are training children to be loyal subjects of the state, not free citizens of a republic. The logic behind support for a government education monopoly and opposition to school choice is chilling and clear."

I only need to read something like this to remind myself of how Baedes thinks, and why he does what he does. So far, he has arrested his political opponent, fabricating charges outright in order to neutralize the political threat. His minions arrested a blatantly innocent man, who just happened to be racially inappropriate. Baedes not only approved but also took advantage of the situation to shore up his own personal power. Then another of his henchmen planted evidence of a non-existent drug crime in order to bring down another innocent man for business reasons. Not only did Baedes defend his henchman, he had personal motive to bring down the Alvarez brothers. Means, motive, opportunity... You connect the dots.

At this point, I am going to take Michael's cue and call the creep Beady-eyes.

Currently, he's using his position to go after those he suspects are part of a breach of confidence in his office. Be assured that if there were such a leak, in his mind, it would be all Mira and Ted's fault. (Yes, Baedes is great at executing a

---

2 http://www.theadvocates.org/liberator/vol-13-num-5.html

plan, but when it comes to investigative work, he's a bit of a bumbler.) Remember, too, that this is only one instance in a long line of pattern abuses of power. We don't even get a clear picture of the pattern. For every reported case, there are a dozen or more unreported ones (just as in real life).

For many people, it can be hard to accept that any protector could be this self-absorbed. Yes, there was Stalin, and Hitler, and Mao Tse Tung. But they were tyrants, not protectors. They were exceptions to the rule. And they didn't live in the U.S. People forget that protectors are just human, and "self-absorbed" is part of the definition of human, because we all assume *prima facie* that everyone sees things the same way we do, and we all tend to project our own images onto others.

A friend of mine and I a few years ago attended a seminar in Boston. We parked the car in the lot behind the convention center. The shuttle to the main entrance was boarding, so we rode to it the front of the building. Afterward, when we were leaving, instead of waiting for the shuttle, we decided to walk down the sidewalk, which led around the building, past the bike racks, to the parking lot. We had made it only a few yards down the sidewalk, when an overweight security guard in a blue uniform asked us where we were going. My friend explained that we were going to the parking lot. The guard told us that we should take the shuttle, and indicated where it would be boarding.

Now, I'm the kind of person who when faced with an unexpected, unexplained, crazy demand by a big man with a gun, who could take me out just by sitting on me, would just do what he asked, steaming and fuming after the fact. But my friend is the kind who would press the issue. He asked the guard why we couldn't just follow the sidewalk. The guard explained that the sidewalk wasn't intended for pedestrian traffic (or something like that), which must be why it was a *sidewalk* with a bike rack there in that space, a bike rack empty and unused. We of course did as the guard asked, me sarcastically asking what he thought we would do, my friend retorting that he thought we had a bomb in our pants (or something like that).

Later, it occurred to me that the guard didn't want a conflict any more than I did, that he was as afraid of us as we were of him, maybe more so. For him, at some level, he was indeed afraid that we had a bomb in our pants, because if we had actually had a bomb, then we also would have had guns and would not have cared about our own personal safety. The abstract paranoia that U.S politicians have fostered in the American people, to this security guard, likely became very concrete, very real, *even though we posed no threat at all to anyone.*

What happens when we take this paranoia to its logical conclusion? What if Sam Baedes not only feels this fear, but also personalizes it? What would he do to innocent people?

In Baedes's case, there's a lot of personal history that makes him a thug. When Sam Baedes was a boy, he lived in the city projects. One of the neighborhood boys, older and bigger than Sam, a bully, swiped Sam's bike, right in front of him. That was the kind of neighborhood he grew up in. This kid taunted Sam. Sam argued with him, tried to get his bike back. But the kid only pushed Sam off, scolded him, and rode off. After the kid had finished joyriding on Sam's bike, he took a baseball bat to it, out of spite.

Baedes was livid and bitter. He picked fights with the boy and his friends, but because he was so much smaller than they, all he could do was taunt them, which only made them angry. Once he even got beat up. But he never forgot. How could he? Many months later, a new teenage kid moved into the neighborhood, even meaner and more criminal than these boys. Baedes lied to him, tricked him, told him that these boys had said something degrading about him... then stood back and let nature take its course. When the ambulance came for the gang,

Baedes was watching, grinning, finally satisfied.

A casual observer (i.e., most voters) would think that Baedes had turned this childhood trauma and its reprises throughout his life into a positive, to fight crime.

Baedes isn't afraid of death. He's afraid of dying a victim.

But Baedes's root flaw is that he believes he can do no wrong. That's why he'll do anything he can get away with. The same applies to most of his crew, all of whom are loyal officers of the state, because honor breeds honor, and contempt breeds contempt. Or as Michael says, "The slime trickles from the top." While Baedes and his department are gods, set on this earth to protect the mortals, you and I are only human. We make mistakes. In his mind, we are guilty until proven— Actually, we're just guilty. Baedes thinks this way, because he's insecure, because he's afraid. And Baedes gets away with it, even prospers from it, because he gets the job done, tough on crime, brings in the criminals, high conviction rate, makes the city streets safe... or so everyone believes. (But more on that later in the story.) The whole situation would be comical, were it not for the fact that innocent people get crushed in the process.

But such is the nature of government.

This is one of the reasons why the framers of the United States wrote the Bill of Rights, and the Second Amendment in particular. As Thomas Jefferson said in this oft-quoted passage from a letter to William S. Smith in 1787:

> God forbid we should ever be twenty years
> without such a rebellion [as Shay's Rebellion in
> Massachusetts]... And what country can preserve
> its liberties, if its rulers are not warned from time
> to time, that this people preserve the spirit of resis-
> tance? Let them take arms... The tree of liberty
> must be refreshed from time to time, with the

blood of patriots and tyrants. It is its natural
manure.

Abe's Turn is a metaphor for this truth. That government is
made up of people, and people are only human. And humans
suffer from short-sightedness and egocentrism and error and
depravity. We like to think that most of us are good people,
that most of us would never steal, for example. However, it is
well known among wise and experienced retail store owners
that almost *anyone* can become a shoplifter, if three conditions
are met: (1) they think they need what you have; (2) they can
rationalize a reason why they should take it from you; and (3)
they think they can get away with it. And shop owners know
that #3 is the only thing you can affect, in order to reduce
shoplifting. You gotta make them think they can't get away
with it.

The same rule applies to governmental power abuse.
Except that many of these abusers do get away with it, and
they know it. That is why James Bovard, in *Feeling Your Pain*,
in his chapter on IRS abuses, can tell tale after horrific tale, as
though he'll never run out—Read it!. I can't relay the stories
here, because there are too many of them. Suffice it to say,
these victims were not criminals. They were not tax cheats.
They were ordinary people like you and me, maybe even more
ordinary, because many of them were weak, because the weak
have the least ability to fight back. So they get raided, have
charges fabricated against them, are threatened unless they rat
on their friends, experience legal stalling tactics designed to
increase the pain, see the law flaunted in their faces. And so-
called reform appears to be useless. As Bovard quoted one IRS
instructor, "Make them cry. We don't give points for being
good scouts..." (p. 35) And when it comes to the Taxpayer Bill
of Rights, "Nothing has changed in our operation in 134
years." (p. 36)

The victims of this abuse are innocent people whose lives were destroyed by puffed up jerkwads, assholes who destroyed these lives because they were vindictive jackasses full of their own shit. If we fear criminals with guns, how much more so criminals with guns *and* authority?

Who knows what the future will hold? The prospects truly terrify me.

Fortunately, influential, connected people both inside and outside of Congress have focused on reining in the executive branch. They face an uphill battle, and so do we, as their masters. As Robert Heinlein noted, there ain't no such thing as a free lunch.

The Birth of Abe's Turn

These thoughts rolled around in my mind, and out came *The Conscience of Abe's Turn*.

At first, I was planning to write it as a short story, then as a novella, then as a series of flash fiction pieces. I finally determined that the story needed to be a much longer series, and that it could go on indefinitely. I decided on telling the story as a series of novelettes or novellas, five chapters per episode, because that's how many segments there are to each story. Then I decided on a three-season initial story arc, using the *Star Wars* trilogy pattern: *A New Hope, The Empire Strikes Back, Return of the Jedi.* That made the first part *The Birth of the Conscience.*

Then I did the math, assuming about a year per season: 52 weeks in a year, one week per chapter, minus some weeks off, 8 episodes per season. That makes for about 2 novel-length volumes per season.

After pursuing this for the first half-season, I have a renewed appreciation for my favorite TV storytellers of the past and present, like Amy Sherman-Palladino, Joss Whedon, and J. Michael Straczynski, who somehow had to produce a full, ready-for-prime-time episode every week.

I chose the name Abe's Turn in honor of the birth of the Republican Party, which also ironically introduced the end of Jefferson's honorable rebellion. Whatever else it was, Lincoln's civil war was a turning point for the United States, and Abe's Turn is a metaphor for that corner in our history.

RECOVERY, RELAPSE, RELATIONSHIP

As I first gazed upon her, the blood rushed from my face, my fingers trembled, my lungs refused to breath, my heart refused to pump. Pity overwhelmed me, then disgust, then anger, then sadness. I could have sworn I smelled vinegar, although I don't know where the smell would have come from. I closed my eyes, to give them a respite, but that only burned the image on the inside of my eyelids.

I had been familiar with cases of violent rape. Hell, they were why I volunteered as a victim's advocate, because I needed to feel I was doing something to help. I saw women come into the hospital with bloody mouths, black eyes, missing teeth, fist-sized bruises, concussions, broken bones... I'd seen it all, or at least I thought I had. The worst case I had ever seen was a girl of 14 they had carried in on a stretcher. A clump of her hair had been torn out; two of her fingers had been broken; and her right hip had been forcibly dislocated. And I won't even try to describe the sexual violence she had suffered, or the injury to her psyche. I had nightmares for a week. But somehow I got through it, stronger for the experience. After that, I thought I could handle anything. So when they asked me to talk to a Clydene Jackson, after her condition had stabilized, I had not sufficiently prepared myself for the shock.

They called me during breakfast, the day after Valentine's Day, 2006, and asked if I could come down to the hospital for a special case. Once there, I met with the doctor and a police detective. We stood around the nurse's station. Dr. Ilic, an athletic woman with medium-length, black hair and a sharply defined chin, reminded me a little of my mother. I missed my mother. But the doctor spoke in an exotic accent I couldn't quite put my finger on. The police detective was a brusque, grizzled, old codger, who wore a suit and tie. It seemed like there were other things he'd rather be doing than talking to me, but such was his job. They filled me in on the situation.

When Clydene had come in late the previous night, she was in pretty bad shape. She had malignant hyperthermia from the anesthesia her attacker had used to knock her out. A friend of mine once almost died from MH, on the operating table, and she would have died if her anesthetist hadn't known what he was doing. Clydene would have died, too, if they hadn't gotten to her in time and if Dr. Ilic had not recognized the symptoms and known what to do.

The "perp" in this case, the detective explained, had gotten a hold of a stash of hospital anesthetic—they were still tracing the source. The guy claimed that he used it because it was safer than the street alternatives, and he didn't want his victims to get hurt. I shook my head in wonder, not that I hadn't heard similar stories in the past. The criminal mind will probably always puzzle me.

Anyways, this guy had done this before—no surprise, because they usually have. Apparently, his attacks had gotten gradually more brutal and more daring—also no surprise, because that also fits the profile of a serial rapist. He was also a bit narcissistic, as if he wanted to get caught. Until they finally did catch him, red-handed at the scene with a belt in one hand and his victim in the other. When they found her, she was in no condition to fight back, even if she had not been tied to that chair.

I swallowed, hard.

"Can you handle this?" the doctor asked.

I nodded casually at her. "Yeah," I said. "No problem." I lied, not because I needed her to believe me, but because I myself needed to believe I could handle it.

"So, we still need a rape kit and her statement," the detective said.

"Okay." I breathed. "Is there anything else I should know."

"Just that her husband is in there with her now," Dr. Ilic said. "His name's Ted. And I don't think he's taking it very well. He's been sitting in there all night."

"Yeah," agreed the detective, nodding. "He may be having regrets. Just get him to see that he didn't do anything wrong."

I had run across similar situations before, both as a victim's advocate and in my practice as a mental health counselor. Loved ones can blame themselves for what happened, even if it was completely out of their control. After they get over the shock of the event itself, they go on an emotional roller coaster ride that can take them through nostalgia, regret, self-blame, and depression. The danger is that they'll never get off the roller coaster. And while they're on the roller coaster, they tend to make poor choices. That could really complicate the situation here, I knew, where Ted was going to have to do things for Clydene that he might not want to do. I also knew he might think me the bad guy, because my primary job was to stick up for Clydene. I hated to be the bad guy.

I quietly pushed open the door to her room and peered inside. The first thing I noticed about Clydene was her face. It was almost recognizably human. Her face was striped with welts and cuts. Her tight, red curls were matted and splotched with blood. Her left eye was covered with a large bruise, which stretched from her cheek across the bridge of her nose.

She wore a hospital gown, and welts sketched an irregular pattern from her cheeks down her neck and past where I could see. A similar pattern of welts and cuts traced her arms, from her hands into the tunnels of her sleeves.

Ted had pulled a chair to the far side of her bed, next to the window, and there he sat, longing after her with love and tenderness. That was the first impression I had of him, and first impressions count. And I'm sure of that impression. Love was clearly what it was. Otherwise, why would he have been there, sitting patiently next to her side? Whatever else he was feeling, he clearly loved her, wretchedly, desperately loved her, lost-without-her loved her. You could see it in his eyes, if you had been there.

He reached out and caressed her hand, not where it was sore and bruised, but along the back of her thumb, slowly, gently. Still asleep, she yanked her hand away. Ted seemed taken aback.

"She may not want you to touch her for awhile," I said, as matter-of-factly as I could.

He regarded me suspiciously.

I added, "But she still needs you." He had been through a traumatic experience of his own, and he needed to know she was not rejecting him.

"And who are you?" He glared at me, annoyed.

"I'm from the Sexual Assault Crisis Center," I answered.

"You have an answer to this crisis?" Ted stood as he said it. He towered over me, still glaring, now with anger.

I instantly sized him up, saw it in his face. He felt guilt, maybe even shame. He blamed himself for some part of what happened, and he would probably blame himself for whatever happened from here on out. Even more, he seemed to be the type who needed to maintain the illusion of being in charge. He was top dog, and he wasn't about to give up that spot voluntarily. The situation was already out of his control, which must have enraged him. And I might need to take what little control he had left away from him, because part of my job was to make sure no one, not the police, not the doctors, nor even he, bullied Clyde into a doing something she didn't want.

His question was more anger than query. Do I have an answer to this crisis? All I could do was to tell the truth and to level with him as best I could. But I also needed to stand up to him, to retain my own authority.

"No, I don't," I replied, again as matter-of-factly as I could.

I had been in situations like this before, but they always made me ill. I did my best to hide that I felt anything but confidence. I absolutely hate being the bad guy.

"So why are you here?" A challenge.

I explained it to him, again as matter-of-factly as I could, without returning his anger, but also without ceding ground. I could see that he loved his wife dearly. That's where his sympathies lay. And that's what I focused on, what she will probably feel, what she will need.

"Because when she wakes up," I said, "she's going to think this was her fault, and she's going to be as angry at herself as you are at yourself."

He stared at me, not in anger now, but in bewilderment. He probably had never considered that Clydene would blame herself. Why would she? He probably couldn't fathom it, even now. He probably thought she would blame him, just as he did. We all tend to project onto others the feelings we feel about ourselves.

"You wouldn't think it," I said, now more tenderly. "But believe it or not, that's the most likely outcome, that Clydene will think it's her fault."

He shook his head. "It's not her fault." He sat back down.

"Who's fault is it?" I heard myself ask. I'm not sure why I asked the question. We both already knew the correct answer.

It was the fault of the rapist. But I also knew the answer Ted—
I was sure—believed, deep in his heart, that it was his fault. At
least I knew, if I were in his situation, I would be searching for
reasons to blame myself. I had even been there, having
suffered loss in my life, knowing all the reasons why it was
my fault. But I didn't want to think about that just then.

He finally answered me. "I don't know you well enough to
answer that question, Miss—"

"Miss Jayson." I introduced myself. "But please call me
Mira." I stepped up and offered my hand for him to shake.

He didn't take my hand, but he looked like he wanted to
say something. Before he could, Clydene groaned. She began
to roll onto her side, but then she stopped and whimpered,
"No." Her eyes were still closed, and I thought that she must
have been dreaming.

Ted stood, gritting his teeth. I felt sorry for him, probably
feeling out of control, probably feeling more vulnerable than
he was used to. But I needed to give first priority to Clydene.

I sidled up next to her. "Sweetie," I said, "it's okay now.
You're safe now. You're in the hospital."

She opened her eyes and stared blankly at me.

Then I added, "Ted is here." I nodded in his direction, on
the other side of her bed.

She looked to him and began to weep. "I'm sorry," she said.

"Could you leave us alone?" he snarled at me. Ted was
clearly struggling to restrain his rage, possibly directed more
at himself than at anyone else.

He reached out to comfort Clydene, and she recoiled. He
pulled back just as Dr. Ilic entered the room. The doctor introduced herself to Clyde. She explained why Clyde had become
sick. Clyde's eyes glazed over. The doctor said the police
wanted to talk to her, and that a Sexual Assault Nurse Examiner would be talking to her about a forensic examination. I
interjected that Clyde should think about whether she wanted

the examination, or to talk to the police, because she didn't have to if she didn't want to. I added that she could have Ted in the room if she wanted, or not, and I would also be happy to stay with her if she wanted.

Ted scowled and mumbled something about "meddling bitch," and the doctor glared at me. I understood Ted's reaction. But that Dr. Ilic glared at me showed that she was not familiar with protocol in a case like this. Either she disagreed with my advice or thought I had overstepped my bounds. All of this saddened me, but I pretended not to notice—or tried to pretend, anyway. Clyde seemed to get what I was saying. She had fondness in her eyes as she nodded quietly, and I felt a little better.

I had a feeling that Clyde was going to want to give an official report. It was something about her expression, or body language—such as there was, even though she barely moved because of her injuries. Something about how she "felt" when I mentioned talking to the police. But I also had a feeling that Ted was going to insist on being there with her, and that could be a problem. Could you imagine having to describe in detail, for the record, how some creep abducted you, humiliated you, sexually assaulted you, and abused you, all in front of your husband? No, I didn't think so. A woman in that situation would be sure to leave out important details, even without meaning to, would soften the account to save herself and her spouse embarrassment.

I needed to speak to Ted, because I needed to talk to him about his role in all this. I strode over next to where he stood. I felt like a little kid standing next to him, because he stood almost two feet taller than me. I valiantly resisted a "How's the air up there?!" joke, because it wasn't the time or place. Still, I tried to talk softly, but I felt as though I needed to shout to be heard.

"How are you holding up?" I asked, and I placed my hand

on the small of his back.

He scoffed. "I'll survive."

I didn't know whether he was trying to belittle me, or whether he thought it was a stupid question, or maybe both. I didn't push the issue any further.

I explained the process to them both. If she decided she wanted to talk to the police, I would arrange it. And she could also have the forensic exam. The more information they got, the greater the chances they would be able to keep him from doing this to anyone else. I also explained that it if Clyde gave a report to the police, that she might want Ted to wait in the hall, because having him there would probably make her uncomfortable, and she would unconsciously tone down her story, and that would give them less to go on.

"Ted, what would you do if Clydene asked you to wait outside while she talked to the police?" I phrased the question carefully, in terms of what Clydene wanted, so that Ted would not have an out, because I knew how he felt about her.

"I'd be fine with that," he replied.

I didn't believe him, but he couldn't go back on it now, not after he committed to it in front of his wife.

Then I added, to Clyde, "I don't want to push you into anything, but..." I was about to try to do just that. "Most of these cases," I explained, "are never reported; and even when it is reported, most of the time, the guy gets away with it; and even when he doesn't get away with it, too many times they get the wrong guy or falsely accuse him. But that hasn't happened here. We know who did this, and... You have a chance to make sure the right result happens."

I stopped there. I didn't want to lay it on too thick. Clyde nodded.

I don't know why I added that part about them getting the wrong guy or falsely accusing an innocent man, except that it's true, and I had to come to terms with the moral ambiguity of rape law a long time ago. I'm sure it didn't bolster my case. But Ted, of all people, seemed to understand exactly what I was saying, as if he had experienced it all before. It wasn't anything he said or did, more what he didn't say. He didn't argue with me. He didn't ask questions. He nodded.

"Have you ever had anything like this happen to you before?" I ventured.

"No." He shook his head. He seemed lost in thought.

The police detective knocked on the door and asked to speak with Ted out in the hall. I sat with Clyde.

"I'm still a bit bubble-headed," Clyde said. "Must be the drugs. What was your name again?"

I smiled, a giggly sort of smile, because in all the excitement, I had forgotten to introduce myself to Clydene. So I did, and I apologized for not doing so earlier.

"Hey, Mira," she said. It's true what they say: the sweetest sound is when someone says your name with kindness.

"Yeah?" I said.

"Will they be able to... get him, without my testimony?"

"I don't know," I told her. "For now, they just want a statement. That is, they just want you to tell them what happened. The more you can tell them, the better. But they're not asking you to testify in court yet. Do you understand?"

She nodded. "Will I have to testify later?"

"Again, I don't know. I've seen it go both ways. I guess it depends on the case and on the evidence they have, and probably on his lawyer, too. You should probably talk to a lawyer yourself, if you're concerned about that. We have time to make that happen, and I know a good lawyer you can talk to. But only if you want."

She shook her head. "No, I have a lawyer. Ted, actually. He's my lawyer."

And Ted started making sense to me.

She suddenly looked upset. "Ted's his lawyer, too."

My face wrinkled with confusion. "I don't understand."

"Ted got the guy off on his last case," Clyde explained, "a rape case."

"The same guy who attacked you?" I asked.

"Yeah," Clyde said.

And Ted started making perfect sense to me.

"Well," I said as tenderly as I could, "I don't think he'll be representing him anymore. And I also think he might be a little too close to handle this particular problem for you. I think he loves you very much, and he may not be able to think clearly because of what's happened. So if you want legal advice, you should probably talk to someone else. Maybe Ted can recommend someone he trusts."

She just looked sad and stared at the wall, deep in thought.

"Look," I said. "There's another way to approach this."

Her expression lifted with hope.

"First of all, no matter what you decide to do, it's going to be hard. I don't think there's any easy way through this. I know that's not what most people want to hear, but I have to level with you. Whether you talk to the police or not, you're going to have to work through your feelings, because there's no way to avoid them. But regardless of whether you talk to the police or not, you can probably get through it, as long as you believe in what you're doing. You have to be able to live with the choice. So why don't you just tell me what you *want* to do? Do you have a gut-level instinct on which course you should take?"

She breathed deeply. "I want to talk to the police."

"Okay." I nodded.

As I stood, she grabbed my hand. There were tears trickling from her eyes. She said, "Could you tell Ted to stay out there?"

I nodded. "Of course. I'll take care of it."

But she didn't let go. Instead she continued, "And would

you stay?"

I sat back down next to her. "I'll stay here as long as you like," I reassured her.

I don't know why I said that. I knew I couldn't stay forever, and some women in this situation might get attached. They might want me to stay forever. If she had been a friend, that would have been different. I would have visited a friend's bedside every day for a month. But I hardly knew Clydene, and I knew the dangers of making promises I couldn't keep.

Still, in my heart, I also knew it was true. I would stay as long as she needed me. Maybe it was pity that made me feel that way. Or maybe it was something more. All I knew for sure is that she needed me, and I needed to be there for her.

"Thanks," she squeaked. She finally released my hand.

A tall, thin, black policewoman took Clyde's statement. Dr. Ilic stood by, occasionally asking questions, occasionally making notes on her medical pad. I told Clyde several times that she could take a break anytime she wanted. I reminded her more because I wanted a break than because she needed one. She wept and wailed through every revolting, infuriating, nauseating detail she could remember, sometimes squeezing my hand, sometimes not, sometimes suffering for 10 or 20 seconds before she could get out the next part of the story.

After her story was told, Clyde curled up in a fetal position, facing the window. I stepped out of the room, found a restroom, and once inside, proceeded to vomit up my breakfast. I sat there in the hospital bathroom, on the floor, next to the bowl, for several minutes, weeping.

After I rinsed my mouth and fixed my face, I returned to Clydene's bedside. The forensic examination went about as well as the interview. Again, Ted waited outside. Again, Clyde asked me to stand next to her. The nurse examiner was sensitive, gentle, and professional. As she took each sample, Clyde squinted and squeezed my hand so hard, I thought she was going to pull it off of my arm. Afterward, I felt another need to use the ladies' room, but the nurse examiner had beat me to it. I slid down the wall outside the bathroom door, until I was sitting on the floor in the hallway. My stomach started to feel better, but sadness overtook me, sadness bordering on depression. Not professional, I know, but— Oh hell. That's a myth.

Dr. Ilic discovered me there. She spoke with a twinge of evil in her voice. "At least the bastard got his."

"What do you mean?" I asked.

She looked puzzled. "I mean... Don't you know. He got beat up pretty bad, resisting arrest or something like that. Not badly enough for all the evil things he did to all those women, if you ask me."

I stared at her, mortified.

"You can sneak up and see him," she said. "He's in room 1404. But I wouldn't if I were you. Not a pretty sight."

That thought disgusted me. I hated what he had done to Clydene and all his other victims. But I also hated that he had been brutalized by the police, and so thoroughly that he needed to be hospitalized. And now that his attackers were the ones charged with guarding him. I felt sick to my stomach again. I changed the subject.

"Is there anything else you need from Clydene Jackson?" I stood up.

"No, I don't think so," she said. "Let's meet with the police lieutenant." And so we did.

By the time I got back to Clyde's room, she and Ted were talking. I didn't mean to eavesdrop, but overhearing a conversation can be like a drug. I paused for a moment outside the partially open door.

"What if I never get over this?" Clyde said. Her voice was quivering. "Will you leave me?"

"Never," Ted said unhesitatingly. Then he did hesitate. "But... you might—"

"I'm not a good wife," she said. "I just can't anymore. I think maybe you should try to find someone else."

"Clyde," Ted said, "no one but you could *ever* be my wife. No matter what. You think I don't know that?"

I teared up a little, as if I were watching a romantic movie, but more real. And loneliness washed through my body. Somehow, at the age of 31, I had avoided meeting the right man, falling in love, moving in together, and all that stuff. Romance has always been an uphill battle for me.

I knocked on the door and swung it open.

Ted had calmed down. He was speaking in quiet, even tones. He looked a little sad, but not angry.

I told them that the police had gotten everything they needed, and I relayed their thanks. I explained that trauma like this could cause lingering issues, and I suggested that they consider talking to a psychologist or counselor who specializes in these types of cases. I offered to recommend someone.

Ted said nothing, and Clyde gave a noncommittal grunt.

"Just think about it, okay?"

They both nodded.

I promised to return the next day to see how Clyde was doing.

I don't remember much of the rest of that day or that night, only a fitful sleep. I remember waking up the next morning, calling my virtual assistant, and having her cancel my morning appointments. Instead of going to work, I raced over to the hospital. Clyde was sitting up in bed, eating breakfast, and Ted was nowhere to be found. Clyde looked refreshed, despite her wounds. She looked happier.

"Good to see you're feeling a little better," I said.

"Yeah. Thank you so much for coming by yesterday," she said. "I probably wouldn't have managed without you."

"You're welcome," I said. "Do you mind," I asked tentatively, "if I sit with you a while?"

We chatted almost as if we were old friends. That is, it felt like we were old friends. We talked about our careers, our interests, hobbies, even politics, religion, and love. Before we knew it, we had spent hours together, and I was glad the nurse had not kicked me out. Clyde asked me if I was married, and I didn't blush when she said, "Because you have guys lined up around the corner and you don't want to jinx it."

I went with the joke. "Are you kidding? Have you seen the slim pickin's out there? The last one I dated made me feel like a trophy wife, and we weren't even married. And let me tell you, he was no prize, either."

Then, after a moment, I got serious. "You're really lucky to have found someone who loves you as much as Ted clearly does."

That apparently was the excuse Clyde needed to tell me all about what had happened after I had left the previous day. She and Ted had discussed everything, including their marriage and their sex life. They decided to wait until she felt a little better, physically, before getting too intimate. But during their talk Clyde had felt more connected to Ted than she ever had before. She didn't blame Ted for having defended the man who attacked her, because that was his job as a criminal defense lawyer. And it was a noble career, because for every one criminal he helped escape, there were a dozen innocents he kept from being victimized. As he left her to go home and get some much-needed sleep, he kissed her, long and tenderly, on the lips, and she did not stop him. She didn't even want him to stop. She even let him goose her behind beneath the sheets, because all her injuries were on her front; her backside was unscathed. In fact, she had felt like getting a lot more randy, but they both knew she couldn't handle it, physically.

"Well," I said, "most erogenous zones are on the posterior surface of the body," something I had read somewhere.

"For a few weeks, that's gonna be kinda fun," she remarked with a salacious twinkle in her eye.

Still, I felt uneasy about her quick psychological recovery. A day earlier, she had been terrified of men, even her loving husband. She recoiled from him more than once. She had not talked to anyone about the incident, not in a mental-health context. Maybe she was on some sort of high. Or maybe she was repressing her feelings, or even the memory of what had happened.

"Have you thought anymore about what I mentioned to you yesterday?" I asked.

"What's that?" she asked.

"About talking to someone."

"You mean seeing a shrink?" Clyde asked.

I giggled, but Clyde giggled along with me, so it must have been all right. "Yes, that's what I mean," I said.

She told me they probably would pass, but thanks for the offer. I asked for permission at least to give her the name of a psychologist, just in case they change their mind, and she was okay with that.

I had Angela Hooper's card in my purse, a psychologist friend of mine, and my own card as well. While I dug through my purse for the business cards, she asked me, "Have you ever gone through anything like this?" She looked serious.

"No, nothing quite as bad," I said. For an instant, I remembered the most traumatic event in my life, the death of my parents. I didn't want to think about that. "I work with people who have had similar experiences all the time, though."

"But you must have had something bad happen to you," she said.

"Yes." I nodded. "I think everybody has something really bad happen to them at least once in their life." I didn't want to think about it.

"What was yours?" she asked. "If you don't mind me

asking."

"Uh, no, I don't mind." I sincerely didn't mind her asking. I just didn't want to answer. "I don't think now is the time, though," I said, "to talk about my problems." I changed subjects. "Just think about meeting with Angela Hooper, at least once, you and Ted both. You may be surprised at what she can do for you, even if you think you're over it. She's very good, insightful."

"More insightful than you?" Clyde asked.

"Well..." I felt both sheepish and suspicious. Sheepish, because I like almost everyone else was embarrassed at being so candidly complemented. Suspicious, because I wondered whether she had an ulterior motive in that comment.

She examined the card. "Do you really think it's that important for me to talk to her?"

"Yes," I admitted. "I do."

Over the following several weeks, I thought about Clyde every few days. I could probably have gotten her phone number—she had not given it to me—but I didn't have a bona-fide reason to call her. It would have been improper for me to do so. She had my phone number, and if she wanted to get in touch with me, she would.

I still don't know exactly why I wanted to talk to her. Maybe because I was still worried about her. She had gone through so great a trauma, and part of me didn't believe that she really had dealt with it, by herself, in just one day. But—I reminded myself—even though we hit it off, I was her advocate, not her friend. I was friendly to her, of course. But it was still a professional relationship. And even though we had shared intimate details of her life, we were still just acquaintances.

Then one day, my office phone rang. I had just finished with a client, and I was preparing for my next appointment. I didn't think anything of it, until I lifted the receiver and from the other end of the line, Clydene's voice spoke to me.

"I'm really sorry about this," she began, "but I didn't know who else to call." She stopped talking.

"That's all right," I reassured her. "I have a few minutes to talk, if you want."

"That psychologist whose name you gave me? Angela Hooper? I made an appointment with her."

"Okay," I acknowledged, noncommittally, because I didn't yet know what she wanted me to say. But inside I was jumping for joy.

"Things have just been so bad between me and Ted lately." Her voice began to tremble. "He's just so angry, and I'm having nightmares, and..." She sniffed loudly. She was obviously crying. "I'm sorry. I thought I could get through this."

"It's okay," I said. "Would like me to come to your appointment with you, introduce you to Angela?"

"Mm hmm."

"I can do that," I reassured her. Stupid, because I didn't yet know when she had made the appointment for, and I didn't know whether I had a schedule conflict. I just wanted to reach through the phone line and hold her and hug her until she felt loved again, and this was as close as I could get to that.

"I'm really sorry to put this on you like this," she explained. "I know we don't know each other very well. It's just that all my other friends are busy, and I don't have anyone else to turn to, and..."

I have to admit, I was a little hurt by the fact that I was her last choice, even though it made sense. After all, I kept reminding myself, she didn't really know me. Our relationship was a professional one, not a personal one.

Ange Hooper's office was in the same building as mine. She is a personal friend and colleague, and I felt very comfortable recommending her. Fortunately, Clyde's appointment fell during a free hour in my schedule, just before lunch. I agreed to meet her there a few minutes early, and I reassured her, there was nothing to be nervous about.

When I saw her, I couldn't help but smile. She looked much better than she had the last time I had seen her. Her wounds were healing nicely, the physical ones anyhow, and makeup covered some of her bruises. She was a beautiful woman, with fair skin and titian hair. She wore red nail polish. I could just barely see the stripes on the back of her hands, but she hid her arms with long sleeves.

"It's so good to see you!" I said.

She beamed back at me, and I gave her a friendly hug, which she returned. I suddenly remembered that she was probably still sore.

"Oh, did I hurt you?"

"No, I'm fine," she said.

"You're looking really good," I told her.

We chatted, again as if we were old friends, as we waited for Ange. At one point, Clyde said, apropos of nothing, "Ted doesn't know I'm here."

"Oh?" I asked.

"O," she answered. "He doesn't think we need our heads shrunk."

I nodded but otherwise listened quietly.

"I'm sorry for how he jumped all over you in the hospital."

"It's okay. He was upset and under stress."

"That doesn't make it okay," Clyde said.

"Well... Let's say, it means we can cut him a little slack."

Clyde nodded. "Still, you stood up to him. I know you did. And... Anyhow, thanks for being there. I really needed a friend. I don't know what I would have done without you."

I pshawed it off, but inside, her words had touched me.

"So," Clyde continued, "I don't know what Ted would say about me being here. But I just thought I needed to give it a try. I've been having trouble concentrating at work, and I've been having... nightmares. And I've been tired and just feeling down. And Ted's gone all the time. He leaves for work early in the morning and doesn't get back home sometimes until after midnight. He says it's just this case he's working on, but that was never a problem before. Not even back in the day, while we were both building our careers and working insane hours. We still found time to be together. Now..."

I understood completely.

Ange's current appointment having finished, she came out to meet Clyde. She saw me there and asked whether Clyde was a client of mine.

"No, no," I said. "She's a friend."

Back up in my own office, I tried to distract myself with a novel, but I couldn't focus on it. I thought about what Clyde had said, that she had needed a friend. I too was thinking of her as a friend. At first, I pitied her, but she was hardly pitiable now. Clydene was not a victim; she was an overcomer. Yet she valued my friendship, whatever that meant. All mental health professionals have had a patient or client develop feelings toward them. And just as often—though not as well known among laymen—every therapist has developed feelings for a patient. Neither one of these is intrinsically bad, as long as professional boundaries are maintained.

But I was not her counselor, and I was not acting like a counselor. A week earlier, Clydene had been repressing her feelings, and maybe even suffering from dissociation. I knew it, but I didn't psychoanalyze her, because I was her friend, not her shrink.

I spent an hour thinking these thoughts. Then came a knock on my office door. It was Clydene. She looked upset.

"Thank you again," Clyde said. "Do you have a minute?"

I did.

She sat in my guest chair and stared at the floor. She clearly wanted to say something, but was upset and didn't know how to begin.

"How did it go with Angela?" I asked.

She nodded, looking like she was about to cry. Then she just said, "I'm sorry. I shouldn't lay this on you." And she started to gather up her purse to leave.

I laid a hand on her shoulder. "What is it? Did something happen during your session?"

She shook her head, tears welling in her eyes.

"Was it something I did?" I asked.

She shook her head again. She looked into my eyes, and I felt how she felt.

"I just don't have anyone I can talk to," she said. And she did cry.

I handed her the box of tissues from my desk. Between sobs, she told me that she didn't want to lay all this on me, because she knows I didn't sign up for it, but no one at work really understood her, and Ted was lashing out at the world and was in no condition to help her. She wiped her eyes, shook her head again, apologized and was again about to leave.

I interrupted her. "Please don't go. Please stay."

She already had a shrink. She didn't need a shrink. She needed a friend, a support system, and I was it. But she was afraid to throw herself on me, gallant of her, but stupid. What were friends for?

"Look, you said it yourself," I continued. "I'm your friend. And if you can't talk to a friend when something's bothering you, well then what are friends for?"

It was worse than she had let on earlier. She and Ted were on the skids. This only added to her depression, and I could well imagine. They were not having sex. They had already missed three of their regular whoopee sessions, which was fine with her, because she really didn't feel like it anyhow. But she also felt guilty for feeling that way. It was complicated.

I just sat and listened.

"How do you get over a trauma like this?" she asked.

I thought of my parents. Ever since they had passed away, I had avoided thinking of them. But I had been thinking of them a lot since I met Clyde. Not big thoughts, but short, fleeting memories, which subconsciously popped into my mind and which I immediately buried again. To this day, I don't understand how she did that to me, when everyone else I knew for years before failed to.

"Well," I began, in answer to her question, "eventually, I guess, you just move on." I was a mental health professional. I knew that wasn't true.

"What were some of the things you did to move on?" she asked.

"Things I did?" I was carefully confused, as if I hadn't been asking myself the same question she had just asked me.

"Yeah. You mentioned that you had experienced a similar trauma. What did you do to move on?"

"I just kind of... got over it," I answered.

A lie. You don't just "get over" a tragedy that rips apart your life. You try your best to go on despite not getting over it.

I shook my head. "You don't actually get over it. You just kind of... get *used* to it."

We were both miserable now, but at least we were miserable together.

I had another hour until my next appointment, and I was getting hungry. So was Clyde. So we decided to get a bite for lunch. We walked to a sub shop across the street. Then we brought our sandwiches to a secluded picnic area in the office park, so we wouldn't have to sit in a restaurant with a bunch of people gawking at the crazy, grieving ladies from Abe's Turn. We ate mostly in silence, occasionally commenting on the food or scenery. "Good sandwiches." Or "Those evergreens are beautiful." Or "Doesn't the air smell fresh?" Or

"What kind of bird was that?" At least we never resorted to "Nice weather we're having, isn't it?"

"So I'm supposed to start spending time with other people besides Ted," Clyde said, apparently having had enough of aimless conversation.

"What do you mean?"

"Dr. Hooper— Ange wants me to put together a support system of friends. I know a few people from work and church, and I can look up some old friends I've fallen out of touch with."

I nodded. I certainly understood how a woman could get wrapped up in her husband's life so deeply that she lost contact with her own circle of friends. Many women, I had a feeling, would just sit and sulk. But Clyde was a survivor.

"Hey, are you doing anything tonight?"

"I don't know. Why?"

"I have a new recipe I wanted to try out, and I usually try them out on—" Her countenance fell. "Anyhow, I haven't cooked in a while, and I wonder if you would like to come over for dinner."

That sounded fun. And what else was I going to do on a Thursday evening by myself? Go to a bar? No thanks. See a movie? Curl up on the couch and get drunk? I took her up on her offer. "What should I bring?" I asked.

"Nothing," she said. "Just bring you."

"Can I bring a salad?"

I think I may have been messing with her menu, or else maybe she just didn't like people bringing food to her dinners. Maybe she liked to be the chef and the hostess.

"Or maybe," I said sheepishly, "I could just bring me."

Clyde grinned and touched my hand. "Bring a salad. Just don't go out of your way, okay?"

I chuckled. "Okay."

Their house was majestic. It looked like a mansion from the

outside. It actually wasn't a mansion, but it was big, with two guest rooms, and they had added a few extras, like a hot tub in the master bath. We ate in the kitchen, not the dining room: I insisted, because it was just her and me, not a dinner party. The food itself was simple but wonderful, some sort of honey curried chicken dish, served with rice and vegetables. And wine, a bottle of French blush from Clydene's wine rack, which she kept in the cellar. Yes, she had an actual, honest to goodness wine rack in the cellar. It was not huge, could hold maybe 20 bottles. Still, I had never seen one of those before.

We had just finished eating and were talking about whether we wanted to move into the other room to finish our wine and maybe watch TV or a movie, when Ted arrived home. We heard him enter the front door, on the other side of the house, and stride down the hallway.

"Ted, you remember Mira," Clyde said, "from the hospital."

Ted said nothing. He glared at me, red-faced. But I saw no reason why he would be embarrassed.

"We left some food for you," Clyde said. "Would you like me to make you up a plate?"

Instead of answering her, he said to me, "What are *you* doing here?"

I felt sick to my stomach, and terrified. And I felt the color drain from my face.

He started in, listing all the ways I was a busybody, butting into their lives, destroying their marriage. I had no idea he felt that way, nor could I think of any reason he would blame me. Yes, he could so easily have fixed the situation himself. But people blame others all the time for things that they could easily fix themselves. So blame work; blame Clyde; blame God. But blame me?

Meanwhile, Clyde watched on in terror.

I felt sad and sick. Still, I pitied him more than I hated him.

He was hurting me, yes, with his anger, but it was out of his own insurmountable hurt that he was doing it. So I tried to remain calm, because that's how you get disturbed people to calm down themselves.

"I know your type," he barked at me. "You were pampered all your life. You parents never told you, 'No.' Spoiled little brat, didn't your mother ever teach you to mind your own business?!"

The mention of my parents hit a nerve. It pricked a spot that had already been rubbed raw by recent memories. I lost it. Like the Incredible Hulk, I transformed—against my will—into a monster. I showed him his soul.

"Your wife is in pain, and all you can think of is yourself. I know you can't stand feeling what you feel; I know you need to feel like you're in control— Well, guess what? You're *not!* And that's not a good enough reason to leave her out to dry! You're being a self-centered, egotistical jerk. Damn it! Don't you feel anything?! Get over the self-pity already, because you know what? No one gives a damn!"

I think that took him aback, because he didn't stop me.

"It wasn't your fault that Clyde got hurt. It's your fault she's still getting hurt. Like that guy who attacked her. It wasn't your fault you got him off. That was what you should have done. That was your *job*. But it's like you're treating me the same way they treated him. You know, just because the police beat him up is no reason to take it out on me!" I was close to tears and only making partial sense.

"You idiot!" he yelled. "They didn't beat him up. I did!"

"Ted, stop it!" Clyde shouted. "This is my friend."

"She's no friend of mine!" Ted said.

"I thought you loved me," Clydene scoffed, hurt and angry.

"He *does* love you!" I shouted. "He's just an ice-hearted jackass!"

"Get out!" Ted growled at me.

I grabbed up my purse and headed quickly and quietly for the door, marched out to my car, and rumbled away before anyone could follow. My skin was still burning hot, as tears began pouring from my eyes. I was lucky not to have gotten in an accident.

Clydene called a few times over the next several days. I always let it go through to voicemail and did not return her calls. She said she wanted to apologize, but I did not want to talk to her, or to her husband. I did not want to talk to her, because I did not want to get further embroiled in their problems. And besides—the real reason—I didn't want to have to explain what had set me off or account for what I had said or how I had said it. That's not what I signed up for.

Then one day, while I was eating lunch and reading another novel, Ange Hooper knocked on my office door. She sat down in my guest chair and sighed. "Ted and Clydene Jackson were in to see me today."

I stared at her and stammered, "Yeah, I— I've been meaning to call her back. I hope she's doing okay." That was only a half-lie.

"Is it true that you called him an ice-hearted jackass?" She had a twinkle in her eye.

"Uh... Yeah, I guess I did."

"I thought maybe he had misunderstood, and you had actually said '*nice*-hearted jackass.'" A giggle in her voice.

"Uh... No, he got it right." I could feel my face getting red.

"Do you want to talk about it?"

"No, I don't think so."

"Might make you feel better."

"You're not my shrink," I reminded her.

"Sure I am," she said, "or who else is going to be one for you?"

"Hmm," I grunted, not wanting to argue with her about whether a mental health worker can counsel a friend, because

I agreed that in many ways, she was my shrink. She was part of my professional and personal support system. She had been a confidant in the past, and all she wanted now was to help me save my professional butt. But I still didn't want to talk about my feelings, not to her, not to anyone.

"What did he say," she asked, "that set you off?"

"What?"

"Something set you off," she explained. "Maybe you've been under stress—I don't know. But something set you off and made you tear into him. That's so unlike you. So what set you off?"

"He disparaged my parents," I admitted.

"Tell me about your parents."

Oh, she was good, and she was clearly wearing her shrink hat.

"I don't want to talk about my parents," I said.

"Why don't you want to talk about your parents?"

"Ange," I said, getting upset, "not now."

"Then when? Tonight? Tomorrow? The day after?"

"You're infuriating, you know that?" I stared at her, fire in my eyes.

"I'm concerned about you, Mira," she said sweetly, with worry in her eyes. "Correct me if I'm wrong, but you look like you're just about to tear into me, and I don't even know what I did. Don't you think you should at least level with me?"

I've never been very good at thinking up excuses under pressure. And I've never been very good at hiding my true feelings. I'm as transparent as a sheet of glass. And I've never been very good at avoiding a direct answer to a direct question. And the answer was that, yes, I did think she deserved an explanation. In retrospect, I could tell you, we both knew "what" she did to upset me. She started poking me in a sensitive spot. But at the time, I wasn't thinking about that. I was thinking that she was right: I was behaving out of character, and I did owe her an explanation.

More than that, a little voice in the back of my mind was telling me that I should talk to her, and that I should do it now, that I'd never encountered the right opportunity to talk about this, that I'd simply gotten used to not talking about it, that if I didn't talk to Ange, right now, she would not force the issue, and that I'd regret staying silent.

"I just don't know where to start," I told her.

"Okay." She nodded. "Why don't you start at the beginning? What's the first thing about your parents that comes to mind?"

So I told her about my father, how he used to tuck me into bed when I was a little girl, how he used to read to me, and how he always understood me and accepted me for who I was, unquestioningly and unconditionally. I didn't get very far through before Ange was handing me the Kleenexes.

Then I told about my mother, how she explained to me the other kids in school, how she helped me get ready for my first date, how she helped me move into my first dorm at college, and all the other firsts she did for me that only a mother can do for a daughter.

"It sounds like you loved your parents very much," Ange said. *Loved,* in the past tense. I had never told her about any of this, but she must have picked up on what was coming. "What happened?" she asked.

And so I took a deep breath, and I told her the story, the short version, because I don't think I could have handled the long version just then, and even the short version was a big step forward for me.

"I was just finishing up my first year of college," I explained. "I planned to go home over the summer to stay with my mom and dad. I was really looking forward to it. What I didn't know was that they were coming to surprise me. But they never made it. They were driving along a curved part of the road, and the pickup truck coming the other way must have been driving too fast and swinging wide around the turn." I shook my head. "They never had a chance."

At that point, I didn't know what to feel. Actually putting the story into words seemed just to make me numb.

"I found out," I said, "when a policeman visited me at my dorm. It was finals week. I was packing for the trip home, planning to take the train. He told me my parents had been in a fatal accident and he needed me to identify the bodies."

I had stopped crying.

"Have you ever told that story to anyone?" Ange asked.

I shook my head. "No," I said.

"Why do you think that is?"

"I just didn't want to think about it."

"What does thinking about it remind you of?" she asked.

I shook my head again, this time in wonder of what they had done, all those years ago. "If they had just called me, I would have told them to stay home and let me take the train. They were going to surprise me. And I guess they did." I stopped a beat. I was hurt and angry, angry at them, angry at me. "They made hotel reservations and everything. They probably planned to help me pack and everything. But damn it, why didn't they just stay home?"

"So how to do feel about that?"

I couldn't put my feelings into words. All I could say was: "They were coming to see *me*. Do you get that? *Me*. Damn it."

"Damn what?" Ange asked, unemotionally. "Damn them? Or damn you?"

I froze for a moment, nausea rising through my heart. "Damn... both."

I felt like spitting, to get the bitter taste of this awful conversation out of my mouth. It tasted like soap.

"I just have one more question for you to mull over," Ange said. "You don't have to answer. Just think about it. Is any of that Clydene's fault?"

"No," I said, answering the question anyway. "It isn't."
Then I said, "I think I owe her an apology." The words felt
dirty, grainy in my mouth, but I knew them to be true. Sometimes, the truth is jagged to swallow and painful to learn.

I brought a bottle of wine to dinner that evening, as a peace
offering. Ted and Clydene were obviously starting to work
things out, and that made me happy. I apologized to Ted, and
he clearly was uncomfortable with that. I think he wanted to
apologize to me, because he looked apologetic, sheepish
almost, but maybe he didn't know how. We discussed the
weather, television, politics, anything but what had originally
brought us together. This was shortly after Sam Baedes had
been promoted to chief, and the memory of Lando Benitez was
still fresh in my mind. I discovered that Ted, being a criminal
defense lawyer, had a unique view into how the system
worked. And hidden well under layer upon layer of tough
outer skin, I also discovered, he had a heart, a big heart made
of pure gold. But that's a different story.

I didn't immediately tell Clyde about my parents. But we
started meeting for lunch, just us two girls, whenever she met
with Ange. As she shared her feelings and realizations, each
prompted a memory of my own, which I shared with her. At
first, I didn't want to, having learned comfort in keeping it all
to myself. And Clyde never pressured me. But I saw how
Clyde struggled to talk out her feelings, and I knew how
healthy it could be, and so I fought to return the favor. She
listened as happily as she talked. Over time, I told her the
whole story, and she seemed to understand perfectly. It felt
good, liberating, to talk things out with her.

I knew I had changed, when found myself saying, "When I
was little, and my father got stressed out, he would ask me,
'Can I have a hug?' and I would be so glad to give him a hug. I
miss hugging my dad."

Needless to say, Clyde and I became close. She invited me over for the occasional dinner. I started to feel self-conscious about having dinner so often over at their house, but Clyde was an excellent cook and a gracious hostess, and she always threw a wonderful dinner. They started inviting other friends over, too, and throwing proper dinner parties, which, I gathered, they had always talked about but never actually tried.

At one of these dinner parties, while Clyde was in the kitchen and the other guests were using the facilities, I noticed Ted staring at me longingly across the dining room table. I didn't know what to make of it, and he was making me a little uncomfortable. Then he said, "I admire the skill with which you empathize with others," in that haughty tone which only Ted has really ever mastered. While I was still trying to figure out what he meant by that, he said, "Thank you for being Clyde's friend. I don't think she would have made it otherwise." And I saw in his eyes the adoration for his bride that I had seen that first awful morning, when I had first met him. Only this time, it wasn't mixed with guilt or defensiveness.

"You may not realize," I answered him, "how lucky she is to have a husband who feels as deep a love as you do for her."

He scoffed, as if it were meaningless, or maybe even offensive.

"Hey." I smiled. "It matters to her, okay?"

"Okay," he said. And I could swear I saw just the faintest peek of a grin behind his otherwise stoic expression.